GALACTIC EMPIRES

VOLUME II

Also in this series:

GALACTIC EMPIRES Volume I

GALACTIC
EMPIRES. (v. 2
VOLUME II

edited by

BRIAN W. ALDISS

ST. MARTIN'S PRESS   NEW YORK

Library of Congress Cataloging in Publication Data
Main entry under title:

Galactic empires.

1. Science fiction, American.   2. Science fiction—
English.   I. Aldiss, Brian Wilson, 1925-
PZ1.G213   1977   [PS648.S3]   813'.0876   77-76626
ISBN O-312-31528-7

ACKNOWLEDGEMENTS

'Escape to Chaos' by John D Macdonald
    Copyright © 1951 by Fictioneers, Inc
'Concealment' by A E van Vogt
    Copyright © 1943 by Street & Smith Publications
    Copyright renewed 1970 by A E van Vogt
'To Civilize' by Algis Budrys
    Copyright © Columbia Publications Inc
    Reprinted by permission of the author and the author's agent Candida
    Conadio and Associates Inc
'Beep' by James Blish
    Copyright © 1954 by James Blish
'Down the River' by Mack Reynolds
    Copyright © Startling Stories 1950, Better Publications Inc
'The Bounty Hunter' by Avram Davidson
    Copyright © 1958 by King-Size Publications Inc
    Reprinted by permission of the author and E J Carnell Literary Agency
'Not Yet the End' by Fredric Brown
    Copyright © 1941 by Captain Future
'Tonight the Stars Revolt' by Gardner F Fox
    Copyright © 1952 by Gardner F Fox
'Final Encounter' by Harry Harrison
    Copyright © 1964 by Galaxy Publishing Corporation
    Reprinted by permission of the author and his agent A P Watt & Son
'Lord of a Thousand Suns' by Poul Anderson
    Copyright © 1951 by Love Romances Publishing Co Inc
'Big Ancestor' by F L Wallace
    Copyright © 1955 by F L Wallace
'The Interlopers' by Roger Dee
    Copyright © 1954 by Roger Dee Aycock

CONTENTS

Introduction vi

Section 2 **Maturity or Bust** (continued)

i '*You Can't Impose Civilization by Force*' 1
Escape to Chaos *John D Macdonald* 8
Concealment *A E van Vogt* 55
To Civilize *Algis Budrys* 72
Beep *James Blish* 82

ii *The Other End of the Stick* 123
Down the River *Mack Reynolds* 126
The Bounty Hunter *Avram Davidson* 135
Not Yet the End *Fredric Brown* 141

Section 3 **Decline and Free Fall**

i *All Things are Cyclic* 145
Tonight the Stars Revolt! *Gardner F Fox* 150
Final Encounter *Harry Harrison* 192

ii *Big Ancestors and Descendants* 215
Lord of a Thousand Sons *Poul Anderson* 219
Big Ancestor *F L Wallace* 251
The Interlopers *Roger Dee* 278

Epilogue 296

INTRODUCTION

There is no point in pretending to distinguish the galactic empire story as a genre. Generally speaking, such stories form part of what is known as 'space opera' – to which the first two anthologies in this series were devoted. The galactic empire is a sort of crystallisation of space opera; there are others, of which Sword-and-Sorcery is one.

Some stories use the imperial background to make a moral point; didacticism is perenially popular in science fiction and Mack Reynolds provides a good example in this volume. But it is the playful aspect of the galactic empire which mainly strikes a reader.

This aspect led many readers, including a lot of sf fans, to despise space opera and the galactic scene. Now, there are good literary reasons why a wide canvas, such as these stories demand, will defeat all but the Michelangelos of sf – and we have too few of them – thus more thoughtful writers (and perhaps the ones we might call the better artists) eschewed the galactic manner. But to dismiss it just because it is playful is not good enough.

The two editors who have wielded most power since sf magazines came into being are undoubtedly Hugo Gernsback, founder of *Amazing Stories* and thus of magazine sf, and John W Campbell, who edited *Astounding Science Fiction* (later *Analog*) for more than thirty years. Both these influential men took a certain attitude to mankind and mankind's activities. Their philosophy was utilitarian. Campbell's was the more formidable intellect, but he believed, no less than Gernsback, that greater human units made for a greater humanity, rather than for less humanity.

Both editors tolerated, nay, fostered space opera in their pages, but it was space opera strongly oriented towards the machine. Campbell saw man as a tool-making animal; he loved to talk about the thumb as the opposed digit which distinguished man from the other primates and gave him a better grasp of weapons, thus setting him on the path to the stars. And his influence was strong on the writers who wrote for him, writers such as Arthur C Clarke. That great imaginative moment in the Kubrick-Clarke film, *2001: A Space Odyssey*, when a bone used by the early man as a killing weapon is hurled triumphantly into the air, to be transformed into a space station, is a Campbell image, the image of *homo faber*.

This Campbellian view of man naturally predisposed him to advocate larger and larger doses of technology. Or perhaps it was the other way round, and his belief in the dosages made him see man as primarily a worker. Whichever way it was, *Astounding* rarely admitted stories which showed mankind growing away from technology. Technology, after all, may merely be a manifestation of racial puberty, rather like motor bikes – to be abandoned for all the rest of our species, life-span. Other races may ascend to a high and creative level of civilization without carrying technics much further than the potter's wheel. But such speculation would have been heresy in *Astounding*. The unorthodox are particularly hot on their own orthodoxies.

Campbell was brilliantly clever. Yet he preferred – and the preference brought his eventual decline as an editor – to ignore the fact that the contents of his beautiful magazine were *play*, mind games, and, in Campbell's heyday, the best mind games in the business. His writers, too, following his example, liked to justify sf in terms of how accurately its predictions were fulfilled, or how well it served as propaganda for the space race, or how strongly it influenced American kids to become physicists when they grew up. This was sf as function, sf as just another tool.

The writers who wrote for other magazines often felt otherwise. They believed that sf should be a game, if a serious one, that its merits were integral, not applied. They understood *homo ludens*; and so their products were denigratingly referred to as escapism by the *faber* brigade.

Some philosophers have argued that *homo ludens* has played a supreme role in history, a role that the upstart *homo faber* has tended to editor out. The most distinguished contribution to this theory is J Huizinga's *Homo Ludens*, which has recently received massive support from Lewis Mumford in *The Myth of the Machine*. In general sf has been approached and evaluated from the utilitarian standpoint, and conscripted willy-nilly under the *faber* banner. The result has been undue encouragement of an sf grounded in a little grey philosophy of man churning away into futurity as a unit of an amorphous technocracy. At least, such has been more or less the official view – in New York as in Moscow – and one which probably played a part in hastening the notorious sf revolt, the New Wave, of the mid-sixties, with its emphasis on doing one's own thing, however obnoxiously. But it is noticeable that when a madman enters the sf field, just plainly enjoying himself, he generates an immediate and enthusiastic following. The early A E van Vogt, Alfred Bester, Michael Moorcock, and R A Lafferty, are examples of this, while public speaking up and down the country has convinced me that probably the most popular of all short story writers is not Ray Bradbury, as commonly supposed, but Robert Sheckley, an imaginative joker whose ramshackle worlds and leaky spaceships have immediate appeal.

A galactic empire, in short, is not intended as a blueprint for a future utopia. That might not be much fun, though no doubt a few trendy sociologists would recommend it to their class. A galactic empire is ramshackle and anachronistic, full of miscegenous worlds, leaky spaceships, and naked slaves working by torchlight in uranium mines. A galactic empire owes more to Cecil B de Mille than to Einstein: it is the Spectacular of sf.

This unashamed escapism is not incompatible with profundity of thought. Here we may recall the question J R R Tolkein asked C S Lewis, 'What class of men would you expect to be most preoccupied with, and most hostile to, the idea of escape?' He answered his own question: 'Jailers.'

I quoted Tolkein's remark in the introduction to the first volume of this anthology. This introduction has been an attempt to restate what I said there in different terms.

There's more than one way of killing a cat, or of sneaking up on a galactic empire.

SECTION 2 (continued)

MATURITY OR BUST

i *'You Can't Impose Civilization by Force'*

John D MacDonald: ESCAPE TO CHAOS   8
A E van Vogt: CONCEALMENT   55
Algis Budrys: TO CIVILIZE   72
James Blish: BEEP   82

The issue of this appalling struggle in the minds of these former imperialists depended on the extent to which specilization for empire had affected them. In a few young worlds, in which specialization had not gone deep, a period of chaos was followed by a period of reorientation and world-planning, and in due season by sane utopia. But in most of these worlds no escape was possible. Either chaos persisted till racial decline set in, and the world sank to the human, the sub-human, the merely animal states; or else, in a few cases only, the discrepancy between the ideal and the actual was so distressing that the whole race committed suicide.

Olaf Stapledon: *Star Maker*

One thing is certain. Men unify only to achieve strength, whether the strength of religion, knowledge, or power. And unification leads to various ills; once you have joined, you are apt to stay joined, whether or not you want out.

Unification also leads to complexity, and in this section mature empires reflect that complexity. Our four distinguished authors, van Vogt, John D MacDonald, Algis Budrys, and James Blish, were writing for the amusement of their readers in generally despised popular magazines, yet they touch on a weird sort of truth. A friendly reviewer of the first book in this series said, 'Space Opera is all good, unpretentious, and proud fun, yet one can't help but suspect that these tales touch some of the mythopoeic archetypal wellsprings deep in every id.' Large words, but I agree – though it may all depend on the circuit diagrams in one's id. These stories seem to me to have the quality described.

Talking of the circuit diagrams of the id, no science fiction writer could boast more elaborate circuits than the late James Blish. All learning was his province. He was a great man for making connections. His splendid Cities in Flight saga explores one of the seminal connections of the modern age, the sibling relationship between space and time; while his formidable life of Roger Bacon, *Doctor Mirabilis*, examines the multitudinous relationships between science and religion – a theme developed in fictional counterpoint in Blish's most famous novel, *A Case of Conscience*, and later in *Black Easter* and *The Day After Judgement*. These threads can also be traced through 'Beep', the slice of galactic history we present here.

One of Blish's preoccupations was with the problem of sin, which he appeared to deal with sometimes as if it were merely an intellectual question. With hindsight, we can observe that sin in 'Beep' is conspicuous by its absence, to deploy that phrase precisely. The story can be interpreted as being about a machine which abolishes sin, root and branch – sin in fact, sin as concept.

'Beep' is a think-piece, and it forms a central think-piece to this volume. It is a story I greatly admire. When I first read it in *Galaxy* I was less impressed by its intellectual qualities than by a haunting image, which embodies much of the glamour of sf, the image contained in these lines:

'I've heard the commander of a worldline cruiser, travelling from 8873 to 8704 along the world-line of the planet Hathshepa, which circles a star on the rim of NGC 4725, calling for help across eleven million light years – but what kind of help he was calling for, or will be calling for, is beyond my comprehension.'

This passage was picked up by Emsh, who illustrated it on its first appearance. He contributed a design showing a whirlpool of space-time, with the cruiser trapped along its spiral.

One of the ingenuities of 'Beep' lies within its title, and in the correspondence of that title to the effect of the story, which unpacks a world of implications from a meaningless seed of noise. 'Beep' tackles headlong one of the central problems of galactic empires: the problem of how to deal with, and if possible overcome, immensely long lines of communication. The Dirac transmitter proves a remarkably effective answer; and Blish shows us what paradoxically

4

good side-effects it generates, including having one of the main characters almost forcibly married to a transvestite lady of mixed ancestry – which marriage he enjoys.

When writing the story, Blish perhaps felt that with free will removed from human affairs there would be no more sin. His assumptions about predestination are interesting and uncomfortable (a lot of Jim's lines of thought were interesting and uncomfortable). He depicts human consciousness as 'just along for the ride'; elsewhere, it is described as 'helpless'. Events rule. I once wrote a story ('Not for an Age') in which I depicted a human consciousness as carried along helpless to interfere with events. It was, and remains, my idea of hell. Yet Blish manages to make it sound almost utopian. The world he portrays in 'Beep' is an extremely happy one, happier than any other world-view in the anthology; as one of the characters says, 'The news is always good'.

To make the connection between instant communication and redemption (freedom from sin) is a remarkable jump. Blish embodies it symbolically by the tender care taken to see that lovers meet as planned. All this is even more remarkable when we consider that most sf writers use the posit of instant communication to further aims of conquest and aggression. In 'Beep', it brings peace. Was Blish trying to equate instant with perfect communication. How else explain why his all-powerful Service is incorruptible?

Science fiction stories often leave strange vapour trails in the skies of our minds. I find myself wondering at the way in which Blish has planted two people in disguise, one in the inner, one in the outer, story; though they assume the disguises for devious purposes, neither meets disapproval or anything stronger when discovered. Perhaps that is how it should be in a utopia. If you remove reasons for aggression, would aggression disappear? But one cannot ask such questions in this construct of Blish's, since cause and effect are proven inoperative by the Dirac transmitter.

If you grant that 'Beep' is utopian in disposition, then you have to grant that it is a very rare sort of story indeed. Although utopias and dystopias are traditionally associated with science fiction, no galactic empire to my knowledge could be remotely regarded as utopian. 'Beep' is the one exception. In his wisdom, James Blish did a lot of strange things.

Algis Budrys' early short stories showed wisdom. Then he stopped writing. He has recently reappeared on the science fiction scene disguised as a reviewer; perhaps that experience will tempt him back to fiction, to show us all how it should be done. Meanwhile, I advise readers to seek out his novel, *Who?* (recently filmed) and, especially, *Rogue Moon*. One line in 'To Civilize' remains in my memory: 'You can't impose civilization by force.' It is something that people, and not only sf writers, tend to forget.

These stories are garnered from obscure magazines, some of which were never published in Britain: *Super Science Stories* did appear over here in an emaciated edition. Above cover scenes showing such delights as New York in flames ran their proud legend, 'Read It Today – Live It Tomorrow'.

It is unlikely that the world of *Escape to Chaos* will ever see actuality, but that is hardly to the point. John D MacDonald – famous for his polished thrillers – posits an amazingly complex civilization, hemmed cheek-by-jowl by other galaxies of similar probability. Among them moves the splendid City of Transition. Van Vogt himself might envy such a grand design.

Not that the Old Master has anything to fear. His Imperial Battleship *Star Cluster* moves through a galaxy inhabited by many races with many different abilities. Will the future see such things? The question remains open. But it should be remembered that space travel itself was once a similar mad dream; science fiction readers were among the scattered few who believed in its possibility. Van Vogt, at this stage of his career, always carried belief, even when his subject matter seemed frankly incredible. Over thirty years later, the magic remains, even if we are less easy to impress.

In this story and ones linked with it, van Vogt captured a sensuous interpretation of space which connects not only with the future but with man's early experience of the cosmos. Van

6

Vogt's great storms in space, his light-year wide streams of particles – so 'modern' when they first appeared – draw us back to ages when our everyday lives were less sundered from the elements and the night skies more omni-present. Technology has weaned us from Mother Nature; electricity and the water closet blacked the mind's eye. Now we have space travel, and we no longer believe in it, except as a quasi-military exercise.

But *once* it was believed in, before we built water-tight bulwarks against sky and moor and forest and sea. Long before science fiction was thought of, great voyages were cosmic in scope, and responsive minds leapt up to embrace the wanderer and his tale. Homer, first voice of the Western psyche, takes us to the margins of the known, where gods and goddesses form part of the traffic of Man, extending the dimensions of his experience. The ancient Epic of Gilgamesh celebrates the belief that if you navigate your ship to the edge of the oceans you may be able to join the great stream of stars and sail upwards into the heavens, where the secret of Creation is. The familiar names of the constellations tell us of an ancient and intimate relationship between man on Earth and the far stars.

One of the impulses behind modern science fiction – particularly the adventure-impulse behind such stories as Poul Anderson's and Gardner Fox's – is extremely ancient. And, we hope, inextinguishable.

At bay against his dissolving skies he fought – the last champion of a star-spanning dynasty which never existed save to die!

ESCAPE TO CHAOS

By John D MacDonald

The third son of Shain, the rebel son, the traitor to Empire, was pursued thrice across the Galaxy, was trapped five times and five times he escaped. Now he stood in the blue and eternal dusk of a cobalt city on Zeran, one of the old planets, a planet of many histories, of many peoples, of the sadness of things lost beyond regaining. Zeran kept its face always toward the vast pink-orange sun that bore it, a half billion miles away.

Three years before, Shain had listened to the reports of the activities of his third son, Andro. Shain lay on the couch and ate of the fruit the women had brought him. He listened. 'Andro said to Telka of Vereen, "How long will you permit my father to oppress you?" Andro said to Clangaron of Lell, "When the uprising comes, you must be ready to join us."'

'Enough!' Shain said in the voice of Empire. He dropped seeds to the soft amber floor, selected another fruit. There was a small wet sound as he bit into it. He chewed, swallowed, yawned. 'Have him killed,' he said languidly.

Three years later Andro stood alone in the dusk of the city of endless blue. He stood alone with heavy shoulders braced against the wall at the end of a forgotten alley. His burns suppurated and they weakened him, but his hand was firm on the grip of the weapon. Forty ships there were, and now there were none. Seven thousand had pledged their loyalty beyond death, and of the seven thousand the last one, the girl, Daylya, had died as he dragged her from the ruin of the last ship.

He was a big man and he waited with a big man's patience. He waited and it was hate that gave him the strength to stand against his hurt. Once he smiled as he thought of what it had

8

cost them. Four times seven thousand. Five times forty ships. Rumor among all the planets of Empire would make those totals greater. The deeds of Andro would be whispered in quiet places. And one day another one would dare, and win. Andro had shown them, shown all of them that revolt, even unsuccessful revolt, was possible, and to many it would seem a good way to die.

The wars of nations on ancient earth had been the rationalization for the founding of what had become galactic empire. For centuries as man had exploded across the star wastes, Empire had been weak. And then when the galactic wars began, star against star, cluster against cluster, Empire had regained its old strength merely by seeming necessary.

And the House of Galvan had ruled Empire for several thousand years. Shain of Galvan was no better and no worse than the average, Andro knew. The House of Galvan had not permitted itself to become weak. The men went to the far wild planets to find the strong-thighed mothers of Empire. The men of the House of Galvan were big. But the House had ruled too long. They had ruled from a time of enlightenment through to a time of superstition and stagnation. Andro, the youngest son, had not been as cleverly and carefully indoctrinated into the mores of Empire as his eldest brother, Larrent, as the middle brother, Masec. He had read much, of the olden times. Then, steeped in the rich traditions of early days, he had looked around him.

He had seen the prancing perfumed artists, claiming an ultimate reality in incomprehensible daubs. He had visited the slave markets of Simpar and Chaigan, and had been sickened. He had seen that the ships were old ships, the weapons old weapons, and the old songs forgotten. He had seen the dusty rotting machines that had been the hope of man, while ten thousand laborers built, by hand and whip a temple to the glory of the House of Galvan.

And he had said, 'This is the dark age of Empire. We have had enough.'

Even as youngest son in the great palaces and fortifications of the heart of Empire, on the green and gold planet called Rael at the heart of the Galaxy, he had only to raise a languid hand to acquire forty slave women, the rarest of wines, or the tax-tribute of a dozen planets for a hundred years.

And he said, 'We have had enough.'

And Shain said, 'Have him killed.'

And Larrent and Masec said, 'Have him killed.'

Death was close. The last ship had crashed near the wall of the empty blue city. The burns on his left side were deep enough to hold his doubled fist, and each time the wave of weakness lasted a bit longer. He wanted to take one more, or two, or three or even a dozen with him. Another fragment to add to the legend, to be said in an awed whisper, 'And when they finally trapped him alone, on Zeran, he . . .'

Andro coughed and it was a cat-weak sound in the eternal dusk. Deralan, Chief of Empire Police, had personally headed this final, successful chase. And Andro knew that wiry, dour Deralan was a cautious man. Andro had felt the streets shudder as the ships had landed in a circle around the blue city. The ring of Deralan's men would be advancing toward the heart of the city, searching each building with care, the ring growing closed, tighter as they neared the center.

When he breathed there was a bubbling in the deepest part of the highest wound on his left side. His legs started to bend. He braced them once more, lifted his heavy head in time to see a flicker of movement at the end of the alley. All weakness was forgotten as he raised the weapon a trifle.

There was hard amusement in him as he thought how the pursuers must feel. Each one of the previous five escapes had bordered on the miraculous. Now they would be expecting a further miracle.

'No miracles this time,' he said, and knew that the borderline of delirium had caused him to speak aloud.

A shadow appeared at the end of the alley. He lifted the weapon, sighted carefully. The firmness on which his feet were braced opened with an oiled abruptness. It wrenched his wounds so that he screamed out in agony. As he fell he saw the vast rim of the orange star directly overhead before the opening clapped shut far above him and he fell through an emptiness that was blacker than deep space.

* * *

Sarrz, Deputy Director of the Bureau of Socionetics, was a round little man with squirrel-bright eyes and a face like a plaster death mask. It was situations exactly like this which made him realize that his EC – Emotional Conditioning – was getting a bit frayed around the edges. He could not prevent a thalamic reaction to such . . . stupidity. There was really no other word for it.

He turned in his chair so that he would not have to look at the two of them, so that he could regain some of his control. Framed in the window, thirty yards across and fifteen yards high, was most of the City of Transition. It looked, Sarrz sometimes thought, like several thousand bridal cakes with raspberry frosting. Beyond the ten thousand foot towers which marked the four corners of the city was darkness.

In the name of energy conservation Transition was now resting on a .8 gravity planet in Era Middle 6 in a high index probability. Transition was imitating a mountain, hence the opacity beyond the slip towers.

Sarrz realized that his pride in the Field Teams was possibly a bit unreasonable. He spoke without turning toward the two members of the team.

'The quality of your indoctrination is questionable,' he said softly. 'I shall conduct this on a primer basis. What is Transition?'

He knew by the voice that the younger of the two, the female, had spoken. She was the atavistic type – a throwback to a higher index of sensuality and emotional sway. A mistake to have ever let her go out.

'Transition,' Calna said, 'is an operational station in probability space-time. There are three such stations. This one operates on the socionetic level through the medium of Field Teams.' She used the exact words of the basic manual.

'Excellent,' he said with a trace of irony. 'Please continue, Agent.'

Her voice faltered a bit. 'There are twenty-six known galactic civilizations with a high probability index, and many thousand more . . . distant.'

He turned and stared at her. With her sturdy figure and

11

overlong hair she looked like one of the old prints. 'Is that the right word?'

'Not distant. Less available,' she corrected.

Sarrz leaned back in his chair. 'Much better. Continue, please.'

The male agent was obviously uncomfortable. He kept fingering the tunic insignia. Calna said, rapidly, 'With the discovery and application of the Oxton Effect, it became apparent that there was no need to limit any galactic civilization to the space-time rigidity previously known. With easy slip between the twenty-six civilizations with high probability index, it was believed that a unification on twenty-six space-time levels could be accomplished. Research had shown that only three space-time levels could be unified immediately. This was done. The unified civilization of three space-time aspects set itself the task of bringing the social level of the remaining twenty-three up to the point where unification could be undertaken.'

'And how could this be done?' Sarrz asked in silky tone.

The girl flushed. 'Field Teams, trained in Socionetics, and based at Transition, were assigned to the twenty-three lagging cultures. It was discovered that if the Field Teams acted openly, as agents from a parallel space-time, their efforts caused a deviation in probability of the culture development so that the civilization resulting became less probable, and hence could not be kept within slip range. It could still be reached, of course, as can the several thousand less probable ones, but only with exorbitant power expenditure.'

'I see,' said Sarrz, as though he were hearing it for the first time. He leaned forward a bit. 'And have we ever lost one of these parallel space-time cultures through too obvious meddling?'

'One,' the girl said. 'Several years ago. It was number seventeen on the program chart.'

Sarrz was ready for the kill. He leaned forward a fraction of an inch more. 'How can you be certain that it isn't two that we have lost, Agent? How can you be certain that your violation of all standing instructions hasn't lost us number four as well?'

The girl flushed and then turned pale. 'You sit here in Transition and lose touch with the Field Team problems,' she said boldly. 'Solin and I have been on the case for over five years. As soon as we were well enough educated in language and customs to walk among them as subjects of the Empire, we found out that our hope was Andro, youngest son of the ruler. You do not know, Deputy Director, how hard we tried to get close enough to Andro to control him, control his rashness, so as to improve his timing. He led the revolt against Empire when his followers were too few, his resources too slim. Five times we managed to save him. I could not stand by and see him killed in an alley. I could not face beginning again. And let me absolve Solin here, my teammate, from any responsibility. He made the strongest protest possible. I went ahead on my own authority. And I do not think we have forced number four out of range, into a low probability index.'

Sarrz closed his eyes for long seconds, opened them suddenly and stared at the girl. ' You were trained, Agent. You were told the danger of obvious meddling. You were told how long these things can continue. You knew that it may be two thousand years before we can steer that culture to the point where acceptance and unification can be considered. Knowing all these things about you, Agent, you leave me with but one conclusion. That you became personally and emotionally so involved with this Andro savage that you lost your head and tried, very sentimentally, to save him. Is that not true?' She turned her eyes from him. 'Answer me!' he said softly.

'I . . . I don't know. Possibly it is true.'

'Agent, there are seven hundred teams operating in that parallel culture. Most of them are attempting to activate a technistic renaissance. Others are directing the subjects of that Empire in equally necessary paths. Other teams, such as the one you two form, have been operating on the socio-political level. Up until now there has not been one violation of security.

Sarrz stood up and walked to the window. He whirled. 'Think of it once! Think of what you've done! One tiny little ship and a galaxy of two billions of habitable planets is pushed forever out of our reach! What did you do with him?'

Solin said in a low tone, 'We cut the passage and as he fell, we resealed it. He was unconscious by the time we floated him down to the chamber. He was badly hurt. Calna stayed with him and I set up the field, returned to our ship and activated the field, removing both of them from the city. He was almost gone. We rebuilt the tissues, took him in deep sleep to the dark side of that planet, to one of the dead cities which they have lost the skill to visit, and placed him on the zero metabolic level. Then we . . . grew worried and came back.'

'So you grew worried, did you?' Sarrz said with acid sweetness. 'What am I to tell the Director?'

'If only they hadn't spotted him as he escaped from the ship,' Solin said.

'I've been going over your detailed reports,' Sarrz said, with a sudden note of hope in his voice. 'This Deralan, he who headed the pursuit, isn't he a very ambitious one?'

'Very,' Solin said.

'Then there's our chance! This sixth escape by Andro will ruin Deralan. Shain will probably have him shot. Shain will want proof of Andro's death. Is there any distinctive mark on this Andro?'

'A tattoo of the royal House of Calvan on the upper portion of the right arm.'

'Go into slip at once, Solin. Take a square of the skin with the tattoo on it. Use your finder to contact the Field Team on Rael. Give the little trophy to either Agent of the Team. It will be placed in Deralan's hand before he has his audience with Shain. I don't think Deralan will ask any questions.'

'But then,' said Calna, in a thin voice, 'when Andro reappears . . .'

'He won't reappear. He'll sleep there for ten thousand years, if it seems necessary.'

The girl stood up, one hand at her throat. 'You can't do that!'

'You have no hand in any more discussion of either policy or procedure, girl. You are no longer an Agent. You will receive all the usual pensions. Report to field five at once. They'll have orders on you. You are being sent back to our own space-time. Any planet preference?'

14

'Earth,' the girl said softly.

For a moment Sarrz forgot his irritation with her. 'Indeed! I guess I never noticed origin on your card. Do you know, this is the first time I have ever actually met anyone from our planet of origin.'

She lifted her chin, with a look of pride. 'It is a good place,' she said. 'It is a good place to know, and a good place to go back to.'

'I am sorry,' Sarrz said with a gentleness. 'Possibly you were never right for this sort of work. I am truly sorry.'

'Why can not Andro be released to recruit new personnel for his revolt?' she asked. 'Wouldn't it save time?'

The irritation came back into Sarrz' voice. 'Release him and he knows that he did not escape through his own powers. He knows he was helped, and to him it would be help through the good offices of the supernatural. He would at once relate this last escape to the previous five, and become, through his new convictions, a son of the gods rather than a revolutionary. Rebellion would change from a social to a quasi-religious basis, and we know that in order to keep number four within the high probability index range, we must hasten development along the *same* lines as would normally occur. We have plotted their culture curve. We can accelerate it without affecting probability, but we cannot redraw the curve on a new basis without losing them forever, or at least until slip becomes possible for lesser probabilities, and our technicians in symbolics say that will never occur.'

'So,' Calna said in a dead tone, 'you will leave him there. A living death.'

'There is no room for sentimentality in our work,' Sarrz said.

Calna turned and left the Deputy Director's headquarters. The door orifice folded softly shut behind her.

Earth was always the origin. Symbolics made that clear. Ten thousand times ten thousand, Earth was the planet of origin. In the beginnings of the science of Symbolic Probability, it was thought all deviations were of equal value. The result would be, if it could be vizualized at all, in the shape of a fan,

15

with an infinity of lines diverging from a fixed point, lines equally spaced.

This concept did not take into account the limitations on culture deviation. Always it was humankind, and reactions – social reactions – are limited, so it became a problem of dividing infinity by the finite. The result is infinity also, but the lines were no longer equally spaced from the common point. They were bundled. Each space-time frame was thus co-existent with its sister probabilities. And as long as they were bundled, grouped, you could slip from one sister probability into the next.

The space-time frame in which the conception originated had tried to jump extra-galactic space and had been hurled back. It was a rigid boundary to further expansion, until, of course, it was found that there were twenty-six superimposed home galaxies in the probability grouping. The small golden pyramidal ships quivered, shimmered, became milky and disappeared in one frame to reappear in the next. So mated were three of the probability frames that the languages, the mores, even the fads and fashions were co-existent. Had it not been possible to slip to one of the other two, the slip would have been accomplished in the other direction within a matter of months rather than years. Three were ready for unification. Twenty-three needed acceleration in their own charted culture line. One was lost. One day it would be twenty-five times two billion planets. Symbolic Probability indicated that there were other bundles of space-time frames in which complete unity and cross travel had been achieved, but their probabilities were so divergent, and on so low an index that slip could not be accomplished.

Slip was the only word that would fit the mode of travel. Travel in a dimension for which there was no name. A dimension folded upon itself, so that the little golden ships were neither up nor down nor sideways. They neither shrank nor expanded. They 'slipped' across a probability matrix into a sister reality without positional change. So close were the co-existences that it explained everything that had ever gone bump in the night, shadows half-seen out of the corner of the eye. You left your own frame and entered the sister frame which had been brushing at the sensory tendrils through generations of superstition. And the frame you left behind was the frame which, through its very closeness, had appeared to rap on tables and speak through trumpets.

Calna stepped from the express strip onto a local strip and then across the increasingly lower strips to the platform of field five. The planet on which Transition rested, was in Era 6, a frame not ready for unification. She had been assigned to Era 4. Eras one, two and three were the unified ones, and, with her loss of Agent standing, the only ones available to her. Possibly, in her lifetime, another would be unified. Era twenty, she had heard, was almost ready. Transition rested in Era 6, next to space stations constructed in Eras one, two and three.

She turned and looked back across the city she would never see again. To the great mass of peoples in Eras one, two, and three, the three great cities constructed to slip across probability lines were more rumor than actuality. Only trained minds could comprehend the enormity of the task the three unified cultures had set themselves. Only highly specialized people could aid in the task.

To the average man and woman of the three basic eras, it was merely a new and wondrous and inexplicable advantage to be able to enjoy three contiguous environments. Those with ample means arranged title to the same piece of property co-existent on three probability levels. The slip field was installed in a central doorway with minimal controls. Each room was three rooms. For the very wealthy, proper positioning of the co-existent homes could result in three climates to be enjoyed. The ideal was a tropic warmth in one, eternal springtime in the next, and a crisp and endless October in the third.

She turned her back on Transition. There was a thickness in her throat. She knew that she should feel shame at the enormity of her mistake – and yet she could not. She knew that her identification with Andro had been too intense, and yet she did not wish it any other way.

'Ex-Agent to Era One,' she said crisply to the routing clerk. He eyed her curiously. Ex-Agents were rare. Dead Agents were not so rare. Resignation was unheard of. And so the

17

routing clerk knew that the change of status had been disciplinary.

The customary respect shown to Agents was markedly lacking. He stared at her until she flushed. 'Why the delay?' she asked angrily.

He winked. 'Are your pensions going to be big enough for two of us?' he asked, leering.

'I can still put you on report,' she said.

'But you won't.' He yawned. 'Take the one at the end of the platform.'

She walked out and down the platform. She saw it and felt lost. It was one of the rooted ships, built only for the slip between frames. Unlike the Agent ships, it could not leap like a golden arrow from planet to planet within any frame. It would contain no survival equipment. The minimal controls would be no more complex than the buttons in an elevator.

Once she was in that stodgy ship there would be no turning back. She slowed her pace as she neared it. The ship beyond was a true Agent's ship, with its double control panel, one for probability change, one for positional change. She could see the new seal beside the insignia and knew that this ship had just been completely checked and re-equipped.

She turned and glanced back. The routing clerk had his back to her. She moved quickly then. It had to be done in seconds. She darted into the Agent's ship. In her mind was the great stabbing pain that came with disobedience. It was the same pain she had felt when overruling Solin and rescuing Andro. Conditioning caused that pain, and should have made disobedience impossible. But, as in the rescue of Andro, there was something in her that fought the pain, made it endurable.

She knew that to slip to Era 4 would mean capture within seconds. She picked Era 18 at random. As she hit the lever with the base of her palm, she heard the suck-snap of the port behind her. As the ship began to fade around her she heard the clangor of the alarm. In thirty seconds they could track her. As the ship shimmered back into life in Era 18, she dropped her hands to the lower panel and shot it straight up at maximum takeoff. As the planet dwindled in the screen, she chopped the ship over onto SL drive, counted slowly to

18

ten, swung it out of SL twenty light-years from the planet, slipped over into Era 22, picked a random course change, put it back into SL for a twenty count. After nine Era shifts in which she kept away from the basic eras and from Era 4, she knew that pursuit was out of the question.

The strain of escape had kept her from thinking of the consequences of her act. Now that she was safe for a time, she felt slack, exhausted. She wept for the first time since she was a child. When there were no more tears, she slept.

II

Calna

Sarrz stood at attention facing the Director. The words that had lashed out at him made him feel faint and dizzy. There was contempt on the Director's gaunt face.

Sarrz tried again. He said, 'But no Agent has disobeyed a—'

'Be still! What order had you started to give when I put you under arrest?'

'I had ordered Agent Solin to go to Era 4 and destroy the body of Andro. I though she would immediately try to . . . you see, there's an emotional attachment . . . seemed logical that . . .'

'Do you remember your history, Sarrz? What, in its simplest sense, was cancer?'

'Why . . . uncontrolled cell growth, starting with one rebel cell and—'

'Any Agent, Sarrz, equipped with an Agent's ship, is very, very close to being impregnable. We are dealing with an unbalanced Agent, for the first time in socionetic history. You would have fixed it so that she would have returned to that place and found this Andro destroyed. Revenge is a typical emotion in an unbalanced mind. What, then, would keep her from using the ship and her mobility to intrude in the most destructive possible way on all probability frames within our reach?'

Sarrz blanched. 'But . . .'

'One rebel cell in our structure, Sarrz. Remember that. If we are not to lose twenty-two sister galaxies, we must eliminate her. Possibly you think this is an alarmist reaction. Agent Calna ceased to be predictable when she prejudiced the entire operation in Era four. Angered and hurt she can force twenty-two cultures off their extrapolated pattern. Saying that she retains enough loyalty to refrain from doing that is mere wishful thinking. I want every available Field Team briefed and assigned to the planet Era four calls Zeran. I want a trap that she won't see on the way in, and can't slip out of. Is that clear?'

'It is clear,' Sarrz said with an effort.

'In the meantime proceed with your plan of presenting Shain, through Solin and the team on Rael, with proof of the death of his youngest son. But warn Solin not to kill Andro. Not under any circumstances. Once we have the girl, Andro can be safely killed.'

When Deralan had been young, he had not feared space flight. He stood as a guest on the bridge of the flagship of the police fleet returning to Rael. He was returning to report to Shain the utter destruction of the remnants of Andro's rebel force. And the sixth escape of Andro himself.

Deralan was a realist. The execution would be swift, and relatively painless. For a time he had considered lying to Shain. But lying led straight to the rooms of evil repute under the main palace, and there Deralan would scream until Shain found the truth and permitted him to die.

In his youth he had accepted the great, roaring, shuddering, thundering ships as a part of life that would never change. Now he knew of the great fields where tens of thousands of the ships moldered away, as no one had the skill to repair them. If the drive failed in flight, the crew and passengers were dead. It was that simple.

And many had failed. Abilities had been lost, somehow. He could see the sign of those lost abilities in the puffy face of the captain of the flag ship now standing before the vast control board, watching his officers complete the intricate procedure for landing. Deralan felt a vast bitterness. They were like monkeys firing a gun. The monkey pulled the trigger and the gun went bang. Ask the monkey to explain the principle of expansion of gasses. The officers pulled switches in the order prescribed in the space flight manuals. The ship landed. It was that simple. If one switch was pulled and somewhere in the guts of the ship a coil failed, that was too bad, and very very fatal.

Routine repairs could be made. New tubes, oxygenation equipment – things on that level. But what made the ship take off, accelerate to ten lights, deaccelerate and land – what induced the normal gravity under any acceleration – what force adapted the view screens to the acceleration – all those things were mysteries, lost in the ancient past when men were wiser, stronger.

Deralan thought sourly that Andro had not been very far-sighted. All he had to do was wait. He could die knowing that within a thousand years there would be no more ships that would function. With no more ships, the House of Galvan would rule one planet rather than a galaxy. Each inhabited planet would be isolated, left to go its own way, to find its own answers, maybe win its way back to space. The ships would die and Empire would die with them.

Now the face of Rael was so close that it filled all of the view screen, the tiny drift of cloud appearing flat against the surface. Deralan's mind kept returning to the report the three men had given him. He could not suppress a thin eerie feeling of awe and concern. 'I saw him. He seemed to be hurt. He had a weapon. As I aimed, he dropped out of sight. We went back there. There was no place for him to get out. There was no hole for him to drop through. He was just . . . gone.'

Shain would not be amused by that story. Three of them had seen it. Deralan had isolated the three who had seen it happen. After considering all sides of the question he had killed them. His power over his men was that of life and death, with no questions asked. Their eye-witness account was an embarrassing factor, an unnecessary factor in the equation. Deralan felt no regret, and no satisfaction over it.

He knew that he did not dare lie to Shain, and yet he wished to continue to live. It was impasse.

The fleet landed, a far smaller fleet than had set out in pursuit of Andro. A guard of honor awaited Deralan as he disembarked. They formed a hollow square around him. Deralan smiled. Shain hadn't been thinking of honor when he sent the guard. Shain had been thinking of escape.

Metal-clad heels struck the paving in harsh cadence as the twelve guards escorted Deralan down the center of the Avenue of Kings. The once-proud street had become a place of bazaars. Rael was a wise and sour old planet. To it had come the dregs of a thousand planets, the sycophants, the cheats, with their smell of depravity, their swaggering insolence. One did not walk alone at night on Rael.

The aimless crowds opened to let the guard through. Some of them jeered at the guards and then fell suddenly silent as they recognized Deralan, feared almost as much as Shain himself and his elder sons.

A drunk reeled too close to the guard. The man at the front left corner of the hollow square reversed his ceremonial short-sword with a practised gesture and smashed the man's skull with the heavy grip.

They marched through the stink of the bazaars, past the crones that vended remedies for every ill, past the street girls in their rags, past men who turned with jerky quickness to hide a wanted face from the keen eye of Deralan. The main palace towered at the end of the Avenue of Kings. They marched through three gates so huge that the men did not have to change formation. Only the fourth gate was so narrow that they shifted to a column of twos. Deralan was midway along the column.

Just as they passed through the gate a screaming girl came racing from the side, her eyes wide with panic. A bearded man chased her. In her fright she ran directly into Deralan, staggering him. The guards cursed and shoved her roughly back into the grasp of the bearded man. Deralan fingered the object the girl had thrust into his hand. It had a soft texture. In the great main hall of the palace he risked a glance at it. For a

22

moment he did not know what it was. When he at last understood what it was, his mind reeled with the shock, and his
mouth went dry.

But Deralan was a realist and an opportunist. They took
him back through the corridors to the private apartments of
Shain. Shain was a ruin of what had been an enormous,
powerful man. Years of debauch had left him looking like a
pig carved of cold lard.

'Your report told me nothing,' Shain said.

Deralan straightened up from the ceremonial bow. 'Forgive
me,' he said. 'I possibly took a childish pleasure in anticipating
this moment.'

"I have some childish pleasures waiting, if I don't like your
report.'

Derelan bowed again, advanced and handed the object to
Shain. 'My proof, your imperial majesty.'

Shain unfolded the soft square. He stared at it. Then he
threw back his great head and began to laugh. He laughed
until tears squeezed out of the small eyes and rolled down
the white heavy cheeks. Deralan took a deep breath. He knew
that he was out of danger.

'How did you do it?' Shain demanded.

'We searched the city. I found him myself, and killed him.
It was your wish.'

'You did well. Tonight we shall celebrate your victory . . .
and . . . and the death of the best of my three sons, the death
of the only one fit to be Emperor.'

Always, in a limited world, the machines grew more powerful. Machines were a form of inbreeding. Man turned his
attentions onto his own pleasures and comforts and the
machines grew, giving sage electronic attention to the complexities of equations with a thousand variables. And man
grew softer within his limitations.

But now, with multiple realities waiting to be merged, the
machines were of little help. Properly guided, the machines
had indicated the possibility of multiple space-time frames,
had assisted in finding a way to reach them. But once reached,
it was once again up to man to work with hands and eyes and

heart to achieve that unity which would weld twenty-five conditional realities into one world.

The Agents were recruited from those who, in less pressing times, would be termed malcontents, would be difficult to control, manage. All of them were, in one sense atavistic.

The Agent was man. His tools were provided by the machines. And no tools in history equaled the golden pyramidial agent ships. They were the extension of the Agent, the way the stone ax fitted the horny palm of the Neanderthal. On SL drive they could span the galaxy in a mouth. The webbed forces, interlocked and convoluted like the surface of a brain, shimmered constantly along the five planes of the ships. They were very close to being invulnerable. They could dive into a planet crust, protecting the Agent in much the way an insect would be protected while held in the palm of an iron fist as the fist was driven into loam. They could move in any direction except time, and at speeds beyond contractive effects. Yet it was the Man and not the Ship.

Calna entered Era 4 at the galactic rim. She was lost. It took long hours of feeding data into the computers to arrive at exact position. Since exact position was only exact in relation to any known object, she calculated her speed in relation to Zeran's sun in the invisible distance. She established course corrections. The ship flickered once and was gone. Twenty hours later the alarm brought her out of deep sleep a hundred million miles from Zeran. She had set the protective web so that light was bent around the tiny ship. She risked observation, in three-second intervals, returning to objective invisibility each time. She knew that she could be detected only by a chance intersection of her path from the galactic rim. It was a risk she had to take.

She stretched the weakness of sleep from her body and tried to think clearly. She was afraid. She suspected weakness in herself that implied an eventual failure. The rescue of Andro was, in Sarrz' terms, weakness. Emotionality. In all probability it would make her reactions predictable. And so she had to fight for a cold objectivity. What made it most difficult was that thoughts of Andro made her heart pound and her face flush. Agents were taught to consider the peoples

24

of backward frames as pawns to be moved at will, sacrificed for the sake of socionetic gambits. But she thought of Andro in the way of a woman rather than an Agent. Yet, even if she were to rescue Andro and take him out of reach of the Field Teams who were undoubtedly waiting, what would he think of her? What would he see in this strong-bodied woman of a more mature culture? This woman with the grey-bright eyes and the hair like ripened grain in a September sun.

She remembered the harsh and shameful joy with which she had seen the death of the woman, Daylya whose beauty had been like a warm cry in the night.

Andro was, above all else, a strong proud man. He would not react kindly to being aided by a woman who, in all except brute muscle, equaled or surpassed his own strength.

The possibility that they had already killed him was like the first rasp of the knifeblade against her throat. She knew how she would plan it were she in charge of those attempting to intercept her. She would make the path to Andro's black and quiet tomb very simple. And escape impossible. By a focus of power five other Agent ships could hold her ship in stasis. She sensed that they were waiting.

She knew the exact location of Andro's body. It was in a crypt in the small room of the highest tower in a frozen city abandoned for half of time. The body would be hard and tough as granite. If there were some way to snatch it up on the run. . . .

Anything could be transferred from planet to ship provided the proper field were built around the item to be transferred. A field was created by a tiny generator no larger than a plum. It could be set to create a field a foot across, or five miles across. But it had to be placed in position.

The item could be received inside the ship, or received within any given range of the ship. She made her plan. It was dependent on deceiving them through apparently descending to land near the crypt. Their reaction times would be trigger-fast. It would be close, and with no possibility of fumbling.

She boldly dropped the ship's screens and streaked toward the dark side of Zeran. She came down through the blackness with her view screens adjusted so that the ruined city stood

25

out as though bathed in a great light. The adjusted generator lay in the small disposal port. The port switch was hooked in with the computer which in turn was hooked up with the aiming screen. She waited without breathing, her hands on the lower panel, fingertips moist on the controls. The interval of drop was to be twenty seconds. The instant she heard the click, she chopped the ship into SL drive and winked away into space. She felt for a fractional part of a second the drag of the focused power of the other Agent ships. It was as though, for that moment, her ship flew through molten lead. For the moment there was nothing for her to do. She had set the ship to come out of SL at exactly twenty seconds from the moment of the drop. The port was ready and skin-gravity set to hold any air that would escape, heat screen ready to combat the cold of space.

She put her hand on the main port control. The moment she felt the tiny, twisting dislocation that meant the end of SL, she tripped the control and the port yawned. The receiving area was set outside the open port. With the suddenness of an explosion the entire top of the tower appeared in the receiving area, swung over and thudded against the ship. Using the top panel she slipped ship and tower into Era 20 to give her a few more moments of grace.

The rough stone of the tower was flat against the open port. Using the hand blower she crumbled a hole through the stone, exposing one corner of the black crypt. She widened the hole, caught the crypt with the focused beam of the attractor, angled it through the port. Ignoring the crumbled stone that had drifted in, she shut the port and tried to flee.

The ship did not move. She cried out, and fought the controls. Her hands flashed across the panels as she tried combinations of controls. Higher and higher rose the thin whine of the ship's screens, fighting the holding force. She applied all power to a straight SL drive, feeling the heat rising within the ship. The ship grew hotter and she waited, her jaw set, until she could scent the acrid odor of the scorched tendrils of her hair. Then, with one fast motion, she cut off everything in the ship. The pursuers were in the position of a man who

26

runs to break down a door when the door opens just before his shoulder touches it. Calna's ship gave a tiny lurch and she was ready to take advantage of it. She slipped to Era 1, and immediately to Era 25, and applied full SL drive the moment the new frame had been attained.

The ship whipped off into freedom, and she laughed aloud with a note of hysteria. She used a completely random pattern of slip and direction, taking no chances, working for long hours on the twin panels until she knew that pursuit was impossible. She knew the danger of awakening Andro in too unfamiliar an environment. The chance of madness was too great.

In Era 11, one of the most backward ones, she found the planet she wanted. In more sophisticated probability frames, it had been turned into a rest planet for Agents. It was uninhabited in all frames except the basic three. The best aspect of it was that it was not the last place they'd look for her. Anticipating her reaction, they would look at once in the last place. It was neither the best nor the worst, thus a median chance in several billion.

She drifted low across the springtime face of the planet and selected a place where a crystal stream came down across rocks to form a pool beside a slant of lush green grass. She tucked the ship between the mighty roots of a fairyland tree so tall that clouds brushed its crown. This was a planet on which one felt elfin. Small and wild and free. The vastness of the trees and the boulders and the utter stillness were the artifacts of magic.

She opened the purloined crypt and laid her fingers against the marble coldness of Andro's cheek. All body functions were suspended. She moved quickly and lightly as she prepared the twin injections that would bring him slowly up to the threshold of life once again. The tips of the needles had to be heated before she could put them into the vein on his inner arm.

She made the injections and then laid her head against his broad chest. It was like listening to a stone. It was the coldness of death and she felt small and afraid. With no circulation of the blood, with the blood itself as still and hard as the red veins in marble, it took a long time for the effect to spread from the point of innoculation.

The heart, at last, gave a slow thud. She counted to thirty before she heard the next thud. Each time the interval decreased by a full second. Body warmth began to return. When he took his first fluttering, shallow breath, she straightened up and smiled down at him. There was color in his face again.

With the help of the small attractor she unhooked from her belt, she lifted him effortlessly and carried him through the port and placed him on the fresh-scented grass at the edge of the deep blue pool.

Then, motivated by a force that was strange to her, she used the cleansing chamber of the ship, webbed fresh garments for herself in a brighter color than ever before.

III

Revolt on Simparl

The slip towers glowed, grew misty and indistinct. The City of Transition gave a delicate shrug of raspberry shoulders and slipped from Era 6 to Era 4. The risk of thus hastening the deviation from plotted culture line was great. But the Director felt that coordination could better be obtained within the target era than from outside. As yet no method of direct communication between eras had been devised. Field Team reports could be received at Transition and orders could go out only if the city were in the era which ex-Agent Calna had made so critical.

Sarrz felt lost. The Director had stepped in to handle direct coordination of Field Teams. Sarrz was left without a function. Though it irked him, it did give him a chance to review the entire picture. As with all directing heads in Socionetics, Sarrz had a good background in Symbolic Probability. With the idle and aimless feeling of mental doodling, he decided to equate the index of probability of the loss of further space-time frames.

He took the small table which held the computor and

swung it around within easy reach. He put it on alphabetic scale and ignored, as he fed in the data, the glow of the 'insufficient data' light. He had the direct loss of one era, the pending loss of a second, plus areas of disturbance in three more.

He read off the index and it startled him. He cleared the computer and tried again. Same result. He sat and listened to the quickening thud of his heart. The index of probability of all sister space-time frames being lost was almost grotesquely high, so high that complete data would have to be within itself improbable in order to level off the result based on incomplete data.

The inference was that some outside factor was at work, some unequated factor. There was a parallel in astronomy. Find the deviation and then look for the cause.

Suddenly Sarrz realized that this matter was of highest importance. The Director must be informed, and at once.

He reached for the switch that would enable him to communicate with the Director.

And that was the way they found him. His heart had stopped as his fingertips had touched the switch.

Animal caution did not desert Andro as he recovered consciousness. He neither stirred nor opened his eyes. He remained quite still and concentrated on bringing all senses up to peak awareness. Hearing – the soft rush and babble of water, a crackling stir, as of wind in leaves. Scent – the spiced smell of brush and forest and wild places. Touch – brush of grass against his arm. Warm air against his body. He remembered the deepness of the burn wounds. He concentrated his sensory attention on the wounded areas and could find no message of pain from the scorched nerve ends. He increased the depth of his respiration and could not detect the quick knives that had stabbed him with each breath as he stood in the blue shadows of the alley.

He remembered those who had joined him, and who had lost. Grief was deep and slow and still. Daylya and all the others. His fault. And born of impatience. Had he waited, grown a bit stronger, planned more thoroughly. . . .

His ear picked up the whisk of grass against an approaching foot. Fingertips touched his chest over his heart. He opened his eyes just enough to see the figure outlined against the sky, bending over him. The equation was simple. Once all your allies are dead, all who remain are enemies.

Andro struck with clenched fist, with a roll that brought the heavy muscles of shoulder and back into the blow. He rolled onto hands and knees and jumped up onto his feet, weaving a little from weakness. He stood under a strange sky near the mightiest tree he had ever seen and looked down on the crumpled unconscious figure of a woman. She wore a toga-like garment of lime yellow, a wide belt from which small unknown devices dangled. Her hair had the clarity and purity of the white fall of water into the deep blue pool a few yards away. On the angle of her jaw was the spreading stain of the force of the blow. He stood and waited and listened for others. There was no sound but the water and the wind. He bent over and fingered her jaw clumsily. The bone did not feel loose and broken under his fingers.

It was then that he remembered his wounds. He looked at his side, and found a strange thing. The skin was clear, firm, healthy over the wounds, and he would have thought he had dreamed the wounds were it not for the untanned pallor of the new skin.

He looked at the woman again, and he frowned. The alley floor had given way under him and he had fallen into darkness. The woman was connected with that phenomenon in some way. At the moment she was helpless. Yet the devices on the belt she wore were a promise that she might not remain helpless. He rolled her over and looked for a place to unhook the belt. It seemed to have no fastening and it fitted too tightly around her slim waist to be slipped down over her hips. He contented himself with unhooking the small devices. He could not guess their uses. Yet they had a gleam that spoke of efficiency, utility. There were six of them. He carried them carefully in his cupped hands and placed them behind a stone. It taxed his strength to tear a strip from the hem of the lime yellow toga. With the strip he bound her hands tightly behind her, placing the knot out of the reach of her fingers. As he

30

tightened the knot, his right arm extended, he saw that the tattoo was gone from his upper arm. It was replaced with another area of that pallid healthy skin.

Andro sat a few feet from the woman and waited for her to regain consciousness. He tried to guess what had happened. He still wore the leather and metal battle skirt, but his cape was gone. He remembered tearing it off as it had started to flame, throwing it aside as he picked up the dying girl and carried her through the great smashed place in the hull of his ship. The battle skirt showed signs of having been scorched. The thongs that bound his sandals were blackened, crisped and the hair had been burned from his calves and ankles. The holster at his right side was empty.

The woman's face was toward him as she opened her eyes. Her eyes were a clear grey and they saw nothing. They focused on him and he did not like the look of intelligence that came into them. In face and body he found her pleasing, but the eyes alarmed him. They spoke too clearly of know-ledge beyond his own – knowledge that made him feel like a child. He saw her test the strength of the strip that bound her wrists, then sit up awkwardly, throw her head back to swing a heavy strand of her hair away from her face. She smiled at him as a conspirator would smile.

'Who are you?' he asked heavily.

She moved her underjaw from side to side and grimaced. 'You are strong, Andro.'

'Who are you?'

'Your friend. Your very good friend. My name is Calna.'

'Calna,' he said, tasting the word carefully. 'I was dying. Now I am whole again. I was trapped, and now I am free. If you did that, it is evidence that you are a friend. But your purposes in doing that may make you enemy rather than friend.'

She glanced down at her belt. 'Untie me, Andro. The bonds are too tight.'

He untied her. She stood up, flexing her hands, rubbing her wrists. The top of her shining head was on a level with his eyes. She smiled at him and there was something in the smile he didn't like.

31

She said, 'I'm helpless now because you took the things from my belt?'

'Of course.'

She put her hands on him and he tried to strike her again. He cried out in sudden agony as her fingers found pressure points. She did not cease smiling. She touched his elbows in what could have almost been a caress and both arms hung slack and useless. Her hand swept across the side of his throat and he fell heavily. He tried to move and though his effort made the sweat stream from his face, he could not move.

She sat beside him and said softly, 'It will go away in a few moments, Andro. And do not let your pride be hurt. Those are methods in which I was carefully trained.' She stood up and glanced around. She went unerringly to the stone behind which he had hid the shining things. She picked them up and hooked them casually onto the belt.

Some of the weakness had left him. He sat up and glared at her. She laughed. 'Don't look so fierce, Andro. You see, I know you very well. I've known you for four long years. There were five escapes before this last one. Probably you thought they were good luck, or even good judgment. I was helping you, Andro. Six times you should have died, and I helped you. The seventh time occurred while you were unconscious and that was the worst time of all, the most dangerous.'

'Why did you help me?'

'I am not from your world, Andro.'

'I have guessed that.'

'My world was interested in your revolt against Shain. It was to our advantage to help you succeed. We helped in many ways, but not enough. I was following orders given to me. When it was seen that our help was not enough, I was ordered to let you die on Zeran. I disobeyed orders.'

'Why?'

Calna frowned. 'I . . . I don't really know. I knew that I was becoming emotionally interested in you, but that in itself should not have been strong enough to enable me to act counter to my training. It just became something I . . . I had to do, Andro. Now I am being hunted by my world.'

'As I am being hunted by mine?'

'No. Your world believes you are dead.'

He stood up as the last increment of his strength flooded back. He looked around.

'Is this your world or mine?'

'Neither.'

He stared at her. 'What are we to do? How did we come here? I wish to go back to my own world. I left . . . many things unfinished.'

'You cannot go back. There is no way.'

Andro watched her for a moment. 'Until that moment, I believe you told the truth. Now why do you start to lie?'

'Listen carefully and understand, if you can. I will say it as simply as I possibly can, Andro. We tried to help your world without making our presence known. If we did it too obviously, your world would grow out of our reach and we could no longer visit it. If you should go back now, the mere fact of your returning from the dead will put your world out of our reach. So I cannot permit that.'

He studied her. 'That seems odd, Calna. You say you are being hunted by your world. Can they hunt for you here?'

'Of course.'

'Then why not return me to my world. You say it will place my world out of reach. Then wouldn't that mean safety for you, in my world?'

'Yes, but it is against all my training, all I believe in, and . . .'

He saw her indecision and for the first time he felt that his strength equaled hers. He put his hands lightly on her shoulders, felt her tense under his touch. He looked into her grey eyes until her glance wavered, dropped. She came into his arms with a small cry in her throat that was like a confession of weakness, that was the sign of the transfer to him of the authority for whatever path they would take into the unknown future.

'We will go to my world,' he said. He felt her acquiescence. 'And before we return,' he said, 'you will teach me how to use the devices of your world. When I return I shall be stronger than Shain and Larrent and Masec, even with no followers.'

33

She stood a little apart from him then, her head lowered. 'My people will be looking for us in your world. They will want to stop us, before the effects of your return have made sufficient change in your world to move it out of their reach.'

At a place which was the essence of no-place, and in a time which, in stasis, was no-time, there was a record of progress in the analysis of paradox, where directed thought maintained the record, where a billion eras moved the record one half-step nearer the point where at last all infinities would become finite. It could not be done on the basis of a controlled experiment, because there is a flaw in that theory. The mere factor of control is an alien factor, a newness added to the other components. Without control, all things must be weighted and all factors considered. The measured counting of high value infinites can only be performed in no-time, and only no-place is vast enough to hold the records.

A child awakens and cries in the night. In its simplest sense the impact of that occurrence can be measured through a thousand generations, given all factors for weighing. What complicates it is that cause and effect are expressions of the same factor. It is more delicate to trace the child's awakening backward for a thousand generations, but still finite and feasible – given enough time and enough space for the keeping of records. Where it becomes paradoxical is when worlds are bridged and all probabilities assume equal values, and in ten thousand co-existent fields of probability where the child awoke at the same instant, the same track can be plotted backward for a thousand generations and be identical for ninety-nine hundred and ninety-nine probabilities, only to diverge at the next to the last generation in the very last of the ten thousand co-existent webs in the matrix. So go back and make that last one similar, and the result will be an increment of divergence which results, most probably, in no child at all, and, less probably, in a night of unbroken rest for the child.

The labor involved makes it essential that the computations be made in no-time, and the records kept in no-space.

And one facet of the endless computation can be – as one

range of probabilities begin to gain mutual access, what happens if such access is denied?

The finite computation of infinities is possible because infinity is merely a function of time and space. Only nothingness becomes endless.

Ever since the dreaded audience with Shain that had been so miraculously saved from disaster, Deralan was obscurely troubled. It was his nature and his profession to learn the background of all events and incidents. Long search for the girl who had handed him the object which had bought his safety was fruitless. He was almost glad that he could not find her. They had returned to Rael from Zeran with all haste possible. Either the object had been brought back on the pursuit ships, or it had arrived at Rael by faster means. And Deralan did not see how it was possible for the object to have been smuggled onto one of the ships. As to faster means of transport – there were none.

As he tried to pick up the threads of his responsibilities that had been disrupted by the revolt of Andro, third son of Shain, he found himself suffering from an inability to give his complete attention to his duties. The capital city was very much like a cage of wild animals. The animals detected the faint inattention of the trainer and crouched a bit lower on their haunches, ready to spring.

When two of his most trusted assistants were torn to bits by a mob, Deralan did not feel the old raw fury with which he had avenged similar previous incidents. His identification, capture and execution of the leaders of the mob was quick and effective, but without heat. His villa, protected almost as well as the very palaces of Shain, no longer was a place of revelry by night. He ceased the entertainment of those close to Shain, and knew that by so doing he was prejudicing his influence at court. He spent more and more time alone, and his thoughts were dark. Many times there was fear in him, but fear of something not quite understood.

He felt that somewhere in the city he would find an answer to all that troubled him. He began to listen more carefully to

35

the talk of odd happenings in the empire. It seemed to be a time of strange occurrences that bordered on the supernatural.

On one sultry afternoon when most of the city slept, Dera-lan questioned a frightened girl who had been brought to him by his agents. She was a dirty, half-wild creature, seemingly poised on the very edge of flight. Her dark red hair was matted with filth and her tip-slanted eyes were of that distinctive lavender shade of the women of Vereen. Her rags barely covered her body. In her left armpit was the telltale gouge where the mark of the slave had been recently removed. Very recently removed.

Though she was frightened to the very borderline of unconsciousness, she would not speak. And such was her emaciation that it was immediately obvious to Deralan she would die at once if force were used. What intrigued him most was the freshness of the blisters along the calf of her left leg. Those were the distinctive blisters carried by one who has traveled in one of the old ships with their defective shielding.

Several isolated bits of information clicked into place in Deralan's mind and convinced him that this girl held a clue to his own bafflement. The increasing numbers of escaped slaves on Rael – the fresh blisters – the girl's obvious fright – the two month delay in customary reports from slave marts – all these things pointed to Simpar, from his agents on that planet of something only she could give him.

Her teeth were small and even and pointed. 'Kill me and watch how a Vereen woman can die!' she whispered to him.

'What made you slave?' he asked, forcing a gentleness into his tone.

'I stabbed my husband. The court sentenced me. They said it was without cause. I was shipped to Simpar with hundreds of others.'

'And you escaped. How?'

She moved restlessly in the thongs which bound her, and turned her head from him, affecting casualness, though the cords stood out like wires in her lean throat.

'How would it feel,' he asked softly, 'to be clean once more. To be scrubbed and clean and scented again. To feel the touch of silk. To recline beside a spiced fountain and have rich foods brought to you. Fine fruit from Vereen. Wines from Lell.'

She did not move. He saw a tear cut a channel of whiteness through the grime of her cheek.

He called the bored attendants and told them to free her and bring her to his villa. He turned his back on their knowing sneers and left. By the time the girl was brought through the innermost gates of the villa all was ready for her. The maids took her in hand. It was dusk in the wide gardens before she was brought to him. She stood with a new pride, tall and silent and quite lovely.

He watched her eat with the precise, almost vicious hunger of a half-starved animal. The wines were brought. She was wary but after a time she lost wariness and her lips grew swollen and her eyes grew vague and she emptied the glass each time he filled it from the flagon. Night came and he sat with her. She laughed with an empty sound as he caressed her.

'It wasn't hard to escape, was it?' he asked.

'No. Not hard. Not with the gates broken and the guards dead and the ships waiting. Not hard.'

'Who broke the gates and killed the guards?'

She giggled. 'Oh, but I am not supposed to tell anyone that, yet. Not until he is ready. Not until we receive word.'

'You can tell me, Leesha. You will stay here with me in comfort and in peace. There will be no secrets between us. You can tell me.' His tone was wheedling.

She giggled emptily again. Her eyes shuttered and she slumped out of the circle of his arm. He grasped her shoulders and shook her hard. 'Tell me!' he shouted.

Her head wobbled loosely. He let her fall to the edge of the fountain. She lay on her back and her breathing was loud between her parted lips.

At noon the next day, heavily guarded, Deralan shuffled up the ramp and through the port of the waiting ship. His face was deeply pocked and scarred, unrecognizable. Around him was the wailing of the newly enslaved. The inner door clanged shut. In the confined space Deralan's nose wrinkled with distaste. At take off there was no warning. They slid into a tangled heap at one end of the lightless room.

As he fought free of the others, found a clear space on the floor, Deralan wondered what would become of him if he could not prove his true identity on Simpar.

Once Calna had committed herself to Andro's plan, she resolutely forgot how far she had veered from the paths of her training. The only remaining indication of the extent of the conflict within her was the splitting headaches which blinded her at times, without warning.

Andro had showed surprising aptness as a pupil. At times she felt that he had taken all of her knowledge and combined it with his own to create a strength beyond anything she had ever before experienced. It was he who had selected Simpar as the symbol of everything he detested about Empire.

They had driven the golden ship deep into the planet crust and waited there for the thrum of directed energy which would tell them that they had been detected. Andro, using the device which collapsed the orbital electrons in matter without releasing the energy, had driven the long slanting corridor to the surface. The ship, completely shielded, lay behind them, deep in the skin of Simpar, utterly undetectable.

Together, disguised by his suggestion as slave buyers from Lell, they had visited the pens, the auction blocks. Though inured through training to the misery on savage planets, Calna felt emotionally staggered by the mere weight of the suffering around her.

Andro, his face altered by her careful surgery, stalked through the open slave marts with an unforgiving grimness in his eyes, in the clamp of his jaw. They knew their danger. Were he to announce his presence too quickly, they would be overpowered by Field Teams before his influence could spread enough to cause a probability deviation.

Calna sensed that Simpar, as well as the other main planets of Empire, was under constant, wary scrutiny. She explained to Andro, saying, 'We must free them in such a way that it will appear to be a natural revolt. I have been trained in that sort of thing. Yet if I do it too cleverly, my presence here will be suspected.'

He thought it over. 'Then why not take this step? As we free them, give them ships and send them away to other planets. And, as they leave, tell them that Andro of Galvan has released them, and to keep that information secret until the word is passed. That will give this influence you talk about, the widest possible chance to operate.'

The Director received the report in person. He immediately beamed it to all Field Teams in Era 4, saying, 'Slave revolt on Simpar indicates help being given by Ex-Agent Calna. Request immediate Team concentration at Simpar.'

Within twenty hours the suspicion was verified by direct report from Simpar. The Field Team reported, 'Ex-Agent Calna and Andro can be immediately eliminated. However, escaped slaves have gone to other planets with information re Andro. Request verification of present probability index, as ship power less responsive than before.'

'Index sagging. Approaching danger point. Immediate elimination ordered. Verify. Verify.'

There was no verification. The Director waited until the last possible moment before ordering the slip back to a stable era. The city slipped back and communication with all Field Teams was thus cut.

It was night on Simpar. The triple moons, blood red, arced across the night sky. There were no more ships. The freed slaves, eyes wide and wild in the torchlight raced through the plundered streets. Throughout Solom, the capitol city of Simpar, Andro and Calna could hear distant crashes, faint screams as the last of the traders and buyers were hunted down and murdered. They had underestimated the unreasoning fury of the slaves, and thus found themselves in danger. Slaves dressed in the fineries of the traders and buyers and were themselves killed by their fellows.

Thrice Andro had to stand and fight and kill in order to clear their path through the city. The first scattered revolts

39

on the planet had been orderly, and the freed slaves had been spirited away on the captured ships without incident. But this past night when the last of the fortified marts and pens and mansions of the traders and the government had fallen completely was nightmare.

Andro found a grim humor in having to stand and do battle with slaves who died screaming his name, as though it were a magic incantation.

At last they were out of the city. Fires burned unchecked in the heart of the city. At one place flames rose hundreds of feet into the air. The dark plain was ahead of them, and in the darkness they meant to find the slanting tunnel down to the hidden ship.

'Now have we won?' Andro demanded as he hurried along beside her.

'I'll know when we reach the ship. If we've won, we cannot reach any other known era.'

The hidden entrance to the tunnel was less than a mile ahead. They ran on, and the night seemed endless as the clamor of the city faded behind them.

Solin's ship, containing the other agent who had replaced Calna, hung poised and invisible fifty feet above the mouth of the tunnel. The screens were adjusted to make the plain that stretched out toward the city as bright and clear as though it were bathed in sunshine.

He watched the tiny figures approaching. He knew who the first two were. The third one, the one who followed them, was unknown to him.

Solin felt the tiny shudder and turned almost in anger to Arla, the woman Agent who had replaced Calna. 'It's pointless to keep trying,' he said, 'we're beyond the point where we can return.'

The woman dropped her hands from the panel and turned toward him. Her expression was bleak and hopeless. Her shoulders sagged. She glanced at the screen. 'Soon they'll be near enough.'

'There seems to be no point in killing them now,' Solin said.

Arla gasped. 'But it was an order! Your service with that

40

Calna has made you a poor Agent, Solin. You heard the order.'

'We're trapped here in Four. They can't reach us and we can't reach them. So why kill them? The damage is already done.'

'It was an order,' the woman said.

Solin sighed. He sometimes wondered if the male-female teams were not a mistake. According to Field Team theory, it made for a more flexible unit, increased the time that could be spent by any single Team on any single assignment. But it did give rise to a great many petty irritations.

'We took so long finding the tunnel,' the woman said. 'That's what trapped us here. We can make it worthwhile now by following orders.'

IV

The Might of Deralan

Deralan, on arrival at Simpar, had been clapped into one of the feeding pens for fattening. He listened to the rumors that brightened the eyes of the one who had been in the pen before his shipment had arrived. Rumors of freedom. Rumors of revolt. They heard violence in the city for many days and nights and at last they were released. The guards were slain and the walls broken down and the gates smashed and the great house where the trader and pen-owner had lived set afire.

Deralan trotted into the city with the rest of them and there he heard the word that he had suspected, that he had not wanted to believe.

'Andro!' they shouted. 'Andro of Galvan!' It was a rallying cry, battle cry, blood scream. 'Andro!'

With sickness in his throat, Deralan dodged into the mouth of an alley and waited until the running steps had thudded into the distance. Dusk had changed slowly to night before he found a lone slave he could overpower.

41

'What of this Andro? Quick, while you live!'

'Please! He is said to be in the city. He has come back. His face is changed, but he has come back.'

'Where can I find him?'

'I don't know. Believe me, I don't know!'

Deralan made a quick and practiced gesture and then flung the body from him. He joined another wolf pack, snatched a torch, held it high, looked endlessly for a man with the huge strong body of Andro of Galvan.

He found a knife with a blade that suited him. He looted and burned and shouted with the others, but always he searched for Andro. He lost track of the hours. And at last he found a big man who stood with a fair-haired girl behind him and fought well, fought with the skill to be expected of any noble of the House of Galvan. He seemed about to be overpowered when the girl stepped to the side and something gleamed in her hand. The three who still faced the big man folded and dropped into absurdly small heaps on the paving stones.

As the big man turned, the torchlight touched his upper arm. Deralan sucked in his breath as he saw the pale rectangular patch. As they hurried on, Deralan looked at the three bodies. He swallowed hard. Something that swept across them, something the girl had used, had apparently completely removed whole sections of the men's torsos. That was why the huddled bodies looked so small.

He flung the torch aside to gutter out and followed the man and the girl through the smoke drift of the streets, his fingers hard and tight on the haft of the knife.

Deralan followed them out of the city and across the dark plain. The three dark moons stretched three vague shadows of his crouched body as he followed them. As the ground grew more uneven, he shortened the distance between them. He reversed the knife in his grasp. It had a good balance. Andro's back was broad. Deralan raised the knife. He poised it. He hurled it with all his strength. In the fractional part of a second before he released it, a great light bathed the entire plain in green-white brilliance. During the last six inches of the swing of his arm it seemed to Deralan that some great outside force had taken his arm and had given it a whip and power beyond anything any man should possess. The odd power snapped the bones of his arm and hurled him screaming into blackness.

Solin sat with his hand on the port control, completely frozen by an astonishment so vast that he could not move. Arla had asked to perform the actual execution. Solin had been glad to comply as he had no heart for it. He opened the port for her and when she had the hand weapon readied, he lighted the target area for her. Andro and Calna were in perfect range, a hundred yards away and fifty feet below them. In the instant of touching the lights he had seen the third figure in the act of hurling what seemed to be a knife at the pair leading him.

The unknown man had hurled the knife. There had been a keening whistle indicative of high velocity and a full-throated chunk. Arla had fallen dead with the knife blade in her brain, the guard of the haft flat against her forehead.

No person could throw a knife that way. Yet they had. He had seen it. The thrower lay crumpled on the ground with both Andro and Calna staring at him.

Solin dropped the ship to the ground beside the hidden tunnel entrance. He stepped over Arla's body and out into the now restricted area of green-white light.

Transition rested in Era 3 beside the endless thunder of the space port.

The Socionetics Board had launched a full scale investigation of the circumstances surrounding the loss of Era 4, and the loss of the thirty-odd Field Teams who had been trapped there when the index of probability dropped below the point where Agent ship power could accomplish the return.

The Board was exercising its prerogative of interviewing the staff members, one at a time. The Board met in the huge central chamber with the luminescent mural depicting the eventual merger of twenty-six co-existent worlds. Though now, of course, there were only twenty-four and thus the mural was, in that sense, a rather wry joke.

After three weeks of review and deliberation, the Director was called in to hear the decision of the Board.

The decision was very simple and very direct. It was given to him in the form of an order. Improper controls and criminal laxness have lost us two complete spheres of eventual cultural expansion. There will no longer be a continuing effort to accelerate the extrapolated cultural pattern of all backward eras simultaneously. All Field Teams will be concentrated on one era. All existing equipment will be immediately altered to make only that era, plus the basic three, available to Agent ships. Era 20 is closest to unity status. All effort is to be concentrated there. If, by any chance, Era 20 should be lost to us, all Field Team activities will be cancelled. No further acceleration of cultures will be attempted. All equipment except one master ship will be altered so as to permit only slip between basic eras. Periodic surveys with the master ship will be made. When each peripheral culture has attained proper probability status, then unity will be undertaken, but it will achieve that status in its own way and in its own time.

'And if unity is achieved with Era 20 without trouble?' the Director asked in a low voice.

'Then all effort will be concentrated on the next era closest to a possible unity status.'

The Director was permitted to leave. He gave the orders he was required to give. He gave an additional one of his own. He called all remaining Field Teams in for complete indoctrination on Era 20, for retraining, for re-analysis.

Thirty-three Field Teams trapped in Era 4. Count Andro and Calna, and subtract Arla. Sixty-seven persons. So few. So very few.

The golden pyramidial ships sat in a closed circle in such a way that the shields combined to form a cone of silence. The cone rose black and tall near the palaces of Rael.

In the streets they said, in hushed tones, 'The Great Ones speak again together.'

Andro had matured in the past months. Authority was stamped on his face, and dignity was imprinted on each movement.

44

'It is time to speak,' he said after a long silence. 'I do not pretend to know how you are trapped here. It has been explained to me. I have been told that my activities caused this era to diverge from some pattern or another. You say that this era has become less probable, in relation to your basic eras. Be that as it may. The damage was done. You were trapped. Through the urging of Solin and Calna you consented to help me impose my will on what is left of Empire. That has been done. There is no more resistance. We are the object of superstitious awe on every inhabited planet of Empire. Now you must feel that your task is ended. I say to you that it is not ended. With your consent, I wish to make you my agents, give each of you an area to govern until such time as self-government is possible. You have been told the things in which I believe. You do not need specific orders. It is not easy to be considered a god, as I now am. If you do your assigned tasks properly, there will come a time when I am no longer considered to be a god. That time will come long after all of us have died. I am urging this course because it seems to me that in this way this era can be gently guided back towards a point where eventually your own people will once again be able to make contact.'

The trapped Agents showed no great enthusiasm.

Calna took Andro's place and spoke. 'I urge you to accept. Through the incident of Arla's death, we have a piece of knowledge that they do not have back at Transition. We know now that while we were attempting to build backward eras up to the point where unity could be achieved, a stronger force was seeking to make all frames divergent. We do not know what that stronger force is. In my own case, I know I was guided when I set this entire pattern in motion. I suspected it then. I know it now. One thing is puzzling. Why was Deralan made the agent of saving Andro and myself from certain death? Divergence had already been achieved. Why was it done in such a way that we would learn of this outside force which interferes with the achievement of unity for our co-existent eras? There is one possible answer. We were saved so that we could be the focal point of this successful effort of the past few months. We were advised of outside inter-

45

ference so that we should be able to content ourselves with these new limitations.'

Solin spoke. 'Content ourselves? How is that meant?'

'Through knowledge that we are part of a master plan guided by some race, some civilization whose abilities make ours look like the efforts of children,' Calna replied.

'What sort of master plan is it which keeps the basic eras from achieving unity with all sister probability frames? That seems like progress in the wrong direction,' another Agent said with a note of anger.

'I say,' said Solin, 'that now that we have given Andro the assistance he asked, we should concentrate on using what skills and talents we have to devise a power source ample enough to enable us to slip back to our own era.'

There was a mutter of agreement. Andro turned to Calna and shrugged.

He said to all of them, 'I see that Solin's suggestion is your wish. So be it.' He looked at Calna. 'You will work with them?'

'I made my choice quite a long time ago,' she said. Together they went back to the palaces where new laws were being written for a galactic race.

Deralan knew at last that the madness was leaving him. It began to leave when he was willing to admit to himself that he had been mad. Something had swept across his brain, twisting it, convulsing it. At last he recognized his environment, knew with a sense of shock that he was in a cell deep under the main palace, a cell that he had filled and emptied many times in what now seemed like a previous incarnation.

Co-mingled with his weariness and lethargy was a new, odd sense of mental power, as though the twisting force had also liberated areas of his brain that had previously been dormant. Throughout the uncounted days of torment he had heard a constant shrill chorus of thin voices, as though he lay in the midst of a vast throng of children at play. Now he could bring back the voices at will, merely by *reaching* to hear them.

When food was brought, one of the shrill voices separated itself from the others and became so distinct that he could

46

understand scattered phrases, '—should be executed – Andro will decide – so many things changed – the Great Ones—'

And slowly Deralan came to know that he was *listening* to the thoughts of those near him. For a long time he listened. With practice he grew more acute, more certain of this new power. Once, when food was brought on an earthen dish, he willed the movement of opening the fingers of his right hand, not opening them, but willing the movement to open them with all his strength. The guard stared stupidly down at the smashed dish and scattered food. He massaged his fingers for a few moments.

With this start, Deralan began to practice with great care, making sure that what he was doing remained undiscovered. He found he could trip those who walked by the cell. At times he wondered if it was merely madness, but there was the evidence of his eyes and ears to be considered.

When he was certain of himself he caused a guard to leave the cell door unlocked. Deralan walked out. It was simplicity itself to cause every other guard to look the other way. He walked through as though invisible. He climbed the flights of stairs up to ground level and went out through all the gates into the streets of the city. He found a man of his own general build and guided the man into a narrow place between two buildings and caused the man to strip and don the prison garments. The man obeyed with an utterly blank expression, with no sign of confusion or fear.

Suddenly Deralan realized how pointless this attempt at escape was. This inexplicable gift which had been thrust upon him at the moment of hurling the knife was too powerful to be used for such a petty affair as escape. He turned soberly and walked back toward the main palace.

He found Andro and the fair-haired girl of the dark plain in the apartments that had once belonged to Shain. He sent the guards striding woodenly down the corridor and entered through the arched doorway.

Andro stared at him, his eyes widening, 'Deralan!' he gasped.

'Where is Shain?'

'Shain is dead by his own hand. Larrent and Masec are in exile.'

'You are Emperor?'

'The last one, Deralan. How did you get by the guards?'

'How do you plan to dispose of me?'

'By trial. You'll receive justice.'

He stood and listened to their thoughts, first sorting out Andro's, then the woman's. Andro was merely puzzled, not afraid. The woman intrigued him. Two voices seemed to come from her. One from here and now. Another background voice that spoke of far places and wondrous things and skills beyond imagining, of others like her who were nearby. He related it immediately to the thoughts of the guards who had spoken of the Great Ones. He changed his plan immediately. He had intended to kill them both, setting them against each other to kill. But these two were not the real opposition.

'Take me to your people,' he said aloud to the woman. She reached for a glittering object which hung from her wide belt. He remembered the three who died so quickly and strangely on Simpar. He made her fling the glittering object into a corner. Her eyes widened with fear and then assumed the familiar blankness. She came with him as he willed her to walk. Andro gave a hoarse cry of alarm and Deralan forced him back into a far corner, left him standing there.

The woman guided him to a place just outside the city where a ring of golden pyramidal objects stood around a building that was new, oddly constructed, covered with hoods and twisted screens of wire.

The woman took him into the building where there were scores of people at work. They stared at him oddly. These were the enemy.

In the center of the floor was the cube on which they worked. Cables as big around as a man's thigh writhed away from the cube. A shining metal column rose upward from the cube through the roof high overhead.

Deralan looked at the cube and he was puzzled. He had a feeling of *wrongness*. He stared at it and saw wrongness, and an obscure clumsiness, and a childish ineffectuality. He walked closer to it and in his mind saw the image of the way it should

48

be. The people were forgotten. Only the power cube was important. He brushed by those who tried to bar the way and reached into the cube where tiny tubes glowed and relays chattered. Slowly at first, and then with increasing dexterity he began to take down circuits. As they tried to pull him away, he turned with impatience and smote them back with a careless easy power of the mind which sent them sprawling. Soon he noted that they were helping him, and he heard his own voice giving instructions that sounded meaningless and yet had a sound of *rightness* as opposed to the *wrongness* he was eliminating.

After fifty hours of ceaseless labor the work was done. The blue cube was like nothing any of the exiled Agents had ever seen before. It utilized only a fractional part of the power they had hooked up to lead into it. It had ceased to be a cube and had become a geometric form which dizzied them as they looked at it. It had nine sides, yet only ten edges. The effect was mildly hypnotic, and the attempt to relate visual evidence to known geometric forms gave it the look of being in constant flux.

Deralan had collapsed the moment the work was finished. They had taken him to a couch. His eyes were wide and he babbled endlessly and sucked at his fingers.

The cables led to one of the Agent ships which had been brought as close as possible to the main entrance to the building.

Calna looked at them all in anger. 'Are we to be superstitious children? Are we to be afraid of this? He was used before, by "them". Now he has been used again. Once he had fulfilled his purpose, he was discarded.'

'What will it do?' Solin asked.

'I say it will do just what it was intended to do. Take us back to our own era,' she said.

Hesitation faded. Two Agents stepped into the ship and port folded shut behind them. The others watched, expecting the mistiness which would indicate that the ship had slipped properly. Instead the ship was just . . . gone. The heavy cables fell to the ground and the air, rushing into the place where

49

the ship had been, made a sound like the cracking of a great whip.

One by one they departed. Solin was last. He left alone in the ship he had shared with Arla. There was one golden ship left. And Calna. Andro had come. He watched her thoughtfully.

'You may go,' he said.

'I shall stay here, Andro. I belong now.'

She went back to the palace with him.'

The long days went by. Often she went to a high window from which she could see the building in which the cube throbbed and shifted. Many times she walked to that place and watched the cube and touched her fingers lightly to the side of the small golden ship.

Andro sensed her discontent. He was busy with the new structure of government which he was building carefully. There was little that they could share.

She remembered other days, and other times, and realized more strongly each day how savage and primitive an era this was.

In a place that was no-place and in a time that was no-time, the thought record halted and waited. It waited, not in the sense of elapsing time, but in the sense of an endless interruption. Impatience was not known to the intelligence directing the record. Other endless computations continued. But the directing intelligence, which did exist in a finite, though variable, space time, felt a subtle irritation.

This particular phase of this particular problem had been completed. The basic questions had been answered. An unseen hand had reached into the remote past, had twisted probabilities to the ultimate degree of distortion. In its simplest sense, false worlds had been created. The historical derivations had been weighed. Cause-effects had been measured in all temporal directions.

And now the ultimate step in the problem was held in stasis, merely because of the almost unpredictable whim of a female who, being a structural portion of an experiment in improbability, was herself improbable. . . .

He came to her as she stood at the high window, and he said, 'You must return. I know that. Come back, if it can be done, and if you have the desire. I can keep you a prisoner no longer.'

'Not a prisoner, Andro.'

'You must go back.'

'I will return if I can. But you're right.'

They went to the golden ship where the cables were already attached, waiting.

She turned as she entered the port, and lifted her hand slowly. Her eyes were misted. She turned quickly to the controls. The port folded shut.

And thus, with the whip crack of her departure, the universe itself, Andro's time and place and cities and suns and planets and wars and history – snapped out as though a quick finger had touched the light switch, leaving a room in darkness. The webs of probability had been pulled tight, twisted. And now the pressure was released. The record had been kept. The experiment was over.

Probability is like a plastic which is formed with a molecular 'memory'. It can be distorted but, once released, it will revert.

The reversion will be a function of time, rather than space. Tangential worlds can be artificially created. So long as the artificial pressure is maintained, they will seem to 'exist.' But with the release of that pressure . . .

The Agent Ship had plunged into the crust of Zeran in Era 4, powerless to save the sole remaining ship, the flagship of Andro's fleet. The crippled flagship swung lower, out of control. Solin, at the controls of the Agent ship, picked up the crippled ship in his screens and swung up through the planet crust in order to be within close range in case anything might be done. He halted the Agent ship twenty feet below ground level just as the crippled ship landed with a tremendous jarring crash.

Calna moved up behind him and watched the screen over Solin's shoulder. A powerful man staggered out through the huge rent in the skin of the ship, dragging an unconscious dark-haired girl. They saw him glance up at the dark skies, his

51

face twisted with fury and anger. He fumbled for a pulse in the girl's throat, then stood silently, shoulders slumped, in stoic grief. Again he searched the blackness overhead, and ran into the city. His wounds had weakened him. He weaved as he ran, but he tugged a weapon from his holster.

'Can we save him once more?' Calna asked calmly.

'Not this time. They've seen him run into the city.'

'At least we could follow. Report the end of it.'

They took the portable screen from the rack, left the ship standing there, sliced through the depths of the city, following Andro in his blundering run. They saw him take refuge in a blind alley, shadowed by the eternal blue dusk. They saw him brace his shoulders against the wall, waiting for them to find him.

Calna and Solin waited directly below him.

Soon the dying man was spotted. He used the weapon well. His last shot was fired from within the boundary of death itself, the finger tightening in the last convulsion. Deralan came and cautiously inspected the body. He signaled to the other to take the body away.

Solin started back along the fresh tunnel, but Calna did not follow. He turned and stared at her. 'What is it?'

'I . . . I don't know. A very odd feeling. As though somehow we have made a mistake that we could not predict. We should have cut up through to him, saved him.'

'And turn a decent rebellion into a pseudo-religious revival?' Solin said.

'I know all that. It was just an odd feeling. But strong, Solin. Very strong.'

Sarrz, Deputy Director of the Bureau of Socionetics, turned in his chair so that he would not have to look at the face of the female Agent who had asked to speak with him after she and Solin had made a rather disappointing, but unavoidable, report on the demise of one Andro, rebel of Era 4.

'You say you are troubled.'

She chose her words carefully. 'I wish to request EC, Deputy Director. I have had odd imaginings. Possibly the strain of the last few months in Era 4.'

52

'Do you care to tell me any of them?'

She shrugged. 'They are all a bit ridiculous. It seemed that in some other existence we had saved Andro rather than permitting him to be killed. I know how unfortunate a mistake it would have been to save him again. Also, I found myself thinking that we had lost some of the eras by permitting too great a probability divergence from our basic eras. And during the last sleep I dreamed that we have a power source which can cause slip to any era, no matter how divergent.'

'Those are concrete examples. But what is your attitude toward them?'

'Awe, I would say. Foreboding. And a feeling of having led other existences.'

Sarrz said, 'All of us have dreams. I dreamed of dying at this desk. I have dreamed of losing all the worlds.'

'And you feel fear?'

'Tension. Doubt. But those, I feel, are the result of our primitive heritage. It is in our blood and our bones to think of only one space and one time. Now we know that there are twenty-six available space-times contiguous to our own which we can reach, and an infinite number of others that we cannot yet reach. I would not worry too much, Agent Calna. We live in a day of oddness, of new philosophic evaluations, of invisible doors which have opened so that we can step through. The first wild dogs that joined savage man in his caves must have had uneasy dreams by the fires of night. And maybe, Agent Calna, we are no higher in our possible evolutionary scale than those dogs were in relation to the man they joined. Even now, at this moment, some inconceivable intelligence from our remote future may be tampering with our acts and the consequences of our acts. Such tampering would leave elusive traces in your mind, in my mind. Possibly every time we enter a strange room and have the feeling that we have been in that room before, it is because we actually *have* been in that room, in some fragmentary part of a vast experiment which was later abandoned. Our present actions, this very conversation, this room . . . it could all be part of an artificially induced environment merely in order to test your reaction and mine. In fact, you may not even exist in

53

the ordinary sense of the word, but only as a manufactured entity thrown into my personal equation as some portion of a test for a solution.'

The girl smiled uncertainly. 'This begins to sound like one of the conversations planned to disprove the existence of everything except the mind of the beholder.'

'I will approve EC if you insist.'

'I think I must insist.'

'You can report to EC at once, if you wish. I will reassign Solin, and give you a new partner when you return.'

The girl left. Sarrz sat in utter stillness for a long time. The girl's request had crystallized some of his own weary doubts as to the rightness of the entire program on which they had embarked.

He sat and felt a sour yearning for the days gone by, the days when man could concern himself with only one environment – back in the functional simplicity of the third atomic era.

He was willing to blow himself and his strange weather station – that watched the movement of millennium-long storms of inter-stellar space – to atoms to conceal the secret of his people. They were safe, concealed in the haystack of a hundred trillion stars – unless he gave a clue!

CONCEALMENT

By A E van Vogt

The Earth ship came so swiftly around the planetless Gisser sun that the alarm system in the meteorite weather station had no time to react. The great machine was already visible when Watcher grew aware of it.

Alarms must have blared in the ship, too, for it slowed noticeably and, still braking, disappeared. Now it was coming back, creeping along, obviously trying to locate the small object that had affected its energy screens.

It loomed vast in the glare of the distant yellow-white sun, bigger even at this distance than anything ever seen by the Fifty Suns, a very hell ship out of remote space, a monster from a semi-mythical world, instantly recognizable from the descriptions in the history books as a battleship of Imperial Earth. Dire had been the warnings in the histories of what would happen someday – and here it was.

He knew his duty. There was a warning, the age-long dreaded warning, to send to the Fifty Suns by the non-directional sub-space radio; and he had to make sure nothing telltale remained of the station.

There was no fire. As the overloaded atomic engines dissolved, the massive building that had been a weather sub-station simply fell into its component elements.

Watcher made no attempt to escape. His brain, with its knowledge, must not be tapped. He felt a brief, blinding spasm of pain as the energy tore him to atoms.

She didn't bother to accompany the expedition that landed

on the meteorite. But she watched with intent eyes through the astroplate.

From the very first moment that the spy rays had shown a human figure in a weather station – a weather station *out here* – she had known the surpassing importance of the discovery. Her mind leaped instantly to the several possibilities.

Weather stations meant interstellar travel. Human beings meant Earth origin. She visualized how it could have happened: an expedition long ago; it must have been long ago because now they had interstellar travel, and that meant large populations on many planets.

His majesty, she thought, would be pleased.

So was she. In a burst of generosity, she called the energy room.

'Your prompt action, Captain Glone,' she said warmly, 'in inclosing the entire meterorite in a sphere of protective energy is commendable, and will be rewarded.'

The man whose image showed on the astroplate, bowed. 'Thank you, noble lady.' He added: 'I think we saved the electronic and atomic components of the entire station. Unfortunately, because of the interference of the atomic energy of the station itself. I understand the photographic department was not so successful in obtaining clear prints.'

The woman smiled grimly, said: 'The *man* will be sufficient, and that is a matrix for which we need no prints.'

She broke the connection, still smiling, and returned her gaze to the scene on the meteorite. As she watched the energy and matter absorbers in their glowing gluttony, she thought:

There had been several storms on the map in that weather station. She'd seen them in the spy ray; and one of the storms had been very large. Her great ship couldn't dare to go fast while the location of that storm was in doubt.

Rather a handsome young man he had seemed in the flashing glimpse she had had in the spy ray, strong-willed, brave. Should be interesting in an uncivilized sort of fashion.

First, of course, he'd have to be conditioned, drained of relevant information. Even now a mistake might make it necessary to begin a long, laborious search. Centuries could be wasted on these short distances of a few light years, where a ship couldn't get up speed, and where it dared not maintain velocity, once attained, without exact weather information.

She saw that the men were leaving the meteorite. Decisively, she clicked off the intership communicator, made an adjustment and stepped through a transmitter into the receiving room half a mile distant.

The officer in charge came over and saluted. He was frowning:

'I have just received the prints from the photographic department. The blur of energy haze over the map is particularly distressing. I would say that we should first attempt to reconstitute the building and its contents, leaving the man to the last.'

He seemed to sense her disapproval, went on quickly:

'After all, he comes under the common human matrix. His reconstruction, while basically somewhat more difficult, falls into the same category as your stepping through the transmitter in the main bridge and coming to this room. In both cases there is dissolution of elements – which must be brought back into the original solution.'

The woman said: 'But why leave him to the last?'

'There are technical reasons having to do with the greater complexity of inanimate objects. Organized matter, as you know, is little more than a hydro-carbon compound, easily conjured.'

'Very well.' She wasn't as sure as he that a man and his brain, with the knowledge that had made the map, was less important than the map itself. But if both could be had – She nodded with decision. 'Proceed.'

She watched the building take shape inside the large receiver. It slid out finally on wings of antigravity, and was deposited in the center of the enormous metal floor.

The technician came down from his control chamber shaking his head. He led her and the half dozen others who had arrived, through the rebuilt weather station, pointing out the defects.

'Only twenty-seven sun points showing on the map,' he said. 'That is ridiculously low, even assuming that these people are organized for only a small area of space. And, besides, notice how *many* storms are shown, some considerably beyond the area of the reconstituted suns and—'

He stopped, his gaze fixed on the shadowy floor behind a machine twenty feet away.

The woman's eyes followed his. A man lay there, his body twisting.

'I thought,' she said frowning, 'the man was to be left to the last.'

The scientist was apologetic: 'My assistant must have misunderstood. They—'

The woman cut him off: 'Never mind. Have him sent at once to Psychology House, and tell Lieutenant Neslor I shall be there shortly.'

'At once, noble lady.'

'Wait! Give my compliments to the senior meteorologist and ask him to come down here, examine this map, and advise me of his findings.'

She whirled on the group around her, laughing through her even, white teeth. 'By space, here's action at last after ten dull years of surveying. We'll rout out these hide-and-go-seekers in short order.'

Excitement blazed inside her like a living force.

The strange thing to Watcher was that he knew before he wakened why he was still alive. Not very long before.

He *felt* the approach of consciousness. Instinctively, he began his normal Dellian preawakening muscle, nerve and mind exercises. In the middle of the curious rhythmic system, his brain paused in a dreadful surmise.

Returning to consciousness? *He!*

It was at that point, as his brain threatened to burst from his head with shock, that the knowledge came of how it had been done.

He grew quiet, thoughtful. He stared at the young woman who reclined on a chaise longue near his bed. She had a fine, oval face and a distinguished appearance for so young a person. She was studying him from sparkling gray eyes. Under that steady gaze, his mind grew very still.

He thought finally: 'I've been conditioned to an easy awakening. What else did they do – find out?'

The thought grew until it seemed to swell his brainpan: WHAT ELSE?

He saw that the woman was smiling at him, a faint, amused smile. It was like a tonic. He grew even calmer as the woman said in a silvery voice:

'Do not be alarmed. That is, not too alarmed. What is your name?'

Watcher parted his lips, then closed them again, and shook his head grimly. He had the impulse to explain then that even answering one question would break the thrall of Dellian mental inertia and result in the revolution of valuable information.

But the explanation would have constituted a different kind of defeat. He suppressed it, and once more shook his head.

The young woman, he saw, was frowning. She said: 'You won't answer a simple question like that? Surely, your name can do no harm.'

His name, Watcher thought, then what planet he was from, where the planet was in relation to the Gisser sun, what about intervening storms. And so on down the line. There wasn't any end.

Every day that he could hold these people away from the information they craved would give the Fifty Suns so much more time to organize against the greatest machine that had ever flown into this part of space.

His thought trailed. The woman was sitting up, gazing at him with eyes that had gone steely. Her voice held a metallic resonance as she said:

'Know this, whoever you are, that you are aboard the Imperial Battleship *Star Cluster*, Grand Captain Laurr at your service. Know, too, that it is our unalterable will that you shall prepare for us an orbit that will take our ship safely to your chief planet.'

She went on vibrantly: 'It is my solemn belief you already know that Earth recognizes no separate governments. Space is indivisible. The universe shall not be an area of countless sovereign peoples squabbling and quarreling for power.

'That is the law. Those who set themselves against it are outlaws, subject to any punishment which may be decided upon in their special case.

'Take warning.'

Without waiting for an answer, she turned her head. 'Lieutenant Neslor,' she said at the wall facing Watcher, 'have you made any progress?'

A woman's voice answered: 'Yes, noble lady. I have set up an integer based on the Muir-Grayson studies of colonial peoples who have been isolated from the main stream of galactic life. There is no historical precedent for such a long isolation as seems to have obtained here, so I have decided to assume that they have passed the static period, and have made some progress of their own.

'I think we should begin very simply, however. A few forced answers will open his brain to further pressures, and we can draw valuable conclusions meanwhile from the speed with which he adjusts his resistance to the brain machine. Shall I proceed?'

The woman on the chaise longue nodded. There was a flash of light from the wall facing Watcher. He tried to dodge, and discovered for the first time that *something* held him in the bed, not rope, or chain, nothing visible. But something as palpable as rubbery steel.

Before he could think further, the light was in his eyes, in his mind, a dazzling fury. Voices seemed to push through it, voices that danced and sang, and spoke into his brain, voices that said:

'A simple question like that – of course I'll answer . . . of course, of course, of course— My name is Gisser Watcher. I was born on the planet Kaider III, of Dellian parents. There are seventy inhabited planets, fifty suns, thirty billion people, four hundred important storms, the biggest at Latitude 473. The Central Government is on the glorious planet, Cassidor VII—'

With a blank horror of what he was doing, Watcher caught his roaring mind into a Dellian knot, and stopped that devastating burst of revelation. He knew he would never be

60

caught like that again but – too late, he thought, too late by far.

The woman wasn't quite so certain. She went out of the bedroom, and came presently to where the middle-aged Lieutenant Neslor was classifying her findings on receptor spools.

The psychologist glanced up from her work, said in an amazed voice: 'Noble lady, his resistance during the stoppage moment registered an equivalent of IQ 800. Now, that's utterly impossible, particularly because he started talking at a pressure point equivalent to IQ 167, which matches with his general appearance, and which you know is average.

'There must be a system of mind training behind his resistance. And I think I found the clue in his reference to his Dellian ancestry. His graph squared in intensity when he used the word.

'This is very serious, and may cause great delay – unless we are prepared to break his mind.'

The grand captain shook her head, said only: 'Report further developments to me.'

On the way to the transmitter, she paused to check the battleship's position. A bleak smile touched her lips, as she saw on the reflector the shadow of a ship circling the brighter shadow of a sun.

Marking time, she thought, and felt a chill of premonition. Was it possible that one man was going to hold up a ship strong enough to conquer an entire galaxy?

The senior ship meteorologist, Lieutenant Cannons, stood up from a chair as she came toward him across the vast floor of the transmission receiving room, where the Fifty Suns weather station still stood. He had graying hair, and he was very old, she remembered, very old. Walking toward him, she thought:

There was a slow pulse of life in these men who watched the great storms of space. There must be to them a sense of futility about it all, a timelessness. Storms that took a century or more to attain their full roaring maturity, such storms and the men who catalogued them must acquire a sort of affinity of spirit.

The slow stateliness was in his voice, too, as he bowed with a measure of grace, and said:

'Grand Captain, the Right Honourable Gloria Cecily, the Lady Laurr of Noble Laurr, I am honoured by your personal presence.'

She acknowledged the greeting, and then unwound the spool for him. He listened, frowning, said finally:

'The latitude he gave for the storm is a meaningless quantity. These incredible people have built up a sun relation system in the Lesser Magellanic Cloud, in which the center is an arbitrary one having no recognizable connection with the magnetic center of the whole Cloud. Probably, they've picked some sun, called it center, and built their whole spatial geography around it.'

The old man whirled abruptly away from her, and led the way into the weather station, to the edge of the pit above which poised the reconstructed weather map.

'The map is utterly worthless to us,' he said succinctly.

'What?'

She saw that he was staring at her, his china-blue eyes thoughtful.

'Tell me, what is your idea of this map?'

The woman was silent, unwilling to commit herself in the face of so much definiteness. Then she frowned, and said:

'My impression is much as you described. They've got a system of their own here, and all we've got to do is find the key.'

She finished more confidently: 'Our main problems, it seems to me, would be to determine which direction we should go in the immediate vicinity of this meteorite weather station we've found. If we chose the wrong direction, there would be vexatious delay, and, throughout, our chief obstacle would be that we dare not go fast because of possible storms.'

She looked at him questioningly, as she ended. And saw that he was shaking his head, gravely:

'I'm afraid,' he said, 'it's not so simple as that. Those bright point-replicas of suns look the size of peas due to light distortion, but when examined through a metroscope they show

62

only a few molecules in diameter. If that is their proportion to the suns they represent—'

She had learned in genuine crises to hide her feelings from subordinates. She stood now, inwardly stunned, outwardly cool, thoughtful, calm. She said finally:

'You mean each one of those suns, their suns, is buried among about a thousand other suns?'

'Worse than that. I would say that they have only inhabited one system in ten thousand. We must never forget that the Lesser Magellanic Cloud is a universe of fifty million stars. That's a lot of sunshine.'

The old man concluded quietly: 'If you wish, I will prepare orbits involving maximum speeds of ten light days a minute to all the nearest stars. We may strike it lucky.'

The woman shook her head savagely: 'One in ten thousand. Don't be foolish. I happen to know the law of averages that relates to ten thousand. We would have to visit a minimum of twenty-five hundred suns if we were lucky, thirty-five to fifty thousand if we were not.

'No, no' – a grim smile compressed her fine lips – 'we're not going to spend five hundred years looking for a needle in a haystack. I'll trust to psychology before I trust to chance. We have the man who understands the map, and while it will take time, he'll talk in the end.'

She started to turn away, then stopped. 'What,' she asked, 'about the building itself? Have you drawn any conclusions from its design?'

He nodded. 'Of the type used in the galaxy about fifteen thousand years ago.'

'Any improvements, changes?'

'None that I can see. One observer, who does all the work. Simple, primitive.'

She stood thoughtful, shaking her head as if trying to clear away a mist.

'It seems strange. Surely after fifteen thousand years they could have added something. Colonies are usually static, but not that static.'

She was examining routine reports three hours later when her astro clanged twice, softly. Two messages—

The first was from Psychology House, a single question: 'Have we permission to break the prisoner's mind?'

'No!' said Grand Captain Laurr.

The second message made her glance across at the orbit board. The board was aglitter with orbit symbols. That wretched old man, disobeying her injunction NOT to prepare any orbits.

Smiling twistedly, she walked over and studied the shining things, and finally sent an order to Central Engines. She watched as her great ship plunged into night.

After all, she thought, there was such a thing as playing two games at the same time. Counterpoint was older in human relations than it was in music.

The first day she stared down at the outer planet of a blue-white sun. It floated in the darkness below the ship, an airless mass of rock and metal, drab and terrible as any meteorite, a world of primeval canyons and mountains untouched by the leavening breath of life.

Spy rays showed only rock, endless rock, not a sign of movement or of past movement.

There were three other planets, one of them a warm, green world where winds sighed through virgin forests and animals swarmed on the plains.

Not a house showed, nor the erect form of a human being.

Grimly, the woman said into the intership communicator: 'Exactly how far can our spy rays penetrate into the ground?'

'A hundred feet.'

'Are there any metals which can simulate a hundred feet of earth?'

'Several, noble lady.'

Dissatisfied, she broke the connection. There was no call that day from Psychology House.

The second day, a giant red sun swam into her impatient ken. Ninety-four planets swung in their great orbits around their massive parent. Two were habitable, but again there was the profusion of wilderness and of animals usually found only on planets untouched by the hand and metal of civilization.

The chief zoological officer reported the fact in his precise voice: 'The percentage of animals parallels the mean for worlds not inhabited by intelligent beings.'

The woman snapped: 'Has it occurred to you that there may have been a deliberate policy to keep animal life abundant, and laws preventing the tilling of the soil even for pleasure?'

She did not expect, nor did she receive, an answer. And once more there was not a word from Lieutenant Neslor, the chief psychologist.

The third sun was farther away. She had the speed stepped up to twenty light days a minute – and received a shocking reminder as the ship bludgeoned into a small storm. It must have been small because the shuddering of metal had barely begun when it ended.

'There has been some talk,' she said afterward to the thirty captains assembled in the captains' pool, 'that we return to the galaxy and ask for an expedition that will uncover these hidden rascals.

'One of the more whining of the reports that have come to my ears suggests that, after all, we were on our way home when we made our discovery, and that our ten years in the Cloud have earned us a rest.'

Her gray eyes flashed; her voice grew icy: 'You may be sure that those who sponsor such defeatism are not the ones who would have to make the personal report of failure to his majesty's government. Therefore, let me assure the faint hearts and the homesick that we shall remain another ten years if it should prove necessary. Tell the officers and crew to act accordingly. That is all.'

Back in the main bridge, she saw that there was still no call from Psychology House. There was a hot remnant of anger and impatience in her, as she dialed the number. But she controlled herself as the distinguished face of Lieutenant Neslor appeared on the plate. She said then:

'What is happening, lieutenant? I am anxiously waiting for further information from the prisoner.'

65

The woman psychologist shook her head. 'Nothing to report.'

'Nothing!' Her amazement was harsh in her voice.

'I have asked twice,' was the answer, 'for permission to break his mind. You must have known that I would not lightly suggest such a drastic step.'

'Oh!' She had known, but the disapproval of the people at home, the necessity for accounting for any amoral action against individuals, had made refusal an automatic action. Now— Before she could speak, the psychologist went on:

'I have made some attempts to condition him in his sleep, stressing the uselessness of resisting Earth when eventual discovery is sure. But that has only convinced him that his earlier revelations were of no benefit to us.'

The leader found her voice: 'Do you really mean, lieutenant, that you have no plan other than violence? Nothing?'

In the astroplate, the image head made a negative movement. The psychologist said simply:

'An 800 IQ resistance in a 167 IQ brain is something new in my experience.'

The woman felt a great wonder. 'I can't understand it,' she complained. 'I have a feeling we've missed some vital clue. Just like that we run into a weather station in a system of fifty million suns, a station in which there is a human being who, contrary to all the laws of self-preservation, immediately kills himself to prevent himself from falling into our hands.

'The weather station itself is an old model galactic affair, which shows no improvements after fifteen thousand years; and yet the vastness of the time elapsed, the caliber of the brains involved suggest that all the obvious changes should have been made.

'And the man's name, Watcher, is so typical of the ancient pre-spaceship method of calling names on Earth according to the trade. It is possible that even the sun, where he is watching, is a service heritage of his family. There's something – depressing – here somewhere that—'

She broke off, frowning: 'What is your plan?' After a minute, she nodded. 'I see . . . very well, bring him to one of the bedrooms in the main bridge. And forget that part about making up one of our strong-arm girls to look like me. I'll do everything that's necessary. Tomorrow. Fine.'

Coldly she sat watching the prisoner's image in the plate. The man, Watcher, lay in bed, an almost motionless figure, eyes closed, but his face curiously tense. He looked, she thought, like someone discovering that for the first time in four days, the invisible force lines that had bound him had been withdrawn.

Beside her, the woman psychologist hissed: 'He's still suspicious, and will probably remain so until you partially ease his mind. His general reactions will become more and more concentrated. Every minute that passes will increase his conviction that he will have only one chance to destroy the ship, and that he must be decisively ruthless regardless of risk.

'I have been conditioning him the past ten hours to resistance to us in a very subtle fashion. You will see in a moment ... ah-h!'

Watcher was sitting up in bed. He poked a leg from under the sheets, then slid forward, and onto his feet. It was an oddly powerful movement.

He stood for a moment, a tall figure in gray pajamas. He had evidently been planning his first actions because, after a swift look at the door, he walked over to a set of drawers built into one wall, tugged at them tentatively, and then jerked them open with an effortless strength, snapping their locks one by one.

Her own gasp was only an echo of the gasp of Lieutenant Neslor.

'Good heavens!' the psychologist said finally. 'Don't ask me to explain how he's breaking those metal locks. Strength must be a by-product of his Dellian training. Noble lady—'

Her tone was anxious; and the grand captain looked at her. 'Yes?'

'Do you think, under the circumstances, you should play such a personal role in his subjection? His strength is obviously such that he can break the body of anyone aboard—'

She was cut off by an imperious gesture. 'I cannot,' said the Right Honourable Gloria Cecily, 'risk some fool making a

67

mistake. I'll take an antipain pill. Tell me when it is time to go in.'

Watcher felt cold, tense, as he entered the instrument room of the main bridge. He had found his clothes in some locked drawers. He hadn't known they were there, but the drawers aroused his curiosity. He made the preliminary Dellian extra energy movements; and the locks snapped before his super strength.

Pausing on the threshold, he flicked his gaze through the great domed room. And after a moment his terrible fear that he and his kind were lost, suffered another transfusion of hope. He was actually free.

These people couldn't have the faintest suspicion of the truth. The great genius, Joseph H Dell, must be a forgotten man on Earth. Their release of him must have behind it some plan of course but—

'Death,' he thought ferociously, 'death to them all, as they had once inflicted death, and would again.'

He was examining the bank on bank of control boards when, out of the corner of his eyes, he saw the woman step from the nearby wall.

He looked up; he thought with a savage joy: The leader! They'd have guns protecting her, naturally, but they wouldn't know that all these days he had been frantically wondering how he could force the use of guns.

Surely to space, they *couldn't* be prepared to gather up his component elements again. Their very act of freeing him had showed psychology intentions.

Before he could speak, the woman said, smilingly: 'I really shouldn't let you examine those controls. But we have decided on a different tactic with you. Freedom of the ship, an opportunity to meet the crew. We want to convince you . . . convince you—'

Something of the bleakness and implacableness of him must have touched her. She faltered, shook herself in transparent self-annoyance, then smiled more firmly, and went on in a persuasive tone:

'We want you to realize that we're not ogres. We want to

68

end your alarm that we mean harm to your people. You must know, now we have found you exist, that discovery is only a matter of time.

'Earth is not cruel, or dominating, at least not any more. The barest minimum of allegiance is demanded, and that only to the idea of a common unity, the indivisibility of space. It is required, too, that criminal laws be uniform, and that a high minimum wage for workers be maintained. In addition, wars of any kind are absolutely forbidden.

'Except for that, every planet or group of planets, can have its own form of government, trade with whom they please, live their own life. Surely, there is nothing terrible enough in all this to justify the curious attempt at suicide you made when we discovered the weather station.'

He would, he thought, listening to her, break her head first. The best method would be to grab her by the feet, and smash her against the metal wall or floor. Bone would crush easily and the act would serve two vital purposes :

It would be a terrible and salutary warning to the other officers of the ship. And it would precipitate upon him the death fire of her guards.

He took a step toward her. And began the faintly visible muscle and nerve movements so necessary to pumping the Dellian body to a pitch of superhuman capability. The woman was saying :

'You stated before that your people have inhabited fifty suns in this space. Why only fifty? In twelve thousand or more years, a population of twelve thousand billion would not be beyond possibility.'

He took another step. And another. Then knew that he must speak if he hoped to keep her unsuspicious for those vital seconds while he inched closer, closer. He said :

'About two thirds of our marriages are childless. It has been very unfortunate, but you see there are two types of us, and when intermarriage occurs as it does without hindrance—'

Almost he was near enough; he heard her say : 'You mean, a mutation has taken place; and the two don't mix?'

He didn't have to answer that. He was ten feet from her;

69

and like a tiger he launched himself across the intervening gap.

The first energy beam ripped through his body too low down to be fatal, but it brought a hot scalding nausea and a dreadful heaviness. He heard the grand captain scream:

'Lieutenant Neslor, what are you doing?'

He had her then. His fingers were grabbing hard at her fending arm, when the second blow struck him high in the ribs and brought the blood frothing into his mouth. In spite of all his will, he felt his hands slipping from the woman. Oh, space, how he would have liked to take her into the realm of death with him.

Once again, the woman screamed: 'Lieutenant Neslor, are you mad? *Cease fire!*'

Just before the third beam burned at him with its indescribable violence, he thought with a final and tremendous sardonicism: 'She still didn't suspect. But somebody did, somebody who at this ultimate moment had guessed the truth.'

'Too late,' he thought, 'too late, you fools! Go ahead and hunt. They've had warning, time to conceal themselves even more thoroughly. And the Fifty Suns are scattered, scattered among a million stars, among—'

Death caught his thought.

The woman picked herself off the floor, and stood dizzily striving to draw her roughly handled senses back into her brain. She was vaguely aware of Lieutenant Neslor coming through a transmitter, pausing at the dead body of Gisser Watcher and rushing toward her.

'Are you all right, my dear? It was so hard firing through an astroplate that—'

'You mad woman!' The grand captain caught her breath. 'Do you realize that a body can't be reconstituted once vital organs have been destroyed. Dissolution or resolution cannot be piecemeal. We'll have to go home without—'

She stopped. She saw that the psychologist was staring at her. Lieutenant Neslor said:

'His intention to attack was unmistakable and it was too

70

soon according to my graphs. All the way through, he's never fitted anything in human psychology.

'At the very last possible moment I remembered Joseph Dell and the massacre of the Dellian supermen fifteen thousand years ago. Fantastic to think that some of them escaped and established a civilization in this remote part of space.

'Do you see now: "Dellian" – Joseph M Dell – the inventor of the Dellian perfect robot.'

After how many years, how many generations, the Earthmen were going home — peacefully submitting to the order of exile. What was the meaning of it all? Why were the Earthlings letting themselves be expelled?

TO CIVILIZE

By Algis Budrys

There was no moon, there were no stars; the sky was overcast. The spacefield lights threw up an umbrella of yellow-white, shot through by the silvered reflections thrown off by the ship on the takeoff stand. The big winches at the ship's cargo-hatches creaked their cables with a disproportionate loudness. Except for the constant undercurrent of the sound of straining metal, the field was quiet.

Is it too *quiet?* Deric thought. Was it the silence that lurks at the van of a storm, waiting to be ripped to tatters as the sudden wind broke out, as the hurricane spun out of the tropics and howled?

Is this how it ends? Deric leaned his weight against the rail of the observation-platform, his whiplash body drawn up into a taut ribbon. The field lights gleamed from the polished blackness of his hide, glinting on the cropped silver follicles of his crest. *Is this the way of Earthmen?*

Except for the graceful bodies of his own people as they operated the silent cargo-carriers streaming out to the ship, there was no life on the field. Even behind the big doors of the cargo-hatches, there was no sign of movement. Under him, at ground-level, the Galactics waited in their big room for the loading to end. Then there would be a procession of figures, loaded with their personal baggage, walking out across the field to the ship. There would be women holding or leading children, and men walking beside them.

In the beginning, when the order had been published, Deric had thought there might be trouble. The Galactics were not a meek lot. While they were independent enough in their

72

everyday affairs, and even occasionally quarrelsome among themselves, he had seen emergencies weld them into a tight, concerted group that operated at high and heedless efficiency. There was every right to expect some sort of demonstration on their part.

Nothing had happened. The Galactics had sold their holdings to the government without a murmur, and disposed of their other non-essential belongings quickly and quietly. Their children had been withdrawn from any classes or special groups they might have attended; goodbyes had been said; and now, a scant GST month after the issuance of the order by the Voroseii, the Galactics were leaving Voroseith, never to return.

Never? Even now, Deric found that impossible to believe. The order was specific, and enforcable, but he had seen other laws relaxed, or evaded with the passage of time.

Or, for that matter, overcome.

Was that it? Deric had heard many stories about the GSN and its big green ships that poured the fire of a sun from their innumerable guns. Were the Earthpeople leaving Voroseith so that the planet would be open to bombardment from outer space?

No, the possibility had been considered before, and rejected. True, no single planet could stand before the Federation. Not even a group of solar systems could do it. The lesson of the Ardath Secession was still fresh, and terrible. But Voroseith's protection lay in the very fact that she was a single planet, and relatively unimportant to the Federation as a whole. Compared to the GSN fleet, her own navy was an insignificant handful of ships. But, ship for ship, it was just as deadly, and the price of conquest would be high – too high for the prize it would bring. There would be no war.

Still – why was there no protest? The Galactics had homes and property on Voroseith. The grandchildren of the Firstcomers were grown and bred on this world. There were friendships, business relations, ties of many kinds by the hundreds. As a lover of the strange composite art form that was opera, Deric would suffer from the loss of new Berkeley libretti, for no one else could work as well with Marto Lihh.

The Federation itself had done nothing beyond dispatching the transport. All reference to the order had been offhand, casual, as a thing that existed without question.

He could not let the Galactics depart and leave him without an answer. He pushed himself back from the rail and slid rapidly down the ramp to the room where the Earthpeople were.

Here, too, there was silence; even the children were quiet. The Galactics sat in rows on benches, facing each other across the narrow aisles. There was no talking, but groups of friends had sat down together, and occasionally there would be a smile or a nod to someone across the aisle.

As Deric entered, several heads turned in his direction. In every case, there was a friendly smile as he was recognized; several people separated themselves from their immediate groups and came over to him.

'Deric!' That was Morris, one of the men who had worked at the museum with him. The Galactic strode up to him rapidly, and laid his hand behind Deric's head with a firm and friendly greeting-stroke. Deric gently touched his right hand to the Earthman's own.

'I thought you'd come down,' Morris said. His face was regretful at the thought of his leaving.

Now that he was here, among them, Deric felt the strangeness of the situation even more strongly than before. He had never seen a group of Galactics before without seeing his own people among them. It felt strange to suddenly realize that this was the winnowing of all the Galactics on Voroseith – that most of these people knew each other less well than they did the individual Voroseii among whom they had lived and worked; but that, nevertheless, they were suddenly a homogenous and segregated group by mere virtue of the fact that they were all Galactics.

It was possible to consider the entire problem as a sort of intellectual puzzle, to be evaluated in the light of the economic factors that had made the order necessary. But Morris was his friend and co-worker, so the situation became one of losing a good friend, of never seeing his family again, and of

74

learning to remember that Day 184, GST, was no longer Susan Morris' birthday.

'I wanted to see you,' Deric said. 'I'm not sure I should be here, but—' He stopped, not sure of his words. 'Well . . .'

Morris smiled. 'Thanks, Deric.'

The other Galactics who had come up exchanged greetings with him in turn. Each of them, like Morris, reflected a regret as great as Deric's own.

He saw Berkeley, sitting by himself at the end of a bench, his eyes somber. *How does he feel?* Deric wondered. He turned back to Morris. 'I – if it's possible, could I talk to him? You know how much I admire his work.'

'Easily done,' Morris said. 'Come on.'

Deric followed his friend across the floor of the waiting room. As he passed among the seated Galactics, he could see the same traces of sadness in their eyes – sadness, but no protest, no rebellion.

Berkeley looked up at Morris' words. 'Deric Liss?' He turned his eyes on Deric. 'Of course.' He reached out and touched Deric's neck warmly. 'I've read your *Cultural History*. One of the most valuable texts I've ever seen.'

'Thank you,' Deric said, his eyes glowing. Completely embarrassed, he felt his body twitch awkwardly. 'I've always admired your work,' he blurted out, conscious of the clumsiness of the statement. Following Berkeley's compliment as it did, it sounded more like back-scratching than anything like the sincere appreciation he had intended to express.

But Berkeley smiled, his eyes crinkling at the corners. 'I'll never have a composer like Marto Lihh to work with again,' he said. A trace of his former brooding look returned to his face.

Deric could hold back his puzzlement no longer. He looked up at Morris and Berkeley. 'I can't understand this,' he said, his voice full of uncertainty. 'Why are you leaving? Or, if you must leave, why aren't you . . .' He let the sentence trail off. One doesn't ask a man why he hasn't been resentful of some injustice you've done him.

'Why aren't we displaying our famous Terrestrial aggressiveness?' Berkeley asked, smiling.

'Yes.' Completely disconcerted, he said, 'And you – a man who's leaving everything he loves and works for. Aren't *you*, at least, angry at what we've done?'

Berkeley shook his head. 'Angry? Your planet's over-crowded. There are no other habitable planets in this system, and we were all competing with you for what room there was. It's only natural that your government has to consider the well-being of its people. After all, we are a foreign race; this is your planet, to do with as you choose. I'd say the order was a very wise move, from the point of view of your people. I'm sure the rest of us feel the same way.'

Morris nodded.

'But the Federation . . .'

'The Federation is exactly that – not an empire. You have the privileges of membership – and the rights, as well,' Berkeley pointed out. If he himself felt a personal loss, he kept it within himself.

'I still don't understand. When the Ardan group seceded, the remainder of the Federation refused to allow it,' Deric said.

Berkeley's face clouded. 'The Ardan Secession was an armed insurrection, born of frustrated ambition and a desire for power. It was motivated only by the Ardans' drive to regain control of the Federation.'

'But they were as justified in their eyes as we are in ours,' Deric protested.

Berkeley cocked his head. 'Perhaps – but what about the Ardan dissolutionists? Was that a sign that even all the Ardans were in agreement with their government's policy?'

'I don't approve of our action, either,' Deric replied.

Berkeley smiled. 'You mean, it strikes you as being some-what peremptory; and this feeling is augmented by the fact that we're submitting to it without any action that would make it seem emotionally justified. If we fought back, you could at least feel that maybe getting rid of the quarrelsome Terrestrials was worthwhile.'

'Yes . . .' Deric admitted slowly, abashed. He had never thought it out that far.

76

'But you're not actively angry at the order,' Berkeley went on. 'You sympathize with us, but you don't feel it's an outrageous situation.'

The Galactic was right. Deric could feel himself twitching with embarrassment again. 'I don't know what to say,' he mumbled.

The librettist smiled again. 'No need for that,' he said warmly. 'We've known from the very beginning that this would happen someday. We've accepted it, so it didn't come as a shock.'

Deric, once again, felt his puzzlement coming to the fore. 'But why did you come at all, then? Look at the history of the last three generations. After we were contacted by the sample ship, your people came here, settled into our culture, and began to live alongside us. More than alongside. You worked for the same goal as we – the progress of Voroseithan culture and civilization. You speak our language. Never once have you done something for the benefit of the Federation, or of Earth. It was as if – as if you were Voroseii yourselves, not as if you were foreigners at all.

'It was difficult to believe. We expected taxes, or levies of *some* kind. We expected you to bring your arts and your sciences, to merge our culture with yours. But none of that happened. And now, though you are Galactics, you are nevertheless Voroseii. If you knew you would someday leave, why did you make Voroseith more truly a home than any other world could possibly be?'

Berkeley, who wrote poetry as a Voroseii would, thinking in terms of a six-tone scale, let a flicker of sorrow cross his face. 'Yes, I imagine that would be what you'd expect. It's what the Ardans did, when they guided the Federation. You're right, and yet, you're wrong, as well.'

He smiled, almost wistfully. 'Yes, Voroseith *is* home to us, and we will miss it. But we were working for the benefit of the Federation, nonetheless. We had to act as though we would always live here – more than act, we had to *believe* we would always live here. We had to devote all our wholehearted energies to working for Voroseith. It was—' He hesitated, and, for a moment, there was a lost look on his face. 'It was a shock when we realized that our job was done, that Voroseith was ready to go out into interstellar space.'

'Interstellar space?' Deric felt his back arch in puzzlement.

Morris nodded. 'It's coming. That's why you've got your navy. You were working out the necessary techniques.'

'But the Federation rules the Galaxy. Will you permit us to go out into your territory?'

Berkeley spoke again. 'The Federation doesn't rule anything; you can't impose civilization by force. It's your turn, as a member of a civilizing movement, to go out and pass on what you have to other people. Space is full of worlds, and people. Earth *guides* the Federation, true, but it doesn't run it – no one does. We work with the common bond of civilization between us – but it is civilization as an abstract concept – not as a rigid, universal pattern of some kind, into which each diverse culture has to be hammered and forced, jammed into a mold for which it was never suited.'

'We didn't try to make you do things our way, did we?' Morris asked.

Deric waved his arm negatively. 'No – no, you didn't. You learned from us, and then you became just so many more individuals working to improve our culture. You brought in a fresh approach to many problems; but it was an approach founded in the roots of our culture, not yours.' He stopped.

The annunciator crackled. 'All cargo has been loaded. Passengers will please embark.' The dispatcher's voice lost its impersonality. Another Vorosei was saying goodbye to his friends. 'Farewell, Earthmen.'

The seated rows of Galactics stood up, still quiet despite the shuffle of feet, the scraping of baggage as it was picked up.

'So now we'll be out in space beside you?' Deric asked Berkeley.

The Galactic nodded. 'When the groups like ours leave a world, that is the historical sign that another race is going out into the stars, civilized, to civilize.'

Deric felt a surge of pride shoot through him. 'Then, this

was a stage, like the time of the sample ship, during which we were trained.'

Morris shook his head. 'Not trained. The sample ship was a test, true – but a test designed to measure nothing more than your ability to conceive of other races beyond your own, and your readiness to accept the fact that interstellar travel was an actuality. Why should we train you? Our culture is not superior to yours in any way – and there are far too many diverse races in space, and far too few Earthmen even remotely to justify any attempt to make you do things the way they're done on Earth.

'No, we were just sent here to accustom you to working beside other races. We weren't instructors – we were co-workers.'

Most of the Galactics were already through the doors that led out to the field. Morris and Berkeley touched Deric's neck again. 'Goodbye, Deric,' Morris said.

Berkeley suddenly reached into his pack and pulled out a sheaf of manuscript. 'I wish you'd take this, Deric.'

Deric looked at the top page. 'But – but this is the original manuscript for the Llersthein Epic!'

Berkeley nodded. 'Take it. I'll remember it, and nobody will really understand it, where I'm going.'

Deric looked up at the Galactic. The somber eyes looked back into his, and, though this was not truly one of his people – theoretically, the facial expressions of one race should be incomprehensible to another – Deric could read what lay in the mind behind the eyes; nor did it occur to him that there was anything remarkable about the fact that he could.

'Thank you,' he said, and let the position of his hands and the twist of his body tell Berkeley what emotions lay behind the words.

The two Galactics picked up their packs and swung them over their shoulders, and joined the waiting groups of their families.

Deric stayed where he was, watching them go, still trying to grasp what it was he had half-seen, half-understood. It was important, too, he knew. It explained, more than sadness, the silence that had overlaid the waiting room, the odd feeling that the Galactics were drawn apart into numerous small groups, each of them turning to his family and immediate friends.

As if they were in danger—

Fear! They were afraid! Morris, Berkeley – all of them. He saw them reach the door and wait for their families to precede them. He coiled his muscles and slid forward in a rapid surge.

'Wait!'

Berkeley and Morris turned back toward him, their faces questioning.

'Where *are* you going?' Deric asked. 'What are you going to do?'

'I don't know,' Berkeley said. 'I don't know,' he repeated slowly. 'We're being taken to Earth.' And now Deric could plainly see the naked uncertainty in their eyes, the hesitation, the clammy tinge of fear.

'We have to get going,' Morris said with sudden harshness – the harshness of nerves strained to the point where they sang and vibrated, waiting for the first new burden to snap and lash back with deadly effect.

Berkeley smiled at Deric – but there were white spots along his own jawline. He laid a gentle hand on Deric's neck. 'I liked it here,' he said wistfully. 'I was born here, like my father was.' He looked up, through the panes of the exit door, and, at that moment, the overcast finally broke, and the starlight flashed through.

Berkeley winced as though something had struck him. Then he shook himself and grinned – the fighting grin that was the Earthman's trademark. Nevertheless, there was something haunted in his voice as he said, 'I wonder what Earth is like.'

'Come on!' Morris said, and half-pushed Berkeley through the door. He raised a hand in a last farewell to Deric, and Berkeley, with Morris' hand on his shoulder, half turned, and waved apologetically for their friend's nervousness.

Deric looked after them, feeling the first beginnings of understanding trickle into his consciousness, knowing that the trickle would swell into a live, leaping torrent. When it came, he had better be very, very busy at some work that was unimportant enough to be spoiled by trembling hands, or clouded vision.

What was it the dispatcher had said? 'Farewell, Earthmen?' He shook his head in the acquired Terrestrial mannerism, turned, and slipped rapidly up the ramp to the observation platform. He watched the last of the Galactics walk into the waiting ship.

'Farewell, Voroseii,' he said softly, as his brothers went unprotestingly into exile.

*Earth's Secret Service kept peace in the Galaxy efficiently
– very efficiently. It was always there . . . before trouble
started!*

BEEP

By James Blish

I

Josef Faber lowered his newspaper slightly. Finding the girl
on the park bench looking his way, he smiled the agonizingly
embarrassed smile of the thoroughly married caught bird-
watching, and ducked back into the paper again.

He was reasonably certain that he looked the part of a
middle-aged, steadily employed, harmless citizen enjoying a
Sunday break in the bookkeeping and family routines. He
was also quite certain, despite his official instructions, that it
wouldn't make the slightest bit of difference if he didn't.
These boy-meets-girl assignments always came off. Jo had
never tackled a single one that had required him.

As a matter of fact, the newspaper, which he was supposed
to be using only as a blind, interested him a good deal more
than his job did. He had only barely begun to suspect the
obvious ten years ago when the Service had snapped him up;
now, after a decade as an agent, he was still fascinated to see
how smoothly the really important situations came off. The
dangerous situations – not boy-meets-girl.

This affair of the Black Hose Nebula, for instance. Some
days ago the papers and the commentators had begun to mention reports of disturbances in that area, and Jo's practiced
eye had picked up the mention. Something big was cooking.

Today it had boiled over – the Black Horse Nebula had
suddenly spewed ships by the hundreds, a massed armada
that must have taken more than a century of effort on the
part of a whole star-cluster, a production drive conducted in
the strictest and most fanatical kind of secrecy—

82

And, of course, the Service had been on the spot in plenty of time. With three times as many ships, disposed with mathematical precision so as to enfilade the entire armada the moment it broke from the nebula. The battle had been a massacre, the attack smashed before the average citizen could even begin to figure out what it had been aimed at – and good had triumphed over evil once more.

Of course.

Furtive scuffings on the gravel drew his attention briefly. He looked at his watch, which said 14:58:03. That was the time, according to his instructions, when boy had to meet girl.

He had been given the strictest kind of orders to let nothing interfere with this meeting – the orders always issued on boy-meets-girl assignments. But, as usual, he had nothing to do but observe. The meeting was coming off on the dot, without any prodding from Jo. They always did.

Of course.

With a sigh, he folded his newspaper, smiling again at the couple – yes, it was the right man, too – and moved away, as if reluctantly. He wondered what would happen were he to pull away the false mustache, pitch the newspaper on the grass, and bound away with a joyous whoop. He suspected that the course of history would not be deflected by even a second of arc, but he was not minded to try the experiment.

The park was pleasant. The twin suns warmed the path and the greenery without any of the blasting heat which they would bring to bear later in the summer. Randolph was altogether the most comfortable planet he had visited in years. A little backward, perhaps, but restful, too.

It was also slightly over a hundred light-years away from Earth. It would be interesting to know how Service headquarters on Earth could have known in advance that boy would meet girl at a certain spot on Randolph, precisely at 14:58:03.

Or how Service headquarters could have ambushed with micrometric precision a major interstellar fleet, with no more preparation than a few days' buildup in the newspapers and video could evidence.

The press was free, on Randolph as everywhere. It reported the news it got. Any emergency concentration of Service ships in the Black Horse area, or anywhere else, would have been noticed and reported on. The Service did not forbid such reports for 'security' reasons or for any other reasons. Yet there had been nothing to report but that (a) an armada of staggering size had erupted with no real warning from the Black Horse Nebula, and that (b) the Service had been ready.

By now, it was a commonplace that the Service was always ready. It had not had a defect or a failure in well over two centuries. It had not even had a fiasco, the alarming-sounding technical word by which it referred to the possibility that a boy-meets-girl assignment might not come off.

Jo hailed a hopper. Once inside, he stripped himself of the moustache, the bald spot, the foreheadcreases – all the make-up which had given him his mask of friendly innocuousness.

The hoppy watched the whole process in the rear-view mirror. Jo glanced up and met his eyes.

'Pardon me, mister, but I figured you didn't care if I saw you. You must be a Service man.'

'That's right. Take me to Service HQ, will you?'

'Sure enough.' The hoppy gunned his machine. It rose smoothly to the express level. 'First time I ever got close to a Service man. Didn't hardly believe it at first when I saw you taking your face off. You sure looked different.'

'Have to, sometime,' Jo said, preoccupied.

'I'll bet. No wonder you know all about everything before it breaks. You must have a thousand faces each, your own mother wouldn't know you, eh? Don't you care if I know about your snooping around in disguise?'

Jo grinned. The grin created a tiny pulling sensation across one curve of his cheek, just next to his nose. He stripped away the overlooked bit of tissue and examined it critically.

'Of course not. Disguise is an elementary part of Service work. Anyone could guess that. We don't use it often, as a matter of fact – only on very simple assignments.'

84

'Oh.' The hoppy sounded slightly disappointed, as melodrama faded. He drove silently for about a minute. Then, speculatively: 'Sometimes I think the Service must have time-travel, the things they pull . . . well, here you are. Good luck, mister.'

'Thanks.'

Jo went directly to Krasna's office. Krasna was a Randolpher, Earth-trained, and answerable to the Earth office, but otherwise pretty much on his own. His heavy, muscular face wore the same expression of serene confidence that was characteristic of Service officials everywhere – even some that, technically speaking, had no faces to wear it.

'Boy meets girl,' Jo said briefly. 'On the nose and on the spot.'

'Good work, Jo. Cigarette?' Krasna pushed the box across his desk.

'Nope, not now. Like to talk to you, if you've got time.'

Krasna pushed a button, and a toadstool-like chair rose out of the floor behind Jo. 'What's on your mind?'

'Well,' Jo said carefully. 'I'm wondering why you patted me on the back just now for not doing a job.'

'You did a job.'

'I did not,' Jo said flatly. 'Boy would have met girl, whether I'd been here on Randolph or back on Earth. The course of true love always runs smooth. It has in all my boy-meets-girl cases, and it has in the boy-meets-girl cases of every other agent with whom I've compared notes.'

'Well, good,' Krasna said, smiling. 'That's the way we like to have it run. And that's the way we expect it to run. But, Jo, we like to have somebody on the spot, somebody with a reputation for resourcefulness, just in case there's a snag. There almost never is, as you've observed. But – if there were?'

Jo snorted. 'If what you're trying to do is to establish preconditions for the future, any interference by a Service agent would throw the eventual result farther *off* the track. I know that much about probability.'

'And what makes you think that we're trying to set up the future?'

'It's obvious even to the hoppies on your own planet; the one that brought me here told me he thought the Service had time-travel. It's especially obvious to all the individuals and governments and entire populations that the Service has bailed out of serious messes for centuries, with never a single failure.' Jo shrugged. 'A man can be asked to safeguard only a small number of boy-meets-girl cases before he realizes, as an agent, that what the Service is safeguarding is the future children of those meetings. Ergo – the Service *knows* what those children are to be like, and has reason to want their future existence guaranteed. What other conclusion is possible?'

Krasna took out a cigarette and lit it deliberately; it was obvious that he was using the manoeuvre to cloak his response.

'None,' he admitted at last. 'We have some foreknowledge, of course. We couldn't have made our reputation with espionage alone. But we have obvious other advantages: genetics, for instance, and operations research, the theory of games, the Dirac transmitter – it's quite an arsenal, and of course there's a good deal of prediction involved in all those things.'

'I see that,' Jo said. He shifted in his chair, formulating all he wanted to say. He changed his mind about the cigarette and helped himself to one. 'But these things don't add up to infallibility – and that's a qualitative difference, Kras. Take this affair of the Black Horse armada. The moment the armada appeared, we'll assume, Earth heard about it by Dirac, and started to assemble a counter-armada. But it takes *finite time* to bring together a concentration of ships and men, even if your message system is instantaneous.

'The Service's counter-armada was *already on hand*. It had been building there for so long and with so little fuss that nobody even noticed it concentrating until a day or so before the battle. Then planets in the area began to sit up and take notice, and be uneasy about what was going to break. But not very uneasy; the Service always wins – that's been a statistical fact for centuries. *Centuries*, Kras. Good Lord, it takes almost as long as that, in straight preparation, to pull some of the tricks we've pulled! The Dirac gives us an advantage of ten to twenty-five years in really extreme cases out on the rim of the Galaxy, but no more than that.'

He realized that he had been fuming away on the cigarette until the roof of his mouth was scorched, and snubbed it out angrily. 'That's a very different thing,' he said, 'than knowing in a general way how an enemy is likely to behave, or what kind of children the Mendelian laws say a given couple should have. It means that we've some way of reading the future in minute detail. That's in flat contradiction to everything I've been taught about probability, but I have to believe what I see.'

Krasna laughed. 'That's a very able presentation,' he said. He seemed genuinely pleased. 'I think you'll remember that you were first impressed into the Service when you began to wonder why the news was always good. Fewer and fewer people wonder about that nowadays; it's become a part of their expected environment.' He stood up and ran a hand through his hair. 'Now you've carried yourself through the next stage. Congratulations, Jo. You've just been promoted!'

'I have?' Jo said incredulously. 'I came in here with the notion that I might get myself fired.'

'No. Come around to this side of the desk, Jo, and I'll play you a little history.' Krasna unfolded the desktop to expose a small visor screen. Obediently Jo rose and went around the desk to where he could see the blank surface. 'I had a standard indoctrination tape sent up to me a week ago, in the expectation that you'd be ready to see it. Watch.'

Krasna touched the board. A small dot of light appeared in the center of the screen and went out again. At the same time, there was a small *beep* of sound. Then the tape began to unroll and a picture clarified on the screen.

'As you suspected,' Krasna said conversationally, 'the Service is infallible. How it got that way is a story that started several centuries back. This tape gives all the dope. You should almost be able to imagine what really happened . . .'

II

Dana Lje – her father had been a Hollander, her mother born in the Celebes – sat down in the chair which Captain Robin Weinbaum had indicated, crossed her legs, and waited, her blue-black hair shining under the lights.

Weinbaum eyed her quizzically. The conqueror Resident who had given the girl her entirely European name had been paid in kind, for his daughter's beauty had nothing fair and Dutch about it. To the eye of the beholder, Dana Lje seemed a particularly delicate virgin of Bali, despite her western name, clothing and assurance. The combination had already proven piquant for the millions who watched her television column, and Weinbaum found it no less charming at first hand.

'As one of your most recent victims,' he said, 'I'm not sure that I'm honored, Miss Lje. A few of my wounds are still bleeding. But I am a good deal puzzled as to why you're visiting me now. Aren't you afraid that I'll bite back?'

'I had no intention of attacking you personally, and I don't think I did,' the video columnist said seriously. 'It was just pretty plain that our intelligence had slipped badly in the Erskine affair. It was my job to say so. Obviously you were going to get hurt, since you're head of the bureau – but there was no malice in it.'

'Cold comfort,' Weinbaum said dryly. 'But thank you, nevertheless.'

The Eurasian girl shrugged. 'That isn't what I came here about, anyway. Tell me, Captain Weinbaum – have you ever heard of an outfit calling itself Interstellar Information?'

Weinbaum shook his head. 'Sounds like a skip-tracing firm. Not an easy business, these days.'

'That's just what I thought when I first saw their letterhead,' Dana said. 'But the letter under it wasn't one that a private-eye outfit would write. Let me read part of it to you.'

Her slim fingers burrowed in her inside jacket pocket, and emerged again with a single sheet of paper. It was plain typewriter bond, Weinbaum noted automatically: she had brought only a copy with her, and had left the original of the letter at home. The copy, then, would be incomplete – probably seriously.

'It goes like this; "Dear Miss Lje: As a syndicated video commentator with a wide audience and heavy responsibilities, you need the best source of information available. We would like you to test our service, free of charge, in the hope of proving to you that it is superior to any other source of news on Earth. Therefore, we offer below several predictions concerning events to come in the Hercules and the so-called 'Three Ghosts' areas. If these predictions are fulfilled 100% – no less – we ask that you take us on as your correspondents for those areas, at rates to be agreed upon later. If the predictions are wrong in *any* respect, you need not consider us further."'

'H'm,' Weinbaum said slowly. 'They're confident cusses – and that's an odd juxtaposition. The Three Ghosts make up only a little solar system, while the Hercules area could include the entire star-cluster – or maybe even the whole constellation, which is a hell of a lot of sky. This outfit seems to be trying to tell you that it has thousands of field correspondents of its own, maybe as many as the government itself. If so, I'll guarantee that they're bragging.'

'That may well be so. But before you make up your mind, let me read you one of the two predictions.' The letter rustled in Dana Lje's hand. ' "At 03:16:10, on Year Day, 2090, the Hess-type interstellar liner *Brindisi* will be attacked in the neighborhood of the Three Ghosts system by four—"'

Weinbaum sat bolt upright in his swivel chair. 'Let me see that letter!' he said, his voice harsh with repressed alarm.

'In a moment,' the girl said, adjusting her skirt composedly. 'Evidently I was right in riding my hunch. Let me go on reading: "—by four heavily armed vessels flying the lights of the navy of Hammersmith II. The position of the liner at that time will be at coded coordinates 88-A-theta-88-aleph-D and-per-se-and. It will—"'

'Miss Lje,' Weinbaum said, 'I'm sorry to interrupt you again, but what you've said already would justify me in jailing you at once, no matter how loudly your sponsors might scream. I don't know about this Interstellar Information outfit, or whether or not you did receive any such letter as the one you pretend to be quoting. But I can tell you that you've shown yourself to be in possession of information that only yours truly and four other men are supposed to know. It's already too late to tell you that everything you say may be held against you; all I can say now is, it's high time you clammed up!'

'I thought so,' she said, apparently not disturbed in the least. 'Then that liner *is* scheduled to hit those coordinates, and the coded time coordinate corresponds with the predicted Universal Time. Is it also true that the *Brindisi* will be carrying a top-secret communications device?'

'Are you deliberately trying to make me imprison you?' Weinbaum said, gritting his teeth. 'Or is this just a stunt, designed to show me that my own bureau is full of leaks?'

'It could turn into that,' Dana admitted. 'But it hasn't, yet. Robin, I've been as honest with you as I'm able to be. You've had nothing but square deals from me up to now. I wouldn't yellow-screen you, and you know it. If this unknown outfit has this information, it might easily have gotten it from where it hints that it got it: from the field.'

'Impossible.'

'Why?'

'Because the information in question hasn't even reached my *own* agents in the field yet – it couldn't possibly have leaked as far as Hammersmith II or anywhere else, let alone to the Three Ghosts system! Letters have to be carried on ships, you know that. If I were to send orders by ultrawave to my Three Ghosts agent, he'd have to wait three hundred and twenty-four years to get them. By ship, he can get them in a little over two months. These particular orders have only been under way to him five days. Even if somebody has read them on board the ship that's carrying them, they could not possibly be sent on to the Three Ghosts any faster than they're traveling now.'

90

Dana nodded her dark head. 'All right. Then what are we left with but a leak in your headquarters here?'

'What, indeed,' Weinbaum said grimly. 'You'd better tell me who signed this letter of yours.'

'The signature is J Shelby Stevens.'

Weinbaum switched on the intercom. 'Margaret, look in the business register for an outfit called Interstellar Information and find out who owns it.'

Dana Lje said, 'Aren't you interested in the rest of the prediction?'

'You bet I am. Does it tell you the name of this communications device?'

'Yes,' Dana said.

'What is it?'

'The Dirac communicator.'

Weinbaum groaned and turned on the intercom again. 'Margaret, send in Dr Wald. Tell him to drop everything and gallop. Any luck with the other thing?'

'Yes, sir,' the intercom said. 'It's a one-man outfit, wholly owned by a J Shelby Stevens, in Rico City. It was first registered this year.'

'Arrest him, on suspicion of espionage.'

The door swung open and Dr Wald came in, all six and a half feet of him. He was extremely blond, and looked awkward, gentle, and not very intelligent.

'Thor, this young lady is our press nemesis, Dana Lje. Dana, Dr Wald is the inventor of the Dirac communicator, about which you have so damnably much information.'

'It's out *already*?' Dr Wald said, scanning the girl with grave deliberation.

'It is, and lots more – *lots* more. Dana, you're a good girl at heart, and for some reason I trust you, stupid though it is to trust anybody in this job. I should detain you until Year Day, videocasts or no videocasts. Instead, I'm just going to ask you to sit on what you've got, and I'm going to explain why.'

'Shoot.'

'I've already mentioned how slow communication is between star and star. We have to carry all our letters on ships, just as we did locally before the invention of the telegraph. The overdrive lets us beat the speed of light, but not by much of a margin over really long distances. Do you understand that?'

'Certainly,' Dana said. She appeared a bit nettled, and Weinbaum decided to give her the full dose at a more rapid pace. After all, she could be assumed to be better informed than the average layman.

'What we've needed for a long time, then,' he said, 'is some virtually instantaneous method of getting a message from somewhere to anywhere. Any time lag, no matter how small it seems at first, has a way of becoming major as longer and longer distances are involved. Sooner or later we must have this instantaneous method, or we won't be able to get messages from one system to another fast enough to hold our jurisdiction over outlying regions of space.'

'Wait a minute,' Dana said. 'I'd always understood that ultrawave is faster than light.'

'Effectively it is; physically it isn't. You don't understand that?'

She shook her dark head.

'In a nutshell,' Weinbaum said, 'ultrawave is radiation, and all radiation in free space is limited to the speed of light. The way we hype up ultrawave is to use an old application of waveguide theory, whereby the real transmission of energy is at light speed, but an imaginary thing called phase velocity is going faster. But the gain in speed of transmission isn't large — by ultrawave, for instance, we get a message to Alpha Centauri in one year instead of nearly four. Over long distances, that's not nearly enough extra speed.'

'Can't it be speeded further?' she said, frowning.

'No. Think of the ultrawave beam between here and Centaurus III as a caterpillar. The caterpillar himself is moving quite slowly, just at the speed of light. But the pulses which pass along his body are going forward faster than he is — and if you've ever watched a caterpillar, you'll know that that's true. But there's a physical limit to the number of pulses you can travel along that caterpillar, and we've already reached that limit. We've taken phase velocity as far as it will go.

'That's why we need something faster. For a long time our relativity theories discouraged hope of anything faster – even the high phase velocity of a guided wave didn't contradict those theories; it just found a limited, mathematically imaginary loophole in them. But when Thor here began looking into the question of velocity of propagation of a Dirac pulse, he found the answer. The communicator he developed does seem to act over long distances, *any* distance, instantaneously – and it may wind up knocking relativity into a cocked hat.'

The girl's face was a study in stunned realization. 'I'm not sure I've taken in all the technical angles,' she said. 'But if I'd had any notion of the political dynamite in this thing—'

'—you'd have kept out of my office,' Weinbaum said grimly. 'A good thing you didn't. The *Brindisi* is carrying a model of the Dirac communicator out to the periphery for a final test; the ship is supposed to get in touch with me from out there at a given Earth time, which we've calculated very elaborately to account for the residual Lorentz and Milne transformations involved in overdrive flight, and for a lot of other time-phenomena that wouldn't mean anything at all to you.

'If that signal arrives here at the given Earth time, then – aside from the havoc it will create among the theoretical physicists whom we decide to let in on it – we will really have our instant communicator, and can include all of occupied space in the same time-zone. And we'll have a terrific advantage over any lawbreaker who has to resort to ultrawave locally and to letters carried by ships over the long haul.'

'Not,' Dr Wald said sourly, 'if it's already leaked out.'

'It remains to be seen how much of it has leaked,' Weinbaum said. 'The principle is rather esoteric, Thor, and the name of the thing alone wouldn't mean much even to a trained scientist. I gather that Dana's mysterious informant didn't go into technical details . . . or did he?'

'No,' Dana said.

'Tell the truth, Dana. I know that you're suppressing some of that letter.'

The girl started slightly. 'All right – yes, I am. But nothing technical. There's another part of the prediction that lists the number and class of ships you will send to protect the *Brindisi* – the prediction says they'll be sufficient, by the way – and I'm keeping that to myself, to see whether or not it comes true along with the rest. If it does, I think I've hired myself a correspondent.'

'If it does,' Weinbaum said, 'you've hired yourself a jail-bird. Let's see how much mind-reading J Whatsit Stevens can do from the sub-cellar of Fort Yaphank.' He abruptly ended the conversation and ushered Dana Lje out with controlled politeness.

III

Weinbaum let himself into Stevens' cell, locking the door behind him and passing the keys out to the guard. He sat down heavily on the nearest stool.

Stevens smiled the weak benevolent smile of the very old, and laid his book aside on the bunk. The book, Weinbaum knew – since his office had cleared it – was only a volume of pleasant, harmless lyrics by a New Dynasty poet named Nims.

'Were our predictions correct, Captain?' Stevens said. His voice was high and musical, rather like that of a boy soprano.

Weinbaum nodded. 'You still won't tell us how you did it?'

'But I already have,' Stevens protested. 'Our intelligence network is the best in the Universe, Captain. It is superior even to your own excellent organization, as events have shown.'

'It's results are superior, that I'll grant,' Weinbaum said glumly. 'If Dana Lje had thrown your letter down her disposal chute, we would have lost the *Brindisi* and our Dirac transmitter both. Incidentally, did your original letter predict accurately the number of ships we would send?'

Stevens nodded pleasantly, his neatly trimmed white beard thrusting forward slightly as he smiled.

'I was afraid so.' Weinbaum leaned forward. 'Do you have the Dirac transmitter, Stevens?'

'Of course, Captain. How else could my correspondents report to me with the efficiency you have observed?'

'Then why don't our receivers pick up the broadcasts of your agents? Dr Wald says it's inherent in the principle that Dirac 'casts are picked up by *all* instruments tuned to receive them, bar none. And at this stage of the game, there are so few such broadcasts being made that we'd be almost certain to detect any that weren't coming from our own operatives.'

'I decline to answer that question, if you'll excuse the impoliteness,' Stevens said, his voice quavering slightly. 'I am an old man, Captain, and this intelligence agency is my sole source of income. If I told you how we operated, we would no longer have any advantage over your own service, except for the limited freedom from secrecy which we have. I have been assured by competent lawyers that I have every right to operate a private investigation bureau, properly licensed, upon any scale that I may choose; and that I have the right to keep my methods secret, as the so-called "intellectual assets" of my firm. If you wish to use our services, well and good. We will provide them, with absolute guarantees on all information we furnish you, for an appropriate fee. But our methods are our own property.'

Robin Weinbaum smiled twistedly. 'I'm not a naive man, Mr Stevens,' he said. 'My service is hard on naivete. You know as well as I do that the government can't allow you to operate on a free-lance basis, supplying top-secret information to anyone who can pay the price, or even free of charge to video columnists on a "test" basis, even though you arrive at every jot of that information independently of espionage – which I still haven't entirely ruled out, by the way. If you can duplicate this *Brindisi* performance at will, we will have to have your services exclusively. In short, you become a hired civilian arm of my own bureau.'

'Quite,' Stevens said, returning the smile in a fatherly way. 'We anticipated that, of course. However, we have contracts with other governments to consider: Erskine, in particular. If we are to work exclusively for Earth, necessarily our price will include compensation for renouncing our other accounts.'

'Why should it? Patriotic public servants work for their government at a loss, if they can't work for it any other way.'

'I am quite aware of that. I am quite prepared to renounce my other interests. But I do require to be paid.'

'How much?' Weinbaum said, suddenly aware that his fists were clenched so tightly that they hurt.

Stevens appeared to consider, nodding his flowery white poll in senile deliberation. 'My associates would have to be consulted. Tentatively, however, a sum equal to the present appropriation of your bureau would do, pending further negotiations.'

Weinbaum shot to his feet, eyes wide. 'You old buccaneer! You know damned well that I can't spend my entire appropriation on a single civilian service! Did it ever occur to you that most of the civilian outfits working for us are on cost-plus contracts, and that our civilian executives are being paid just a credit a year, by their own choice? You're demanding nearly two thousand credits an hour from your own government, and claiming the legal protection that the government affords you at the same time, in order to let those fanatics on Erskine run up a higher bid!'

'The price is not unreasonable,' Stevens said. 'The service is worth the price.'

'That's where you're wrong! We have the discoverer of the machine working for us. For less than half the sum you're asking, we can find the application of the device that you're trading on – of that you can be damned sure.'

'A dangerous gamble, Captain.'

'Perhaps. We'll soon see!' Weinbaum glared at the placid face. 'I'm forced to tell you that you're a free man, Mr Stevens. We've been unable to show that you came by your information by any illegal method. You had classified facts in your possession, but no classified documents, and it's your privilege as a citizen to make guesses, no matter how educated.

'But we'll catch up with you sooner or later. Had you been reasonable, you might have found yourself in a very good position with us, your income as assured as any political income can be, and your person respected to the hilt. Now, however, you're subject to censorship – you have no idea how humiliating that can be, but I'm going to see to it that you find out. There'll be no more newsbeats for Dana Lje, or for anyone else. I want to see every word of copy that you file with any client outside the bureau. Every word that is of use to me will be used, and you'll be paid the statutory one cent a word for it – the same rate that the FBI pays for anonymous gossip. Everything I don't find useful will be killed without clearance. Eventually we'll have the modification of the Dirac that you're using, and when that happens, you'll be so flat broke that a pancake with a hare lip could spit right over you.'

Weinbaum paused for a moment, astonished at his own fury.

Stevens' clarinetlike voice began to sound in the windowless cavity. 'Captain, I have no doubt that you can do this to me, at least incompletely. But it will prove fruitless. I will give you a prediction, at no charge. It is guaranteed, as are all our predictions. It is this: *You will never find that modification.* Eventually, I will give it to you, on my own terms, but you will never find it for yourself, nor will you force it out of me. In the meantime, not a word of copy will be filed with you; for, despite the fact that you are an arm of the government, I can well afford to wait you out.'

'Bluster,' Weinbaum said.

'Fact. Yours is the bluster – loud talk based on nothing more than a hope. I, however, *know* whereof I speak . . . But let us conclude this discussion. It serves no purpose; you will need to see my points made the hard way. Thank you for giving me my freedom. We will talk again under different circumstances on – let me see; ah, yes, on June 9th of the year 2091. That year is, I believe, almost upon us.'

Stevens picked up his book again, nodding at Weinbaum, his expression harmless and kindly, his hands showing the marked tremor of *paralysis agitans.* Weinbaum moved helplessly to the door and flagged the turnkey. As the bars closed behind him, Stevens' voice called out: 'Oh, yes; and a Happy New Year, Captain.'

* * *

97

Weinbaum blasted his way back into his own office, at least twice as mad as the proverbial nest of hornets, and at the same time rather dismally aware of his own probable future. If Stevens' second prediction turned out to be as phenomenally accurate as his first had been Capt Robin Weinbaum would soon be peddling a natty set of secondhand uniforms.

He glared down at Margaret Soames, his receptionist. She glared right back; she had known him too long to be intimidated. 'Anything?' he said.

'Dr Wald's waiting for you in your office. There are some field reports, and a couple of Diracs on your private tape. Any luck with the old codger?'

'That,' he said crushingly, 'is Top Secret.'

'Poof. That means that nobody still knows the answer but J Shelby Stevens.'

He collapsed suddenly. 'You're so right. That's just what it does mean. But we'll bust him wide open sooner or later. We've *got* to.'

'You'll do it,' Margaret said. 'Anything else for me?'

'No. Tip off the clerical staff that there's a half-holiday today, then go take in a stereo or a steak or something yourself. Dr Wald and I have a few private wires to pull . . . and unless I'm sadly mistaken, a private bottle of aquavit to empty.'

'Right,' the receptionist said. 'Tie one on for me, Chief. I understand that beer is the best chaser for aquavit – I'll have some sent up.'

'If you should return after I am suitably squiffed,' Weinbaum said, feeling a little better already, 'I will kiss you for your thoughtfulness. *That* should keep you at your stereo at least twice through the third feature.'

As he went on through the door of his own office, she said demurely behind him, 'It certainly should.'

As soon as the door closed, however, his mood became abruptly almost as black as before. Despite his comparative youth – he was now only fifty-five – he had been in the service a long time, and he needed no one to tell him the possible consequences which might flow from possession by a private citizen of the Dirac communicator. If there was ever

98

to be a Federation of Man in the Galaxy, it was within the power of J Shelby Stevens to ruin it before it had fairly gotten started. And there seemed to be nothing at all that could be done about it.

'Hello, Thor,' he said glumly. 'Pass the bottle.'

'Hello, Robin. I gather things went badly. Tell me about it.'

Briefly, Weinbaum told him. 'And the worst of it,' he finished, is that Stevens himself predicts that we won't find the application of the Dirac that he's using, and that eventually we'll have to buy it at his price. Somehow I believe him – but I can't see how it's possible. If I were to tell Congress that I was going to spend my entire appropriation for a single civilian service, I'd be out on my ear within the next three sessions.'

'Perhaps that isn't his real price,' the scientist suggested. 'If he wants to barter, he'd naturally begin with a demand miles above what he actually wants.'

'Sure, sure . . . but frankly, Thor, I'd hate to give the old reprobate even a single credit if I could get out of it.' Weinbaum sighed. 'Well, let's see what's come in from the field.'

Thor Wald moved silently away from Weinbaum's desk while the officer unfolded it and set up the Dirac screen. Stacked neatly next to the ultraphone – a device Weinbaum had been thinking of, only a few days ago, as permanently outmoded – were the tapes Margaret had mentioned. He fed the first one into the Dirac and turned the main toggle to the position labeled *Start*.

Immediately the whole screen went pure white and the audio speakers emitted an almost instantly end-stopped blare of sound – a *beep* which, as Weinbaum already knew, made up a continuous spectrum from about 30 cycles per second to well above 18,000 cps. Then both the light and the noise were gone as if they had never been, and were replaced by the familiar face and voice of Weinbaum's local ops chief in Rio City.

'There's nothing unusual in the way of transmitters in Stevens' office here,' the operative said without preamble.

'And there isn't any local Interstellar Information staff, except for one stenographer, and she's as dumb as they come. About all we could get from her is that Stevens is "such a sweet old man." No possibility that she's faking it; she's genuinely stupid, the kind that thinks Betelgeuse is something Indians use to darken their skins. We looked for some sort of list or code table that would give us a line on Stevens' field staff, but that was another dead end. Now we're maintaining a 24-hour Dinwiddie watch on the place from a joint across the street. Orders?'

Weinbaum dictated to the blank stretch of tape which followed: 'Margaret, next time you send any Dirac tapes in here, cut the damnable *beep* off them first. Tell the boys in Rio City that Stevens had been released, and that I'm proceeding for an Order In Security to tap his ultraphone and his local lines – this is one case where I'm sure we can persuade the court that tapping's necessary. Also – and be damned sure you code this – tell them to proceed with the tap immediately and to maintain it regardless of whether or not the court okays it. I'll thumbprint a Full Responsibility Confession for them. We can't afford to play patty-cake with Stevens – the potential is just too damned big. And oh, yes, Margaret, send the message by carrier, and send out general orders to everybody concerned not to use the Dirac again except when distance and time rule every other medium out. Stevens has already admitted that he can receive Dirac 'casts.'

He put down the mike and stared morosely for a moment at the beautiful Eridanean scrollwood of his desktop. Wald coughed inquiringly and retrieved the aquavit.

'Excuse me, Robin,' he said, 'but I should think that would work both ways.'

'So should I. And yet the fact is that we've never picked up so much as a whisper from either Stevens or his agents. I can't think of any way that could be pulled, but evidently it can.'

'Well, let's rethink the problem, and see what we get,' Wald said. 'I didn't want to say so in front of the young lady, for obvious reasons – I mean Miss Lje, of course, not Margaret – but the truth is that the Dirac is essentially a simple mechanism in principle. I seriously doubt that there's any way to transmit a message from it which can't be detected – and an examination of the theory with that proviso in mind might give us something new.'

'What proviso?' Weinbaum said. Thor Wald left him behind rather often these days.

'Why, that a Dirac transmission doesn't *necessarily* go to all communicators capable of receiving it. If that's true, then the reasons why it is true should emerge from the theory.'

'I see. Okay, proceed on that line. I've been looking at Stevens' dossier while you were talking, and it's an absolute desert. Prior to the opening of the office in Rio City, there's no dope whatever on J Shelby Stevens. The man as good as rubbed my nose in the fact that he's using a pseud when I first talked to him. I asked him what the "J" in his name stood for, and he said, "Oh, let's make it Jerome." But who the man behind the pseud *is*—'

'Is it possible that he's using his own initials?'

'No,' Weinbaum said. 'Only the dumbest ever do that, or transpose syllables, or retain any connection at all with their real names. Those are the people who are in serious emotional trouble, people who drive themselves into anonymity, but leave clues strewn all around the landscape – those clues are really a cry for help, for discovery. Of course we're working on that angle – we can't neglect anything – but J Shelby Stevens isn't that kind of case, I'm sure.' Weinbaum stood up abruptly. 'Okay, Thor – what's first on your technical program?'

'Well . . . I suppose we'll have to start with checking the frequencies we use. We're going on Dirac's assumption – and it works very well, and always has – that a positron in motion through a crystal lattice is accompanied by de Broglie waves which are transforms of the waves of an electron in motion somewhere else in the Universe. Thus if we control the frequency and path of the positron, we control the placement of the electron – we cause it to appear, so to speak, in the circuits of a communicator somewhere else. After that, reception

101

is just a matter of amplifying the bursts and reading the signal.'

Wald scowled and shook his blond head. 'If Stevens is getting out messages which we don't pick up, my first assumption would be that he's worked out a fine-tuning circuit that's more delicate than ours, and is more or less sneaking his messages under ours. The only way that could be done, as far as I can see at the moment, is by something really fantastic in the way of exact frequency control of his positron-gun. If so, the logical step for us is to go back to the beginning of our tests and re-run our diffractions to see if we can refine our measurements of positron frequencies.'

The scientist looked so inexpressibly gloomy as he offered this conclusion that a pall of hopelessness settled over Weinbaum in sheer sympathy. 'You don't look as if you expected that to uncover anything new.'

'I don't. You see, Robin, things are different in physics now than they used to be in the Twentieth Century. In those days, it was always presupposed that physics was limitless – the classic statement was made by Weyl, who said that "It is the nature of a real thing to be inexhaustible in content." We know now that that's not so, except in a remote, associational sort of way. Nowadays, physics is a defined and self-limited science; its scope is still prodigious, but we can no longer think of it as endless.

'This is better established in particle physics than in any other branch of the science. Half of the trouble physicists of the last century had with Euclidean geometry – and hence the reason why they evolved so many re-complicated theories of relativity – is that it's a geometry of lines and thus can be subdivided infinitely. When Cantor proved that there really is an infinity, at least mathematically speaking, that seemed to clinch the case for the possibility of a really infinite physical universe, too.'

Wald's eyes grew vague, and he paused to gulp down a slug of the licorice-flavored aquavit which would have made Weinbaum's every hair stand on end.

'I remember,' Wald said, 'the man who taught me theory

of sets at Princeton, many years ago. He used to say: "Cantor teaches us that there are many kinds of infinities". *There* was a crazy old man!'

Weinbaum rescued the bottle hastily. 'So go on, Thor.'

'Oh.' Wald blinked. 'Yes. Well, what we know now is that the geometry which applies to ultimate particles, like the positron, isn't Euclidean at all. It's Pythagorean – a geometry of points, not lines. Once you've measured one of those points, and it doesn't matter what kind of quantity you're measuring, you're down as far as you can go. At that point, the Universe becomes discontinuous, and no further refinement is possible.

'And I'd say that our positron-frequency measurements have already gotten that far down. There isn't another element in the Universe denser than plutonium, yet we get the same frequency-values by diffraction through plutonium crystals that we get through osmium crystals – there's not the slightest difference. If J Shelby Stevens is operating in terms of fractions of those values, then he's doing what an organist would call "playing in the cracks" – which is certainly something you can *think* about doing, but something that's in actuality impossible to do. *Hoop.*'

'Hoop?' Weinbeaum said.

'Sorry. A hiccup only.'

'Oh. Well, maybe Stevens has rebuilt the organ?'

'If he has rebuilt the metrical frame of the Universe to accommodate a private skip-tracing firm,' Wald said firmly, 'I for one see no reason why we can't counter-check him – *hoop* – by declaring the whole cosmos null and void.'

'All right, all right,' Weinbaum said, grinning. 'I didn't mean to push your anology right over the edge – I was just asking. But let's get to work on it anyhow. We can't just sit here and let Stevens get away with it. If this frequency angle turns out to be as hopeless as it seems, we'll try something else.'

Wald eyed the aquavit bottle owlishly. 'It's a very pretty problem,' he said. 'Have I ever sung you the song we have in Sweden called "Nat-og-Dag?"'

'*Hoop,*' Weinbaum said, to his own surprise, in a high falsetto.

'Excuse me. No. Let's hear it.'

The computer occupied an entire floor of the Security building, its seemingly identical banks laid out side by side on
the floor along an advanced pathological state of Peano's
'space-filling curve'. At the current business end of the line
was a master control board with a large television screen at its
center, at which Dr Wald was stationed, with Weinbaum
looking, silently but anxiously, over his shoulder.

The screen itself showed a pattern which, except that it
was drawn in green light against a dark gray background,
strongly resembled the grain in a piece of highly polished
mahogany. Photographs of similar patterns were stacked on
a small table to Dr Wald's right; several had spilled over onto
the floor.

'Well, there it is,' Wald sighed at length. 'And I won't
struggle to keep myself from saying "I told you so." What
you've had me do here, Robin, is to reconfirm about half the
basic postulates of particle physics – which is why it took so
long, even though it was the first project we started.' He
snapped off the screen. 'There are no cracks for J Shelby
to play in. That's definite.'

'If you'd said "That's flat," you would have made a joke,'
Weinbaum said sourly. 'Look . . . isn't there still a chance of
error. If not on your part, Thor, then in the computer? After
all, it's set up to work only with the unit charges of modern
physics; mightn't we have to disconnect the banks that contain that bias before the machine will follow the fractional-
charge instructions we give it?'

'Disconnect, he says,' Wald groaned, mopping his brow re-
flectively. 'The bias exists everywhere in the machine, my
friend, because it functions everywhere on those same unit
charges. It wasn't a matter of subtracting banks; we had to
add one with a bias all of its own, to counter-correct the corrections the computer would otherwise apply to the instructions. The technicians thought I was crazy. Now, five months
later, I've proved it.'

Weinbaum grinned in spite of himself. 'What about the
other projects?'

'All done – some time back, as a matter of fact. The staff and I checked every single Dirac tape we've received since you released J Shelby from Yaphank, for any sign of intermodulation, marginal signals, or anything else of the kind. There's nothing, Robin, absolutely nothing. That's our net result, all around.'

'Which leaves us just where we started,' Weinbaum said. "All the monitoring projects came to the same dead end; I strongly suspect that Stevens has not risked any further calls from his home office to his field staff, even though he seemed confident that we'd never intercept such calls – as we haven't. Even our local wiretapping hasn't turned up anything but calls made by Stevens' secretary, making appointments for him with various clients, actual and potential. Any information he's selling these days he's passing on in person – and not in his office, either, because we've got bugs planted all over that and haven't heard a thing.'

'That must limit his range of operation enormously,' Wald objected.

Weinbaum nodded.

'Without a doubt – but he shows no signs of being bothered by it. He can't have sent any tips to Erskine recently, for instance, because our last tangle with that crew came out very well for us, even though we had to use the Dirac to send the orders to our squadron out there. If he overheard us, he didn't even try to pass the word. Just as he said, he's sweating us out—' Weinbaum paused. 'Wait a minute, here comes Margaret. And by the length of her stride, I'd say she's got something particularly nasty on her mind.'

'You bet I do,' Margaret Soames said vindictively. 'And it'll blow plenty of lids around here, or I miss my guess. The ID squad has finally pinned down J Shelby Stevens. They did it with the voice-comparator alone.'

'How does that work?' Wald said interestedly.

'Blink microphone,' Weinbaum said impatiently. 'Isolates inflections on single, normally stressed syllables and matches them. Standard ID searching technique, on a case of this kind, but it takes so long that we usually get the quarry by other means before it pays off. Well, don't stand there like a dummy, Margaret. Who is he?'

' "He," ' Margaret said, 'is your sweetheart of the video waves, Miss Dana Lje.'

'They're crazy!' Wald said, staring at her.

Weinbaum came slowly out of his first shock of stunned disbelief. 'No, Thor,' he said finally. 'No, it figures. If a woman is going to go in for disguises, there are always two she can assume outside her own sex: a young boy, and a very old man. And Dana's an actress; that's no news to us.'

'But – but why did she do it, Robin?'

'That's what we're going to find out right now. So we wouldn't get the Dirac modification by ourselves, eh? Well, there are other ways of getting answers besides particle physics. Margaret, do you have a pick-up order out for that girl?'

'No,' the receptionist said. 'This is one chestnut I wanted to see you pull out for yourself. You give me the authority, and I send the order – not before.'

'Spiteful child. Send it, then, and glory in my gritted teeth. Come on, Thor – let's put the nutcracker on this chestnut.'

As they were leaving the computer floor, Weinbaum stopped suddenly in his tracks and began to mutter in an almost inaudible voice.

Wald said, 'What's the matter, Robin?'

'Nothing. I keep being brought up short by those predictions. What's the date?'

'M'm ... June 9th. Why?'

'It's the exact date that "Stevens" predicted we'd meet again, damn it! Something tells me that this isn't going to be as simple as it looks.'

If Dana Lje had any idea of what she was in for – and considering the fact that she was 'J Shelby Stevens' it had to be assumed that she did – the knowledge seemed not to make her at all fearful. She sat as composedly as ever before Weinbaum's desk, smoking her eternal cigarette, and waited, one dimpled knee pointed directly at the bridge of the officer's nose.

'Dana,' Weinbaum said, 'this time we're going to get all the answers, and we're not going to be gentle about it. Just in case you're not aware of the fact, there are certain laws relating to giving false information to a security officer, under which we could heave you in prison for a minimum of fifteen years. By application of the statutes on using communications to defraud, plus various local laws against transvestism, pseudonymity and so on, we could probably pile up enough additional short sentences to keep you in Yaphank until you really *do* grow a beard. So I'd advise you to open up.'

'I have every intention of opening up,' Dana said. 'I know practically word for word, how this interview is going to proceed, what information I'm going to give you, just when I'm going to give it to you – and what you are going to pay me for it. I knew all that many months ago. So there would be no point in my holding out on you.'

'What you're saying, Miss Lje,' Thor Wald said in a resigned voice, 'is that the future is fixed, and that you can read it, in every essential detail.'

'Quite right, Dr Wald. Both those things are true.'

There was a brief silence.

'All right,' Weinbaum said grimly. 'Talk.'

'All right, Captain Weinbaum, pay me,' Dana said calmly.

Weinbaum snorted.

'But I'm quite serious,' she said. 'You still don't know what I know about the Dirac communicator. I won't be forced to tell it, by threat of prison or ·by any other threat. You see, I know for a fact that you aren't going to send me to prison, or give me drugs, or do anything else of that kind. I know for a fact, instead, that you are going to pay me – so I'd be very foolish to say a word until you do. After all, it's quite a secret you're buying. Once I tell you what it is, you and the entire service will be able to read the future as I do, and then the information will be valueless to me.'

Weinbaum was completely speechless for a moment. Finally he said, 'Dana, you have a heart of purest brass, as well as a knee with an invisible gunsight on it. I say that I'm *not* going to give you my appropriation, regardless of what the future may or may not say about it. I'm not going to give it to you because the way my Government – and yours – runs things makes such a price impossible. Or is that really your price?'

'It's my real price . . . but it's also an alternative. Call it my second choice. My first choice, which means the price I'd settle for, comes in two parts: (a), to be taken into your service as a responsible officer; and, (b), to be married to Capt Robin Weinbaum.'

Weinbaum sailed up out of his chair. He felt as though copper-coloured flames a foot long were shooting out of each of his ears.

'Of all the—' he began. There his voice failed completely.

From behind him, where Wald was standing, came something like a large, Scandinavian-model guffaw being choked into insensibility.

Dana herself seemed to be smiling a little.

'You see,' she said, 'I don't point my best and most accurate knee at every man I meet.'

Weinbaum sat down again, slowly and carefully. 'Walk, do not run, to nearest exit,' he said. 'Women and childlike security officers first. Miss Lje, are you trying to sell me the notion that you went through this elaborate hanky-panky – beard and all – out of a burning passion for my dumpy and underpaid person?'

'Not entirely,' Dana Lje said. 'I want to be in the bureau, too, as I said. Let me confront you, though, Captain, with a fact of life that doesn't seem to have occurred to you at all. Do you accept as a fact that I can read the future in detail, and that that, to be possible at all, means that the future is fixed?'

'Since Thor seems able to accept it, I suppose I can too – provisionally.'

'There's nothing provisional about it,' Dana said firmly. 'Now, when I first came upon this – uh, this gimmick – quite a while back, one of the first things that I found out was that I was going to go through the "J Shelby Stevens" masquerade, force myself onto the staff of the bureau, and marry you, Robin. At the time, I was both astonished and completely rebellious. I did not want to be on the bureau staff; I liked

108

my free-lance life as a video commentator. I did not want to marry you, though I wouldn't have been averse to living with you for a while – say a month or so. And above all, the masquerade struck me as ridiculous.

'But the facts kept staring me in the face. I *was* going to do all those things. There were no alternatives, no fanciful "branches of time", no decision-points that might be altered to make the future change. My future, like yours, Dr Wald's, and everyone else's, was fixed. It didn't matter a snap whether or not I had a decent motive for what I was going to do; I was going to do it anyhow. Cause and effect, as I could see for myself, just don't exist. One event follows another because events are just as indestructible in space-time as matter and energy are.

'It was the bitterest of all pills. It will take me many years to swallow it completely, and you too. Dr Wald will come around a little sooner, I think. At any rate, once I was intellectually convinced that all this was so, I had to protect my own sanity. I knew that I couldn't alter what I was going to do, but the least I could do to protect myself was to supply myself with motives. Or, in other words, just plain rationalizations. That much, it seems, we're free to do; the consciousness of the observer is just along for the ride through time, and can't alter events – but it can comment, explain, invent. That's fortunate, for none of us could stand going through motions which were truly free of what we think of as personal significances.

'So I supplied myself with the obvious motives. Since I was going to be married to you and couldn't get out of it, I set out to convince myself that I loved you. Now I do. Since I was going to join the bureau staff, I thought over all the advantages that it might have over video commentating, and found that they made a respectable list. Those are my motives.

'But I had no such motives at the beginning. Actually, there are never motives behind actions. All actions are fixed. What we called motives evidently are rationalizations by the helpless observing consciousness, which is intelligent enough to smell an event coming – and, since it cannot avert the event, instead cooks up reasons for wanting it to happen.'

'Wow,' Dr Wald said, inelegantly but with considerable force.

'Either "wow" or "balderdash" seems to be called for – I can't quite decide which,' Weinbaum agreed. 'We know that Dana is an actress, Thor, so let's not fall off the apple tree quite yet. Dana, I've been saving the *really* hard question for the last. That question is: *How?* How did you arrive at this modification of the Dirac transmitter? Remember, we know your background, where we didn't know that of "J Shelby Stevens." You're not a scientist. There were some fairly high-powered intellects among your distant relatives, but that's as close as you come.'

'I'm going to give you several answers to that question,' Dana Lje said. 'Pick the one you like best. They're all true, but they tend to contradict each other here and there.

'To begin with, you're right about my relatives, of course. If you'll check your dossier again, though, you'll discover that those so-called "distant" relatives were the last surviving members of my family besides myself. When they died, second and fourth and ninth cousins though they were, their estates reverted to me, and among their effects I found a sketch of a possible instantaneous communicator based on de Broglie-wave inversion. The material was in very rough form, and mostly beyond my comprehension, because I am, as you say, no scientist myself. But I was interested; I could see, dimly, what such a thing might be worth – and not only in money.

'My interest was fanned by two coincidences – the kind of coincidences that cause-and-effect just can't allow, but which seem to happen all the same in the world of unchangeable events. For most of my adult life, I've been in communications industries of one kind or another, mostly branches of video. I had communications equipment around me constantly, and I had coffee and doughnuts with communications engineers every day. First I picked up the jargon; then, some of the procedures; and eventually, a little real knowledge. Some of the things I learned can't be gotten any other way. Some other things are ordinarily available only to highly educated people like Dr Wald here, and came to me by accident, in horseplay, between kisses, and a hundred other ways – all natural to the environment of a video network.'

Weinbaum found, to his own astonishment, that the 'between kisses' clause did not sit very well in his chest. He said, with unintentional brusqueness: 'What's the other coincidence?'

'A leak in your own staff.'

'Dana, you ought to have that set to music.'

'Suit yourself.'

'I can't suit myself,' Weinbaum said petulantly. 'I work for the Government. Was this leak direct to you?'

'Not at first. That was why I kept insisting to you in person that there might be such a leak, and why I finally began to hint about it in public, on my program. I was hoping that you'd be able to seal it up inside the bureau before my first rather tenuous contact with it got lost. When I didn't succeed in provoking you into protecting yourself, I took the risk of making direct contact with the leak myself – and the first piece of secret information that came to me through it was the final point I needed to put my Dirac communicator together. When it was all assembled, it did more than just communicate. It predicted. And I can tell you why.'

Weinbaum said thoughtfully, 'I don't find this very hard to accept, so far. Pruned of the philosophy, it even makes some sense of the "J Shelby Stevens" affair. I assume that by letting the old gentleman become known as somebody who knew more about the Dirac transmitter than I did, and who wasn't adverse to negotiating with anybody who had money, you kept the leak working through you – rather than transmitting data directly to unfriendly governments.'

'It did work out that way,' Dana said. 'But that wasn't the genesis or the purpose of the Stevens masquerade. I've already given you the whole explanation of how that came about.'

'Well, you'd better name me that leak, before the man gets away.'

'When the price is paid, not before. It's too late to prevent a getaway, anyhow. In the meantime, Robin, I want to go on and tell you the other answer to your question about how I was able to find this particular Dirac secret, and you didn't. What answers I've given you up to now have been cause-and-effect answers, with which we're all more comfortable. But I want to impress on you that all apparent cause-and-effect relationships are accidents. There is no such thing as a cause, and no such thing as an effect. I found the secret because I found it; that event was fixed; that certain circumstances seem to explain why I found it, in the old cause-and-effect terms, is irrelevant. Similarly, with all your superior equipment and brains, you didn't find it for one reason, and one reason alone: because you didn't find it. The history of the future says you didn't.'

'I pays my money and I takes no choice, eh?' Weinbaum said ruefully.

'I'm afraid so – and I don't like it any better than you do.'

'Thor, what's your opinion of all this?'

'It's just faintly flabbergasting,' Wald said soberly. 'However, it hangs together. The deterministic Universe which Miss Lje paints was a common feature of the old relativity theories, and as sheer speculation has an even longer history. I would say that in the long run, how much credence we place in the story as a whole will rest upon her method of, as she calls it, reading the future. If it is demonstrable beyond any doubt, then the rest becomes perfectly credible – philosophy and all. If it doesn't, then what remains is an admirable job of acting, plus some metaphysics which, while self-consistent, are not original with Miss Lje.'

'That sums up the case as well as if I'd coached you, Dr Wald,' Dana said. 'I'd like to point out one more thing. If I can read the future, then "J Shelby Stevens" never had any need for a staff of field operatives, and he never needed to send a single Dirac message which you might intercept. All he needed to do was to make predictions from his readings, which he knew to be infallible; no private espionage network had to be involved.'

'I see that,' Weinbaum said dryly. 'All right, Dana, let's put the proposition this way: *I do not believe you.* Much of what you say is probably true, but in totality I believe it to be false. On the other hand, if you're telling the whole truth, you certainly deserve a place on the bureau staff – it would be dangerous as hell *not* to have you with us – and the marriage is a more or less minor matter, except to you and me. You can have that with no strings attached; I don't want to be bought, any more than you would.

'So: if you will tell me where the leak is, we will consider that part of the question closed. I make that condition not as a price, but because I don't want to get myself engaged to somebody who might be shot as a spy within a month.'

'Fair enough,' Dana said. 'Robin, your leak is Margaret Soames. She is an Erskine operative, and nobody's bubble-brain. She's a highly trained technician.'

'Well, I'll be damned,' Weinbaum said in astonishment. 'Then she's already flown the coop – she was the one who first told me we'd identified you. She must have taken on that job in order to hold up delivery long enough to stage an exit.'

'That's right. But you'll catch her, day after tomorrow. And you are now a hooked fish, Robin.'

There was another suppressed burble from Thor Wald.

'I accept the fate happily,' Weinbaum said, eyeing the gun-sight knee. 'Now, if you will tell me how you work your swami trick, and it it backs up everything you've said to the letter, as you claim, I'll see to it that you're also taken into the bureau and that all charges against you are quashed. Otherwise, I'll probably have to kiss the bride between the bars of a cell.'

Dana smiled. 'The secret is very simple. It's in the beep.'

Weinbaum's jaw dropped. 'The beep? The Dirac noise?'

'That's right. You didn't find it out because you considered the beep to be just a nuisance, and ordered Miss Soames to cut it off all tapes before sending them in to you. Miss Soames, who had some inkling of what the beep meant, was more than happy to do so, leaving the reading of the beep exclusively to "J Shelby Stevens" – who she thought was going to take on Erskine as a client.'

'Explain,' Thor Wald said, looking intense.

'Just as you assumed, every Dirac message that is sent is picked up by every receiver that is capable of detecting it.

113

Every receiver – including the first one ever built, which is yours, Dr Wald, through the hundreds of thousands of them which will exist throughout the Galaxy in the Twenty-Fourth Century, to the untold millions which will exist in the Thirtieth Century, and so on. The Dirac beep is the simultaneous reception of *every one of the Dirac messages which have ever been sent, or ever will be sent.* Incidentally, the cardinal number of the total of those messages is a relatively small and of course finite number; it's far below really large finite numbers such as the number of electrons in the Universe, even when you break each and every message down into individual "bits" and count those.'

'Of course,' Dr Wald said softly. 'Of course! But, Miss Lje . . . how do you tune for an individual message? We tried fractional positron frequencies, and got nowhere.'

'I didn't even know fractional positron frequencies existed,' Dana confessed. 'No, it's simple – so simple that a lucky layman like me could arrive at it. You tune individual messages out of the beep by time-lag, nothing more. All the messages arrive at the same instant, in the smallest fraction of time that exists, something called a "chronon."'

'Yes,' Wald said. 'The time it takes one electron to move from one quantum-level to another. That's the Pythagorean point of time-measurement.'

'Thank you. Obviously no gross physical receiver can respond to a message that brief, or at least that's what I thought at first. But because there are relay and switching delays, various forms of feedback and so on in the apparatus itself, the beep arrives at the output end as a complex pulse which has been "splattered" along the time axis for a full second or more. That's an effect which you can exaggerate by recording the "splattered" beep on a high-speed tape, the same way you would record any event that you wanted to study in slow motion. Then you tune up the various failure-points in your receiver, to exaggerate one failure, minimize all the others, and use noise-suppressing techniques to cut out the background.'

Thor Wald frowned. 'You'd still have a considerable garble

114

when you were through. You'd have to sample the messages—'

'Which is just what I did; Robin's little lecture to me about the ultrawave gave me that hint. I set myself to find out how the ultrawave channel carries so many messages at once, and I discovered that you people sample the incoming pulses every thousandth of a second and pass on one pip only when the wave deviates in a certain way from the mean. I didn't really believe it would work on the Dirac beep, but it turned out just as well: 90% as intelligible as the original transmission after it came through the smearing device. I'd already got enough from the beep to put my plan in motion, of course – but now every voice message in it was available, and crystal-clear: If you select three pips every thousandth of a second, you can even pick up an intelligible transmission of music – a little razzy, but good enough to identify the instruments that are playing – and that's a very close test of any communications device.'

'There's a question of detail here that doesn't quite follow,' said Weinbaum, for whom the technical talk was becoming a little too thick to fight through. 'Dana, you say that you knew the course this conversation was going to take – yet it isn't being Dirac-recorded, nor can I see any reason why any summary of it would be sent out on the Dirac afterwards.'

'That's true, Robin. However, when I leave here, I will make such a transcast myself, on my own Dirac. Obviously I will – because I've *already* picked it up, from the beep.'

'In other words, you're going to call yourself up – months ago.'

'That's it,' Dana said. 'It's not as useful a technique as you might think at first, because it's dangerous to make such broadcasts while a situation is still developing. You can safely "phone back" details only after the given situation has gone to completion, as a chemist might put it. Once you know, however, that when you use the Dirac you're dealing with time, you can coax some very strange things out of the instrument.'

She paused and smiled. 'I have heard,' she said conversationally, 'the voice of the President of our Galaxy, in 3480,

115

announcing the federation of the Milky Way and the Magellanic Clouds. I've heard the commander of a worldline cruiser, traveling from 8873 to 8704 along the world-line of the planet Hathshepa, which circles a star on the rim of NGC 4725, calling for help across eleven million light-years – but what kind of help he was calling for, or will be calling for, is beyond my comprehension. And many other things. When you check on me, you'll hear these things too – and you'll wonder what many of them mean.

'And you'll listen to them even more closely than I did, in the hope of finding out whether or not anyone was able to understand in time to help.'

Weinbaum and Wald looked dazed.

Her voice became a little more somber. 'Most of the voices in the Dirac beep are like that – they're cries for help, which you can overhear decades or centuries before the senders get into trouble. You'll feel obligated to answer every one, to try to supply the help that's needed. And you'll listen to the succeeding messages and say: "Did we – will we get there in time? Did we understand in time?"

'And in most cases you won't be sure. You'll know the future, but not what most of it means. The farther into the future you travel with the machine, the more incomprehensible the messages become, and so you're reduced to telling yourself that time will, after all, have to pass by at its own pace, before enough of the surrounding events can emerge to make those remote messages clear.

'The long run effect, as far as I can think it through, is not going to be that of omniscience – of our consciousness being extracted entirely from the time-stream and allowed to view its whole sweep from one side. Instead, the Dirac in effect simply slides the bead of consciousness forward from the present a certain distance. Whether it's five hundred or five thousand years still remains to be seen. At that point the law of diminishing returns sets in – or the noise-factor begins to overbalance the information, take your choice – and the observer is reduced to traveling in time at the same old speed. He's just a bit ahead of himself.'

'You've thought a great deal about this,' Wald said slowly. 'I dislike to think of what might have happened had some less conscientious person stumbled on the beep.'

'That wasn't in the cards,' Dana said.

In the ensuing quiet, Weinbaum felt a faint, irrational sense of let-down, of something which had promised more than had been delivered – rather like the taste of fresh bread as compared to its smell, or the discovery that Thor Wald's Swedish 'folk-song' *Nat-og-Dag* was only Cole Porter's *Night and Day* in another language. He recognized the feeling: it was the usual emotion of the hunter when the hunt is over, the born detective's professional version of the *post coitum triste*. After looking at the smiling, supple Dana Lje a moment more, however, he was almost content.

'There's one more thing,' he said. 'I don't want to be insufferably skeptical about this – but I want to see it work. Thor, can we set up a sampling and smearing device such as Dana describes and run a test?'

'In fifteen minutes,' Dr Wald said. 'We have most of the unit in already assembled form on our big ultrawave receiver, and it shouldn't take any effort to add a high-speed tape unit to it. I'll do it right now.'

He went out. Weinbaum and Dana looked at each other for a moment, rather like strange cats. Then the security officer got up, with what he knew to be an air of somewhat grim determination, and seized his fiancee's hands, anticipating a struggle.

That first kiss was, by intention at least, mostly *pro forma*. But by the time Wald padded back into the office, the letter had been pretty thoroughly superseded by the spirit.

The scientist harrumphed and set his burden on the desk. 'This is all there is to it,' he said, 'but I had to hunt all through the library to find a Dirac record with a beep still on it. Just a moment more while I make connections . . .'

Weinbaum used the time to bring his mind back to the matter at hand, although not quite completely. Then two tape spindles began to whir like so many bees, and the end-stopped sound of the Dirac beep filled the room. Wald stopped the

117

apparatus, reset, and started the smearing tape very slowly in the opposite direction.

A distant babble of voices came from the speaker. As Weinbaum leaned forward tensely, one voice said clearly and loudly above the rest:

'Hello, Earth bureau. Lt T L Matthews at Hercules Station NGC 6341, transmission date 13-22-2091. We have the last point on the orbit-curve of your dope-runners plotted, and the curve itself points to a small system about 25 light-years from the base here; the place hasn't even got a name on our charts. Scouts show the home planet at least twice as heavily fortified as we anticipated, so we'll need another cruiser. We have a "can-do" from you in the beep for us, but we're waiting as ordered to get it in the present. NGC 6341 Matthews out.'

After the first instant of stunned amazement – for no amount of intellectual willingness to accept could have prepared him for the overwhelming fact itself – Weinbaum had grabbed a pencil and begun to write at top speed. As the voice signed out he threw the pencil down and looked excitedly at Dr Wald.

'Seven months ahead,' he said, aware that he was grinning like an idiot. 'Thor, you know the trouble we've had with that needle in the Hercules haystack! This orbit-curve trick must be something Matthews has yet to dream up – at least he hasn't come to me with it yet, and there's nothing in the situation as it stands now that would indicate a closing-time of six months for the case. The computers said it would take three more years.'

'It's new data,' Dr Wald agreed solemnly.

'Well, don't stop there, in God's name! Let's hear some more!'

Dr Wald went through the ritual, much faster this time. The speaker said:

'Nausentampen. Eddettompic. Berobsilom. Aimkaksetchoc. Sanbetogmow. Datdectamset. Domatrosmin. Out.'

'My word,' Wald said, 'What's all that?'

'That's what I was talking about,' Dana Lje said. 'At least

118

half of what you get from the beep is just as incomprehensible. I suppose it's whatever has happened to the English language, thousands of years from now.'

'No, it isn't,' Weinbaum said. He had resumed writing, and was still at it, despite the comparative briefness of the transmission. 'Not this sample, anyhow. That, ladies and gentlemen, is code – no language consists exclusively of four-syllable words, of that you can be sure. What's more, it's a version of our code. I can't break it down very far – it takes a full-time expert to read this stuff – but I get the date and some of the sense. It's March 12, 3022, and there's some kind of a mass evacuation taking place. The message seems to be a routing order.'

'But why will we be using code?' Dr Wald wanted to know. 'It implies that we think somebody might overhear us – somebody else with a Dirac. That could be very messy.'

'It could indeed,' Weinbaum said. 'But we'll find out, I imagine. Give her another spin, Thor.'

'Shall I try for a picture this time?'

Weinbaum nodded. A moment later, he was looking squarely into the green-skinned face of something that looked like an animated traffic signal with a helmet on it. Though the creature had no mouth, the Dirac speaker was saying quite clearly, 'Hello, Chief. This is Thammos NGC 2287, transmission date Gor 60, 302 by my calendar, July 2, 2973 by yours. This is a lousy little planet. Everything stinks of oxygen, just like Earth. But the natives accept us and that's the important thing. We've got your genius safely born. Detailed report coming later by paw. NGC 2287 Thammos out.'

'I wish I knew my New General Catalogue better,' Weinbaum said. 'Isn't that M 41 in Canis Major, the one with the red star in the middle? And we'll be using non-humanoids there! What *was* that creature, anyhow? Never mind, spin her again.'

Dr Wald spun her again. Weinbaum, already feeling a little dizzy, had given up taking notes. That could come later. All that could come later. Now he wanted only scenes and voices, more and more scenes and voices from the future. They were better than aquavit, even with a beer chaser.

IV

The indoctrination tape ended, and Krasna touched a button. The Dirac screen darkened, and folded silently back into the desk.

'They didn't see their way through to us, not by a long shot,' he said. 'They didn't see, for instance, that when one section of the government becomes nearly all-knowing – no matter how small it was to begin with – it necessarily becomes all of the government that there is. Thus the bureau turned into the Service and pushed everyone else out.

'On the other hand, those people did come to be afraid that a government with an all-knowing arm might become a rigid dictatorship. That couldn't happen and didn't happen, because the more you know, the wider your field of possible operation becomes and the more fluid and dynamic a society you need. How could a rigid society expand to other star-systems, let alone other galaxies? It couldn't be done.'

'I should think it could,' Jo said slowly. 'After all, if you know in advance what everybody is going to do—'

'But we don't, Jo. That's just a popular fiction – or, if you like, a red herring. Not all of the business of the cosmos is carried on over the Dirac, after all. The only events we can ever overhear are those which transmitted as a message. Do you order your lunch over the Dirac? Of course you don't. Up to now, you've never said a word over the Dirac in your life.

'And there's much more to it than that. All dictatorships are based on the proposition that government can somehow control a man's thoughts. We know now that the consciousness of the observer is the only free thing in the Universe. Wouldn't we look foolish trying to control that, when our entire physics shows that it's impossible to do so? That's why the Service is in no sense a thought police. We're interested only in acts. We're an Event Police.'

'But why,' Jo said. 'If all history is fixed, why do we bother with these boy-meets-girl assignments, for instance? The meetings will happen anyhow.'

'Of course they will,' Krasna agreed immediately. 'But look, Jo. Our interests as a government depend upon the future. We operate *as if* the future is as real as the past, and so far we haven't been disappointed: the Service is 100 percent successful. But that very success isn't without its warnings. What would happen if we *stopped* supervising events? We don't know, and we don't dare take the chance. Despite the evidence that the future is fixed, we have to take on the role of the caretaker of inevitability. We believe that nothing can possibly go wrong . . . but we have to act on the philosophy that history helps only those who help themselves.

'That's why we safeguard huge numbers of courtships right through to contract, and even beyond it. We have to see to it that *every single person who is mentioned in any Dirac 'cast gets born*. Our obligation as Event Police is to make the events of the future possible, because those events are crucial to our society – even the smallest of them. It's an enormous task, believe me, and it gets bigger every day. Apparently it always will.'

'Always?' Jo said. 'What about the public? Isn't it going to smell this out sooner or later? The evidence is piling up at a terrific rate.'

'Yes and no,' Krasna said. 'Lots of people are smelling it out right now, just as you did. But the number of new people we need in the Service grows faster – it's always ahead of the number of laymen who follow the clues to the truth.'

Jo took a deep breath. 'You take all this as if it were as commonplace as boiling an egg, Kras,' he said. 'Don't you ever wonder about some of the things you can get from the beep? That 'cast Dana Lje picked up from Canes Venatici, for instance, the one from the ship that was travelling backward in time? How is that possible? What could be the purpose? Is it—'

'*Pace, pace*,' Krasna said. 'I don't know, and I don't care. Neither should you. That event is too far in the future for us

121

to worry about. We can't possibly know its context yet, so there's no sense in trying to understand it. If an Englishman of around 1600 had found out about the American Revolution, he would have thought it a tragedy; an Englishman of 1950 would have a very different view of it. We're in the same spot. The messages we get from the really far future have no contexts yet.'

'I think I see,' Jo said. 'I'll get used to it in time, I suppose, after I use the Dirac for a while. Or does my new rank authorize me to do that?'

'Yes, it does. But, Jo, first I want to pass on to you a rule of Service etiquette that must never be broken. You won't be allowed anywhere near a Dirac mike until you have it burned into your memory beyond any forgetfulness.'

'I'm listening, Kras, believe me.'

'Good. This is the rule: *The date of a Serviceman's death must never be mentioned in a Dirac 'cast.*'

Jo blinked, feeling a little chilly. The reason behind the rule was decidedly tough-minded, but its ultimate kindness was plain. He said, 'I won't forget that. I'll want that protection myself. Many thanks, Kras. What's my new assignment?'

'To begin with,' Krasna said, grinning, 'as simple a job as I've ever given you, right here on Randolph. Skin out of here and find me that cab-driver – the one who mentioned time-travel to you. He's uncomfortably close to the truth; closer than you were in one category.

'Find him, and bring him to me. The Service is about to take in a new raw recruit!'

Mack Reynolds: DOWN THE RIVER   126
Avram Davidson: THE BOUNTY HUNTERS   135
Fredric Brown: NOT YET THE END   141

Heady stuff, galactic empires, when you identify with the ruling classes. One of the delights of science fiction is the ease with which it changes viewpoints and attitudes. In this section, we are set among the losers.

A word here from Arnold Toynbee comes in appropriately. In his volume *Surviving the Future*, he has this comment on a world state which applies equally to galactic unification: 'It is most unlikely, I fear, that it will be established by the will, or even with the acquiescence of the majority of mankind. It seems to me likely to be imposed on the majority by a ruthless, efficient, and fanatical minority, inspired by some ideology or religion.' Mack Reynolds has a few words to say on that subject.

The Davidson and Brown offerings are the shortest in the book. Brevity generally makes its point with wit. Avram Davidson, who lives in an exotic part of the world – as does Mack Reynolds – has written a number of amusing stories, often with a Jewish flavour. Fredric Brown was another wit, known to the thriller field for such novels as *The Fabulous Clip Joint*, and to sf readers for his crazy comic novel, *What Mad Universe*. *Not Yet the End* is the oldest story in this anthology, but it still makes its amusing point.

When the aliens come, Earth finds itself a mere barbarian pawn in the game of galactic empire!

DOWN THE RIVER

By Mack Reynolds

The space-ship was picked up by Army radar shortly after it entered the atmosphere over North America. It descended rather slowly and by the time it hovered over Connecticut a thousand fighter planes were in the air.

Wires sizzled hysterically between captains of State Police and colonels of the National Guard, between Army generals and cabinet members, between admirals and White House advisers. But before anything could be decided in the way of attack upon the intruder or defense against him the space-ship had settled gently into an empty Connecticut field.

Once it had landed all thought of attack left the minds of everyone concerned with North American defense. The craft towered half a mile upward and gave an uncomfortable impression of being able to take on the armed forces of the United States all by itself, if it so desired, which seemingly it didn't. As a matter of fact it showed no signs of life whatsoever for the first few hours of its visit.

The governor arrived about noon, beating the representative from the State Department by fifteen minutes and the delegates from the United Nations by three hours. He hesitated only briefly at the cordon which State Police and National Guardsmen had thrown up about the field and decided that any risk he might be taking would be worth the publicity value of being the first to greet the visitors from space.

Besides, the television and newsreel cameras were already set up and trained upon him. 'Honest Harry' Smith knew a good thing when he saw it. He instructed the chauffeur to approach the ship.

As the car came closer, escorted cautiously by two motorcycle troopers and the newsreel and television trucks, the problem arose of just how to make known his Excellency's presence. There seemed to be no indication of a means of entrance to the spectacular craft. It presented a smooth mother-of-pearl effect that was breathtakingly beautiful – but at the same time cold and unapproachable in appearance.

Happily the problem was solved for them as they came within a few yards of the vessel. What seemed a solid part of the craft's side swung inward and a figure stepped lightly to the ground.

Governor Smith's first shocked impression was that it was a man wearing a strange mask and a carnival costume. The alien, otherwise human and even handsome by our standards, had a light green complexion. It tucked the Roman-like toga it wore about its lithe figure and approached the car smilingly. Its English had only a slight touch of accent. Grammatically it was perfect.

'My name is Grannon Tyre Eighteen-Hundred and Fifty-two K,' the alien said. 'I assume that you are an official of this – er – nation. The United States of North America, is it not?'

The governor was taken aback. He'd been rehearsing inwardly a pantomime of welcome – with the television and newsreel men in mind. He had pictured himself as holding up his right arm in what he conceived to be the universal gesture of peace, of smiling broadly and often and, in general, making it known that the aliens were welcome to the earth and to the United States in general and to the State of Connecticut in particular. He hadn't expected the visitors to speak English.

However he had been called upon to speak off the cuff too often not to be able to rise to the occasion.

'Welcome to Earth,' he said with a flourish that he hoped the TV boys got. 'This is an historical occasion indeed. Without doubt future generations of your people and mine will look back on this fateful hour and . . .'

Grannon Tyre 1852K smiled again. 'I beg your pardon but was my assumption correct? You are an official of the government?'

'Eh? Er – humph – yes, of course. I am Governor Harry Smith, of Connecticut, this prosperous and happy state in which you have landed. To go on—'

The alien said, 'If you don't mind, I have a message from the Graff Marin Sidonn Forty-eight L. The Graff has commanded me to inform you that it is his pleasure that you notify all the nations, races and tribes upon Earth that he will address their representatives exactly one of your Earth months from today. He has an important message to deliver?'

The governor gave up trying to hold command of the situation. 'Who?' he asked painfully. 'What kind of a message?'

Grannon Tyre 1852K still smiled but it was the patient smile you used with a backward or recalcitrant child. His voice was a bit firmer, there was a faint touch of command.

'The Graff requests that you inform all nations of the world to have their representatives gather one month from today to receive his message. Is that clear?'

'Yeah. I guess so. Who—'

'Then that is all for the present. Good day.' The green alien turned and strode back to the space-ship. The portal closed behind him silently.

'I'll be double blessed,' said Governor Harry Smith a fraction of a second before the television cameras could cut him off the air.

Never before had there been anything like the following month. It was a period of jubilation and fear, of anticipation and foreboding, of hope and despair. As the delegates from all over Earth gathered to hear the message of the visitor from space tension grew throughout the world.

Scientist and savage, politician and revolutionist, banker and beggar, society matron and street walker, awaited that which they knew would influence the rest of their lives. And each hoped for one thing and feared another.

Newspaper columnists, radio commentators and soap-box speakers dwelt on the possibilities of the message endlessly. Although there were some who viewed with alarm, as a whole it was believed that the aliens would open up a new era for earth.

Scientific secrets beyond the dreams of man were expected

128

to be revealed. Disease was to be wiped out overnight. Man would take his place with this other intelligence to help rule the universe.

Preparations were made for the delegates to meet at Madison Square Garden in New York. It had early been seen that the United Nations buildings would be inadequate. Representatives were coming from races, tribes and countries which had never dreamed of sending delegates to the international conferences so prevalent in the last few decades.

The Graff Marin Sidonn 48L was accompanied to the gathering by Grannon Tyre 1852K and by a score of identically uniformed green complexioned aliens, who could only be taken for guards although they carried no evident weapons either defensive or offensive.

The Graff himself appeared to be an amiable enough gentleman, somewhat older than the other visitors from space. His step was a little slower and his toga more conservative in color than that of Grannon Tyre 1852K, who was evidently his aide.

Although he gave every indication of courtesy, the large number of persons confronting him seemed irritating and the impression was gained that the sooner this was over the more pleased he would be.

President Hanford of the United States opened the meeting with a few well chosen words, summing up the importance of the conference. He then introduced Grannon Tyre 1852K, who was also brief but who threw the first bombshell, although a full half of the audience didn't at first recognize the significance of his words.

'Citizens of Earth,' he began, 'I introduce to you Marin Sidonn Forty-eight L, Graff of the Solar System by appointment of Modren One, Gabon of Carthis, and, consequently, Gabon of the Solar System including the planet Earth. Since the English language seems to be nearest to a universal one upon this world, your Graff has prepared himself so that he may address you in that tongue. I understand that translating devices have been installed so that representatives of other languages will be able to follow.'

129

He turned to the Graff, held the flat of his right hand against his waist and then extended it toward his chief. The Graff returned the salute and stepped before the microphone.

The delegates arose to their feet to acclaim him and the cheers lasted a full ten minutes, being stilled finally when the alien from space showed a slight annoyance. President Hanford got to his feet, held up his hands and called for order.

The clamor died away and the Graff looked out over his audience. 'This is a strange meeting indeed,' he began. 'For more than four decals, which roughly comes to forty-three of your Earth years, I have been Graff of this Solar System, first under Toren One, and, more recently, under his successor, Modren One, present Gabon of Carthis, which, as has already been pointed out by my assistant, makes him Gabon of the Solar System and of Earth.'

Of all those present in the Garden, Larry Kincaid, of Associated Press, was the first to grasp the significance of what was being said. 'He's telling us we're property. Shades of Charlie Fort!'

The Graff went on. 'In all of this four decals, however, I have not visited Earth but have spent my time on the planet you know as Mars. This, I assure you, has not been because I was not interested in your problems and your welfare as an efficient Graff should be.

'Rather it has been traditional with the Gabons of Carthis not to make themselves known to the inhabitants of their subject planets until these subjects have reached at least an H-Seventeen development. Unfortunately, Earth has reached but an H-Four development.'

A low murmur was spreading over the hall. The Graff paused for a moment and then said kindly, 'I imagine that what I have said thus far is somewhat of a shock. Before we go on, let me sum it up briefly.

'Earth has been for a longer period than your histories record, a part of the Carthis Empire, which includes all of this Solar System. The Gabon, or perhaps you would call him Emperor, of Carthis appoints a Graff to supervise each of his sun systems. I have been your Graff for the past forty-three

130

years, making my residence on Mars, rather than on Earth, because of your low state of civilization.

'In fact,' he went on, half musingly, 'Earth hasn't been visited more than a score of times by representatives of Carthis in the past five thousand years. And, as a rule, these representatives were taken for some supernatural manifestation by your more than usually superstitious people. At least it is well that you have got over the custom of greeting us as gods.'

The murmur increased within the large auditorium to reach the point where the Graff could no longer be heard. Finally President Hanford, pale of face, stepped before the microphones and held up his hands again. When a reasonable quiet had been obtained, he turned back to the green man.

'Undoubtedly, it will take considerable time for any of us fully to assimilate this. All of the assembled delegates probably have questions which they would like to ask. However, I believe that one of the most pressing and one that we all have in mind is this—

'You say that ordinarily you wouldn't have made yourself known to us until we had reached a development of, I think you said, H-Seventeen – and that now we are but H-Four. Why have you made yourself known to us now? What special circumstances called for this revelation?'

The Graff nodded. 'I was about to dwell upon that, Mr. President.' He turned again to the quieted world delegates.

'My purpose in visiting Earth at this time was to announce to you that an interstellar arrangement has been made between the Gabon of Carthis and the Gabon of Wharis whereby the Solar System becomes part of the Wharis Empire, in return for certain considerations among the Aldebaran planets. In short, you are now subjects of the Gabon of Wharis. I am being recalled and your new Graff, Belde Kelden Forty-eight L, will arrive in due order.'

He let his eyes go over them gently. There was a touch of pity in them. 'Are there any other questions you wish to ask?'

Lord Harricraft stood up at his table directly before the microphones. He was obviously shaken. 'I cannot make an official statement until I have consulted with my government but I would like to ask this – what difference will it make to us, this change in Graffs, or even this change in – er – Gabons? If the policy is to leave Earth alone until the race has progressed further it will affect us little, if at all, for the time being, will it not?'

The Graff spoke sadly. 'While that has always been the policy of the Gabons of Carthis, your former rulers, it is not the policy of the present Gabon of Wharis. However, I can only say that your new Graff, Belde Kelden Forty-eight L, will be here in a few weeks and will undoubtedly explain his policies.'

Lord Harricraft remained on his feet. 'But you must have some idea of what this new Gabon wants of Earth.'

The Graff hesitated then said slowly, 'It is widely understood that the Gabon of Wharis is badly in need of uranium and various other rare elements to be found here on Earth. The fact that he has appointed Belde Kelden Forty-eight L, as your new Graff is also an indication, since this Graff has a wide reputation for success in all-out exploitation of new planets.'

Larry Kincaid grinned wryly at the other newspapermen at the press table. 'We've been sold down the river.'

Monsieur Pierre Bart was on his feet. 'Then it is to be expected that this Graff Belde Kelden Forty-eight L, under the direction of the Gabon of Wharis, will begin wholesale exploitation of this planet's resources, transporting them to other parts of the Gabon's empire?'

'I am afraid that is correct.'

President Hanford spoke again. 'But are we to have nothing to say about this? After all—'

The Graff said, 'Even in Carthis and under the benevolent rule of Modren One, the most progressive Gabon in the galaxy, a planet has no voice in its own rule until it has reached a development of H-Forty. You see, each Gabon must consider the welfare of his empire as a whole. He cannot be affected by the desires or even needs of the more primitive life forms on his various backward planets. Unfortunately—'

Lord Harricraft was beet red with indignation. 'But this is

preposterous,' he sputtered. 'It is unheard of that a—'

The Graff held up his hand coldly. 'I have no wish to argue with you. As I have said I am no longer Graff of this planet. However, I might point out to you a few facts which make your indignation somewhat out of place. In spite of my residence on Mars I have gone to the effort of investigating to some extent the history of Earth. Correct me if I am wrong in the following—

'This nation in which we hold our conference is the United States. Is it not true that in eighteen-hundred-three the United States bought approximately one million square miles of its present territory from the French Emperor Napoleon for fifteen million dollars? I believe it is called the Louisiana Purchase.

'I also believe that at that time the Louisiana Territory was inhabited almost exclusively by Amerindian tribes. Had these people ever heard of Napoleon or the United States? What happened to these people when they tried to defend their homes against the encroaching white man?'

He indicated Lord Harricraft. 'Or perhaps I should come closer to home. I understand that you represent the powerful British Empire. Tell me, how was Canada originally acquired? Or South Africa? Or India?'

He turned to Pierre Bart. 'And you, I believe, represent France. How were your North Africa colonies acquired? Did you consult with the nomadic peoples who lived there before you took over control of them?'

The Frenchman sputtered. 'But these were backward barbarians! Our assuming government over the area was to their benefit and to the benefit of the world as a whole.'

The Graff shrugged sadly. 'I am afraid that that is exactly the story you will hear from your new Graff Belde Kelden Forty-eight L.'

Suddenly half the hall was on its feet. Delegates stood on chairs and tables. Shouts rose, threats, hysterical defiance.

'We'll fight!'

'Better death than slavery!'

'We'll unite for all-out defense against the aliens!'

'Down with other-world interference!'

'WE'LL FIGHT!'

The Graff waited until the first fire of protest had burnt itself out, then held up his hands for quiet.

'I strongly recommend that you do nothing to antagonize Belde Kelden Forty-eight L, who is known to be a ruthless Graff when opposed by his inferiors. He strictly carries out the orders of the Gabon of Wharis, who usually makes a policy of crushing such revolts and then removing the population remaining to less desirable planets, where they are forced to support themselves as best they can.

'I can only add, that on some of the Wharis Empire planets, this is quite difficult, if not impossible.'

The din throughout the hall was beginning to rise again. The Graff shrugged and turned back to President Hanford. 'I am afraid I must go now. There is nothing more for me to say.' He motioned to Grannon Tyre 1852K and his guard.

'One moment,' the President said urgently. 'Isn't there anything else? Some advice, some word of assistance?'

The Graff sighed. 'I am sorry. It is now out of my hands.' But he paused and considered a moment. 'There is one thing I can suggest that might help you considerably in your dealings with Belde Kelden Forty-eight L. I hope that in telling you of it, I don't hurt your feelings.'

'Of course not,' the president muttered hopefully. 'The fate of the whole world is at stake. Anything that will help—'

'Well then, I might say that I consider myself completely without prejudice. It means nothing to me if a person has a green skin, a yellow one or is white, brown, black or red. Some of my best friends are unfortunately colored.

'However – well, don't you have any races on this planet with a green complexion? Graff Belde Kelden Forty-eight L is known to be extremely prejudiced against races of different colors. If you had some green representatives to meet him—'

The president stared at him dumbly.

The Graff was distressed. 'You mean that you have no races at all on Earth of green complexion? Or, at very least, blue?'

Gently ironic and bearded Avram Davidson is one of the most interesting among the newcomers to the field. A beautiful stylist, Davidson has gained rapid recognition for his sensitive studies of very human and very credible Tomorrows. . . .

THE BOUNTY HUNTER

By Avram Davidson

There was a whirring noise and a flurry and part of the snow-bank shot up at a 45-degree angle – or so it seemed – and vanished in the soft grey sky. Orel stopped and put out his arm, blocking his uncle's way.

'It's a bird . . . only a bird . . . *get* on, now, Orel,' Councillor Garth said, testily. He gave his nephew a light shove. 'They turn white in the winter-time. Or their feathers do. Anyway, that's what Trapper says.'

They plodded ahead, Orel, partly distracted by the pleasure of seeing his breath, laughed a bit. 'A bird outside of a cage. . . .' The councillor let him get a few feet ahead, then he awkwardly compressed a handful of snow and tossed it at his nephew's face when he turned it back. The first startled cry gave way to laughter. And so they came to the trapper's door.

The old fellow peered at them, but it was only a thing he did because it was expected of him; there was nothing wrong with his eyes. Garth had known him for many years, and he was still not sure how many of his mannerisms were real, how many put on. Or for that matter, how much of the antique stuff, cluttering up the cabin was actually part of the trapper's life and how much only there for show. Not that he cared: the trapper's job was as much to be quaint and amusing as to do anything else.

Orel, even before the introductions were over, noticed the cup and saucer on the top shelf of the cabinet, but not till his two elders paused did he comment, 'Look, Uncle: earthenware!'

135

'You've got a sharp eye, young fellow,' the trapper said, approvingly. 'Yes, it's real pottery. Brought over by my who knows how many times removed grandfather from the home planet. . . . Yes, my family, they were pretty important people on the home planet,' he added, inconsequentially. He stood silent for a moment, warmed with pride, then made a series of amiable noises in his throat.

'Well, I'm glad to meet you, young fellow. Knew your uncle before he was councillor, before you were born.' He went to the tiny window, touched the defroster, looked out. 'Yes, your machine is safe enough.' He turned around. 'I'll get the fire started, if there's no objection? And put some meat on to grill? Hm?'

The councillor nodded with slow satisfaction; Orel grinned widely.

The trapper turned off the heating unit and set the fire going. The three men gazed into the flames. The meat turned slowly on the jack. Orel tried to analyse the unfamiliar smells crowding around him – the wood itself, and the fire: no, fire had no smell, it was *smoke*; the meat, the furs and hides . . . he couldn't even imagine what they all were. It was different from the cities, that was sure. He turned to ask something, but his uncle Garth and Trapper weren't attending. Then he heard it – a long, drawn-out, faraway sort of noise. Then the trapper grunted and spat in the fire.

'What was it?' Orel asked.

The old fellow smiled. 'Never heard it before? Not even recorded, in a nature studies course? That's one of the big varmints – the kind your uncle and the other big sportsmen come out here to hunt – in season – the kind I trap in any season.' Abruptly, he turned to Councillor Garth. 'No talk of their dropping the bounty, is there?' Smilingly, the councillor shook his head. Reassured, the trapper turned his attention to the meat, poked it with a long pronged fork.

Orel compared the interior of the cabin to pictures and 3-D plays he had observed. Things looked familiar, but less – smooth, if that was the word. There was more disorder, an absence of symmetry. Hides and pelts – not too well cured, if

136

the smell was evidence – were scattered all around, not neatly tacked up or laid in neat heaps. Traps and parts of traps sat where the old man had evidently last worked at mending them.

'Council's not in session, I take it?' the trapper asked. Orel's uncle shook his head. 'But – don't tell me school's out, too? Thought they learned right through the winter.'

Garth said, 'I was able to persuade the Dean that our little trip was a genuine – if small – field expedition – and that Orel's absence wouldn't break the pattern of learning.'

The trapper grunted. *Pattern!* Orel thought. The mention of the word annoyed him. Everything was part of a pattern: Pattern of learning, pattern of earning, pattern of pleasure. . . . Life in the city went by patterns, deviations were few; people didn't even *want* to break the patterns. They were afraid to.

But it was obvious that the trapper didn't live by patterns. This . . . disorder.

'Do you have any children, Trapper?' he asked. The old man said he didn't. 'Then who will carry on your work?'

The trapper waved his hand to the west. 'Fellow in the next valley has two sons. When I get too old – a long time from now,' he said, defiantly; '—one of them will move in with me. Help me out. Split the bounties with me.

'I was married once.' He gazed into the fire. 'City woman. She couldn't get used to it out here. The solitude. The dangers. So we moved to the cities. *I* never got used to *that*. Got to get up at a certain time. Got to do everything a certain way. Everything has to be put in its place, neatly. All the people would look at you otherwise. Breaking the patterns? They didn't like it. Well, she died. And I moved back here as fast as I could get the permission. And here I've stayed.'

He took down plates, forks, knives, carved the meat. They ate with relish.

'Tastes better than something out of a factory lab, doesn't it?'

Orel's mind at once supplied him with an answer: that synthetics were seven times more nutritious than the foods they imitated. But his mouth was full and besides, it *did* taste better. Much better. . . . After the meal there was a sort of lull. The trapper looked at Councillor Garth in an expectant sort of way. The councillor smiled. He reached over into the pocket of his hunting jacket and took out a flask. Orel, as he smelled it (even before: after all, everyone knew that the bounty-hunters drank – the flask was part of every 3-D play about them), framed a polite refusal. But none was offered him.

'The purpose of this two-man field expedition,' his uncle said, after wiping his mouth, 'is to prepare a term paper for Orel's school showing how, in the disciplined present, the bounty-hunters maintain the free and rugged traditions of the past, on the Home Planet . . . let me have another go at the flask, Trapper.'

Orel watched, somewhat disturbed. Surely his uncle knew how unhealthy. . . .

'My family, they were pretty important people back on the Home Planet.' The Old Trapper, having had another drink, began to repeat himself. Outside – the dusk had begun to set in – that wild, rather frightening, sound came again. The old man put the flask down. 'Coming nearer,' he said, as if to himself. He got to his feet, took up his weapon. 'I won't be gone long . . . they don't generally come so near . . . but it's been a hard winter. This one sounds kind of hungry. But don't you be frightened, young fellow,' he said to Orel, from the door; 'there's no chance of its eating *me*.'

'Uncle . . .' Orel said, after a while. The councillor looked up. 'Don't be offended, but . . . does it ever strike you that we lead rather useless lives in the city – compared, I mean, to *him*?'

The councillor smiled. 'Oh, come now. Next you'll be wanting to run away and join the fun. Because that's all it is, really: fun. These beasts – the big "varmints", as he calls them – are no menace to us any longer. Haven't been since we switched from meat to synthetics. So it's not a truly useful life the old man leads. It's only our traditional reluctance to admit things have changed which keeps us paying the bounty. . . .' He got up and walked a few steps, stretched.

138

'We *could* get rid of these creatures once and for all, do it in one season's campaign. Drop poisoned bait every acre through the whole range. Wipe them out.'

Orel, puzzled, asked why they didn't.

'And I'll tell you something else – but don't put it in your report. The old fellow, like all the trappers, sometimes cheats. He often releases females and cubs. He takes no chances of having his valley trapped out. "Why don't we?" you ask – why don't we get rid of the beasts once and for all, instead of paying bounties year after year? Well, the present cost is small. And as for getting an appropriation for an all-out campaign – who'd vote for it? *I* wouldn't.

'No more hunting – no more 3-D plays about the exciting life in the wild country – no more trappers – why, it would just about take what spirit is left away from us. And we are dispirited enough – tired enough – as it is.'

Orel frowned. 'But why are we like that? We weren't always. A tired people could never have moved here from the Home Planet, could never have conquered this one. Why are we so – so played out?'

The councillor shrugged. 'Do you realize what a tremendous effort it was to move such a mass of people such a distance? The further effort required to subdue a wild, new, world? The terrible cost of the struggle against colonialism – and finally the Civil Wars? We don't even like to think about it – we create our myths instead out of the life out here in the wilds – and all the time, we retreated farther and farther, back into our cities. We are tired. We've spent our energies, we've mortgaged them, in fact. We eat synthetics because it's easier, not because it's healthier.'

A gust of cold wind blew in on them. They whirled around. The Old Trapper came in, dragging his kill by the forelimbs. He closed the door. The two city folk came up close. The beast was a huge male, gaunt from the poor hunting which winter meant to the wild creatures.

'See here—' the trapper pointed. 'Lost two toes there. *Old* wound. Must've gnawed his way out of a trap one time. *There* – got *these* scars battling over a mate, I suppose. This *here's*

139

a burn. Bad one. When was the last big forest fire we had? – one too big to outrun—' He figured with moving lips. '*That* long ago? How the time does pass. . . . Let me have that knife there, young fellow—' Orel glanced around, located the knife, handed it to him; gazed down in fascination and revulsion. The wild life did not seem so attractive at this moment.

'Watch close, now, and I'll show you how to skin and dress a big varmint,' the Old Trapper said. He made the initial incision. 'Dangerous creatures, but when you know their habits as well as *I* do . . . Can't expect to wipe them out altogether—' He looked at the two guests. Orel wondered how much he knew or guessed of what had been said in his absence. 'No. Keep their numbers down, is all you can expect to do.' He tugged, grunted. 'I *earn* my bounty, I can tell you.' He turned the creature on its back.

Orel struck by something, turned to the councillor.

'You know, Uncle, if this beast were cleaned up and shaved and—' he laughed at the droll fancy – 'and dressed in clothes, it—'

Councillor Garth finished the sentence for him. 'Would bear a faint, quaint resemblance to *us*? Hm, yes . . . in a way . . . of course, but their external ears and their having only five digits on each—' He clicked his tongue and stepped aside. The Old Trapper, who didn't care how much blood he got on things or people, worked away, but the Councillor took his nephew closer to the fire to finish what he had to say.

There was a vacancy for the dirtiest job in the galaxy. But were those terrestrial layabouts bright enough to qualify?

NOT YET THE END

By Fredric Brown

There was a greenish, hellish tinge to the light within the metal cube. It was a light that made the dead-white skin of the creature seated at the controls seem faintly green.

A single, faceted eye, front center in the head, watched the seven dials unwinkingly. Since they had left Xandor that eye had never once wavered from the dials. Sleep was unknown to the galactic race to which Kar-388Y belonged. Mercy, too, was unknown. A single glance at the sharp, cruel features below the faceted eye would have proved that.

The pointers on the fourth and seventh dials came to a stop. That meant the cube itself had stopped in space relative to its immediate objective. Kar reached forward with his upper right arm and threw the stabilizer switch. Then he rose and stretched his cramped muscles.

Kar turned to face his companion in the cube, a being like himself. 'We are here,' he said. 'The first stop, Star Z-5689. It has nine planets, but only the third is habitable. Let us hope we find creatures here who will make suitable slaves for Xandor.'

Lal-16B, who had sat in rigid immobility during the journey, rose and stretched also. 'Let us hope so, yes. Then we can return to Xandor and be honoured while the fleet comes to get them. But let's not hope too strongly. To meet with success at the first place we stop would be a miracle. We'll probably have to look a thousand places.'

Kar shrugged. 'Then we'll look a thousand places. With the Lounacs dying off, we must have slaves else our mines must close and our race will die.'

He sat down at the controls again and threw a switch that activated a visiplate that would show what was beneath them.

141

He said, 'We are above the night side of the third planet. There is a cloud layer below us. I'll use the manuals from here.'

He began to press buttons. A few minutes later he said, 'Look, Lal, at the visiplate. Regularly spaced lights – a city! The planet *is* inhabited.'

Lal had taken his place at the other switchboard, the fighting controls. Now he too was examining dials. 'There is nothing for us to fear. There is not even the vestige of a force field around the city. The scientific knowledge of the race is crude. We can wipe the city out with one blast if we are attacked.'

'Good,' Kar said. 'But let me remind you that destruction is not our purpose – yet. We want specimens. If they prove satisfactory and the fleet comes and takes as many thousand slaves as we need, then will be time to destroy not a city but the whole planet. So that their civilization will never progress to the point where they'll be able to launch reprisal raids.'

Lal adjusted a knob. 'All right. I'll put on the megrafield and we'll be invisible to them unless they see far into the ultraviolet, and, from the spectrum of their sun, I doubt that they do.'

As the cube descended the light within it changed from green to violet and beyond. It came to a gentle rest. Kar manipulated the mechanism that operated the airlock.

He stepped outside, Lal just behind him. 'Look,' Kar said, 'two bipeds. Two arms, two eyes – not dissimilar to the Lounacs, although smaller. Well, here are our specimens.'

He raised his lower left arm, whose three-fingered hand held a thin rod wound with wire. He pointed it first at one of the creatures, then at the other. Nothing visible emanated from the end of the rod, but they both froze instantly into statuelike figures.

'They're not large, Kar,' Lal said. 'I'll carry one back, you carry the other. We can study them better inside the cube, after we're back in space.'

Kar looked about him in the dim light. 'All right, two is enough, and one seems to be male and the other female. Let's get going.'

A minute later the cube was ascending and as soon as they were well out of the atmosphere, Kar threw the stabilizer switch and joined Lal, who had been starting a study of the specimens during the brief ascent.

'Viviparous,' said Lal. 'Five-fingered, with hands suited to reasonably delicate work. But – let's try the most important test, intelligence.'

Kar got the paired headsets. He handed one pair to Lal, who put one on his own head, one on the head of one of the specimens. Kar did the same with the other specimen.

After a few minutes, Kar and Lal stared at each other bleakly.

'Seven points below minimum,' Kar said. 'They could not be trained even for the crudest labor in the mines. Incapable of understanding the most simple instructions. Well, we'll take them back to the Xandor museum.'

'Shall I destroy the planet?'

'No,' Kar said. 'Maybe a million years from now – if our race lasts that long – they'll have evolved enough to become suitable for our purpose. Let us move on to the next star with planets.'

The make-up editor of the *Milwaukee Star* was in the composing room, supervising the closing of the local page. Jenkins, the head make-up compositor, was pushing in leads to tighten the second last column.

'Room for one more story in the eighth column, Pete,' he said. 'About thirty-six picas. There are two there in the overset that will fit. Which one shall I use?'

The make-up editor glanced at the type in the galleys lying on the stone beside the chase. Long practice enabled him to read the headlines upside down at a glance. 'The convention story and the zoo story, huh? Oh, hell, run the convention story. Who cares if the zoo director thinks two monkeys disappeared off Monkey Island last night?'

SECTION 3

DECLINE AND FREE FALL

i All Things are Cyclic

Gardner F Fox: TONIGHT THE STARS REVOLT!   150
Harry Harrison: FINAL ENCOUNTER   192

The sense of the fated incompleteness of all creatures and of their achievements gave the Galactic Society of Worlds a charm, a sanctity, as of some short-lived and delicate flower.
Olaf Stapledon: *Star Maker.*

One thing we learn from science fiction is that pleasure can be derived from the worst catastrophe.

Magazine sf – never let it be forgotten – was written in the main for an underprivileged audience. It was grass roots literature, a child of the pulp magazines. If you were under-paid and under-educated and worked in a dingy office in London or New York, commuting home at the end of the day to a drab flat in a mean street, then the fictional destruction of your capital city could be a good cathartic read. Or write. One of the great nineteenth century disaster novels, *After London,* was written by a naturalist and journalist called Richard Jefferies, who found himself caught up with London and hated the place. His evocative novel, which totally erases London, was written as a kind of revenge.

The man to ask about this subject is Harry Harrison, who lived many years of his life in New York, only to flee it forever when he made his first big science fiction sale. He sat in an elegant house in Denmark and wrought the ruin of his home town in a now-famous novel, *Make Room! Make Room!*, later made into a film called Soylent Green, starring Charlton Heston, which does not do justice to Harrison's panoramic view of urban over-population.

Harrison specialises in ramshackle worlds which never quite fall apart; his style is generally unmistakable, in person as in his books. But the story included here, *Final Encounter*, is, ex-ceptionally, about a world coming together. It marks, I sup-pose, the logical end of the galactic empire. The two hands are folded about the apple.

It could be that the same atavistic urge which moves sf writers to destroy what they love or loathe prompts them so often to marry their galactic empire with an extraordinary feudal system, loaded with lords, beautiful ladies, and sweat-

147

ing peasants. Computers are rare; jewels are everyday currency.

In this respect, Gardner Fox's gloriously extravagant story runs true to form, right down to the lovely Moana, of whom it has been said that 'the thin stuff of her gown clung to supple haunches and proud breasts'. Down in the swill-wet streets, revolt is brewing. We also have super-science and talk of 'compulsory interracial wedlock'. And we surge symbolically from the mire and filth of Lower City to the clean white reaches of the Citadel. So the cycle of being is completed, as in the Harrison story.

The use of feudalism in so many stories like Fox's is not just caprice. In Volume One we remarked on the minting of steel currency in Isaac Asimov's *Foundation*. Asimov freely admits that he took the Roman Empire as pattern and exemplar for his galactic empire. But in general empires of the skies use such feudal backgrounds as we have described. This of course provides all the trappings of glamour and the contrasts between high life and squalor which are clear to a reader's heart. But there may be a less calculated reason for embracing such an anachronistic model.

For the operation of what Lewis Mumford calls 'the invisible machine' or 'the megamachine' of human endeavour and achievement, our present culture needs money as the individual needs blood. We are creatures of economics and we must work while we are able or perish, just as did our ancestors generations back; we are ruled by money, the endless necessity for which forms the circuitry that keeps workforce and nation functional. (True, there are rare individuals who stand outside this invisible machine; they are dictators – Stalin, owning Russia, never had a coin in his pocket – royalty, the very rich, or the extremely poor; gipsies are shunned since they contribute no power to the invisible machine.)

The capitalist system enjoys comparatively effective circuitry. That is to say, its pressures are constant but, when its units are functioning smoothly, not all that insistent on the majority.

All the same, it is difficult to imagine any present-day coercion system, not capitalism, certainly not communism, work-

148

ing effectively to embrace several planetary systems light years apart. Relativity, which affects space and time, would certainly affect cash-flow. Cash-flow has two aspects; it works both as coercive and incentive. A more coercive system would be more effective. Like dictatorship. Or even feudalism.

Feudalism was a cruder version of the invisible machine, yet the sort of feudalism practised in Ancient Egypt produced, in the shape of the Great Pyramids, some of the most lasting and impressive monuments on this planet.

The number of nutty attemps to explain the pyramids, or the memorials of the Incas or of any other great vanished race, in terms of some superstitious theory – an example is von Daniken's notion that all the great achievements on our planet were built by galactic astronauts – simply shows lack of understanding of how other invisible machines than ours functioned in the past. All invisible machines make human and/or mechanical energy available in strength where it is needed; under our present system, we all work to accumulate stockpiles of military hardware, as the feudal world worked to accumulate stones for the dead Pharoahs. We can empathise with that world no more than it could empathise with ours.

But we can empathise with the abolition of money! Oh, yes! This is what makes feudal systems attractive in escapist literature. It frees the way for adventure, which has little to do with cash-flow. And I think the sf writers' basic instincts are right: money will have to fade out when we move into the galaxy.

Or could it be that those sinister dark pools of energy in *Tonight the Stars Revolt!*, guarded by the ancient god Stasor, are symbolic representations of your local Barclay's Bank?

*In the Black Pools he found the 50,000-year-lost wisdom of
the Ancients. For a day Red Angus held victory in his sword-
hand. But it was too short a glimpse, too elusive a thought
to bolster the star-rabble against the Citadel's iron guard.*

TONIGHT THE STARS REVOLT!

By Gardner F. Fox

*The pools were like the gaping mouth of space itself, dark
and fathomless, extending into bottomless wells, the depths
of which the people of Karr could only guess. Some said the
god Stasor dwelt in the glistening black depths. Others
claimed the emptiness was the hollow interior of the planet.
None of them was right.*

*All men feared the pools. Only a man fifty thousand years
old knew their incredible secret, and he lived in an invisible
city. . . .*

Red Angus fled like a frightened hound through the twisted
alleys of the Lower City. Dim lamplight from the towering
white walls of the Citadel threw glowing brilliance across his
naked chest, glinted on the metal studs of his broad leather
belt, and on the rippling muscles of his long legs. He skidded
on a patch of slops, righted himself and dove for the darkness of an arched doorway. He drew back in the shadows,
barely feeling the burn of the new brand on his shoulder that
stamped him as a pirate.

Faintly, he heard the shouts and drumming feet of the
Diktor's police as they ravened in the streets, hunting him.
His heart thudded swiftly under the high arch of his ribcase.
Red Angus smiled wryly.

He was a hunted space pirate, just free of the cell blocks
below the palace. But he was more than that to the Diktor of
Karr. He was a Karrvan noble who had gone bad, who had
fled into space and established an eyrie on a wandering

asteroid, who had set himself up as a one-man crusade against Stal Tay, ruler of Karr by the grace of the god Stasor.

'I'll find a way,' the pirate swore in the shadows, listening to the shouts and running of the guards, the sharp, barking blasts of their heatguns.

There was a faint sound behind the thick oaken door. Angus moved his naked back, still welt and scarred, away from the damp wood. He clenched a big fist and stood silent, waiting.

He was a tall man, lean in the belly and wide about the shoulders. His mouth was thin but curved at the corners as though used to smiling. Close-cropped reddish hair gave his hard, tanned face a fiery look. Dark blue eyes glistened in the half-squint of the habitual spaceman.

The oaken door swung open. A cowled form stood in the darkness of the archway putting out a thin, old hand toward him. Where the cowl hung there was only a faint white dimness for a face.

'The Hierarch will see you, and save you, Red Angus,' said the old man. 'Come in. He hopes you'll listen to reason.'

'The Hierarch?' snorted the lean man in disbelief. 'He's hand in arm with Stal Tay. He'd land me back with my ankles in a manacle chain.'

The cowled man shook his head and whispered, 'Hurry, hurry. There's no time to argue!'

A shout from a street less than sixty feet away decided the half-naked, winded Angus. He moved his shoulders in a bitter shrug and slid inside the door. The latch clicked on the door and a hand caught his. A voice, gentle with age, said softly, 'Follow me.'

Two hundred feet from the door the walls began to glow. Angus looked at his guide and saw an old man, a member of the Hierachy, a priestly cult of scientists who were honored and protected by the Diktor. Thirty years before, when the people of the Lower City had been ravaged by disease, they had stormed the block of buildings where the scientists worked.

They had wrecked machines and killed men.

The people of the Lower City were no better than savages

151

and the pagan superstitions they boasted were encouraged by Stal Tay. It pleased the Diktor to believe that science was something only the rich deserved. So Stal Tay stepped in. He withdrew the scientists from the world of men and gave them a little world of their own that was called the Citadel.

Red Angus and the scientist went through corridors that bent and twisted in subtle fashion. It was quiet in this underground tunnel. Once Angus heard the subterranean rush of a hidden river seeking an outlet in the great Car Carolan Sea. Water condensed in oozing droplets on the cold stone walls.

Then they were going up handhewn stone steps toward an archway in which a thick, soot-blackened door was opening. Lights glared beyond the doorway in a large room with a high, groined ceiling.

He saw Tandor first, standing big and massive among the cowled priests, the wall light glinting from his bald head. They had had a time taking him from the Lower City, Angus saw. There were cut marks on him, and the blood here and there on his rough wool tunic had dried.

A tall man in a white cowl that was bordered with purple came toward them. He said, 'I saved your man from the Diktor's torturers. Money will do much in the Citadel. Even a pirate's first captain is not as valuable as a handful of *sestelins*.'

Red Angus shrugged. 'What do you want from me?'

The Hierarch nodded. 'They told me you were a sensible man. Tonight I will free Tandor after you do me a service.'

'What service?'

The Hierarch studied him carefully. 'Kill the Diktor!'

Angus barked derisive laughter. 'As well ask me to find the Book of Nard. I'd stand as much chance!'

'I may well ask that too, before you and I are through.'

'Suppose I refuse?'

The Hierarch sighed. His black eyes glittered in the shadow of his cowl. 'I'll smash your legs so you can't run, and let Stal Tay send his men for you. I'll put red-hot daggers in Tandor's eyes until he confesses your crimes. I—'

Angus scowled. 'I thought the Diktor was your friend.'

'He keeps us penned in the Citadel as his slaves. The

152

scientific discoveries we make he claims as his own. He sent the diseases that the people blamed on the scientists.'

Angus said, 'I will kill him.' But he thought to himself, I only play for time. It's promise or get my legs broken.

They led Angus to a little room where a cowled man waited for him with garments that were living reds and ochres, braided with gold and ornate with jewels. The scientist said coldly, 'You are to impersonate the Ambassador of Nowk. He's red-headed and big with a scar on his face like your own.'

The night air was crisp as Angus stepped with the cowled scientist through a stone gateway and into a long, sleek wheeler. He gathered his cloak of black sateenis about him and sank into the foamisal unholstery.

The cowled man whispered, 'Everything is arranged. A woman dancer, Berylla by name, will dance for the Diktor. Right after that he plans to call you to his side to discuss the new trade agreement with Nowk. The dancer will give you the signal as she leaves. When you're summoned strike at the Diktor's neck. A divertissement in the form of drunken revellers has been planned. In the excitement, you will be spirited away.'

Angus touched the slim dagger at his side and nodded.

The Diktor of Karr was a big man. He was solid in the shoulder and slim at the waist. His head was bald, and there was a jagged scar across his right temple. He sat on his jewelled throne and drummed restless fingers against the hand-carved arm.

Beside him sat a woman with sloe eyes and hair the color of a raven's wing. The thin stuff of her gown clung to supple haunches and proud breasts. She watched the new Ambassador from Nowk thread a path through the guests, unable to decide whether the man was ugly or ruggedly handsome. But he was big, with long, heavily-muscled arms and legs, and he had the look of a fighter.

Moana laughed softly. There was music in her voice and art in the manner of her movement as he drew closer. Her eyes ran over his big frame slowly, slumberously.

153

Red Angus came to a stop at the base of the dais and bowed low. He was a pirate but he had been in the great capitals of the Six Worlds.

'Your first visit to Karr?' smiled Stal Tay.

'The first, excellency.'

'You like the court we keep?'

Red Angus knew of the taverns and swill-wet streets of the Lower City. He knew the people were slaves to the Hierarchy and to the Diktor and his little coterie. Girls danced and pandered to the desires of the rich – if they did not, things were done to them in secret. He knew men grew old before their time, working to pay for the rare jewels that Moana and others like her flaunted.

But he murmured, 'Plegasston of Nowk has said, "For the good of the State, the greatest number of its people must enjoy the greatest amount of its highest rewards." But Plegasston was a dreamer.'

Moana gestured Angus to the golden chair beside her. She let her fingertips brush his hand as he took the seat. 'Tell me about yourself, Ben Tal.'

Angus grinned, 'I'm a relative of his Eminence of Nowk. That explains all about me. But you. You're priestess to the god Stasor. You've gone into the black pool to face him. You've heard his pronouncements.'

Moana made a wry face and shrugged. Strains of music swept down from the fluted ceiling, diffused throughout the room. Her black eyes glowed. 'Don't talk religion to me, Ben Tal. Take me in your arms and let us dance.'

She was warm and fragrant, following his movements. Her dark eyes enticed as her hands fluttered from his arm to his shoulder to his neck. She made the moments fly. Seated with her at a table, letting her feed him playfully, he almost forgot his mission.

And then. . . .

The room darkened. The hidden musicians made their stringed instruments dance with savage rhythm. And in a circle of golden light, her white flesh gleaming fitfully through a garment of diamonds, a woman swayed out onto the cleared floor.

154

And Angus remembered. He was here to kill a man.

The woman in the service of the Hierarchs was a fireflame out there with the jeweled dress cloud of living rainbows swirling about her. She pirouetted, dipped, and leaped. She was motionless – and a storm of movement. She laughed. She wept. She taunted and cajoled. She was everything any woman ever was.

Angus saw her eyes darting, hunting him. They slid over his deep chest and long legs, square jaw and close-cropped red hair many times without recognition. Only toward the end, as the beam of light that spotlighted her dance touched him too, did she know him.

Her surprise made her stumble but she recovered swiftly. She whirled around the room, diamonds tinkling faintly to the stamping of her bare feet. She threw herself into the Dance of the Garland of Gems, and made it a living thing. When she came to the black curtains she posed for an instant, moved her arm in the agreed signal, and was gone.

The Diktor lifted a hand and gestured. Angus bowed to Moana and got to his feet. With all the iron control he had developed on the lonely star-trails he fought to keep his hand from his knife-haft.

He bent to take his seat. Now his right hand was sheltered by his body and he put it on the dagger.

The thin blade whispered, coming out of the scabbard.

Red Angus leaned forward and thrust at the throat before him.

Four hands came out of midair and fastened to his wrist. They dragged him down by surprise and by the weight of their bodies. He went off his chair in a rolling fall, hitting the man to his left, toppling him backwards into Stal Tay.

Men were shouting. A woman screamed. Angus brought his hard left fist up in a short arc, drove it into the stomach-muscles of the man on his right. The man grunted and went backwards. Red Angus stood free, his clean blade still naked in his hand.

He leaped for Stal Tay but other guards had come running. One threw himself before the dagger, both hands catching at

155

it. Another hit the pirate across the legs with his hurtling body. A third man clawed himself to a position astride his back, hooking a hairy forearm under his chin. That was when the rest of them hit him.

Angus went back off his feet into a mass of struggling, cursing flesh. The guards yelped triumphantly but Red Angus had fought in tavern brawls in the Lower City, had wrestled with salt slavers on the desert dunes, had fought fights from Karr to Rimeron. He surged up. His fists went up and down. His right hand flashed out, closing on a guard's wrist. The guard screamed and fell away, moaning.

Angus breathed through distended nostrils, dancing back, fists thudding into rib and jaw. He fought to get room and he almost made it. But a guard left his feet in a wild dive before the pirate could brace himself. The man hit his knees and took them out from under him. Angus went down under a dozen leaping warriors. Grimy, blooded, Red Angus shook his head and gave up.

Moana was standing above him, laughing scorn through the queer, awed light in her eyes. Her white breasts rose and fell swiftly under their scant covering. 'The little dancer knew you, Ben Tal. I saw that. But she's never been out of Karr City. And this is your first visit. Who are you?'

Red Angus shrugged as the guardsman lifted him to his feet and sat him roughly down in a chair before the Diktor. He made a wry face. There was a taste like bitter ashes dragging down the corners of his mouth. His belly quivered under the glistening cloth of his breeches. He seemed to hear the Hierarch's drawling voice, 'If you fail, you die.'

The Diktor waved a hand. The guards lifted him, dragged him behind velveteen drapes and along a stone corridor, into a small room. The Diktor and Moana followed at his heels. It was the Diktor who turned the key in the lock.

'Who sent you?' the stocky ruler asked softly. 'Who paid for my death? Tell me that, and you'll walk out of here a free man.'

Red Angus shook his head. He met the hazel eyes of the Diktor grimly.

156

Stal Tay smiled. 'Berylla the dancer knows you. I can always have her brought in, you know.'

Moana had been walking around Angus. She came close, put a hand on the tunic that fitted his chest like a glove, and ripped. His heavily muscled shoulder was laid bare, where the inflamed interlocking triangles gleamed.

Moana cried out. 'A pirate!'

The Diktor opened his eyes wide. 'Of course. Now I know you. Red Angus. My men captured you a week ago. But how in Stasor's name did you get free?'

Angus said briefly, 'Does it matter?'

'No.' Stal Tay went and sat on a curved sigellis-chair and crossed his heavy legs. He drummed short, powerful fingers against the beethel-wood arm. 'But the fact that you came back after getting free – that is important. You wouldn't have stayed in Karr City unless you had to. Who made you stay? Certainly you didn't hate me enough to risk your neck on such a long chance.'

Angus grinned through the fear in him. 'A million people hate you, if you want to know. You keep the lower-city men and women in filthy poverty to buy you and your kind jewels and luxury. You subsidize the Hierarchy, using their science to make your life easier and safer. Why deny those poor devils down below what you could give them so cheaply? Heat. Light. Power to operate a few machines. Let them taste something from life besides slops and sweaty clothes and hard beds.'

'Oho,' laughed the Diktor softly. 'Plegasston of Nowk made a convert. What else did he say, Angus?'

'He said that government and science should serve the people, not enslave them. Doesn't Stasor teach that?'

Moana laughed softly. Her black eyes taunted him. She said, 'You want to hear what Stasor says about government and science and people, Angus the Red? Let me take him through the Veil, Eminence. Let the god himself tell the fool.'

The Diktor smiled thinly, looking from man to woman. He shook his head. Moana moved to one side of the square-set

157

ruler. Her black eyes bored straight at Angus. He tried to understand their expression.

The Diktor stood up. 'I've used reason, Angus. You're a pirate. You've preyed on my space-caravans. You've stolen and plundered from me. I tell you again, I'll forgive all that – even reward you – if you tell me who sent you here this night.'

The black eyes burned at him in Moana's pale white face. She touched her full upper lip with a red tongue-tip.

'If I could see Stasor,' fumbled Angus, trying to fathom what Moana wanted him to say. When she nodded almost imperceptibly, he went on, 'perhaps he could make me change my mind. If Stasor says I've been a fool, why then everything I've believed in will have gone smash. In that case I'd like to serve your Eminence.'

Moana's black eyes laughed, silently applauding him. The Diktor scowled thoughtfully. He swung around on the girl. 'Will you be his vow-companion?'

Angus knew what that meant. If he found a way to escape, the Diktor would stretch that lovely white body on the rack in place of his own, give those thighs and breasts and face to the red-hot pincers, the nails, the barbed hooks. He would never let her suffer that fate.

Maybe the Diktor knew that. He smiled a little as Moana promised. He went, without another glance at Angus.

Moana said softly, 'It was all I could do, Red Angus. He would have taken you to the Pits tonight if I hadn't delayed it.'

'You don't owe me anything,' he told her crisply.

'I do, though. My brother angered the Diktor a year ago. He was sent to the salt marshes of Ptixt. You raided the caravan that carried him and set him free. My brother lives safely hidden today in one of your pirate cities. I remember that, Angus. Sometimes good deeds do pay off. What does Plegasston say about that?'

She went past him and through the doorway.

He followed her swaying body along the drape-hung corridors, into small rooms and past oak-beamed doors. She came to a blank wall, reached up and pressed pink fingertips against a rose-red stone.

'The whorls at the tips of my fingers set off a light-switch mechanism within the stone,' she explained. 'It's better than any key.'

Somewhere an engine hummed faintly and the rock wall began to turn. It swung aside to reveal a narrow corridor leading downwards. The walls were coated with a luminescent blueness that glowed brightly, lighting the way.

Angus saw the pool long before he came to it. A round metal collar bordered the glistening blackness, that seemed to press upward as though striving to burst free of whatever held it. It shimmered and quivered. It pulsed and throbbed with something close to life itself.

Angus came to a stop, staring at it. He put out a hand and thrust it into the darkness. It felt light, biting, and he thought it might taste like heady wine.

Moana took his other hand. She whispered, 'Come,' and stepped down into the pool.

The darkness swam all around Angus. He felt it on his skin, in the pores of his arms and hands and legs. It made him giddy, so that he wanted to laugh. It was like walking on air, to stride in this thing.

They went down into the pool and stood in a strange space, where there was only blackness, unrelieved by light. It was cold. Faintly, Angus could hear what he thought was music.

'Will yourself ahead,' he heard a musical voice whisper.

He floated effortlessly.

'Where are we?' he wondered aloud.

'Out of space. Out of time. In the abode of the god. Soon now, we shall see Stasor.'

A bright point of red glowed faintly, as a pinhead might gleam when heated in a fire. It grew swiftly to the size of a fist, to the size of a head.

The red glow burst, and sent streamers of flame out into the darkness.

Where the red had been was Stasor.

His face floated in a white mist, ancient and wise and sorrowful. The dimly veined lids were shut. The forehead was high, rounded, surmounted by snowy hair. On either side of the

159

great hawk-nose, high cheekbones protruded. The eyelids quivered, slowly arose.

Angus stared dumbly into living wisdom. He wondered deep inside him how old Stasor must be, to know what those eyes knew; how many worlds he must have gazed on, how many peoples he must have seen grow to statehood, to degeneracy, to death.

'You entered the pool. I felt your emanations. What do you wish?'

Moana said, 'I am your priestess, Stasor. I have brought a man to see you.'

'Let the man speak.'

Angus wet his lips. He scowled, trying to find words. He mumbled, 'I've been sentenced to die for attempting to kill the Diktor of Karr. He's an evil man.'

'What is evil, my son? Is a man bad becauses he opposes your will?'

Angus growled, 'He's a curse to his race. He sends disease and death on his people when they disobey him. He keeps improvement from them. He makes them slaves when they might be gods.'

'That is your belief. What says the Book of Nard?'

Moana whispered, 'The Book of Nard is lost, High One.'

Stasor was silent a long time. He said, finally, 'The Book must be found. In it are the secrets of the Elder Race. Go to the City of the Ancients. There you will find the Book.'

'No one today knows where the City is, either. It is lost, with all the secrets of the Elder Race.'

'The City lies across the Car Carolan Sea, through the Land of Living Flame. Go there.'

The lips closed. The eyelids shut. Swiftly the old face faded into nothingness. The blackness came and pressed around them.

Angus turned slowly, as in a dream. Still in that dreamlike trance he found himself staring at three tall, cowled forms that stood like sentinels.

Moana screamed.

One of the cowled figures lifted an arm and gestured assurance. 'There is no cause for fear. The Hierarch sent us to bring you before him.'

Moana shuddered. Angus felt her cold hand seeking his, trying to hide itself in his palm. Hand in hand they willed themselves after the cowled forms. They swam bodily through the blackness, moving eerily, without muscular movement.

A round curtain of shimmering bluish motes ahead of them was like a glowing patch in the darkness. One of the cowled forms turned and waited. He said, 'Another pool, Moana. The pool of the Hierarchy. We, too, know the way into this world.'

'What is the blackness?' wondered Angus.

'What man knows? It was formed and built by the Elder Ones before they went on.'

They were in the pool, passing upward through its queer surface. It sizzled and bubbled all around them, tingling on the skin.

They passed the pool and stood in a low-ceilinged, bare room.

A cowled man opened a door for them and stood aside.

The Hierarch sat in a curved chair ornate with gold edgings. His pale, ascetic face gloomed from the shadow of his big cowl. He stared at them, a thin smile touching his lips. He stared so long that Angus asked impatiently, 'What do you want with us? Tandor, is he free?'

Moana gasped, sudden understanding waking her mind. The Hierarch brushed her with his eyes and sighed.

'Tandor is free. I fulfill my promises. You tried and failed, yet you tried. Now—'

He paused, fingertips pressed together, brooding down at Angus.

'Many thousands of eons ago, before our race came into existence, all Karr belonged to the Elder Race. It lived a long time on this world, before it went on.'

Angus grinned, 'Your priest said that. You and he mean—'

The Hierarch spoke patiently, as if lecturing a child. 'It did not die out. It went on, to another plane of existence. Everything must progress. That is the immutable law of nature. The First Race progressed, far beyond our understanding, beyond the natural laws as we know them. They exist today – somewhere outside.

'Stasor, now. Take him, for instance.' The Hierarch flicked burning black eyes at Moana. 'Some think he is a god. He is a member of the Elder Race.'

Moana said harshly. 'Blasphemy! You speak blasphemy of Stasor.'

The Hierarch shrugged. 'I tell you Stasor is a four-plane man, one not bound by our three dimensions. He and his kind have gone on to that other world. They left behind them rules to guide those who came after them. They left the pools. They were a great race, the Elders, and the black pools are their greatest discovery. Those rules they gave us are contained in the Book of Nard. I want that book!'

'Why?'

The Hierarch smiled gently. 'With the secrets of the Elders at my fingertips do you think the Diktor could keep us penned here in the Citadel?'

A faint hope burned in Angus' chest. 'You mean, you wouldn't be cloistered any more? That you'd give your science to the people and help them up?'

'Pah!' snapped the Hierarch. 'The people? Pigs! They wallow in their filths and love it.' His burning black eyes glittered fanatically. 'No. I mean I – and not the Diktor – will rule all Karr!'

He is mad, too, thought Angus. He and the Diktor – mad with the lust for power. If the Diktor dies and the Hierarch rules the people will change a bootheel for a mortar and pestle. *Even the stars must revolt against that.*

II

The street was dark, except for the moonlight shining faintly through the serrated rooftops, and reflected grey and dismal from the rounded edges of the cobblestones. Angus and a cowled man made a short dash, ran into the shadows, and trotted at a slow pace.

Above them a sign creaked on rusty chains. Angus looked

behind at the huge stone bulk of the Citadel where it rose from solid rock, wall piled on wall, and turret on tower, and battlement upon bastion. Beyond the Citadel the thin, delicate spires of the palaces towered above the clean, fragrantly perfumed Upper City. Up above, there was no swill. There was no stench of rotting garbage. The patricians did not know what roast derstite looked like on a greasy platter, or how broiled colob smelled or what awful stuff the vintners sold in the big Mart.

Angus said, 'I still don't see why the Hierarch bothers sending me after the Book. He has a lot of scientists who'd do a better job of finding it.'

The lips of the man twisted in the darkness of the cowl. 'How do you think the Diktor keeps us penned in the Citadel, red-man? He has spectragrams of each of us in his palace, attached to central controls. Every once in a while he has his captains check on our locations. When the vibratory beams touch us, they reflect our spectrums on the visi-screens. If one of us is out of place – beyond the limits of Karr City, that is – he sends a patrol to find and capture us. We lost several good men that way before we grew resigned. Once a scientist is captured by the Diktor he is destroyed. Instantly.'

'Isn't there anyone else to help you?'

The scientist showed his disdain by a twitch of the lips. 'Who? One of the people? They'd run so fast to betray us a theto-hound couldn't catch them. They hate the Diktor, but I think they hate us more.'

Behind them the shadow of a man with a zigzag scar on his face disengaged himself from beneath an overhanging cornice and silently followed.

Angus and the scientist went through the narrow streets, down stone steps and across a great square. To one side the red lanterns of the Spotted Stag tavern glowed and the shouts and roistering laughter of men mingled with the shrill excited laughter of a woman.

The scientist glanced about him nervously, wet his lips with his tongue. 'I don't like this section. It's too near the wharves. There are other rats than the four-legged kind.'

A blackish, blunt instrument in the hand of a half-naked

163

man bounced from the skull of the cowled one. Angus went forward, left hand hooking. He caught the big man on the side of the mouth and drove his head sideways. His right fist was crossing as his left landed. He hit the man with his right hand and the man went backwards into a brick wall.

'Easy, Angus,' growled a voice in back of him, with a hint of laughter in it.

Angus whirled, teeth bared. When he saw the bald head of the giant in front of him he laughed harshly.

'By the gods! Tandor. The Hierarch did keep his promise, then!'

'We heard you'd missed killing that scum that lives in the palace by an inch. Tsk! The Hierarch felt that, with luck, Stal Tay would be dead by now. He let me go, yes. As soon as he learned that you and that priestess were in the black pool.'

Angus bent and threw back the cowl of the scientist. There was a swelling lump on the back of his head. Angus said, 'I thought you broke his skull when you hit him.' He looked at the man stirring against the brick wall. 'Sorry, friend. I thought you a footpad.'

'Tandor told me you were fast. He wasn't lying.' The man grinned ruefully, feeling his jaw.

Tandor shouldered Angus aside and picked up the cowled man. He led the way up through the streets, the limp man's legs and arms dangling inertly. Tandor asked, 'Where was he taking you?'

'To a hidden globe-ship. I'm supposed to find the Book of Nard. The Hierarch is holding Moana as hostage for my success.'

Tandor whistled softly, eyes round. 'He exchanged me for the girl. A smart man, the High Priest!'

Laughter came out at them from the ill-lighted interior of the tavern together with the dry smell of wine and the stench of sweating flesh. Tandor kicked the oak door open and went along the wall with his burden. A girl with a rag around her middle ran for Angus, tipsily pressing wet lips to his. She threw up a wooden goblet, the red wine splashing over its

164

rim, crying, 'The Anvil! To Red Angus the Anvil – the only friend we have!'

The roar echoed in his ears as Angus stepped into the little side room. Tandor kicked a chair toward Angus, reaching for a wooden pitcher. He growled, 'Are you going hunting for the Book?'

Angus stretched out his legs and dragged a full goblet toward him. He stared at the dark liquor. Finally he said, 'Yes, I'm going.'

'Why?'

'Because I've seen the way they live in the Upper City. I've seen the life they lead and I've seen the life those people out there in the big room lead.'

Tandor made a rumbling sound in his throat. 'You don't think they'll appreciate your changing it, do you?'

Angus looked thoughtful. He smiled, 'I know what our race is heading toward, now. We will be like Stasor – the man behind the veil – eventually. The longer the Diktor stays in power, and others like him, the longer will the rest of us be kept from that goal.'

Tandor grinned like a wolf. 'Some men like to be martyrs. It's a weakness of the brain.' He scowled, and brought the flat of his ham-like hand down on the wooden tabletop. 'I say it's madness. Let the Hierarch and the Diktor slit each other's throats. Let's go back to the star trails, Angus. Out where a man can breathe and stretch himself.'

Angus shook his head. 'Take the ship yourself. Go raiding, if you want. I stay. I want to answer a question.'

'What question?'

'Why is science?'

'Why is— You're crazy, now. I know it. Of all the stupid questions. Science is an art designed to better the life standards of the patrician class. There. That answer you?'

'I say science is something that should benefit all. Why do we have torches while the Hierarchy and the patricians use illumilamps and incandescent walls? Why don't we have stoves instead of hearths or electronizers instead of percussion guns?'

Tandor smirked. 'It's safer.'

165

Angus got to his feet and walked about the smoky, oak-beamed room. In the reddish light his chest and thickly muscled arms seemed coated with crimson. The crop of red hair on his rounded, square-jawed skull added to the illusion. He planted his hands on his hips and stood in front of his lieutenant.

'I turned pirate when the last Diktor executed my father for leniency with his servants. The Diktor said he was undermining governmental discipline. I took my mother and fled into space. I found a safe spot on Yassinan. I built a pirate empire with your help. I'd offer up all that – all the wealth we've amassed in Yassinan – to smash the setup here!'

Tandor spat on his hand and rubbed his palm on the flat of his bald dome. He said drily, 'You make me mad, Angus. You aren't satisfied with things. Always you have to change them. Isn't life full enough for you now?'

Angus ignored him. 'If I could get the Book of Nard and free Moana and take her away to safety we might stand a chance. If we could develop science undisturbed on Yassinan we could do it.'

'Why fret about Moana?'

'She became my vow-companion. You know what that means to somebody like the Diktor.' Angus slapped his broad leather belt decisively. 'I'll do it. I'll go in his globe-ship and try and find the Book. Tandor, you stay here. Raise men to fight for us.'

The big man with the bald head nodded gloomily. He poured wine from the wooden tankard, downed the brimming goblet in one long gulp. He wiped his lips on the palm of his hand and rubbed it dry on his bald head. 'I hear you. I think you're mad but I hear you. What are you going to do with that?'

His thumb jerked at the limp scientist in the long cowled robe. Angus shrugged. 'He'll come around. When he does I'll pretend I've fought off his assailant. Meanwhile, you find out which globe-ship he means to give me. Can you do that?'

The big man rumbled. 'Tandor can do anything. I'll find out without leaving the room.' He lifted his voice and bellowed. When the door opened and a face peered in, Tandor grinned, 'Find that wharf-rat Plisket and send him in here.'

Plisket limped in, grinning at Angus, bobbing his head. His eyes opened when he heard what Tandor wanted. He chuckled, 'The hierarchy plot like a pack of fools. Everybody outside the Citadel hates them. It happens I hate the Diktor more. They gave me gold to build a ship.'

'The Skimmer?' asked Tandor. 'That wonder-boat you were telling me about?'

'It is a wonder-boat. It incorporates the—'

'Never mind the details,' rapped Angus, leaning his palms on the table. 'Is that the boat the hierarchy want me to use?'

'It must be. It's the only one unchartered. And Angus – if you are to control it – remember that it will submerge. And it has four speeds, two more than . . .'

Tandor slapped the table with his palm, making the goblets bounce. 'Enough, enough. Plisket, your tongue wags like a hound's tail. Angus, are you ready?'

Angus stretched his tall, heavily shouldered body. He went and bent his lean height over the shallow-breathing scientist and swung him up in a fireman's hitch. He walked firmly, steadily, as he headed for the oaken door.

The man with the zigzag scar on his cheek drew back into the darkness of a jutting second storey as a door creaked open down the street. His eyes glittered, watching Angus emerge with a cowled body atop a shoulder. The hidden man touched a glittering knob strapped to his wrist, turned the knob and lifted it to his mouth.

Angus did not see him, did not hear him whisper into the voxbeamer. He heaved up, settling the body on his shoulder. He began to trot, with space-devouring strides. He went by the spot where Tandor's bully had struck down the cowled man. He went ten paces beyond it, and halted. He lowered the man to the ground and began to shake him.

'Wake up . . . he didn't hit you that hard. Come on. Man, stir yourself . . . that's better . . . see me, do you? Who am I? Angus. Good. You're better? All right . . . on your feet . . . I'll give you a hand.'

The scientist teetered weakly, tried to smile. 'I told you it was a place for rats. What happened?'

'I beat him off. I carried you a bit, thinking he might come back. We've lost some time.'

'Sorry. I'll make a report to the Hierarch. He'll be glad to know you didn't run out on him.'

Red Angus clipped coldly, 'I wouldn't leave Moana to that Diktor devil. The Hierarch knows that.'

The cowled man nodded. 'Just the same, I'll tell him. I like you, Angus. If I can ever help you, remember Thordad.'

'You're all right? Sure you can go on?'

'I can go on. Hurry. Never mind me. I'll make it.'

They saw the towering ball of the globe-ship as they broke from the squat buildings framing the square at the waterfront. It was a ball of golden brilliance, riding the slight sea-swell despite its bulk, occasionally rubbing against the soft snubbers attached to the dock. In the moonlight it loomed majestic and awe-inspiring above the wet, rounded stones of the quay. Its soft *slip-slup* motion on the waves made it seem alive in the salt-laden breeze moving in from the sea.

The scientist halted. 'I leave you here. You know how to get to the Flaming Land? Good.'

Thordad held out his bony hand. Angus grinned and clasped it. He chuckled, 'Tell the Hierarch to dust off a shelf in his Literatum. I'll fill it with the Book of Nard.'

Thordad smiled, turned on a heel and strode off into the darkness of an alleyway. Angus went on, eyes gleaming up at the hulk of the ship. He heard the wind whistling in the rooftops, and across the flat stretch of the square. With eyes and ears already occupied, he did not hear the sobbed cry Thordad managed as a hand closed on his throat, nor did he see the dagger dripping crimson in the hand of the man with the zig-zag scar, rising to fall again and again in Thordad's body.

Angus went across the gangplank into the curved port. He pressed a stud and the door slid into place. Lights sprang to full illumination, revealing shimmering metal beams and cross-braces, glittering crimson floor, and long banks of control panels. Glowing tubes, slowly warming, flooded the gigantic room with a soft blue color.

Angus studied the meters. He drew down a red-handled lever. Far below the plasticine-sheltered engines throbbed, roared their power. Slowly the great hull of the globe-ship began to revolve, circling the inner ball. The fine margin of air-space, charged with electronically regulated magnets, made a soft, swooshing sound as the outer ball rotated faster. The inner ball, gigantic gyroscope set in a magnetic field, held steady, while the outer globe swirled rapidly.

The globe-ship seemed a huge ball that some giant's hand was shoving through the water. It flipped water from it as it raced. Its bulk, designed for the minimum amount of friction in water, danced across the waves with terrific speed.

Angus watched the great bulk of swaying, restless water ahead of him, saw combers flee by, watched huge swells come and go, split by the globular hull. He flipped over the light-map and studied his progress, making changes in the directional needle.

He headed out across the heaving Car Carolan Sea toward the Flaming Lands, where no living man had ever gone before.

The Diktor turned from a contemplation of the serried bands of light glistening across the beaded spectragraph screen. A young attendant in golden jacket and breeches touched a button at his command and the screen went dead.

The drapes over the arched doorway at the end of the room billowed aside as an officer entered, clicked heels and bowed. His voice was hoarse. 'Teoman has returned, Eminence. He bears news of the pirate.'

The Diktor came striding across the floor, sweeping his cloak behind him with a short, thickly muscled arm. He gestured peremptorily and the billowing curtains lifted. A man with a zigzag scar on his cheek bobbed his head up and down, sidling into the room.

'The pirate has gone in a globe-ship across the Car Carolan Sea, Highest One. A scientist of the Dragon Class was assisting him. I daggered the scientist but I could not reach Angus in time.'

169

The Diktor bit his lip. 'Moana?'

The spy shook his sparsely-haired head. 'No sign of her, Eminence. She was not with him.'

The Diktor tossed a bag of coins to Teoman, gestured the man out. He snapped an order and went striding back and forth across the room as the officer hurried out.

The officer came back with two red-clad attendants who wheeled a squat engine, bulbs and gears locked inside a transparent jacket, before them. High on the gleaming metal top of the machine stood a vox-phone.

The Diktor bent and put his lips to the vox-phone. He said irritably, 'Subject: the Car Carolan Sea and adjacent territories. Query: What, if anything, of scientific value is reputedly found in that region?'

There was a faint hum of the gears and pistons. A soft, gentle voice replied, 'The Flaming Land and the Desert of Dead White Stones border the Car Carolan Sea to the west. To the east is the continent of Karr Major. To the south the ice floes that are barren. To the north, the polar regions. Beyond the Flaming Land is an inland sea fed underground by waters from the Car Carolan. Beyond that sea lies the desert. It is an uninhabited land. There is nothing of scientific import there aside from the volcanic region of the Flaming Land.'

The machine clicked and died. The Diktor sighed. He would have to go and see Stasor. He did not want to do that because he had a feeling that the members of the Elder Race did not approve of him and his methods.

Even far out at sea Angus felt the heat coming toward him in surging waves. Mists, formed from water heated to the boiling point, rose like a white pall to shelter the Flaming Lands from his eyes. But here and there, through a breeze-made rift, he could see huge tongues of fire, red and sullen, rising from the ground.

Angus drove the globe-ship into the white fog. Gigantic bubbles broke under it, flung mists and steam up over the ship. Inside the glober the heat was fierce.

Angus was clammy with the sweat running down his cheeks and ribs. It was sapping his energies. When the controls started to blur in his eyes he knew he had enough. His fingers touched the warm control lever and threw it forward.

He fled miles from the mist and slowed to a stop, riding the ocean's swell. He muttered, 'I'm through. Finished. I can't go over and I can't go under . . . or can I? Didn't Plisket say something about that? Wait . . . wait . . . sure! He said this thing will submerge.'

Angus got up and crossed the room. There was a small literatum inset in the metal wall. He ran his eyes over titles, reached up and brought down a thick book on geophysiology.

He bent, consulting pages on subterranean oceanology. His finger pointed out a paragraph. 'From the Car Carolan Sea an underground river feeds the inland sea that lies between the Flaming Lands and the Desert of Dead White Stones'.

It took him a long time, hunting blindly in the heated water all around him. He went deep, trundling across the jagged ocean bottom. The oxygenerators were laboring when he found the great dark orifice looming ahead in his sea-lights.

It was close work, maneuvering the glober through the sea-tunnel. All around was the muted booming of volcanic fires sending up hot jets of molten lava, flame and ashes. Water swirled, black and thickish, past the rounded hull.

When the water lightened, he knew they were out of the tunnel. Angus sent the glober rocketing upward. It burst through the water into clean air. The Flaming Lands lay behind. Ahead, across the bluish expanse that was the inland sea, lay a vast stretch of sand and rock.

Angus anchored the globe-ship. He dove overboard and swam to the whitish sands. The sun was warm above and the hot sand bit through his boots. Angus threw a canteen across his shoulder and fastened a packet of food tablets around his waist.

He walked for two days and a night before he found the half-sunken road that arched across the desert. The road ended four days later, in the barrens. His water was gone and the leathern pocket that had held food tablets was empty.

'I can't turn back,' he thought. 'I've been gone a whole week from the inland sea.'

Angus turned and stumbled on. The sun beat down on his

171

naked shoulders, on the remnants of the sun-worn rags about his middle. With each puff of sand his feet kicked up, something went out of his spirit.

Angus saw a brown rock uplifting its jagged tip from the sand. He ran awkwardly toward it, hoping that from its top he might see the spires of a distant, nebulous city. But there was only sand and more twisted, curving dunes, and the faint azure tint of the horizon.

He stood on the naked finger of rock and swore. He invoked the olden gods – the fecund Ashtal, goddess of love and sex; Grom who fought with warriors; Jethad who loved the wise. He called on them for their attention and he cursed them, upwards and down, forward and back.

In his rage he took the empty canteen and hurled it.

Choking, he broke off in mid-curse.

The canteen had disappeared in mid-air!

The Hierarch made fists out of his taloned hands. The cowled man, bent before his carven chair, trembled. The Hierarch whispered, 'Are you sure?'

'We followed his spectragraph in the screen, Excellency. We followed it until it disappeared!'

The black orbs in the thin white face of the chief scientist burned with fanatical ardor. Through thin lips he rasped, 'He tricked me. He had those pirates of his pick him up when he was safely out of my hands.'

'He went through the Flaming Lands,' quavered the cowled man. 'We saw him do that. Would he go to all that trouble to be picked up in the desert? He could have escaped from the Car Carolan Sea.'

'Evidence of his cunning. He wanted to make sure he was a good distance away from the power of the Diktor.'

'The Diktor?'

'You fool! I'm going to the Diktor and turn Moana over to his torturers. I'll tell him Angus planned with Moana to kill him. Ha! The torturers will work over her for a long time, I think. When Angus hears of that . . .'

The Hierarch brooded. He smiled, 'I might even turn that

into a trap for him. When he returns, having heard what has happened to Moana, I'll be waiting for him.'

Angus slid down from the rock with his heart in his mouth. *The canteen flew out into the air*, he thought. *It went high, and as it came down it disappeared!*

There was something just ahead of him. Perhaps a force field hidden in the shifting and eddying mists rising from the desert lands.

If he could find the canteen and discover what made it invisible . . .

Angus was weak. His knees crumpled as he tried to take a forward step. He summoned the muscles and the nerves of his big, gaunt body. He went forward one step, then two.

At the third step he fell. He put out his hands.

They parted the grey mists in front of him but did not break his fall. His naked knees hit rounded stones and then his palms went out and touched the worn pavings of a city street.

'Gods!' the pirate whispered, lifting his head, blue eyes burning like coals in his tanned face.

The gray mists shifted, fading. From their wisps, as though like the flesh of a naked woman revealed by smoky veils, shone queerly rounded and smoothly curved walls of amaranthine and ochre, red and jonquil yellow. Here and there a dome of pearly champagne stood tipped with a knob of vermilion. The houses on the edge of the city were low, seeming to rise higher and higher toward the center where a tall, slender building reared its spire.

Red Angus drew a deep breath, running his hands down the ridged muscles of his thighs. He turned and stared behind him where the hot sands ought to be. He saw only mists, shifting and shimmering.

Angus went down the street, past empty-windowed buildings, across bare intersections, his foot-falls loud in the stillness of the dead city.

He walked until the entrance to the central tower was in front of him. Crested with heraldic devices – Red Angus recognized the flame-eyed Stallion of forgotten Shallar and the

173

rampant Dragon of Domeer – the wide door was a glittering mass of emeralds embedded in carvings so delicate they seemed sheared from paper.

The doors opened at a touch, revealing red-and-yellow squares of metal stretching forward beneath a glittering dome of translucent jade. In the center of the hall stood a low metal rim about a bubble of grayish green iridescence. He went toward the rim, bent over and stared down.

'One of the black pools!' whispered Angus.

Through the luminescent bubble he could see only blackness, a jet nothingness that seemed alive.

A step sounded on the metal flagging behind him.

Angus whirled.

A man stood there, leaning on a bent staff, smiling gently. He was clad in a loose woollen garment, white as falling snow. His arms and legs were bare and brown. His face, though lined and creased, seemed almost youthful.

'I have waited many years,' he said softly, 'and no one ever came. Now – at last – there is someone who has found the city. Welcome. I bid you welcome to the Tower of the Ancients!'

'Stasor!' cried Angus in sudden recognition.

'The Stasor you know, yes. One of my race is chosen to spend a hundred years as Guardian of the City, to wait for any who might come to seek its treasures. You are the first who ever found it.'

Angus said, 'A lifetime of loneliness. Are we worth it?'

The old man laughed. 'We do not die – not as your race knows death. It's one of our attainments. Like the blackness where you first saw me.'

'The blackness?' Angus turned, stared down at the metal collar encasing the jet black pool. 'What is it? It must be all over the planet. No one knows what the pool is.'

'It is the greatest product of my race. Many eons ago a scientist discovered that an atom may be split to create ravening energy. For years the mightiest scientists of the Elders studied that fact. Eventually they built machines that could

174

house such awful power. Finally, after many centuries, they developed the pools.

'The pools are nothing more than that atomic radiation – sheer energy – bottled up in vast chambers lined with *stalabasil*. Ready for use at any time.

'In the early days men died from such radioactivity. As time went on and we handled it more and more, our bodies evolved, so that the painful burns that caused death became as mere tinglings along the nerve-ends. Your own race, that evolved on Karr after the Elders went on, is also immune to it.'

'Reservoirs of energy,' murmured Angus, rubbing hand on thigh. 'If you could harness that energy and turn it into channels of production . . .'

His blue eyes widened as breath caught in his throat. Stasor smiled, his old head nodding. 'That's what we Elders used. We powered our machines with it. We needed no fuel, no refilling of bins or tanks. It was always there, ready to tap.'

'Does the Book of Nard mention it?'

The old man nodded. 'All our secrets are contained in the Book of Nard. Do you want to see it?'

They went up a flight of spiralling steps and into a room where heavy golden drapes hung bright and splendid. On a wooden rest lay a closed book, its covers solid gold, its parchment leaves tinted a pale rose.

'Open it,' said the Guardian.

Angus bent and lifted the cover. He gazed on the archaic lettering etched into the thick vellum.

Each man has in him the seeds of his own immortality. He must progress or he must die. And the race is like the man. Who shall say what path that progression shall take? A man cannot know his own future. Neither does the race. This is the Book of Nard, first of the Elder Race. With encouragement to all peoples who come after us, we leave this short transcript of our past.

Angus lifted his eyes. He stared at the smiling Guardian, who nodded. Quickly the pirate touched the parchment, spread pages wide. His keen blue eyes scanned the etchings while he read the record of those who had gone on. He

175

scanned mathematical and astronomical formulae, chemical equations, biological charts.

He whispered, 'The entire history of the race, told in the achievements of its scientists!'

'It is all that lives.'

'I don't understand it, of course. I catch a thought, here and there. But the entire equation . . .'

'You don't understand it?'

'No.'

The old man smiled. He said suddenly, 'Would you like to see some of those achievements in action? Would you like to see the worlds in three-dimensional space, the island universes, the galaxies, the stars and their planets?'

Angus said, 'I've been out among the Six Worlds. I've seen other systems through telescopes.'

The old man laughed. It was a spontaneous, happy sort of laugh. 'I don't mean that way. Come, let me show you what my race can do.' Angus caught him smiling oddly, the corners of his lips drawing down, as though he shared a queer joke only with himself.

They did not use the stairway this time. They stepped into a bare room walled and ceilinged and floored with shining steel. The old man touched a stud on the door.

The room of the book was gone.

In its stead, there was a round chamber with a transparent dome that revealed stars twinkling uncounted miles above. In the middle of the otherwise unfurnished room stood a low, flat dais set with chairs riveted on their curving metal legs into the dais. A bank of controls was set flush in the floor of the platform.

The old man led him to the dais. He smiled, bending over the control panel, 'This is the kind of observatory your race will have, someday. You won't have to depend on polished mirrors and light and thick lenses. Basically the principle of the thing is the same as that of the teleport room we used to come over here. We just make use of coordinated space and time factors. It's like steering a boat on an uncharted ocean. If you know where your lodestar is you can go anywhere you want.'

176

He turned and reached for a chair. We're ready now. You are perfectly safe, no matter what you see, or think you see. Just relax.'

The reflected light in the room was fading. Blackness came down through the transparent dome and surrounded them. It was like the Staratarium Red Angus had visited on Mawk – or it was, until Angus saw stars beside and below him.

A nebula that was uncounted light years away came rushing toward them. It was a spinning silver wheel at a distance, but it broke into great blotches of black space to dissolve into just another star system without form or noticeable nebulosity.

They swooped over a reddish planet and dropped through its atmosphere. They studied great buildings of stone and metal that towered high into the clouds. Tiny fliers and great air-freighters dotted the skies. The old man said, 'This people used their science wisely. They built a civilization that gives every man all he wants which is, in effect, all he can understand.'

They left the red planet, swept light years away and down through heavy mists to a greenish globe whirling majestically in the light of its distant sun. Beneath them lush, tropical jungles lifted fronds and branches to the steaming mists. Somewhere in that massed carpet of vegetation an animal screamed in its dying agonies. Through a break in the trees Angus saw a naked man squat and hairy and with a stone-bladed spear in his hand, fleeing before the bounding fury of a gigantic tiger. The great cat was making its last leap, spreading its talons into the man's shivering flesh, as the mists crept up and hid them.

'A young world,' Stasor said softly, 'with all its life ahead of it in which to find its destiny.'

They went out into space and found a planet where giant insects ruled, where a lumbering thing in the shape of a man, but mindless, was used for heavy labor. Another planet showed lizards dwelling in strangely wrought mansions. A third showed mind-beings that looked like crimson jellyfish hanging in midair by some means of mental suspension.

'All these,' explained Stasor with a wave of his palm,' are

freaks. Life throughout the whole universe, across all of its uncountable light-years, follows mainly a pattern like our own. Creatures that we call man, with two arms, two legs, two eyes, a nose and mouth, breathing atmosphere into lungs, have been the ruling race because of circumstances like gravity and atmosphere, over which they themselves have no control.

'One more example, then we're done....'

They fled across star galaxies, through sprawling universe where binaries and dwarf stars and red giants alternated against the black void like a spangled curtain. They went through the Megellanic Cluster and the Andromeda nebula. They came swooping down so swiftly that the stars blurred a little, even at their incredible distances, toward another galaxy.

Stasor found a little star. It was surrounded by nine planets. He chose the third planet outward from the star, and dropped his observational platform through the heaviside and ionosphere.

Angus craned forward. He liked this world. It reminded him vaguely of Karr, with its green grasses and rolling oceans.

'Its inhabitants call it the Earth. A peaceful place. Look over there – you can see the city clearer now.'

It had graceful spires and round, lovely dwellings. Giant ships rested beside white, sparkling wharves. People went back and forth clad in light, airy garments. There was an air of glowing contentment.

Stasor said, 'This is their golden age. It will last a long time. Soon they will colonize other planets near them. In the end – some million years from now – these people will rule almost all the known universes. And yet, compared to ours, their science is just a crawling child.'

Angus felt a touch of jealousy. 'Why should they rule the worlds? We people of Karr . . .'

'Wait, not yet. I want to show you this world three hundred years ago.'

He touched a lever. The world below them grew away, shot backward and out into space. Angus cried out in amazement. 'It's receding from us.'

'I'm going back in time. Remember, this is an expanding universe. It's come a long way in the past three centuries, going toward the fixed star, Vega. We have to follow it.'

This time, there was no lovely world. There was only blackened earth, charred and scorched. Great humps of steel stuck up from the ground like the fire-blackened ribs of some giant fallen in swamp-muck. From the west came seven thin, lean shapes, speeding through the air. From the blackened ground came thinner, smaller shapes to intercept them. The small shapes were like wasps in their darting and their speed. The big shapes never had a chance. They went down in masses of red flame, spinning.

Stasor announced, 'This is their Last War. It is to go on ten more years. The seven shapes you saw were bombers loaded to their wings with atomic bombs. The smaller ships were fighters, their armaments mounted with fission-guns, an invention of an American scientist.'

'Ten more years!' flinched Angus. 'There's only blackened ground for them to live on.'

'They live underground,' explained Stasor.

Angus mused, 'There's such a sharp difference between this world and what it's to be like three hundred years from this time.'

'The American who invented the fission-gun,' explained Stasor, 'will lead their world to that pinnacle. He is going to organize the remnants of the civilization left after the last war, compel interracial wedlock and births. The biological result of that will be, naturally, a new and different race in the course of the years. It is that race that will go out from Earth to the stars.'

Angus regarded Stasor thoughtfully. 'You're thinking that what the American did with his people, I can do with mine.'

The old man shrugged. He reached out and twisted the dials. He murmured, 'Karr fights a war just as deadly as the one you see below. There's a difference. Instead of death, Karr's enemies deal it stagnation and degeneration.'

'If I could get the Diktor to give the Hierarch's sciences to the people,' Angus mused.

'Where there is hope you have new life,' smiled Stasor

gently. 'Without science to benefit their lives the people of Karr have no hope.'

Angus lashed out bitterly, 'The Diktor is too powerful. There isn't any way to beat him.'

'I will show you a way,' murmured the old man.

III

Stal Tay held court before his ruby throne. He sat with right hand on his knee, bent forward, thin lips smiling. Before him stood the Hierarch, rigid with rage, black eyes burning under the shadow of his white cowl. To the Hierarch's left an almost naked Moana was crumpled on the cold stone floor, manacles rivetted to her wrists and ankles, her white flesh gleaming through torn garments.

Stal Tay taunted, 'You come too late, Hierarch. I know where Red Angus went, what he went for, and who sent him.'

'It was done in your interests,' rasped the scientist. 'I brought her to you that you might know the truth.'

Stal Tay glanced at the weeping Moana. 'So many odd things are done in my supposed interests these days. At that, I'm almost inclined to believe you but what really bothers me is this – did Angus find . . .'

The Diktor snapped off his speech abruptly. He rose half out of his throne, fingers clutching the jeweled arms. The Hierarch whirled. Even Moana turned her head to look, the sobs still racking her body.

A yellow glow was forming in midair a foot above the stone tiles of the Audience Chamber. The yellow glittered, coruscated and faded away. Where the color was now stood a flat black dais with three chairs whose curving legs were rivetted to the floor of the dais. A man turned from the control panel that rose between the seats, a man with red hair and a tanned body. The man looked at them and laughed.

'Angus,' whimpered Moana.

'Seize him,' raged Stal Tay.

Angus bent and lifted something and held it up. It glittered

180

in the light filtering through the arched windows of the Audience Chamber. Angus said, 'This is the Book of Nard. I've come to bargain with you, Stal Tay.'

The Diktor sank back into his throne, gesturing his guards aside. He said, 'What do you want for the Book?'

'Moana.'

'Moana,' said the Diktor in surprise. 'Is that all? Take her . . . but wait. How do I know this isn't a trick? How do I know I'll get the Book?'

Angus stepped from the dais to the floor of the chamber. He placed the book in its golden covers on the floor. 'I went to the City of the Ancients. I met Stasor and took the Book of Nard from him. I came to bring it to you. I see I came just in time to save Moana.'

Stal Tay came to his feet. 'That thing you ride. What is it? Tell me its secret and I'll pardon you.'

Angus laughed in his face. 'Stasor calls it a teleportator. It shifts space, draws sectors of space together in an instant. In it a man can move from here to anywhere on Karr. Stasor knows many things, Stal Tay. One of them is how to bring you off that throne!'

The Diktor's face purpled. He started to talk but his eyes caught the golden covers of the Book of Nard and he controlled his anger. 'Take her,' he said, 'before I decide the Book isn't worth your insults!'

Irons clanking, the girl stepped to Angus' side, let him lift her to the dais. Then Angus turned and studied the Diktor through narrowed eyelids.

'I'm giving you the Book now, Stal Tay. But it's only fair to warn you – I'll be back for it!'

He stepped onto the dais, turned a knob on the control panel. The dais fled and the golden bubble came back, and then that, too, disappeared.

Moana sobbed as the dais fled through shifting white mists. Angus knelt beside her, using his disintegrator on the links of her manacles. She said, 'The Diktor will send men for you. He'll never let you get away with this. You've only won a temporary victory.'

Angus chuckled, 'He'll be too busy with the Hierarch and

181

the Book of Nard to go after me for a while. When he does, it will be too late.' He dropped the severed chains to the floor of the dais. 'You see, none of the scientists in the Citadel will understand the sciences in the book. They'll tell Stal Tay that and he won't believe them. There'll be a minor war between the Diktor and the Hierarchy. Once a breach between them is made, we'll step into it.'

The dais settled on something solid. The golden veil dissipated as before a wind, to reveal the smoke-blackened beams of a tavern room. Tandor was there, a wooden mug in one hand, straining forward from the tableside, his other hand clutching its edge, staring at them.

Angus helped Moana down. Tandor drained the mug and slammed it on the tabletop. He demanded, 'Well? Got a bellyful of it? Ready for the star trails?'

'Not yet, Tandor.'

Tandor growled and rubbed his palm on his bald head. He grumbled, 'You'll be a martyr yet. You watch. You'll see. Red Angus – who died saving nothing!'

The pirate grinned at him, leaning his palms flat on the tabletop. 'If I win, you know what'll happen, don't you? You and I will have to rule Karr. You'll be my majordomo. You'll wear fine clothes and make decisions and listen to people bellyache.'

Tandor howled, leaping up so suddenly that his chair went skidding. He slammed his palms on the table. 'Not me!' he bellowed. 'I want no office and no snivelling folk to spoil my days! I—'

Angus moved a hand. He put it flat to Tandor's chest and held it there. The bald giant snapped his lips together. He grew silent as a clam, and as still.

The door was opening.

Something that looked like a man, that was swathed in white bandages from toes to head, with two slits for eyes and a hole for a mouth, was coming in the room. Tandor's hand swooped and lifted with a disintegrator.

'Angus,' whispered the apparition. 'Red Angus! I need help.'

The pirate was across the room, catching the bandaged

182

figure in cradling arms, lowering him to the couch. He whispered, 'This is the second time you've been on that couch, Thordad. What happened to you?'

'When I left you at the globe-ship dock one of Stal Tay's spies knifed me and left me for dead. The Hierarch sent men to find me. They doctored me and were carrying me to the Citadel when the Diktor jumped us. He sent me to his torture dungeons.'

The man shuddered under the bandages. The eyes, through the slits, were wide with horror and remembered pain. 'The Diktor wanted to learn what the Hierarch was after. I wouldn't tell him. Before that he confronted me with the Hierarch who disowned me. He told Stal Tay to do with me what he wanted!'

The raw hate throbbed in Thordad's voice. It sent a cold ripple down Angus' spine. The pirate leaned closer to the bandaged mouth: 'The Diktor let his beasts at me for three days. It was horrible. But I got away. I think I went mad with the pain. I crept to my cousin's house and was bandaged and partially healed there. Then I came here. You're the only hope any of us have. You've got to do something – anything – to stop that madman and the Hierarch!'

Angus wiped his hands on his jacket. 'You, Tandor. What news have you?'

'I've been busy too,' Tandor growled, eyeing Thordad curiously. 'I've roused the men and women of the Lower City. I've sent for the pirates on Yassanin, sent for warriors from the cities of Streeth and Fayalat. We've a crew of fighting men with swords and spears and a few disintegrators. But with the scientific might of Stal Tay and the Hierarch we're beaten before we start.'

Angus laughed. 'Not yet. Stasor has promised help. We're to meet him and get the weapons he told me about. Into the teleportator on the double – all of you.'

When they were in the chairs fastened to the dais, Angus threw over the lever. A golden mist formed about them, hardened. There was an instant of coldness . . .

The golden mist disappeared. The teleportator stood before the fountain in the Tower of the Ancients. Angus sprang from the machine. 'Stasor, I'm back!'

There was no answer. Only the silence of the dead walls of the dead city replied.

It was Moana who found the blood-stained bit of silk that had been ripped from Stasor's garment. Wordlessly she held it out to Angus.

His belly turned over when he saw it. He looked at the girl, then at Tandor.

'The Diktor's come for him. With Stasor to unravel the secrets in the Book of Nard, Stal Tay can't be beaten!'

Tandor shrugged massive shoulders. 'I knew that a long time ago. We'll all die. It's just a matter of when and where.'

In the time Angus had allotted him, Tandor had thrown up a small city of tents and wickiups along the stone ridges of the Bloody Cliffs. Here came the pirates from Yassinan, the starved soldiery from the star cities of Fayalat and Kor. Here were half-naked gypsy girls and camp followers, fighting men and muckers. Here were dishonored captains and untried youths who owned swords and a hot hunger to use them.

In the red fire of an armorer's forge, Red Angus handled a ring-barreled gun that was powered by a portable dynamo set up on a small, two-wheeled cart.

The armorer said, 'It's weak and it's clumsy, but it's the best I could do. The electroray gets its power from the dynamo in the cart. Power travels along the fuel line to the breach. A tiny converter translates it into a thin beam of force. I've seen them in the museums. I made sketches. Given more time I could do better.'

Red Angus put a grin on his lips and held it there by sheer will-power. His hand clapped the man on the back. He told him, 'You've done fine, Yoth! Keep it up. Turn out as many as you can!'

The armorer shook his head glumly. 'They won't be much alongside the disintegrators that Stal Tay will have. Even their sonic-beams will do more damage than this!'

Tandor came swaggering up through the half-naked, hairy chested men who fought with blunted sabres and war-spears.

There was dirt on his face, and runnels of sweat ran on his barrel chest. He planted his legs apart, and glowered at Red Angus.

'You're mad as a priest of Grom. You keep us here when we'd do better by scattering to the six worlds.'

Angus said, 'These are the toughest fighting men in the galaxy. If they can't take the Citadel no one can. Once we get within sword-sweep of the Diktor's guards . . .'

Tandor bellowed. He went up on his toes and waved his arms, and his veins stood out on his bald head. 'As well get within sword-sweep of Ashtal the Shameless!' he roared. 'The Diktor will sweep the streets with disintegrator beams when he sees us coming. Maybe you want to play martyr, but I've better uses for my life. Take that gypsy girl . . .'

Angus caught him by the fur of his cloak and shook him. 'Forget your gypsy wenches. We go into the Lower City at night. All of us, over a week's time. We bed down in different homes. Loyal homes. A fortnight from now will be the Night of the Serpent. Singing and dancing in the streets. Wine. Women.'

Tandor grinned. 'Aie, that sounds good.'

'At the hour of the Dog we hit the Citadel. There'll be so much roistering going on we'll belt-whip every mother's son into the streets that night, and make 'em yell to cover our movements. No one'll notice us!

'We hit the Citadel from every street. Some of us will get through. Ten streets, ten companies, each of them a flying wedge to get inside and kill Stal Tay. That's our first job. After that . . .'

Red Angus talked on, sketching in the hot sands. He did not see a bandaged Thordad come out of a tent and stand there, watching them, and listening. Thordad turned away after a while and went back into the tent where he sat shivering and staring down at his hands.

Neither did Red Angus see him that night when he daggered a guard and fled on a haml across the desert for Karr City. They found the guard but guessed him a victim of a jealous lover for he had a reputation as a lady's man.

The days slid into weeks, and the fires burned and metal

185

glowed, and the forges and the anvils never stopped. Swords and shields and spears, daggers and clumsy electrorays were turned out for eager hands.

They broke camp in the faint mists of an early dawn. On ewe-necked haml and on foot, by cart and by stolen jetcar, they left the base of the Bloody Cliffs. They came into Karr City by twos and threes and hid themselves in the taverns and in the thatch-roofed houses. The city knew them and the city swallowed them, and the city slumbered, waiting.

In the tavern of the Spotted Stag, Red Angus paced the floor. Tandor, an arm around his gypsy girl, was sampling a new tun of imported wine. Moana was white-faced, pale and silent at the table.

Angus said, 'I don't like it. I don't like it. I have the feel of a wolf sniffing at the jaws of a trap.'

Tandor drew his lips from the gypsy's neck long enough to say, 'It's quiet, isn't it. What more do you want?'

'That's just it. It's too quiet. There are no Citadel guards out hunting me. No arrests for five days. No street patrols, even!'

'Good. Then let's call it off and go back to Yassanin. You'll like Yassanin, honey.' Tandor nuzzled the girl's throat, 'I have a big house there. Much wine. Better wine than this!'

Angus stared at the man through slitted eyes, reached for a goblet and lifted it. His hand poised the goblet, about to throw. Angus swore and buried his nose in the cup. He flung it from him, and it broke against the wall.

The city stayed quiet for five days. On the morning of the Night of the Serpent it exploded with energy. Men and women, in masks and costumes, paraded and sang. They drank and danced and the Citadel brooded down on them.

The day wore on. Tandor and Angus were busy, keeping some semblance of order in their fighting crews, keeping the men from the wine-barrels, readying them for their assignments. Tandor went stalking into the taverns and the wine shops with heavy hands, striking out as he walked, often upending an unfortunate into a wine-tun after knocking in its head with the head of the man he held upside down in his hands.

Red Angus went more circumspectly, fighting off the tipsy women and armed footpads who waxed rich in the torchlight gatherings during the long Night of the Serpent. He rounded up his crews and found them their weapons.

'Tonight the stars revolt!'

At the hour of the Dog ten companies of hard-eyed fighting men came out of the shadows of the ten cobblestoned streets that led by twisting tiers to the Citadel. They went up the curving stone stairs to the smooth Citadel streets and started forward . . .

And then the Diktor struck.

The sonicbeams came first, cutting the front ranks to bloody pulp. Disintors rayed into action. Men went down silently under the lightning-swift impact of purplish lances.

It was a rout.

Here, a naked mercenary from Fayalat would flesh his blade in a few necks as he drove in behind a wall of dead flesh. There, a warrior from Kor might take three of Stal Tay's soldiers with him before he touched hands with his ancestors. But the beams and the rays slew in the darkness and the rabble was driven back.

Where Red Angus fought with an electroray cart, sweeping the ringed nozzle of his weapon in and out of the shadows. the men of the Lower City stood a while. They fought with the ferocity of trapped thots, for the pits of Stal Tay yawned for them.

'Hold firm!' roared Tandor, his sword a sweeping line of death where it circled and darted.

'Fall back,' cried Angus. 'Back to reform! They've trapped us well, the tricky dogs.'

A man with a bandaged face stood out a moment from the shadows, pointing. He cried, 'Half a hundred *oblis* to the man who brings down Red Angus!'

'Thordad!' shouted Angus, and he knew now the manner of his betrayal. Thordad had seen a chance for reinstatement and had taken it. He had seen the rabble that served Red Angus and knew the disciplined power of the Diktor's guards.

He had gone with news of Angus' plans. This trap was the result.

Red Angus forgot the others. He sighted the electroray carefully. A thin beam of brilliance lanced out. It touched Thordad on face and neck. A headless corpse rolled at the guards' feet as they came forward.

Their rush caught Angus and the men with him. It swept them backward through the streets, rolled up their flanks. It clubbed the center with sonicbeams until men screamed in the agony of mashed legs and caved-in chests.

Angus fought like a maddened griff. He used the electroray like a broom, sweeping it before him. He kicked the two-wheeled cart ahead for without the dynamo in the cart the electroray was useless.

A sudden rush of guards caught Angus in a maelstrom of cursing, howling men.

They hit him and drove him back against the glittering metal collar of one of the black pools, yawning grim and silent in the cobblestoned square. They hammered him with swordblades and pounded the cart with metal-headed axes.

Angus stumbled, fell. He came up slowly, his back to the cold metal collar of the pool, the ringed barrel of the useless electroray still in his hands.

It's all over, he told himself, staring at the swords coming for him. *I've failed, and I'll die, and so will Moana, and Tandor, and all the rest of this motley crew who tried to pull themselves up by their bootstraps.*

Angus clubbed with the ringed barrel and a man fell whimpering at his feet.

'Come on!' the pirate roared. 'Here's my last stand, here at the edge of the pool! You're done with Red Angus. See how a free man dies.'

Angus broke off, eyes wide.

The pool!

One of the black pools of Karr . . .

What was it Stasor had said of those pools? 'The pools are nothing more than atomic radiation – sheer energy – bottled up in vast chambers lined with stalahasil. Ready for use at any time.'

Ready for use.

With the savage fury of the barbarian, Angus slammed the ringed barrel at the faces pressing in on him. They wanted him alive and that gave him the precious moment he needed.

He whipped the electroray high in the air, swung it so the weighted powercord flailed high and far over the metal rim of the pool's collar. It dropped down and down into the black depths.

Angus pressed the stud.

A ravening stream of black mist shot from the ringed nozzle. It touched the oncoming soldiers of the Diktor, touched them, and . . .

Ate them!

When the black mist faded the Diktor's soldiers faded, too. They were gone in that desolation of yawning street and crumpled walls. Where the black mist had touched nothing remained.

Tandor bellowed.

The star-pirates roared their glee.

Angus moved the weapon and touched the stud again. The black mist fled outward, up one street, down another. When he was finished there were no soldiers facing them. The streets to the Citadel lay empty, beckoning.

They went forward in a ravening wave of fury, the fury of roused fighting men, who had looked the eyeless sockets of Death's skull in the face and lived. The night held no more terrors for them for their nostrils were tasting the fragrance of victory. Other men came up from the Lower City to join them, men who bore home-made weapons, crude clubs and axes.

Angus caught a sweat-streaked Tandor by the arm. 'This gun! The powercord that fell in the black pool. That's what did it. It's a weapon of the Elders. The pool feeds it, gives it power . . .'

'What matters that?' bellowed Tandor, shaking a new sword in his hand. 'It worked!'

'But it won't work if I can't keep the powercord inside the pool.'

Tandor blinked, grunting as understanding came to him. 'Huh. That's different. Pask. Gatl. Sonal. At the double, you riff-raff. To me.'

He gave orders crisply, then swung to Angus. 'They'll scour the Lower City for copper wire. We'll couple an extension to the cord so you can take it wherever you want.'

Angus nodded. 'Put a file of men on either side of it. Keep them there. Make them fight for that cord with their lives. If they fail us, we die.'

Tandor handpicked his men, big men all, with the scars of many battles speaking their experience. The cord was slit and fitted with gleaming copper cable-lengths, insulated, and welded tightly.

Weapon in hands, Red Angus led his rabble army up the stone-block roadway steps, upward from the mire and filth of the Lower City, upward to the clean white reaches of the Citadel.

The Diktor's personal guards made a sortie against them, but the black mist swept them away. When the Hierarch sent his troops to join those of the Diktor the mist swirled around them once, and then blew away, leaving the Citadel gardens empty of opposition.

It was over.

They walked through the gardens, into the halls and corridors of the Palace. Men stood weaponless, fright tightening the lines of their faces.

Tandor roared, 'The Diktor, you foul hounds. Where is he?'

Men pointed and at the end of their fingers loomed the great golden bulk of the Audience Chamber.

The Diktor and the Hierarch stood before the ruby throne. They were beaten men, expecting death, their cheeks washed an ashen grey.

Angus said, 'If you've harmed Stasor you'll take a year to die.'

The Diktor gestured wearily. 'He's in chains, in the lower pits. We haven't harmed him. He would not translate the Book

190

of Nard. But even so, dead he was useless to us. Alive, he might have changed his mind.'

He went on to explain how he had traced Angus' journey in the spectragraph, how his men had followed Angus' course in globe ships to bring the god of Karr to the Citadel. He said, 'You were beaten. Whipped. My messengers told me that you were hemmed in, your men chopped to thumbits. And yet – yet you come here—'

Madness glinted in the Diktor's eyes. His right hand moved like lightning, and the blue metal of a disintor caught fire from the soft luminescence of the walls.

The Diktor was swift but Tandor was faster. His hand blurred and a glittering longsword jumped the five feet that separated them. It drove the dead body of the Diktor back three steps to the ruby throne. He fell at its base and a pool of blood grew on the floor.

The Hierarch shrugged and put a pellet to his mouth. The poison acted with incredible speed. He was falling as the chamber door opened and a gently smiling Stasor entered, leaning on his staff.

Angus and Moana stood on the heights of the Citadel and looked down at the Lower City. They saw the thatched roofs no longer, but instead tidy houses, clean streets and healthy children. Men and women walked with pride, their bodies clean, enjoying the new life that Stasor and the Book of Nard could bring them. It would take time, all that. But it would come.

Moana moved gently. Her hand caught his. He turned her head up and his lips settled on hers.

A hundred feet away, Tandor grinned. 'A martyr, I called him,' he told the night.

He thought of a black-haired noblewoman who had been widowed in the night's fighting. Tandor rubbed his head again and chuckled. He tiptoed from the gardens.

191

Far in the future, they discovered a new natural law: what goes up must come round. Even Hautamaki came round to the idea.

FINAL ENCOUNTER

By Harry Harrison

I

Hautamaki had landed the ship on a rubble-covered pan of rock, a scored and ancient lava flow on the wrong side of the glacier. Tjond had thought, but only to herself, that they could have landed nearer; but Hautamaki was shipmaster and made all the decisions. Then again, she could have stayed with the ship. No one had forced her to join in this hideous scramble across the fissured ice. But of course staying behind was out of the question.

There was a radio beacon of some kind over there – on this uninhabited planet – sending out squeals and cracklings on a dozen frequencies. She *had* to be there when they found it.

Gulyas helped her over a difficult place and she rewarded him with a quick kiss on his windburned cheek.

It was too much to hope that it could be anything other than a human beacon, though their ship was supposed to be covering an unexplored area. Yet there was the slimmest chance that some *others* might have built the beacon. The thought of not being there at the time of a discovery like that was unbearable. How long had mankind been looking now, for how many time-dimmed centuries?

She had to rest, she was not used to this kind of physical effort. She was roped between the two men and when she stopped they all stopped. Hautamaki halted and looked when he felt her hesitant tug on the rope, staring down at her and saying nothing. His body said it for him, arrogant, tall, heavily muscled, bronzed and nude under the transparent atmosphere suit. He was breathing lightly and normally, and his face never changed expression as he looked at her desperately heaving

192

breast. Hautamaki! What kind of a man are you, Hautamaki, to ignore a woman with such a deadly glance?

For Hautamaki it had been the hardest thing he had ever done. When the two strangers had walked up the extended tongue of the ship's boarding ramp he had felt violated.

This was his ship, his and Kiiskinen's. But Kiiskinen was dead and the child that they had wanted to have was dead. Dead before birth, before conception. Dead because Kiiskinen was gone and Hautamaki would never want a child again. Yet there was still the job to be done; they had completed barely half of their survey swing when the accident had occurred. To return to survey base would have been prodigiously wasteful of fuel and time, so he had called for instructions – and this had been the result. A new survey team, unfledged and raw.

They had been awaiting first assignment – which meant they at least had the training if not the experience. Physically they would do the work that needed to be done. There would be no worry about that. But they were a team, and he was only half a team; and loneliness can be a terrible thing.

He would have welcomed them if Kiiskinen had been there. Now he loathed them.

The man came first, extending his hand. 'I'm Gulyas, as you know, and my wife Tjond.' He nodded over his shoulder and smiled, the hand still out.

'Welcome aboard my ship,' Hautamaki said and clasped his own hands behind his back. If this fool didn't know about the social customs of Men, he was not going to teach him.

'Sorry. I forgot you don't shake hands or touch strangers.' Still smiling, Gulyas moved aside to make room for his wife to enter the ship.

'How do you do, shipmaster?' Tjond said. Then her eyes widened and she flushed, as she saw for the first time that he was completely nude.

'I'll show you your quarters,' Hautamaki said, turning and walking away, knowing they would follow. A woman! He had seen them before on various planets, even talked with them, but never had he believed that there would some day

193

be one on his ship. How ugly they were, with their swollen bodies! It was no wonder that on the other worlds everyone wore clothes, to conceal those blubbery, bobbing things and the excess fat below.

'Why – he wasn't even wearing *shoes*!' Tjond said indignantly as he closed the door. Gulyas laughed.

'Since when has nudity bothered you? You didn't seem to mind it during our holidays on Hie. And you knew about the Men's customs.'

'That was different. Everyone was dressed – or undressed – the same. But this, it's almost indecent!'

'One man's indecency is another's decency.'

'I bet you can't say that three times fast.'

'Nevertheless it's true. When you come down to it he probably thinks that we're just as socially wrong as you seem to think he is.'

'I don't think – I *know*!' she said, reaching up on tiptoes to nip his ear with her tiny teeth, as white and perfectly shaped as rice grains. 'How long have we been married?'

'Six days, nineteen hours standard, and some odd minutes.'

'Only odd because you haven't kissed me in such a terribly long time.'

He smiled down at her tiny, lovely figure, ran his hand over the warm firmness of her hairless skull and down her straight body, brushing the upturned almost vestigial buds of her breasts.

'You're beautiful,' he said, then kissed her.

II

Once they were across the glacier the going was easier on the hard-packed snow. Within an hour they had reached the base of the rocky spire. It stretched above them against the green-tinted sky, black and fissured. Tjond let her eyes travel up its length and wanted to cry.

'It's too tall! *Impossible* to climb. With the gravsled we could ride up.'

'We have discussed this before,' Hautamaki said, looking

194

at Gulyas as he always did when he talked to her. 'I will bring no radiation sources near the device up there until we determine what it is. Nothing can be learned from our aerial photograph except that it appears to be an untended machine of some kind. I will climb first. You may follow. It is not difficult on this type of rock.'

It was not difficult – it was downright impossible. She scrambled and fell and couldn't get a body's-length up the spire. In the end she untied her rope. As soon as the two men had climbed above her she sobbed hopelessly into her hands. Gulyas must have heard her, or he knew how she felt being left out, because he called back down to her.

'I'll drop you a rope as soon as we get to the top, with a loop on the end. Slip your arms through it and I'll pull you up.'

She was sure that he wouldn't be able to do it, but still she had to try. The beacon – it might *not* be human made!

The rope cut into her body, and surprisingly enough he could pull her up. She did her best to keep from banging into the cliff and twisting about: then Gulyas was reaching down to help her. Hautamaki was holding the rope . . . and she knew that it was the strength of those corded arms, not her husband that had brought her so quickly up.

'Hautamaki, thank you for—'

'We will examine the device now,' he said, interrupting her and looking at Gulyas while he spoke. 'You will both stay here with my pack. Do not approach unless you are ordered to.'

He turned on his heel, and with purposeful stride went to the outcropping where the machine stood. No more than a pace away from it he dropped to one knee, his body hiding most of it from sight, staying during long minutes in this cramped position.

'What is he doing?' Tjond whispered, hugging tight to Gulyas' arm. 'What is it? What does he see?'

'Come over here!' Hautamaki said, standing. There was a ring of emotion in his voice that they had never heard before. They ran, skidding on the ice-glazed rock, stopping only at the barrier of his outstretched arm.

'What do you make of it?' Hautamaki asked, never taking

195

his eyes from the squat machine fixed to the rock before them.

There was a central structure, a half sphere of yellowish metal that clamped tight to the rock, its bottom edge conforming to the irregularities beneath it. From this projected stubby arms of the same material, arranged around the circumference close to the base. On each arm was a shorter length of metal. Each one was shaped differently, but all were pointing sky-wards like questing fingers. An arm-thick cable emerged from the side of the hemisphere and crawled over to a higher shelf of rock. There it suddenly straightened and stood straight up, rearing into the air above their heads. Gulyas pointed to this.

'I have no idea what the other parts do, but I'll wager that is the antenna that has been sending out the signals we picked up when we entered this system.'

'It might be,' Hautamaki admitted. 'But what about the rest?'

'One of those things that's pointing up towards the sky looks like a little telescope,' Tjond said. 'I really believe it is.'

Hautamaki gave an angry cry and reached for her as she knelt on the ground, but he was too late. She pressed one eye to the bottom of the tube, squinted the other shut and tried to see.

'Why – yes, it is a telescope!' She opened the other eye and examined the sky. 'I can see the edge of the clouds up there very clearly.'

Gulyas pulled her away, but there was no danger. It was a telescope, as she had said, nothing more. They took turns looking through it. It was Hautamaki who noticed that it was slowly moving.

'In that case – all of the others must be turning too, since they are parallel,' Gulyas said, pointing to the metal devices that tipped each arm. One of them had an eyepiece not unlike the telescope's, but when he looked into it there was only darkness. 'I can't see a thing through it,' he said.

'Perhaps *you* weren't intended to,' Hautamaki said, rub-bing his jaw while he stared at the strange machine, then turned away to rummage in his pack. He took a multi-radiation tester from its padded carrying case and held it before the eyepiece that Gulyas had been trying to look through. 'Infra-red radiation only. Everything else is screened out.'

Another of the tube-like things appeared to focus ultra-violet rays, while an open latticework of metal plates concentrated radio waves. It was Tjond who voiced the thought they all had.

'If I looked through a telescope – perhaps all these other things are telescopes too! Only made for alien eyes, as if the creatures who built the thing didn't know who, or what, would be coming here and provided all kinds of telescopes working on all kinds of wavelengths. The search is over! We ... mankind ... we're not alone in the universe after all!'

'We mustn't leap to conclusions,' Hautamaki said, but the tone of his voice belied his words.

'Why not?' Gulyas shouted, hugging his wife to him in a spasm of emotion. 'Why shouldn't we be the ones to find the aliens? If they exist at all we knew we would come across them some time! The galaxy is immense – but finite. *Look and you shall find.* Isn't that what it says over the entrance to the academy?'

'We have no real evidence yet,' Hautamaki said, trying not to let his own growing enthusiasm show. He was the leader, he must be the devil's advocate. 'This device could have been human made.'

'Point one,' Gulyas said, ticking off on his finger. 'It resembles nothing that any of us have ever seen before. Secondly, it is made of a tough unknown alloy. And thirdly it is in a section of space that, as far as we know, has never been visited before. We are light-centuries from the nearest inhabited system, and ships that can make this sort of trip and return are only a relatively recent development. . . .'

'And here is *real* evidence – without any guesswork!' Tjond shouted, and they ran over to her.

She had followed the heavy cable that transformed itself into the aerial. At the base, where it was thickened and fastened to the rock, were a series of incised characters. There must have been hundreds of them, rising from ground level

197

to above their heads, each one clear and distinct.

'Those aren't human,' Tjond said triumphantly. 'They do not bear the slightest resemblance to any written characters of any language known to man. They are *new*!'

'How can you be sure?' Hautamaki said, forgetting himself enough to address her directly.

'I know, shipmaster, because this is my specialty. I trained in comparative philology and specialized in abbicciology – the study of the history of alphabets. We are probably the only science that is in touch with earth—'

'Impossible.'

'No, just very slow. Earth must be halfway around the galaxy from where we are now. If I remember correctly, it takes about four hundred years for a round-trip communication. Abbicciology is a study that can grow only at the outer fringes; we deal with a hard core of unalterable fact. The old Earth alphabets are part of history and cannot be changed. I have studied them all, every character and every detail, and I have observed their mutations through the millennia. It can be observed that no matter how alphabets are modified and changed they will retain elements of their progenitors. That is the letter "L" as it has been adapted for computer input.' She scratched it into the rock with the tip of her knife, then incised a wavy character next to it. 'And this is the Hebrew *lamedh*, in which you can see the same basic shape. Hebrew is a proto-alphabet, so ancient as to be almost unbelievable. Yet there is the same right-angle bend. But these characters – there is *nothing* there that I have ever seen before.'

The silence stretched on while Hautamaki looked at her, studied her as if the truth or falsity of her words might be written somehow on her face. Then he smiled.

'I'll take your word for it. I'm sure you know your field very well.' He walked back to his pack and began taking out more test instruments.

'Did you see that,' Tjond whispered in her husband's ear, 'he *smiled* at me.'

'Nonsense. It is probably the first rictus of advanced frostbite.'

Hautamaki had hung a weight from the barrel of the telescope and was timing its motion over the ground. 'Gulyas,' he asked, 'do you remember this planet's period of rotation?'

'Roughly eighteen standard hours. The computation wasn't exact. Why?'

'That's close enough. We are at about 85 degrees north latitude here, which conforms to the angle of those rigid arms, while the motion of these scopes . . .'

'Counteracts the planet's rotation, moving at the same speed in the opposite direction. Of course! I should have seen it.'

'What are you two talking about?' Tjond asked.

'They point to the same spot in the sky all the time,' Gulyas said. 'To a star.'

'It could be another planet in this system,' Hautamaki said, then shook his head. 'No, there is no reason for that. It is something outside. We will tell after dark.'

They were comfortable in the atmosphere suits and had enough food and water. The machine was photographed and studied from every angle and they theorized on its possible power source. In spite of this the hours dragged by until dusk. There were some clouds, but they cleared away before sunset. When the first star appeared in the darkening sky Hautamaki bent to the ocular of the telescope.

'Just sky. Too light yet. But there is some sort of glowing grid appearing in the field, five thin lines radiating in from the circumference. Instead of crossing they fade as they come to the centre.'

'But they'll point out whatever star is in the centre of the field – without obscuring it?'

'Yes. The stars are appearing now.'

It was a seventh-magnitude star, isolated near the galactic rim. It appeared commonplace in every way except for its location with no nearby neighbours even in stellar terms. They took turns looking at it, marking it so they could not possibly mistake it for any other.

'Are we going there?' Tjond asked, though it was more of a statement than a question that sought an answer.

'Of course,' Hautamaki said.

III

As soon as their ship had cleared atmosphere, Hautamaki sent a message to the nearest relay station. While they waited for an answer they analyzed the material they had.

With each result their enthusiasm grew. The metal was no harder than some of the resistant alloys they used, but its composition was completely different and some unknown process of fabrication had been used that had compacted the surface molecules to a greater density. The characters bore no resemblance to any human alphabet. And the star towards which the instruments had been pointed was far beyond the limits of galactic exploration.

When the message arrived, *signal recorded,* they jumped the ship at once on the carefully computed and waiting course. Their standing instructions were to investigate anything, report everything, and this they were doing. With their planned movements recorded they were free. They, *they*, were going to make a first contact with an alien race – had already made contact with one of its artifacts. No matter what happened now, the honour was irrevocably theirs. The next meal turned naturally into a celebration, and Hautamaki unbent enough to allow other intoxicants as well as wine. The results were almost disastrous.

'A toast!' Tjond shouted, standing and wobbling just a bit.

'To Earth and mankind – no longer alone!'

No longer alone, they repeated, and Hautamaki's face lost some of the party gaiety that it had reluctantly gained.

'I ask you to join me in a toast,' he said, 'to someone you never knew, who should have been here to share this with us.'

'To Kiiskinen,' Gulyas said. He had read the records and knew about the tragedy that was still fresh in Hautamaki's thoughts.

'Thank you. To Kiiskinen.' They drank.

'I wish we could have met him,' Tjond said, a tendril of feminine curiosity tickling at her.

'A fine man,' Hautamaki said, seeming anxious to talk now that the subject had been broached for the first time since the accident. 'One of the very finest. We were twelve years on this ship.'

'Did you have . . . children?' Tjond asked.

'Your curiosity is not fitting,' Gulyas snapped at his wife. 'I think it would be better if we dropped. . .'

Hautamaki held up his hand. 'Please. I understand your natural interest. We Men have settled only a dozen or so planets and I imagine our customs are curious to you; we are only in a minority as yet. But if there is any embarrassment it is all your own. Are you embarrassed about being bi-sexual? Would you kiss your wife in public?'

'A pleasure,' Gulyas said, and did.

'Then you understand what I mean. We feel the same way and at times act the same way, though our society is mono-sexual. It was a natural result of ectogenesis.'

'Not natural,' Tjond said, a touch of colour in her cheeks. 'Ectogenesis needs a fertile ovum. Ova comes from females; an ectogenetic society should logically be a female society. An all-male one is unnatural.'

'Everything we do is unnatural,' Hautamaki told her without apparent anger. 'Man is an environment-changing animal. Every person living away from Earth is living in an "un-natural" environment. Ectogenesis on these terms is no more unnatural than living, as we are now, in a metal hull in an unreal manifestation of space-time. That this ectogenesis should combine the germ plasm from two male cells rather than from an egg and a sperm is of no more relevancy than your vestigial breasts.'

'You are being insulting,' she said, blushing.

'Not in the least. They have lost their function, therefore they are degenerative. You bisexuals are just as natural – or unnatural – as we Men. Neither is viable without the "un-natural" environment that we have created.'

The excitement of their recent discovery still possessed them, and perhaps the stimulants and the anger had lowered Tjond's control. 'Why – how dare you call me unnatural – you—'

'You forget yourself, woman!' Hautamaki boomed, drowning out the word, leaping to his feet. 'You expected to pry into the intimate details of my life and are insulted when I mention some of your own taboos. The Men are better off without your kind!' He drew a deep, shuddering breath, turned on his heel and left the room.

Tjond stayed in their quarters for almost a standard week after that evening. She worked on her analysis of the alien characters and Gulyas brought her meals. Hautamaki did not mention the events, and cut Gulyas off when he tried to apologize for his wife. But he made no protest when she appeared again in the control section, though he reverted to his earlier custom of speaking only to Gulyas, never addressing her directly.

'Did he actually want me to come too?' Tjond asked, closing her tweezers on a single tiny hair that marred the ivory sweep of her smooth forehead and skull. She pulled it out and touched her brow. 'Have you noticed that he really has eyebrows? Right *here*, great shabby things like an atavism. Even hair around the base of his skull. Disgusting. I'll bet you that the Men sort their genes for hirsuteness, it couldn't be accident. You never answered – did he ask for me to be there?'

'You never gave me a chance to answer,' Gulyas told her, a smile softening his words. 'He didn't ask for you by name. That would be expecting too much. But he did say that there would be a full crew meeting at nineteen hours.'

She put a touch of pink make-up on the lobes of her ears and the bottoms of her nostrils, then snapped her cosmetic case shut. 'I'm ready whenever you are. Shall we go see what the shipmaster wants?'

'In twenty hours we'll be breaking out of jump-space,' Hautamaki told them when they had met in the control section. 'There is a very good chance that we will encounter the people – the aliens – who constructed the beacon. Until we discover differently we will assume that they are peacefully inclined. Yes, Gulyas?'

'Shipmaster, there has been a good deal of controversy on

the intentions of any hypothetical race that might be encountered. There has been no real agreement . . .'

'It does not matter. I am shipmaster. The evidence so far indicates a race looking for contact, not conquest. I see it this way. We have a rich and very old culture, so while we have been searching for another intelligent life form we have also been exploring and recording with ships like this one. A poorer culture might be limited in the number of ships that they could apply to this kind of occupation. Therefore the beacons. Many of them could be easily planted by a single ship over a large area of space. There are undoubtedly others. All of them serve to draw attention to a single star, a rendezvous point of some type.'

'This doesn't prove peaceful intentions. It could be a trap.'

'I doubt it. There are far better ways to satisfy warlike tendencies than to set elaborate traps like this. I *think* their intentions are peaceful, and that is the only factor that matters. Until we actually encounter them any action will have to be based on a guess. Therefore I have already jettisoned the ship's armament—'

'You *what*?'

'—and I'll ask you to surrender any personal weapons that you might have in your possession.'

'You're risking our lives – without even consulting us,' Tjond said angrily.

'Not at all,' he answered, not looking at her. 'You risked your own life when you entered the service and took the oath. You will obey my instructions. All weapons here within the hour; I want the ship clean before we break through. We will meet the strangers armed only with our humanity. . . . You may think the Men go naked for some perverse reason, but that is wrong. We have discarded clothes as detrimental to total involvement in our environment, a both practical and symbolic action.'

'You aren't suggesting that *we* remove our clothes as well, are you?' Tjond asked, still angry.

'Not at all. Do as you please. I am just attempting to explain my reasons so we will have some unanimity of action when we encounter the intelligent creatures who built the beacon. Survey knows now where we are. If we do not return, a later contact team will be protected by mankind's complete armoury of death. So we will now give our aliens every opportunity to kill us – if that is what they are planning. Retribution will follow. If they do not have warlike intentions we will make peaceful contact. That, in itself, is reason enough to risk one's life a hundred times over. I don't have to explain to you the monumental importance of such a contact.'

The tension grew as the time for break-through approached. The box of handguns, explosive charges, poisons from the laboratory – even the large knives from the kitchen – had long since been jettisoned. They were all in the control area when the bell pinged softly and they broke through, back into normal space. Here, at the galactic rim, most of the stars were massed to one side. Ahead lay a pit of blackness with a single star glowing.

'That's it,' Gulyas said, swinging back the spectral analyzer, 'but we're not close enough for clear observation. Are we going to take another jump now?'

'No,' Hautamaki said, 'I want a clevs observation first.'

The sensitive clevs screen began to glow as soon as the pressure dropped, darkening slowly. There were occasional bursts of light from their surface as random molecules of air struck them, then this died away. The forward screen deepened to the blackness of outer space and in its centre appeared the image of the star.

'It's impossible!' Tjond gasped from the observer's seat behind them.

'Not impossible,' Hautamaki said. 'Just impossible of natural origin. Its existence proves that what we see can – and has – been constructed. We will proceed.'

The star image burned with unreality. The star itself at the core was normal enough – but how to explain the three interlocking rings that circled it? They had the dimensions of a planetary orbit. Even if they were as tenuous as a comet's tail their construction was an incredible achievement. And what could be the significance of the coloured lights on the rings, apparently orbiting the primary like insane electrons?

The screen sparkled and the image faded.

'It could only be a beacon,' Hautamaki said, removing his helmet. 'It is there to draw attention, as was the radio beacon that drew us to the last planet. What race with the curiosity to build spaceships could possibly resist the attraction of a thing like that?'

Gulyas was feeding the course corrections into the computor. 'It is still baffling,' he said. 'With the physical ability to construct that why haven't they built an exploring fleet to go out and make contacts – instead of trying to draw them in?'

'I hope that we will discover that answer soon. Though it probably lies in whatever composes their alien psychology. To their way of thinking this might be the obvious manner. And you will have to admit that it has worked.'

IV

This time when they made the transition from jump-space the glowing rings of light filled the front ports. Their radio receivers were on, automatically searching the wavelengths.

They burst into sound on a number of bands simultaneously. Gulyas lowered the volume.

'This is the same kind of broadcast we had from the beacon,' he said. 'Very directional. All of the transmissions are coming from that golden planetoid, or whatever it is. It's big, but doesn't seem to have a planetary diameter.'

'We're on our way,' Hautamaki told him. 'I'll take the controls, see if you can get any image on the video circuits.'

'Just interference. But I'm sending out a signal, a view of this cabin. If they have the right equipment there they should be able to analyse our signal and match it. . . . Look, the screen is changing! They're working fast.'

The viewscreen was rippling with colour. Then a picture appeared, blurred, then steadied. Tjond focused and it snapped into clear life. The two men looked, stared. Behind them Tjond gasped.

'At least no snakes or insects, praise fortune for that!'

The being on the screen was staring at them with the same intensity. There was no way to estimate its relative size, but it was surely humanoid. Three long fingers, heavily webbed, with an opposed thumb. Only the upper part of its figure was visible, and this was clothed so that no physical details could be seen. But the being's face stood out clearly on the screen, golden in colour, hairless, with large, almost circular eyes. Its nose, had it been a human one, would be said to be broken, spread over its face, nostrils flaring. This, and the cleft upper lip, gave it a grim appearance to human eyes.

But this yardstick could not be applied. By alien standards it might be beautiful.

'S'bb'thik,' the creature said. The radio beacons carried the matching audio now. The voice was high-pitched and squeaky.

'I greet you as well,' Hautamaki said. 'We both have spoken languages and we will learn to understand each other. But we come in peace.'

'Maybe we do, but I can't say the same thing for these aliens,' Gulyas interrupted. 'Look at screen three.'

This held an enlarged view taken from one of the forward pickups, locked onto the planetoid they were approaching. A group of dark buildings stood out from the golden surface, crowned with a forest of aerials and antennae. Ringed about the building were circular structures mounted with squat tubular devices that resembled heavy-bore weapons. The similarity was increased by the fact that the numerous emplacements had rotated. The open orifices were tracking the approaching ship.

'I'm killing our approach velocity,' Hautamaki said, stabbing the control buttons in rapid sequence. 'Set up a repeater plate here and switch on a magnified view of those weapons. We'll find out their intentions right now.'

Once their motion relative to the golden planetoid had been stopped, Hautamaki turned and pointed to the repeater screen, slowly tapping the image of the weapons. Then he tapped himself on the chest and raised his hands before him, fingers spread wide, empty. The alien had watched this dumb show with glistening, golden eyes. It rocked its head from side to side and repeated Hautamaki's gesture, tapping itself on the chest with its long central finger, then pointed into the screen.

'He understood at once,' Gulyas said. 'Those weapons – they're turning away, sinking out of sight.'

'We'll continue our approach. Are you recording this?'

'Sight, sound, full readings from every instrument. We've been recording since we first saw the star, with the tapes being fed into the armoured vault as you ordered. I wonder what the next step is?'

'They've already taken it – look.'

The image of the alien reached off the screen and brought back what appeared to be a metal sphere that it held lightly in one hand. From the sphere projected a pipe-like extrusion of metal with a lever half way up its length. When the alien pressed the lever they heard a hissing.

'A tank of gas,' Gulyas said. 'I wonder what it is supposed to signify? No – it's not gas. It must be a vacuum. See, the pipe is sucking up those grains sprinkled on the table.' The alien kept the lever depressed until the hissing stopped.

'Ingenious,' Hautamaki said. 'Now we know there is a sample of their atmosphere inside that tank.'

There was no mechanical propulsion visible, but the sphere came swooping up towards their ship where it swung in orbit above the golden planetoid. The sphere stopped, just outside the ship and clearly visible from the viewports, bobbing in a small arc.

'Some sort of force beam,' Hautamaki said, 'though nothing registers on the hull instruments. That's one thing I hope we find out how to do. I'm going to open the outer door on the main hatch.'

As soon as the door opened the sphere swooped and vanished from sight and they saw, through the pickup inside the air lock, that it fell gently to the deck inside. Hautamaki closed the door and pointed to Gulyas.

'Take a pair of insulated gloves and carry that tank to the lab. Run the contents through the usual air examination procedures that we use for testing planetary atmosphere. As soon as you have taken the sample evacuate the tank and fill it with our own air, then throw it out through the lock.'

The analysers worked on the sample of alien air, and presumably the aliens were doing the same with their tank of ship's atmosphere. The analysis was routine and fast, the report appearing in coded form on the panel in control.

'Unbreathable,' Gulyas said, 'at least for us. There seems to be enough oxygen, more than enough, but any of those sulphurated compounds would eat holes through our lungs. They must have rugged metabolisms to inhale stuff like that. One thing for certain, we'll never be in competition for the same worlds. . . .'

'Look! The picture is changing,' Tjond said, drawing their attention back to the viewing screen.

The alien had vanished and the viewpoint appeared to be in space above the planetoid's surface. A transparent bulge on its surface filled the screen and while they watched the alien entered it from below. The scene shifted again, then they were looking at the alien from inside the clear-walled chamber. The alien came toward the pickup, but before reaching it the alien stopped and leaned against what appeared to be thin air.

'There's a transparent wall that divided the dome in half,' Gulyas said. 'I'm beginning to get the idea.'

The pickup panned away from the alien, swept around to the opposite direction where there was an entrance cut into the clear fabric of the wall. The door was open into space.

'That's obvious enough,' Hautamaki said, rising to his feet. 'That central wall must be airtight, so it can be used for a conference chamber. I'll go. Keep a record of everything.'

'It looks like a trap,' Tjond said, fidgeting with her fingers while she looked at the invitingly open door on the screen. 'It will be a risk. . . .'

Hautamaki laughed, the first time they had ever heard him do it, as he climbed into his pressure suit. 'A trap! Do you believe they have gone to all this to set a trap for me? Such ego is preposterous. And if it were a trap – do you think it possible to stay out of it?'

* * *

He pushed himself free of the ship. His suited figure floated away, getting smaller and smaller.

Silently, moving closer together without realizing they did so, they watched the meeting on the screen. They saw Hautamaki drawn gently in through the open doorway until his feet touched the floor. He turned to look as the door closed, while from the radio they heard a hissing, very dimly at first, then louder and louder.

'It sounds like they are pressurizing the room,' Gulyas said.

Hautamaki nodded. 'Yes, I can hear it now, and there is a reading on the external pressure gauge. As soon as it reaches atmospheric normal I'm taking my helmet off.'

Tjond started to protest, but stopped when her husband raised his hand in warning. This was Hautamaki's decision to make.

'Smells perfectably breathable,' Hautamaki said, 'though it has a metallic odour.'

He laid his helmet aside and stripped his suit off. The alien was standing at the partition and Hautamaki walked over until they stood face to face, almost the same height. The alien placed his palm flat against the transparent wall and the human put his hand over the same spot. They met, as close as they could, separated only by a centimetre of substance. Their eyes joined and they stared for a long time, trying to read intent, trying to communicate. The alien turned away first, walking over to a table littered with a variety of objects. It picked up the nearest one and held it for Hautamaki to see. '*Kilt*,' the alien said. It looked like a piece of stone.

Hautamaki for the first time took notice of the table on his side of the partition. It appeared to hold the identical objects as the other table, and the first of these was a lump of ordinary stone. He picked it up.

'Stone,' he said, then turned to the television pickup and the unseen viewers in the ship. 'It appears that a language lesson is first. This is obvious. See that this is recorded separately. Then we can programme the computor for machine translation in case the aliens aren't doing it themselves.'

The language lesson progressed slowly once the stock of simple nouns with physical referents had been exhausted.

Films were shown, obviously prepared long before, showing simple actions, and bit by bit verbs and tenses were exchanged. The alien made no attempt to learn their language, he just worked to ensure accuracy of identity in the words. They were recording too. As the language lesson progressed Gulyas's frown deepened, and he started to make notes, then a list that he checked off. Finally he interrupted the lesson.

'Hautamaki – this is important. Find out if they are just accumulating a vocabulary or if they are feeding a MT with this material.'

The answer came from the alien itself. It turned its head sideways, as if listening to a distant voice, then spoke into a cup-like device at the end of a wire. A moment later Hautamaki's voice spoke out, toneless since each word had been recorded separately.

'I talk through a machine . . . I talk my talk . . . a machine talk your talk to you . . . I am Liem . . . we need have more words in machine before talk well.'

'This can't wait,' Gulyas said. 'Tell them that we want a sample of some of their body cells, any cells at all. It is complex, but try to get it across.'

The aliens were agreeable. They did not insist on a specimen in return, but accepted one. A sealed container brought a frozen sliver of what looked like muscle tissue over to the ship. Gulyas started towards the lab.

'Take care of the recordings,' he told his wife. 'I don't think this will take too long.'

V

It didn't. Within the hour he had returned, coming up so silently that Tjond, intent on listening to the language lesson, did not notice him until he stood next to her.

'Your face,' she said. 'What is wrong? What did you discover?'

He smiled dryly at her. 'Nothing terrible, I assure you. But things are very different from what we supposed.'

210

'What is it?' Hautamaki asked from the screen. He had heard their voices and turned towards the pickup.

'How has the language progressed?' Gulyas asked. 'Can you understand me, Liem?'

'Yes,' the alien said, 'almost all of the words are clear now. But the machine has only a working force of a few thousand words so you must keep your speech simple.'

'I understand. The things I want to say are very simple. First a question. Your people, do they come from a planet orbiting about a star near here?'

'No. We have travelled a long way to this star, searching. My home world is there, among those stars there.'

'Do all your people live on that world?'

'No, we live on many worlds, but we are all children of children of children of people who lived on one world very long ago.'

'Our people have also settled many worlds, but we all come from one world,' Gulyas told him, then looked down at the paper in his hands. He smiled at the alien in the screen before him, but there was something terribly sad about this smile. 'We came originally from a planet named Earth. That is where your people came from too. We are brothers, Liem.'

'What madness is this?' Hautamaki shouted at him, his face swollen and angry. 'Liem is humanoid, not human! It cannot breathe our air!'

'*He* cannot breath our air, or perhaps she,' Gulyas answered quietly. 'We do not use gene manipulation, but we know that it is possible. I'm sure we will eventually discover just how Liem's people were altered to live under the physical conditions they do now. It might have been natural selection and normal mutation, but it seems too drastic a change to be explained that way. But that is not important. *This* is.' He held up the sheets of notes and photographs. 'You can see for yourself. This is the DNR chain from the nucleus of one of my own cells. This is Liem's. They are identical. His people are as human as we are.

'They can't be!' Tjond shook her head in bewilderment. 'Just look at him, he is so different, and their alphabet – what about that? I cannot be wrong about that?'

211

'There is one possibility you did not allow for, a totally independent alphabet. You yourself told me that there is not the slightest similarity between the Chinese ideographs and western letters. If Liem's people suffered a cultural disaster that forced them to completely reinvent writing you would have your alien alphabet. As to the way they look – just consider the thousands of centuries that have passed since mankind left Earth and you will see that his physical differences are minor. Some are natural and some may have been artificially achieved, but germ plasm cannot lie. We are all the sons of man.'

'It is possible,' Liem said, speaking for the first time. 'I am informed that our biologists agree with you. Our points of difference are minor when compared to the points of similarity. Where is this Earth you come from?'

Hautamaki pointed at the sky above them, at the star-filled sweep of the Milky Way, burning with massed stars. 'There, far out there on the other side of the core, roughly half way around the lens of the galaxy.'

'The galactic core explains partially what must have happened,' Gulyas said. 'It is thousands of light-years in diameter and over 10,000 degrees in temperature. We have explored its fringes. No ship could penetrate it or even approach too closely because of the dust clouds that surround it. So we have expanded outwards, slowly circling the rim of the galaxy, moving away from Earth. If we stopped to think about it we should have realized that mankind was moving the other way too, in the opposite direction around the wheel.'

'And sometime we would have to meet,' Liem said. 'Now I greet you, brothers. And I am sad, because I know what this means.'

'We are alone,' Hautamaki said, looking at the massed trillions of stars. 'We have closed the circle and found only ourselves. The galaxy is ours, but we are alone.' He turned about not realizing that Liem, the golden alien – the man – had turned at the same time in the same manner.

They faced outwards, looking at the infinite depth and infinite blackness of intergalactic space, empty of stars. Dimly,

212

distantly, there were spots of light, microscopic blurs against the darkness, not stars but island universes, like the one at whose perimeter they stood.

These two beings were different in many ways: in the air they breathed, the colour of their skins, their languages, mannerisms, cultures. They were as different as the day is from the night: the flexible fabric of mankind had been warped by the countless centuries until they could no longer recognize each other. But time, distance and mutation could not change one thing; they were still men, still human.

'It is certain then,' Hautamaki said, 'we are alone in the galaxy.'

'Alone in *this* galaxy.'

They looked at each other, then glanced away. At that moment they measured their humanness against the same rule and were equal.

For they had turned at the same instant and looked outward into intergalactic space, towards the infinitely remote light that was another island galaxy.

'It will be difficult to get there,' someone said.

They had lost a battle. There was no defeat.

ii   *Big Ancestors and Great Descendants*

Poul Anderson: LORD OF A THOUSAND SUNS   219
F L Wallace: BIG ANCESTOR   251
Roger Dee: THE INTERLOPERS   278
EPILOGUE   296

It was not just starships and communication and pageantry which flashed across the galaxy from planet to planet. It was also a stream of blood. In that stream of blood was born man's genetic inheritance, shaping him even as he shaped his heritage.

As the stream of blood carried the taste of the primaeval ocean from which life was born, it also carried the message from which future life – unimaginable and perhaps incomprehensible to us – would spring.

What is our place in the galaxy? It is a serious question, and no very serious answer is attempted in this volume. Olaf Stapledon attempted a serious answer and for those who are interested his mighty chronicle-novel, *Star Maker*, is strongly recommended. It is the great fictional work about the galaxy and the universe, and the destiny of mankind.

Working in a much lighter vein, Roger Dee and F L Wallace present opposed speculations on the subject. In Dee's story, an Earthman speaks: 'A hundred thousand races from rim to rim of the galaxy – the least of them, so far as Clowdis had seen, older and wiser and infinitely stronger that his own upstart culture – suspended opinion when the T'sai spoke.' The T'sai are the galactic masters. Note how the cyclic pattern once more imposes itself.

At least indirectly, *The Interlopers* is about what we may become, and so forms a fitting conclusion to our history. In contrast, *Big Ancestor* looks back on what we were – and by so doing reflects on our future role in galactic terms. A nice story, and as nasty as they come.

Both these stories run on logic, lubricated by a little prejudice. Whereas *Lord of a Thousand Suns* is an extravagant emotional exercise in the youthful Poul Anderson's best vein. It is crammed full of those mythopoeic archetypes to which our friendly reviewer, previously quoted, made mention. 'I who was Daryesh of Tollogh, lord of a thousand suns and lover of Ilorna the Fair, immortalized noble of the greatest empire the universe has ever seen – I am now trapped in the

217

half-evolved body of a hunted alien, a million years after the death of all which mattered . . .'

We all experience, on one level or another, similar dualities in our being. Perhaps that is what attracts us to galactic empire-building in the first place. The hope of establishing against the loneliness and majesty of the cosmos a few humble warm-blooded, human institutions appeases the two sides of our nature – the individual side which responds with affection to other individuals, and the evolutionary side which we can never properly know, since its time-scale is not ours, as it burns like a green fuse towards whatever remote destiny awaits humankind on whatever remote mountainside.

Blood's a rover, as they say. Where it will take us is anyone's guess.

A Man without a World, this 1,000,000-year-old Daryesh!
Once Lord of a Thousand Suns, now condemned to rove the
spaceways in alien form, searching for love, for life, for the
great lost Vwyrdda.

LORD OF A THOUSAND SUNS

By Poul Anderson

'Yes, you'll find almost anything man has ever imagined,
somewhere out in the Galaxy,' I said. 'There are so damned
many millions of planets, and such a fantastic variety of surface conditions and of life evolving to meet them, and of
intelligence and civilization appearing in that life. Why, I've
been on worlds with fire-breathing dragons, and on worlds
where dwarfs fought things that could pass for the goblins
our mothers used to scare us with, and on a planet where a
race of witches lived – telepathic pseudohypnosis, you know –
oh, I'll bet there's not a tall story or fairy tale ever told which
doesn't have some kind of counterpart somewhere in the universe.'

Laird nodded. 'Uh-huh,' he answered, in that oddly slow
and soft voice of his. 'I once let a genie out of a bottle.'

'Eh? What happened?'

'It killed me.'

I opened my mouth to laugh, and then took a second glance
at him and shut it again. He was just too dead-pan serious
about it. Not poker-faced, the way a good actor can be when
he's slipping over a tall one – no, there was a sudden misery
behind his eyes, and somehow it was mixed with the damned-
est cold humor.

I didn't know Laird very well. Nobody did. He was out
most of the time on Galactic Survey, prowling a thousand
eldritch planets never meant for human eyes. He came back
to the Solar System more rarely and for briefer visits than
anyone else in his job, and had less to say about what he had
found.

A huge man, six-and-a-half feet tall, with dark aquiline
features and curiously brilliant greenish-grey eyes, middle-

aged now though it didn't show except at the temples. He was courteous enough to everyone, but shortspoken and slow to laugh. Old friends, who had known him thirty years before when he was the gayest and most reckless officer in the Solar Navy, thought something during the Revolt had changed him more than any psychologist would admit was possible. But he had never said anything about it, merely resigning his commission after the war and going into Survey.

We were sitting alone in a corner of the lounge. The Lunar branch of the Explorers' Club maintains its building outside the main dome of Selene Center, and we were sitting beside one of the great windows, drinking Centaurian sidecars and swapping the inevitable shop-talk. Even Laird indulged in that, though I suspected more because of the information he could get than for any desire of companionship.

Behind us, the long quiet room was almost empty. Before us, the window opened on the raw magnificence of moonscape, a sweep of crags and cliffs down the crater wall to the riven black plains, washed in the eerie blue of Earth's light. Space blazed above us, utter black and a million sparks of frozen flame.

'Come again?' I said.

He laughed, without much humor. 'I might as well tell you,' he said. 'You won't believe it, and even if you did it'd make no difference. Sometimes I tell the story – alcohol makes me feel like it – I start remembering old times . . .'

He settled farther back in his chair. 'Maybe it wasn't a real genie,' he went on. 'More of a ghost, perhaps. That was a haunted planet. They were great a million years before man existed on Earth. They spanned the stars and they knew things the present civilization hasn't even guessed at. And then they died. Their own weapons swept them away in one burst of fire, and only broken ruins were left – ruins and desert, and the ghost who lay waiting in that bottle.'

I signalled for another round of drinks, wondering what he meant, wondering just how sane that big man with the worn rocky face was. Still – you never know. I've seen things out beyond that veil of stars which your maddest dreams

220

never hinted at. I've seen men carried home mumbling and empty-eyed, the hollow cold of space filling their brains where something had broken the thin taut wall of their reason. They say spacemen are a credulous breed. Before Heaven, they have to be!

'You don't mean New Egypt?' I asked.

'Stupid name. Just because there are remnants of a great dead culture, they have to name it after an insignificant valley of ephemeral peasants. I tell you, the men of Vwyrdda were like gods, and when they were destroyed whole suns were darkened by the forces they used. Why, they killed off Earth's dinosaurs in a day, millions of years ago, and only used one ship to do it.'

'How in hell do you know that? I didn't think the archeologists had deciphered their records.'

'They haven't. All our archeologists will ever know is that the Vwyrddans were a race of remarkably humanoid appearance, with a highly advanced interstellar culture wiped out about a million Earth-years ago. Matter of fact, I don't really know that they did it to Earth, but I do know that they had a regular policy of exterminating the great reptiles of terrestroid planets with an eye to later colonization, and I know that they got this far, so I suppose our planet got the treatment too.' Laird accepted his fresh drink and raised the glass to me. 'Thanks. But now do be a good fellow and let me ramble on in my own way.

'It was – let me see – thirty-three years ago now, when I was a bright young lieutenant with bright young ideas. The Revolt was in full swing then, and the Janyards held all that region of space, out Sagittari way you know. Things looked bad for Sol then – I don't think it's ever been appreciated how close we were to defeat. They were poised to drive right through our lines with their battle-fleets, slash past our frontiers, and hit Earth itself with the rain of hell that had already sterilized a score of planets. We were fighting on the defensive, spread over several million cubic light-years, spread horribly thin. Oh, bad!

'Vwyrdda – New Egypt – had been discovered and some excavation done shortly before the war began. We knew about

221

as much then as we do now. Especially, we knew that the so-called Valley of the Gods held more relics than any other spot on the surface. I'd been quite interested in the work, visited the planet myself, even worked with the crew that found and restored that gravitomagnetic generator – the one which taught us half of what we know now about g-m fields.

'It was my young and fanciful notion that there might be more to be found, somewhere in that labyrinth – and from study of the reports I even thought I knew about what and where it would be. One of the weapons that had novaed suns, a million years ago—

'The planet was far behind the Janyard lines, but militarily valueless. They wouldn't garrison it, and I was sure that such semi-barbarians wouldn't have my idea, especially with victory so close. A one-man sneakboat could get in readily enough – it just isn't possible to blockade a region of space; too damned inhumanly big. We had nothing to lose but me, and maybe a lot to gain, so in I went.

'I made the planet without trouble and landed in the Valley of the Gods and began work. And that's where the fun started.'

Laird laughed again, with no more mirth than before.

There was a moon hanging low over the hills, a great scarred shield thrice the size of Earth's, and its chill white radiance filled the Valley with colorless light and long shadows. Overhead flamed the incredible sky of the Sagittarian regions, thousands upon thousands of great blazing suns swarming in strings and clusters and constellations strange to human eyes, blinking and glittering in the thin cold air. It was so bright that Laird could see the fine patterns of his skin, loops and whorls on the numbed fingers that groped against the pyramid. He shivered in the wind that streamed past him, blowing dust devils with a dry whisper, searching under his clothes to sheathe his flesh in cold. His breath was ghostly white before him, the bitter air felt liquid when he breathed.

Around him loomed the fragments of what must have been a city, now reduced to a few columns and crumbling walls held up by the lava which had flowed. The stones reared high in the unreal moonlight, seeming almost to move as the shadows and the drifting sand passed them. Ghost city. Ghost planet. He was the last life that stirred on its bleak surface.

But somewhere above that surface—

What was it, that descending hum high in the sky, sweeping closer out of stars and moon and wind? Minutes ago the needle on his gravitomagnetic detector had wavered down in the depths of the pyramid. He had hurried up and now stood looking and listening and feeling his heart turn stiff.

No, no, no, – not a Janyard ship, not now – it was the end of everything if they came.

Laird cursed with a hopeless fury. The wind caught his mouthings and blew them away with the scudding sand, buried them under the everlasting silence of the valley. His eyes travelled to his sneakboat. It was invisible against the great pyramid – he'd taken that much precaution, shoveling a low grave of sand over it – but, if they used metal detectors that was valueless. He was fast, yes, but almost unarmed; they could easily follow his trail down into the labyrinth and locate the vault.

Lord if he had led them here – if his planning and striving had only resulted in giving the enemy the weapon which would destroy Earth—

His hand closed about the butt of his blaster. Silly weapon, stupid popgun – what could he do?

Decision came. With a curse, he whirled and ran back into the pyramid.

His flash lit the endless downward passages with a dim bobbing radiance, and the shadows swept above and behind and marched beside, the shadows of a million years closing in to smother him. His boots slammed against the stone floor, *thud-thud-thud* – the echoes caught the rhythm and rolled it boomingly ahead of him. A primitive terror rose to drown his dismay; he was going down into the grave of a thousand millennia, the grave of the gods, and it took all the nerve he had to keep running and never look back. He didn't dare look back.

Down and down and down, past this winding tunnel, along this ramp, through this passageway into the guts of the planet. A man could get lost here. A man could wander in the cold and the dark and the echoes till he died. It had taken him weeks to find his way into the great vault, and only the clues given by Murchison's reports had made it possible at all. Now—

He burst into a narrow ante-chamber. The door he had blasted open leaned drunkenly against a well of night. It was fifty feet high, that door. He fled past it like an ant and came into the pyramid storehouse.

His flash gleamed off metal, glass, substances he could not identify that had lain sealed against a million years till he came to wake the machines. What they were, he did not know. He had energized some of the units, and they had hummed and flickered, but he had not dared experiment. His idea had been to rig an antigrav unit which would enable him to haul the entire mass of it up to his boat. Once he was home, the scientists could take over. But now—

He skinned his teeth in a wolfish grin and switched on the big lamp he had installed. White light flooded the tomb, shining darkly back from the monstrous bulks of things he could not use, the wisdom and techniques of a race which had spanned the stars and moved planets and endured for fifty million years. Maybe he could puzzle out the use of something before the enemy came. Maybe he could wipe them out in one demoniac sweep – just like a stereofilm hero, jeered his mind – or maybe he could simply destroy it all, keep it from Janyard hands.

He should have provided against this. He should have rigged a bomb, to blow the whole pyramid to hell—

With an effort, he stopped the frantic racing of his mind and looked around. There were paintings on the walls, dim with age but still legible, pictographs, meant perhaps for the one who finally found this treasure. The men of New Egypt were shown, hardly distinguishable from humans – dark of skin and hair, keen of feature, tall and stately and robed in living light. He had paid special attention to one representation. It showed a series of actions, like an old time comic-strip – a man taking up a glassy object, fitting it over his head,

224

throwing a small switch. He had been tempted to try it, but – gods, what would it do?

He found the helmet and slipped it gingerly over his skull. It might be some kind of last-ditch chance for him. The thing was cold and smooth and hard, it settled on his head with a slow massiveness that was strangely – *living*. He shuddered and turned back to the machines.

This thing now with the long coil-wrapped barrel – an energy projector of some sort? How did you activate it? Hell-fire, which was the muzzle end?

He heard the faint banging of feet, winding closer down the endless passageways. Gods, his mind groaned. They didn't waste any time, did they?

But they hadn't needed to . . . a metal detector would have located his boat, told them that he was in this pyramid rather than one of the dozen others scattered through the valley. And energy tracers would spot him down here . . .

He doused the light and crouched in darkness behind one of the machines. The blaster was heavy in his hand.

A voice hailed him from outside the door. 'It's useless, Solman. Come out of there!'

He bit back a reply and lay waiting.

A woman's voice took up the refrain. It was a good voice, he thought irrelevantly, low and well modulated, but it had an iron ring to it. They were hard, these Janyards, even their women led troops and piloted ships and killed men.

'You may as well surrender, Solman. All you have done has been to accomplish our work for us. We suspected such an attempt might be made. Lacking the archeological records, we couldn't hope for much success ourselves, but since my force was stationed near this sun I had a boat lie in an orbit around the planet with detectors wide open. We trailed you down, and let you work, and now we are here to get what you have found.'

'Go back,' he bluffed desperately. 'I planted a bomb. Go back or I'll set it off.'

The laugh was hard with scorn. 'Do you think we wouldn't know it if you had? You haven't even a spacesuit on. Come out with your hands up or we'll flood the vault with gas.'

225

Laird's teeth flashed in a snarling grin. 'All right,' he shouted, only half aware of what he was saying. 'All right, you asked for it!'

He threw the switch on his helmet.

It was like a burst of fire in his brain, a soundless roar of splintering darkness. He screamed, half crazy with the fury that poured into him, feeling the hideous thrumming along every nerve and sinew, feeling his muscles cave in and his body hit the floor. The shadows closed in, roaring and rolling, night and death and the wreck of the universe, and high above it all he heard – laughter.

He lay sprawled behind the machine, twitching and whimpering. They had heard him, out in the tunnels, and with slow caution they entered and stood over him and watched his spasms jerk toward stillness.

They were tall and well-formed, the Janyard rebels – Earth had sent her best out to colonize the Sagittarian worlds, three hundred years ago. But the long cruel struggle, conquering and building and adapting to planets that never were and never could be Earth, had changed them, hardened their metal and frozen something in their souls.

Ostensibly it was a quarrel over tariff and trade rights which had led to their revolt against the Empire; actually, it was a new culture yelling to life, a thing born of fire and loneliness and the great empty reaches between the stars, the savage rebellion of a mutant child. They stood impassively watching the body until it lay quiet. Then one of them stooped over and removed the shining glassy helmet.

'He must have taken it for something he could use against us,' said the Janyard, turning the helmet in his hands; 'but it wasn't adapted to his sort of life. The old dwellers here looked human, but I don't think it went any deeper than their skins.'

The woman commander looked down with a certain pity. 'He was a brave man,' she said.

'Wait – he's still alive, ma'm – he's sitting up—'

Daryesh forced the shaking body to hands and knees. He felt its sickness, wretched and cold in throat and nerves and muscles, and he felt the roiling of fear and urgency in the brain. These were enemies. There was death for a world and a civilization here. Most of all, he felt the horrible numbness of the nervous system, deaf and dumb and blind, cut off in its house of bone and peering out through five weak senses . . .

Vwyrdda, Vwyrdda, he was a prisoner in a brain without a telepathy transceiver lobe. He was a ghost reincarnated in a thing that was half a corpse!

Strong arms helped him to his feet. 'That was a foolish thing to try,' said the woman's cool voice.

Daryesh felt strength flowing back as the nervous and muscular and endocrine systems found a new balance, as his mind took over and fought down the gibbering madness which had been Laird. He drew a shuddering breath. Air in his nostrils after – how long? How long had he been dead?

His eyes focused on the woman. She was tall and handsome. Ruddy hair spilled from under a peaked cap, wide-set blue eyes regarded him frankly out of a face sculptured in clean lines and strong curves and fresh young coloring. For a moment he thought of Ilorna, and the old sickness rose – then he throttled it and looked again at the woman and smiled.

It was an insolent grin, and she stiffened angrily. 'Who are you, Solman?' she asked.

The meaning was clear enough to Daryesh, who had his – host's – memory patterns and linguistic habits as well as those of Vwyrdda. He replied steadily, 'Lieutenant John Laird of the Imperial Solar Navy, at your service. And your name?'

'You are exceeding yourself,' she replied with frost in her voice. 'But since I will wish to question you at length . . . I am Captain Joana Rostov of the Janyard Fleet. Conduct yourself accordingly.'

Daryesh looked around him. This wasn't good. He hadn't the chance now to search Laird's memories in detail, but it was clear enough that this was a force of enemies. The rights and wrongs of a quarrel ages after the death of all that had been Vwyrdda meant nothing to him, but he had to learn more of the situation, and be free to act as he chose. Especially since Laird would presently be reviving and start to resist.

The familiar sight of the machines was at once steadying and unnerving. There were powers here which could smash

227

planets! It looked barbaric, this successor culture, and in any event the decision as to the use of this leashed hell had to be his. His head lifted in unconscious arrogance. *His!* For he was the last man of Vwyrdda, and they had wrought the machines, and the heritage was his.

He had to escape.

Joana Rostov was looking at him with an odd blend of hard suspicion and half-frightened puzzlement. 'There's something wrong about you, Lieutenant,' she said. 'You don't behave like a man whose project has just gone to smash. What was that helmet for?'

Daryesh shrugged. 'Part of a control device,' he said easily. 'In my excitement I failed to adjust it properly. No matter. There are plenty of other machines here.'

'What use to you?'

'Oh – all sorts of uses. For instance, that one over there is a nucleonic disintegrator, and this is a shield projector, and—'

'You're lying. You can't know any more about this than we do.'

'Shall I prove it?'

'Certainly not. Come back from there!'

Coldly, Daryesh estimated distances. He had all the superb psychosomatic coordination of his race, the training evolved through millions of years, but the subcellular components would be lacking in this body. Still – he had to take the chance.

He launched himself against the Janyard who stood beside him. One hand chopped into the man's larynx, the other grabbed him by the tunic and threw him into the man beyond. In the same movement, Daryesh stepped over the falling bodies, picked up the machine rifle which one had dropped, and slammed over the switch of the magnetic shield projector with its long barrel.

Guns blazed in the dimness. Bullets exploded into molten spray as they hit that fantastic magnetic field. Daryesh, behind it, raced through the door and out the tunnel.

They'd be after him in seconds, but this was a strong long-legged body and he was getting the feel of it. He ran easily, breathing in coordination with every movement, conserving his strength. He couldn't master control of the involuntary functions yet, the nervous system was too different, but he could last for a long while at this pace.

He ducked into a remembered side passage. A rifle spewed a rain of slugs after him as someone came through the magnetic field. He chuckled in the dark. Unless they had mapped every labyrinthine twist and turn of the tunnels, or had life-energy detectors, they'd never dare trail him. They'd get lost and wander in here till they starved.

Still, that woman had a brain. She'd guess he was making for the surface and the boats, and try to cut him off. It would be a near thing. He settled down to running.

It was long and black and hollow here, cold with age. The air was dry and dusty, little moisture could be left on Vwyrdda. How long has it been? How long has it been?

John Laird stirred back toward consciousness, stunned neurones lapsing into familiar pathways of synapse, the pattern which was personality fighting to restore itself. Daryesh stumbled as the groping mind flashed a random command to his muscles, cursed, and willed the other self back to blankness. Hold on, Daryesh, hold on, a few minutes only—

He burst out of a small side entrance and stood in the tumbled desolation of the valley. The keen tenuous air raked his sobbing lungs as he looked wildly around at sand and stone and the alien stars. New constellations – Gods, it had been a long time! The moon was larger than he remembered, flooding the dead landscape with a frosty argence. It must have spiraled close in all those uncounted ages.

The boat! Hellblaze, where was the boat?

He saw the Janyard ship not far away, a long lean torpedo resting on the dunes, but it would be guarded – no use trying to steal it. Where was this Laird's vessel, then?

Tumbling through a confusion of alien memories, he recalled burying it on the west side . . . No, it wasn't he who had done that but Laird. Damnation, he had to work fast. He plunged around the monstrous eroded shape of the pyramid, found the long mound, saw the moongleam where the wind had blown sand off the metal. What a clumsy pup this Laird was.

He shoveled the sand away from the airlock, scooping with his hands, the breath raw in throat and lungs. Any second now they'd be on him, any instant, and now that they really believed he understood the machines—

The lock shone dully before him, cold under his hands. He spun the outer dog, swearing with a frantic emotion foreign to old Vwyrdda, but that was the habit of his host, untrained psychosomatically, unevolved— There they came!

Scooping up the stolen rifle, Daryesh fired a chattering burst at the group that swarmed around the edge of the pyramid. They tumbled like jointed dolls, screaming in the death-white moonlight. Bullets howled around him and ricocheted off the boat-hull.

He got the lock open as they retreated for another charge. For an instant his teeth flashed under the moon, the cold grin of Daryesh the warrior who had ruled a thousand suns in his day and led the fleets of Vwyrdda.

'Farewell, my lovelies,' he murmured, and the remembered syllables of the old planet were soft on his tongue.

Slamming the lock behind him, he ran to the control room, letting John Laird's almost unconscious habits carry him along. He got off to a clumsy start – but then he was climbing for the sky, free and away—

A fist slammed into his back, tossed him in his pilot chair to the screaming roar of sundered metal. Gods, O gods, the Janyards had fired a heavy ship's gun, they'd scored a direct hit on his engines and the boat was whistling groundward again.

Grimly, he estimated that the initial impetus had given him a good trajectory, that he'd come down in the hills about a hundred miles north of the valley. But then he'd have to run for it, they'd be after him like beasts of prey in their ship – and John Laird would not be denied, muscles were twitching and sinews tightening and throat mumbling insanity as the resurgent personality fought to regain itself. That was one battle he'd have to have out soon!

Well – mentally, Daryesh shrugged. At worst, he could

230

surrender to the Janyards, make common cause with them. It really didn't matter who won this idiotic little war. He had other things to do.

Nightmare. John Laird crouched in a wind-worn cave and looked out over hills lit by icy moonlight. Through a stranger's eyes, he saw the Janyard ship landing near the down-glided wreck of his boat, saw the glitter of steel as they poured out and started hunting. Hunting *him*.

Or was it him any longer, was he more than a prisoner in his own skull? He thought back to memories that were not his, memories of himself thinking thoughts that were not his own, himself escaping from the enemy while he, Laird, whirled in a black abyss of half-conscious madness. Beyond that, he recalled his own life, and he recalled another life which had endured a thousand years before it died. He looked out on the wilderness of rock and sand and blowing dust, and remembered it as it had been, green and fair, and remembered that he was Daryesh of Tollogh, who had ruled over whole planetary systems in the Empire of Vwyrdda. And at the same time he was John Laird of Earth, and two streams of thought flowed through the brain, listening to each other, shouting at each other in the darkness of his skull.

A million years! Horror and loneliness and a wrenching sorrow were in the mind of Daryesh as he looked upon the ruin of Vwyrdda. A million years ago!

Who are you? cried Laird. What have you done to me? And even as he asked, memories which were his own now rose to answer him.

It had been the Erai who rebelled, the Erai whose fathers came from Vwyrdda the fair but who had been strangely altered by centuries of environment. They had revolted against the static rule of the Immortals, and in a century of warfare they had overrun half the Empire and rallied its populations under them. And the Immortals had unleashed their most terrible powers, the sun-smashing ultimate weapons which had lain forbidden in the vaults of Vwyrdda for ten million years. Only – the Erai had known about it. And they had had the weapons too.

In the end, Vwyrdda went under, her fleets broken and her armies reeling in retreat over ten thousand scorched planets. The triumphant Erai had roared in to make an end of the mother world, and nothing in all the mighty Imperial arsenals could stop them now.

Theirs was an unstable culture, it could not endure as that of Vwyrdda had. In ten thousand years or so, they would be gone, and the Galaxy would not have even a memory of that which had been. Which was small help to us, thought Laird grimly, and realized with an icy shock that it had been the thought of Daryesh.

The Vwyrddan's mental tone was, suddenly, almost conversational, and Laird realized what an immensity of trained effort it must have taken to overcome that loneliness of a million years. 'See here, Laird, we are apparently doomed to occupy the same body till one of us gets rid of the other, and it is a body which the Janyards seem to want. Rather than fight each other, which would leave the body helpless, we'd better cooperate.'

'But – Lord, man! What do you think I am? Do you think I want a vampire like you up there in my brain?'

The answer was fierce and cold. 'What of me, Laird? I, who was Daryesh of Tollogh, lord of a thousand suns and lover of Ilorna the Fair, immortalized noble of the greatest empire the universe has ever seen – I am now trapped in the half-evolved body of a hunted alien, a million years after the death of all which mattered. Better be glad I'm here, Laird. I can handle those weapons, you know.'

The eyes looked out over the bleak windy hillscape, and the double mind watched distance-dwarfed forms clambering in the rocks, searching for a trail. 'A hell of a lot of good that does us now,' said Laird. 'Besides, I can hear you thinking, you know, and I can remember your own past thoughts. Sol or Janya, it's the same to you. How do I know you'll play ball with me?'

The answer was instant, but dark with an unpleasant laughter. 'Why – read my mind, Laird! It's your mind too, isn't it?' Then, more soberly: 'Apparently history is repeating itself in the revolt of the barbarians against the mother planet,

232

though on a smaller scale and with a less developed science. I do not expect the result to be any happier for civilization than before. So perhaps I may take a more effective hand than I did before.'

It was ghostly, lying here in the wind-grieved remnants of a world, watching the hunters move through a bitter haze of moonlight, and having thoughts which were not one's own, thoughts over which there was no control. Laird clenched his fists, fighting for stability.

'That's better,' said Daryesh's sardonic mind. 'But relax. Breathe slowly and deeply, concentrate only on the breathing for a while – and then search my mind which is also yours.'

'Shut up! Shut up!'

'I am afraid that is impossible. We're in the same brain, you know, and we'll have to get used to each other's streams of consciousness. Relax, man, lie still; think over the thing which has happened to you and know it for the wonder it is.'

Man, they say, is a time-binding animal. But only the mighty will and yearning of Vwyrdda had ever leaped across the borders of death itself, waited a million years that that which was a world might not die out of all history.

What is the personality? It is not a thing, discreet and material, it is a pattern and a process. The body starts with a certain genetic inheritance and meets all the manifold complexities of environment. The whole organism is a set of re-actions between the two. The primarily mental component, sometimes called the ego, is not separable from the body but can in some ways be studied apart.

The scientists had found a way to save something of that which was Daryesh. While the enemy was blazing and thundering at the gates of Vwyrdda, while all the planet waited for the last battle and the ultimate night, quiet men in laboratories had perfected the molecular scanner so that the pattern of synapses which made up all memory, habit, re-flex, instinct, the continuity of the ego, could be recorded upon the electronic structure of certain crystals. They took the pattern of Daryesh and of none other, for only he of the remaining Immortals was willing. Who else would want a pattern to be repeated, ages after he himself was dead, ages

233

after all the world and all history and meaning were lost? But Daryesh had always been reckless, and Ilorna was dead, and he didn't care much for what happened.

Ilorna, Ilorna! Laird saw the unforgotten image rise in his memory, golden-eyed and laughing, the long dark hair flowing around the lovely suppleness of her. He remembered the sound of her voice and the sweetness of her lips, and he loved her. A million years, and she was dust blowing on the night wind, and he loved her with that part of him which was Daryesh and with more than a little of John Laird . . . O Ilorna . . .

And Daryesh the man had gone to die with his planet, but the crystal pattern which reproduced the ego of Daryesh lay in the vault they had made, surrounded by all the mightiest works of Vwyrdda. Sooner or later, sometime in the infinite future of the universe, someone would come; someone or something would put the helmet on his head and activate it. And the pattern would be reproduced on the neurones, the mind of Daryesh would live again, and he would speak for dead Vwyrdda and seek to renew the tradition of fifty million years. It would be the will of Vwyrdda, reaching across time – But Vwyrdda is *dead*, thought Laird frantically. Vwyrdda is gone – this is a new history – you've got no business telling us what to do!

The reply was cold with arrogance. 'I shall do as I see fit. Meanwhile, I advise that you lie passive and do not attempt to interfere with me.'

'Cram it, Daryesh!' Laird's mouth drew back in a snarl. 'I won't be dictated to by anyone, let alone a ghost.'

Persuasively, the answer came. 'At the moment, neither of us has much choice. We are hunted, and if they have energy trackers – yes, I see they do – they'll find us by this body's thermal radiation alone. Best we surrender peaceably. Once aboard the ship, loaded with all the might of Vwyrdda, our chance should come.'

Laird lay quietly, watching the hunters move closer, and the sense of defeat came down on him like a falling world. What else could he do? What other chance was there?

'All right,' he said at last, audibly. 'All right. But I'll be watching your every thought, understand? I don't think you can stop me from committing suicide if I must.'

'I think I can. But opposing signals to the body will only neutralize each other, leave it helplessly fighting itself. Relax, Laird, lie back and let me handle this. I am Daryesh the warrior, and I have come through harder battles than this.'

They rose and began walking down the hillside with arms lifted. Daryesh's thought ran on, 'Besides – that's a nice-looking wench in command. It could be interesting!'

His laughter rang out under the moon, and it was not the laughter of a human being.

'I can't understand you, John Laird,' said Joana.

'Sometimes,' replied Daryesh lightly, 'I don't understand myself very well – or you, my dear.'

She stiffened a little. 'That will do, Lieutenant. Remember your position here.'

'Oh, the devil with our ranks and countries. Let's be live entities for a change.'

Her glance was quizzical. 'That's an odd way for a Solman to phrase it.'

Mentally, Daryesh swore. Damn this body, anyway! The strength, the fineness of coordination and perception, half the senses he had known, were missing from it. The gross brain structure couldn't hold the reasoning powers he had once had. His thinking was dull and sluggish. He made blunders the old Daryesh would never have committed. And this young woman was quick to see them, and he was a prisoner of John Laird's deadly enemies, and the mind of Laird himself was tangled in thought and will and memory, ready to fight him if he gave the least sign of—

The Solarian's ego chuckled nastily. Easy, Daryesh, easy!

Shut up! his mind snapped back, and he knew drearily that his own trained nervous system would not have been guilty of such a childishly emotional response.

'I may as well tell you the truth, Captain Rostov,' he said aloud. 'I am not Laird at all. Not any more.'

She made no response, merely drooped the lids over her eyes and leaned back in her chair. He noticed abstractedly how long her lashes were – or was that Laird's appreciative mind, unhindered by too much remembrance of Ilorna?

They sat alone, the two of them, in her small cabin aboard the Janyard cruiser. A guard stood outside the door, but it was closed. From time to time they would hear a dull thump or clang as the heavy machines of Vwyrdda were dragged aboard – otherwise they might have been the last two alive on the scarred old planet.

The room was austerely furnished, but there were touches of the feminine here and there – curtains, a small pot of flowers, a formal dress hung in a half-open closet. And the woman who sat across the desk from him was very beautiful, with the loosened ruddy hair streaming to her shoulders and the brilliant eyes never wavering from his. But one slender hand rested on a pistol.

She had told him frankly, 'I want to talk privately with you. There is something I don't understand . . . but I'll be ready to shoot at the first suspicion of a false move. And even if you should somehow overpower me, I'd be no good as a hostage. We're Janyards here, and the ship is more than the life of any one of us.'

Now she waited for him to go on talking.

He took a cigarette from the box on her desk – Laird's habits again – and lit it and took a slow drag of smoke into his lungs. *All right, Daryesh, go ahead. I suppose your idea is the best, if anything can be made to work at all. But I'm listening, remember.*

'I am all that is left of this planet,' he said tonelessly. 'This is the ego of Daryesh, of Tollogh, Immortal of Vwyrdda, and in one sense I died a million years ago.'

She remained quiet, but he saw how her hands clenched and he heard the sharp small hiss of breath sucked between the teeth.

Briefly, then, he explained how his mental pattern had been preserved, and how it had entered the brain of John Laird.

'You don't expect me to believe that story,' she said contemptuously.

'Do you have a lie detector aboard?'

'I have one in this cabin, and I can operate it myself.' She

236

got up and fetched the machine from a cabinet. He watched her, noticing the grace of her movements. *You died long ago, Ilorna – you died and the universe will never know another like you. But I go on, and she reminds me somehow of you.*

It was a small black thing that hummed and glowed on the desk between them. He put the metal cap on his head, and took the knobs in his hands, and waited while she adjusted the controls. From Laird's memories, he recalled the principle of the thing, the measurement of activity in separate brain centers, the precise detection of the slight extra energy needed in the higher cerebral cortex to invent a falsehood.

'I have to calibrate,' she said. 'Make up something I know to be a lie.'

'New Egypt has rings,' he smiled, 'which are made of Limburger cheese. However, the main body of the planet is a delicious Camembert—'

'That will do. Now repeat your previous statements.'

Relax, Laird, damn it – blank yourself! I can't control this thing with you interfering.

He told his story again in a firm voice, and meanwhile he was working within the brain of Laird, getting the feel of it, applying the lessons of nerve control which had been part of his Vwyrddan education. It should certainly be possible to fool a simple electronic gadget, to heighten activity in all centers to such an extent that the added effort of his creative cells could not be spotted.

He went on without hesitation, wondering if the flickering needles would betray him and if her gun would spit death into his heart in the next moment: 'Naturally, Laird's personality was completely lost, its fixed patterns obliterated by the superimposition of my own. I have his memories, but otherwise I am Daryesh of Vwyrdda, at your service.'

She bit her lip. 'What service! You shot four of my men.'

'Consider my situation, woman. I came into instantaneous existence. I remember sitting in the laboratory under the scanner, a slight dizziness, and then immediately I was in an alien body. Its nervous system was stunned by the shock of my entry, I couldn't think clearly. All I had to go on was

Laird's remembered conviction that these were deadly foes surrounding me, murderous creatures bent on killing me and wiping out my planet. I acted half-instinctively. Also, I wanted, in my own personality, to be a free agent, to get away and think this out for myself. So I did. I regret the death of your men, but I think they will be amply compensated for.'

'H'm – you surrendered when we all but had you anyway.'

'Yes, of course, but I had about decided to do so in all events.' Her eyes never lifted from the dials that wavered life or death. 'I was, after all, in your territory, with little or no hope of getting clear, and you were the winning side of this war, which meant nothing to me emotionally. Insofar as I have any convictions in this matter, it is that the human race will best be served by a Janyard victory. History has shown that when the frontier cultures – which the old empire calls barbaric but which are actually new and better adapted civilizations – when they win out over the older and more conservative nations, the result is a synthesis and a period of unusual achievement.'

He saw her visibly relaxing, and inwardly he smiled. It was so easy, so easy. They were such children in this later age. All he had to do was hand her a smooth lie which fitted in with the propaganda that had been her mental environment from birth, and she could not seriously think of him as an enemy.

The blue gaze lifted to his, and the lips were parted. 'You will help us?' she whispered.

Daryesh nodded. 'I know the principles and construction and use of those engines, and in truth there is in them the force that molds planets. Your scientists would never work out the half of all that there is to be found. I will show you the proper operation of them all.' He shrugged. 'Naturally, I will expect commensurate rewards. But even altruistically speaking, this is the best thing I can do. Those energies should remain under the direction of one who understands them, and not be misused in ignorance. That could lead to unimaginable catastrophes.'

238

Suddenly she picked up her gun and shoved it back into its holster. She stood up, smiling, and held out her hand.

He shook it vigorously, and then bent over and kissed it. When he looked up, she stood uncertain, half afraid and half glad.

It's not fair! protested Laird. The poor girl has never known anything of this sort. She's never heard of coquetry. To her love isn't a game, it's something mysterious and earnest and decent—

I told you to shut up, answered Daryesh coldly. Look, man, even if we do have an official safe-conduct, this is still a ship full of watchful hostility. We have to consolidate our position by every means at hand. Now relax and enjoy this.

He walked around the desk and took her hands again. 'You know,' he said, and the crooked smile on his mouth reminded him that this was more than half a truth, 'you make me think of the woman I loved, a million years ago on Vwyrdda.'

She shrank back a little. 'I can't get over it,' she whispered. 'You – you're old, and you don't belong to this cycle of time at all, and what you must think and know makes me feel like a child – Daryesh, it frightens me.'

'Don't let it, Joana,' he said gently. 'My mind is young, and very lonely.' He put a wistfulness in his voice. 'Joana, I need someone to talk to. You can't imagine what it is to wake up a million years after all your world is dead, more alone than – oh, let me come in once in a while and talk to you, as one friend to another. Let's forget time and death and loneliness. I need someone like you.'

She lowered her eyes, and said with a stubborn honesty, 'I think that would be good too, Daryesh. A ship's captain doesn't have friends, you know. They put me in this service because I had the aptitude, and that's really all I've ever had. Oh, comets!' She forced a laugh. 'To space with all that self-pity. Certainly you may come in whenever you like. I hope it'll be often.'

They talked for quite a while longer, and when he kissed her goodnight it was the most natural thing in the universe.

239

He walked to his bunk – transferred from the brig to a tiny unused compartment – with his mind in pleasant haze.

Lying in the dark, he began the silent argument with Laird anew. 'Now what?' demanded the Solarian.

'We play it slow and easy,' said Daryesh patiently – as if the fool couldn't read it directly in their common brain. 'We watch our chance, but don't act for a while yet. Under the pretext of rigging the energy projectors for action, we'll arrange a setup which can destroy the ship at the flick of a switch. They won't know it. They haven't an inkling about subspatial flows. Then, when an opportunity to escape offers itself, we throw that switch and get away and try to return to Sol. With my knowledge of Vwyrddan science, we can turn the tide of the war. It's risky – sure – but it's the only chance I see. And for Heaven's sake let me handle matters. You're supposed to be dead.'

'And what happens when we finally settle this business? How can I get rid of you?'

'Frankly, I don't see any way to do it. Our patterns have become too entangled. The scanners necessarily work on the whole nervous system. We'll just have to learn to live together.' Persuasively: 'It will be to your own advantage. Think, man! We can do as we choose with Sol. With the Galaxy. And I'll set up a life-tank and make us a new body to which we'll transfer the pattern, a body with all the intelligence and abilities of a Vwyrddan, and I'll immortalize it. Man, you'll never die!'

It wasn't too happy a prospect, thought Laird skeptically. His own chances of dominating that combination were small. In time, his own personality might be completely absorbed by Daryesh's greater one.

Of course – a psychiatrist – narcosis, hypnosis—

'No you don't!' said Daryesh grimly. 'I'm just as fond of my individuality as you are.'

The mouth which was theirs twisted wryly in the dark. 'Guess we'll just have to learn to love each other,' thought Laird.

The body dropped into slumber. Presently Laird's cells were asleep, his personality faded into a shadowland of

dreams. Daryesh remained awake a while longer. Sleep –
waste of time – the Immortals had never been plagued by
fatigue—

He chuckled to himself. What a web of lies and counterlies
he had woven. If Joana and Laird both knew—

The mind is an intricate thing. It can conceal facts from itself,
make itself forget that which is painful to remember, persuade its own higher components of whatever the subconscious deems right. Rationalization, schizophrenia, autohypnosis, they are but pale indications of the self-deception which
the brain practices. And the training of the Immortals included full neural coordination; they could consciously utilize
the powers latent in themselves. They could by an act of conscious will stop the heart, or block off pain, or split their own
personalities.

Daryesh had known his ego would be fighting whatever
host it found, and he had made preparations before he was
scanned. Only a part of his mind was in full contact with
Laird's. Another section, split off from the main stream of
consciousness by deliberate and controlled schizophrenia, was
thinking its own thoughts and making its own plans. Self-
hypnotized, he automatically reunited his ego at such times
as Laird was not aware, otherwise there was only subconscious
contact. In effect a private compartment of his mind, inaccessible to the Solarian, was making its own plans.

That destructive switch would have to be installed to satisfy
Laird's waking personality, he thought. But it would never
be thrown. For he had been telling Joana that much of the
truth – his own advantage lay with the Janyards, and he meant
to see them through to final victory.

It would be simple enough to get rid of Laird temporarily.
Persuade him that for some reason it was advisable to get
dead drunk. Daryesh's more controlled ego would remain
conscious after Laird's had passed out. Then he could make
all arrangements with Joana, who by that time should be
ready to do whatever he wanted.

Psychiatry – yes, Laird's brief idea had been the right one.
The methods of treating schizophrenia could, with some

modifications, be applied to suppressing Daryesh's extra personality. He'd blank out that Solarian . . . permanently.

And after that would come his undying new body, and centuries and millennia in which he could do what he wanted with this young civilization.

The demon exorcising the man – He grinned drowsily. Presently he slept.

The ship drove through a night of stars and distance. Time was meaningless, was the position of the hands on a clock, was the succession of sleeps and meals, was the slow shift in the constellations as they gulped the light-years.

On and on, the mighty drone of the second-order drive filling their bones and their days, the round of work and food and sleep and Joana. Laird wondered if it would ever end. He wondered if he might not be the Flying Dutchman, outward bound for eternity, locked in his own skull with the thing that had possessed him. At such times the only comfort was in Joana's arms. He drew of the wild young strength of her, and he and Daryesh were one. But afterward—

'We're going to join the Grand Fleet. You heard her, Daryesh. She's making a triumphal pilgrimage to the gathered power of Janya, bringing the invincible weapons of Vwyrdda to her admiral.

Why not? She's young and ambitious, she wants glory as much as you do. What of it?'

We have to escape before she gets there. We have to steal a lifeboat and destroy this ship and all in it soon.

All in it? Joana Rostov, too?

Damn it, we'll kidnap her or something. You know I'm in love with the girl, you devil. But it's a matter of all Earth. This one cruiser has enough stuff in it now to wreck a planet. I have parents, brothers, friends – a civilization. We've got to act!

All right, all right, Laird. But take it easy. We have to get the energy devices installed first. We'll have to give them enough of a demonstration to allay their suspicions. Joana's the only one aboard here who trusts us. None of her officers do.

The body and the double mind labored as the slow days passed, directing Janyard technicians who could not understand what it was they built. Laird, drawing on Daryesh's memories, knew what a giant slept in those coils and tubes and invisible energy-fields. Here were forces to trigger the great creative powers of the universe and turn them to destruction – distorted space-time, atoms dissolving into pure energy, vibrations to upset the stability of force-fields which maintained order in the cosmos. Laird remembered the ruin of Vwyrdda, and shuddered.

They got a projector mounted and operating, and Daryesh suggested that the cruiser halt somewhere that he could prove his words. They picked a barren planet in an uninhabited system and lay in an orbit fifty thousand miles out. In an hour Daryesh had turned the facing hemisphere into a sea of lava.

'If the dis-fields were going,' he said absent-mindedly, 'I'd pull the planet into chunks for you.'

Laird saw the pale taut faces around him. Sweat was shining on foreheads, and a couple of men looked sick. Joana forgot her position enough to come shivering into his arms.

But the visage she lifted in a minute was exultant and eager, with the thoughtless cruelty of a swooping hawk. 'There's an end of Earth, gentlemen!'

'Nothing they have can stop us,' murmured her exec dazedly. 'Why, this one ship, protected by one of those space-warp screens you spoke of, sir – this one little ship could sail in and lay the Solar System waste.'

Daryesh nodded. It was entirely possible. Not much energy was required, since the generators of Vwyrdda served only as catalysts releasing fantastically greater forces. And Sol had none of the defensive science which had enabled his world to hold out for a while. Yes, it could be done.

He stiffened with the sudden furious thought of Laird: *That's it, Daryesh! That's the answer.*

The thought-stream was his own too, flowing through the same brain, and indeed it was simple. They could have the whole ship armed and armored beyond the touch of Janya. And since none of the technicians aboard understood the machines, and since they were now wholly trusted, they could install robotcontrols without anyone's knowing.

Then – the massed Grand Fleet of Janya – a flick of the main switch – man-killing energies would flood the cruiser's interior, and only corpses would remain aboard. Dead men and the robots that would open fire on the Fleet. This one ship could ruin all the barbarian hopes in a few bursts of incredible flame. And the robots could then be set to destroy her as well, lest by some chance the remaining Janyards manage to board her.

And we – we can escape in the initial confusion, Daryesh. We can give orders to the robot to spare the captain's gig, and we can get Joana aboard and head for Sol! There'll be no one left to pursue!

Slowly, the Vwyrddan's thought made reply: A good plan. Yes, a bold stroke. We'll do it!

'What's the matter, Daryesh?' Joana's voice was suddenly anxious. 'You look—'

'Just thinking, that's all. Never think, Captain Rostov. Bad for the brain.'

Later, as he kissed her, Laird felt ill at thought of the treachery he planned. Her friends, her world, her cause – wiped out in a single shattering blow, and he would have struck it. He wondered if she would speak to him ever again, once it was over.

Daryesh, the heartless devil, seemed only to find a sardonic amusement in the situation.

And later, when Laird slept, Daryesh thought that the young man's scheme was good. Certainly he'd fall in with it. It would keep Laird busy till they were at the Grand Fleet rendezvous. And after that it would be too late. The Janyard victory would be sealed. All he, Daryesh, had to do when the time came was keep away from that master switch. If Laird tried to reach it their opposed wills would only result in nullity – which was victory for Janya.

He liked this new civilization. It had a freshness, a vigor and hopefulness which he could not find in Laird's memories of Earth. It had a tough-minded purposefulness that would get it far. And being young and fluid, it would be

244

amenable to such pressures of psychology and force as he chose to apply.

Vwyrdda, his mind whispered. Vwyrdda, we'll make them over in your image. You'll live again!

Grand Fleet!

A million capital ships and their auxiliaries lay marshaled at a dim red dwarf of a sun, massed together and spinning in the same mighty orbit. Against the incandescent whiteness of stars and the blackness of the old deeps, armored flanks gleamed like flame as far as eyes could see, rank after rank, tier upon tier, of titanic sharks swimming through space — guns and armor and torpedoes and bombs and men to smash a planet and end a civilization. The sight was too big, imagination could not make the leap, and the human mind had only a dazed impression of vastness beyond vision.

This was the great spearhead of Janya, a shining lance poised to drive through Sol's thin defense lines and roar out of the sky to rain hell on the seat of empire. They can't really be human any more, thought Laird sickly. Space and strangeness have changed them too much. No human being could think of destroying Man's home. Then, fiercely: All right Daryesh. This is our chance!

Not yet, Laird. Wait a while. Wait till we have a legitimate excuse for leaving the ship.

Well — come up to the control room with me. I want to stay near that switch. Lord, Lord, everything that is Man and me depends on us now!

Daryesh agreed with a certain reluctance that faintly puzzled the part of his mind open to Laird. The other half, crouching deep in his subconscious, knew the reason: It was waiting the posthypnotic signal, the key event which would trigger its emergence into the higher brain-centers.

The ship bore a tangled and unfinished look. All its conventional armament had been ripped out and the machines of Vwyrdda installed in its place. A robot brain, half-alive in its complexity, was gunner and pilot and ruling intelligence of the vessel now, and only the double mind of one man knew what orders had really been given it. *When the main*

245

switch is thrown, you will flood the ship with ten units of disrupting radiation. Then, when the captain's gig is well away, you will destroy this fleet, sparing only that one boat. When no more ships in operative condition are in range, you will activate the disintegrators and dissolve this whole vessel and all its contents to basic energy.

With a certain morbid fascination, Laird looked at that switch. An ordinary double-throw knife type – Lord of space, could it be possible, was it logical that all history should depend on the angle it made with the control panel? He pulled his eyes away, stared out at the swarming ships and the greater host of the stars, lit a cigaret with shaking hands, paced and sweated and waited.

Joana came to him, a couple of crewmen marching solemnly behind. Her eyes shone and her cheeks were flushed and the turret light was like molten copper in her hair. No woman, thought Laird, had ever been so lovely, and he was going to destroy that to which she had given her life.

'Daryesh!' Laughter danced in her voice. 'Daryesh, the high admiral wants to see us in his flagship. He'll probably ask for a demonstration, and then I think the fleet will start for Sol at once with us in the van. Daryesh – oh, Daryesh, the war is almost over!'

Now! blazed the thought of Laird, and his hand reached for the main switch. Now – easily, casually, with a remark about letting the generators warm up – and then go with her, overpower those guardsmen in their surprise and head for home!

And Daryesh's mind reunited itself at that signal, and the hand froze . . .

No!

What? But—

The memory of the suppressed half of Daryesh's mind was open to Laird, and the triumph of the whole of it, and Laird knew that his defcat was here.

So simple, so cruelly simple – Daryesh could stop him, lock the body in a conflict of wills, and that would be enough. For while Laird slept, while Daryesh's own major ego was uncon-

246

scious, the trained subconscious of the Vwyrddan had taken over. It had written, in its self-created somnambulism, a letter to Joana explaining the whole truth, and had put it where it would easily be found once they started looking through his effects in search of an explanation for his paralysis. And the letter directed, among other things, that Daryesh's body should be kept under restraint until certain specified methods known to Vwyrddan psychiatry – drugs, electric waves, hypnosis – had been applied to eradicate the Laird half of his mind.

Janyard victory was near.

'Daryesh!' Joana's voice seemed to come from immensely far away; her face swam in a haze and a roar of fainting consciousness. 'Daryesh, what's the matter? Oh, my dear, what's wrong?'

Grimly, the Vwyrddan thought: Give up, Laird. Surrender to me, and you can keep your ego. I'll destroy that letter. See, my whole mind is open to you now – you can see that I mean it honestly this time. I'd rather avoid treatment if possible, and I do owe you something. But surrender now, or be wiped out of your own brain.

Defeat and ruin – and nothing but slow distorting death as a reward for resistance. Laird's will caved in, his mind too chaotic for clear thought. Only one dull impulse came: I give up. You win, Daryesh.

The collapsed body picked itself off the floor. Joana was bending anxiously over him. 'Oh, what is it, what's wrong?'

Daryesh collected himself and smiled shakily. 'Excitement will do this to me, now and then. I haven't fully mastered this alien nervous system yet. I'm all right now. Let's go.'

Laird's hand reached out and pulled the switch over.

Daryesh shouted, an animal roar from the throat, and tried to recover it, and the body toppled again in a stasis of locked wills.

It was like a deliverance from hell, and still it was but the inevitable logic of events, as Laird's own self reunited. Half of him still shaking with defeat, half realizing its own victory, he thought savagely:

None of them noticed me do that. They were paying too

247

much attention to my face. Or if they did, we've proved to them before that it's only a harmless regulating switch. And – the lethal radiations are already flooding us! If you don't cooperate now, Daryesh, I'll hold us here till we're both dead!

So simple, so simple. Because, sharing Daryesh's memory, Laird had shared his knowledge of self-deception techniques. He had anticipated, with the buried half of his mind, that the Vwyrddan might pull some such trick, and had installed a posthypnotic command of his own. In a situation like this, when everything looked hopeless, his conscious mind was to surrender, and then his subconscious would order that the switch be thrown.

Cooperate, Daryesh! You're as fond of living as I. Cooperate, and let's get the hell out of here!

Grudgingly, wryly: You win, Laird.

The body rose again, and leaned on Joana's arm, and made its slow way toward the boat blisters. The undetectable rays of death poured through them, piling up their cumulative effects. In three minutes, a nervous system would be ruined.

'Too slow, too slow. Come on, Joana. Run!'

'Why—' She stopped, and a hard suspicion came into the faces of the two men behind her. 'Daryesh – what do you mean? What's come over you?'

'Ma'm . . .' One of the crewmen stepped forward. 'Ma'm, I wonder . . . I saw him pull down the main switch. And now he's in a hurry to leave the ship. And none of us really know how all that machinery ticks.'

Laird pulled the gun out of Joana's holster and shot him. The other gasped, reaching for his own side arm, and Laird's weapon blazed again.

His fist leaped out, striking Joana on the angle of the jaw, and she sagged. He caught her up and started to run.

A pair of crewmen stood in the corridor leading to the boats. 'What's the matter, sir?' one asked.

'Collapsed – radiation from the machines – got to get her to a hospital ship,' gasped Daryesh.

They stood aside, wonderingly, and he spun the dogs of

248

the blister valve and stepped into the gig. 'Shall we come, sir?' asked one of the men.

'No!' Laird felt a little dizzy. The radiation was streaming through him, and death was coming with giant strides. 'No—' He smashed a fist into the insistent face, slammed the valve back, and vaulted to the pilot's chair.

The engines hummed, warming up. Fists and feet battered on the valve. The sickness made him retch.

O Joana, if this kills you—

He threw the main-drive switch. Acceleration jammed him back as the gig leaped free.

Staring out the ports, he saw fire blossom in space as the great guns of Vwyrdda opened up.

My glass was empty. I signalled for a refill and sat wondering just how much of the yarn one could believe.

'I've read the histories,' I said slowly. 'I do know that some mysterious catastrophe annihilated the massed fleet of Janya and turned the balance of the war. Sol speared in and won inside of a year. And you mean that you did it?'

'In a way. Or Daryesh did. We were acting as one personality, you know. He was a thoroughgoing realist, and the moment he saw his defeat he switched wholeheartedly to the other side.'

'But – Lord, man! Why've we never heard anything about this? You mean you never told anyone, never rebuilt any of those machines, never did anything?'

Laird's dark, worn face twisted in a bleak smile. 'Certainly. This civilization isn't ready for such things. Even Vwyrdda wasn't, and it'll take us millions of years to reach their stage. Besides, it was part of the bargain.'

'Bargain?'

'Just as certainly. Daryesh and I still had to live together, you know. Life under suspicion of mutual trickery, never trusting your own brain, would have been intolerable. We reached an agreement during that long voyage back to Sol, and used Vwyrddan methods of autohypnosis to assure that it could not be broken.'

He looked somberly out at the lunar night. 'That's why I

249

said the genie in the bottle killed me. Inevitably, the two personalities merged, became one. And that one was, of course, mostly Daryesh, with overtones of Laird.

'Oh, it isn't so horrible. We retain the memories of our separate existences, and the continuity which is the most basic attribute of the ego. In fact, Laird's life was so limited, so blind to all the possibilities and wonder of the universe, that I don't regret him very often. Once in a while I still get nostalgic moments and have to talk to a human. But I always pick one who won't know whether or not to believe me, and won't be able to do much of anything about it if he should.'

'And why did you go into Survey?' I asked, very softly.

'I want to get a good look at the universe before the change. Daryesh wants to orient himself, gather enough data for a sound basis of decision. When we – I – switch over to the new immortal body, there'll be work to do, a galaxy to remake in a newer and better pattern by Vwyrddan standards! It'll take millennia, but we've got all time before us. Or I do – what do I mean, anyway?' He ran a hand through his gray-streaked hair.

'But Laird's part of the bargain was that there should be as nearly normal a human life as possible until this body gets inconveniently old. So—' He shrugged. 'So that's how it worked out.'

We sat for a while longer, saying little, and then he got up. 'Excuse me,' he said. 'There's my wife. Thanks for the talk.'

I saw him walk over to greet a tall, handsome red-haired woman. His voice drifted back: 'Hello, Joana—'

They walked out of the room together in perfectly ordinary and human fashion.

I wonder what history has in store for us.

*Man's family tree was awesome enough to give every galactic
race an inferiority complex – but then he tried to climb it!*

BIG ANCESTOR

By F L Wallace

In repose, Taphetta the Ribboneer resembled a fancy giant
bow on a package. His four flat legs looped out and in, the
ends tucked under his wide, thin body, which constituted
the knot at the middle. His neck was flat, too, arching out in
another loop. Of all his features, only his head had appreci-
able thickness and it was crowned with a dozen long though
narrower ribbons.

Taphetta rattled the head fronds together in a surprisingly
good imitation of speech. 'Yes, I've heard the legend.'

'It's more than a legend,' said Sam Halden, biologist. The
reaction was not unexpected – non-humans tended to dismiss
the data as convenient speculation and nothing more. 'There
are at least a hundred kinds of humans, each supposedly
originating in strict seclusion on as many widely scattered
planets. Obviously there was no contact throughout the ages
before space travel – *and yet each planetary race can interbreed with a minimum of ten others!* That's more than a
legend – one hell of a lot more!'

'It is impressive,' admitted Taphetta. 'But I find it mildly
distasteful to consider mating with someone who does not
belong to my species.'

'That's because you're unique,' said Halden. 'Outside of
your own world, there's nothing like your species, except
superficially, and that's true of all other creatures, intelligent
or not, with the sole exception of mankind. Actually, the
four of us here, though it's accidental, very nearly represent
the biological spectrum of human development.

'Emmer, a Neanderthal type and our archaeologist, is
around the beginning of the scale. I'm from Earth, near the
middle, though on Emmer's side. Meredith, linguist, is on

the other side of the middle. And beyond her, toward the far end, is Kelburn, mathematician. There's a corresponding span of fertility. Emmer just misses being able to breed with my kind, but there's a fair chance that I'd be fertile with Meredith and a similar though lesser chance that her fertility may extend to Kelburn.'

Taphetta rustled his speech ribbons quizzically. 'But I thought it was proved that some humans did originate on one planet, that there was an unbroken line of evolution that could be traced back a billion years.'

'You're thinking of Earth,' said Halden. 'Humans require a certain kind of planet. It's reasonable to assume that, if men were set down on a hundred such worlds, they'd seem to fit in with native life-forms on a few of them. That's what happened on Earth; when Man arrived, there was actually a manlike creature there. Naturally our early evolutionists stretched their theories to cover the facts they had.

'But there are other worlds in which humans who were there before the Stone Age aren't related to anything else there. We have to conclude that Man didn't originate on any of the planets on which he is now found. Instead, he evolved elsewhere and later was scattered throughout this section of the Milky Way.'

'And so, to account for the unique race that can interbreed across thousands of light-years, you've brought in the big ancestor,' commented Taphetta dryly. 'It seems an unnecessary simplification.'

'Can you think of a better explanation?' asked Kelburn. 'Something had to distribute one species so widely and it's not the result of parallel evolution – not when a hundred human races are involved, and *only* the human race.'

'I can't think of a better explanation.' Taphetta rearranged his ribbons. 'Frankly, no one else is much interested in Man's theories about himself.'

It was easy to understand the attitude. Man was the most numerous though not always the most advanced – Ribboneers had a civilization as high as anything in the known section of the Milky Way, and there were others – and humans were more than a little feared. If they ever got together – but they hadn't except in agreement as to their common origin.

Still, Taphetta the Ribboneer was an experienced pilot and could be very useful. A clear statement of their position was essential in helping him make up his mind. 'You've heard of the adjacency mating principle?' asked Sam Halden.

'Vaguely. Most people have if they've been around men.'

'We've got new data and are able to interpret it better. The theory is that humans who can mate with each other were once physically close. We've got a list of all our races arranged in sequence. If planetary race F can mate with race E back to A and forward to M, and race G is fertile only back to B, but forward to O, then we assume that whatever their positions are now, at one time G was actually adjacent to F, but was a little further along. When we project back into time those star systems on which humans existed prior to space travel, we get a certain pattern. Kelburn can explain it to you.'

The normally pink body of the Ribboneer flushed slightly. The colour change was almost imperceptible, but it was enough to indicate that he was interested.

Kelburn went to the projector. 'It would be easier if we knew all the stars in the Milky Way, but though we've explored only a small portion of it, we can reconstruct a fairly accurate representation of the past.'

He pressed the controls and stars twinkled on the screen. 'We're looking down on the plane of the Galaxy. This is one arm of it as it is today and here are the human systems.' He pressed another control and, for purposes of identification, certain stars became more brilliant. There was no pattern, merely a scattering of stars. 'The whole Milky Way is rotating. And while stars in a given region tend to remain together, there's also a random motion. Here's what happens when we calculate the positions of stars in the past.'

Flecks of light shifted and flowed across the screen. Kelburn stopped the motion.

'Two hundred thousand years ago,' he said.

253

There was a pattern of the identified stars. They were spaced at fairly equal intervals along a regular curve, a horseshoe loop that didn't close, though if the ends were extended, the lines would have crossed.

Taphetta rustled. 'The math is accurate?'

'As accurate as it can be with a million-plus body problem.'

'And that's the hypothetical route of the unknown ancestor?'

'To the best of our knowledge,' said Kelburn. 'And whereas there are humans who are relatively near and not fertile, they can always mate with those they were adjacent to *two hundred thousand years ago!*'

'The adjacency mating principle. I've never seen it demonstrated,' murmured Taphetta, flexing his ribbons. 'Is that the only era that satisfies the calculations?'

'Plus or minus a hundred thousand years, we can still get something that might be the path of a spaceship attempting to cover a representative section of territory,' said Kelburn. 'However, we have other ways of dating it. On some worlds on which there are no other mammals, we're able to place the first human fossils chronologically. The evidence is sometimes contradictory, but we believe we've got the time right.'

Taphetta waved a ribbon at the chart. 'And you think that where the two ends of the curve cross is your original home?'

'We think so,' said Kelburn. 'We've narrowed it down to several cubic light years – then. Now it's far more. And, of course, if it were a fast-moving star, it might be completely out of the field of our exploration. But we're certain we've got a good chance of finding it this trip.'

'It seems I must decide quickly.' The Ribboneer glanced out the visionport, where another ship hung motionless in space beside them. 'Do you mind if I ask other questions?'

'Go ahead,' Kelburn invited sardonically. 'But if it's not math, you'd better ask Halden. He's the leader of the expedition.'

Halden flushed; the sarcasm wasn't necessary. It was true that Kelburn was the most advanced human type present, but while there were differences, biological and in the scale of intelligence, it wasn't as great as once was thought. Anyway, non-humans weren't trained in the fine distinctions that men made among themselves. And, higher or lower, he was as good a biologist as the other was a mathematician. And there was the matter of training; he'd been on several expeditions and this was Kelburn's first trip. Damn it, he thought, that rated some respect.

The Ribboneer shifted his attention. 'Aside from the sudden illness of your pilot, why did you ask for me?'

'We didn't. The man became sick and required treatment we can't give him. Luckily, a ship was passing and we hailed it because it's four months to the nearest planet. They consented to take him back and told us that there was a passenger on board who was an experienced pilot. We have men who could do the job in a makeshift fashion, but the region we're heading for, while mapped, is largely unknown. We'd prefer to have an expert – and Ribboneers are famous for their navigational ability.'

Taphetta crinkled politely at the reference to his skill. 'I had other plans, but I can't evade professional obligations, and an emergency such as this should cancel out any previous agreements. Still, what are the incentives?'

Sam Halden coughed. 'The usual, plus a little extra. We've copied the Ribboneer's standard nature, simplifying it a little and adding a per cent here and there for the crew pilot and scientist's share of the profits from any discoveries we may make.'

'I'm complimented that you like our contract so well,' said Taphetta, 'but I really must have our own unsimplified version. If you want me, you'll take my contract. I came prepared.' He extended a tightly bound roll that he had kept somewhere on his person.

They glanced at one another as Halden took it.

'You can read it if you want,' offered Taphetta. 'But it will take you all day – it's micro printing. However, you needn't be afraid that I'm defrauding you. It's honoured everywhere we go and we go nearly everywhere in this sector – places men have never been.'

There was no choice if they wanted him, and they did.

Besides, the integrity of Ribboneers was not to be questioned. Halden signed.

'Good,' Taphetta crinkled. 'Send it to the ship; they'll forward it for me. And you can tell the ship to go on without me.' He rubbed his ribbons together. 'Now if you'll get me the charts, I'll examine the region toward which we're heading.'

Firmon of hydroponics slouched in, a tall man with scanty hair and an equal lack of grace. He seemed to have difficulty in taking his eyes off Meredith, though, since he was a notch or so above her in the mating scale, he shouldn't have been so interested. But his planet had been inexplicably slow in developing and he wasn't completely aware of his place in the human hierarchy.

Disdainfully, Meredith adjusted a skirt that, a few inches shorter, wouldn't have been a skirt at all, revealing, while doing so, just how long and beautiful a woman's legs could be. Her people had never given much thought to physical modesty and, with legs like that, it was easy to see why.

Muttering something about primitive women, Firmon turned to the biologist. 'The pilot doesn't like our air.'

'Then change it to suit him. He's in charge of the ship and knows more about these things than I do.'

'More than a man?' Firmon leered at Meredith and, when she failed to smile, added plaintively, 'I did try to change it, but he still complains.'

Halden took a deep breath. 'Seems all right to me.'

'To everybody else, too, but the tapeworm hasn't got lungs. He breathes through a million tubes scattered over his body.'

It would do no good to explain that Taphetta wasn't a worm, that his evolution had taken a different course, but that he was in no sense less complex than Man. It was a paradox that some biologically higher humans hadn't developed as much as lower races and actually weren't prepared for the multitude of life-forms they'd meet in space. Firmon's reaction was quite typical.

'If he asks for cleaner air, it's because his system needs it,'

256

said Halden. 'Do anything you can to give it to him.'

'Can't. This is as good as I can get it. Taphetta thought you could do something about it.'

'Hydroponics is your job. There's nothing *I* can do.' Halden paused thoughtfully. 'Is there something wrong with the plants?'

'In a way, I guess, and yet not really.'

'What is it, some kind of toxic condition?'

'The plants are healthy enough, but something's chewing them down as fast as they grow.'

'Insects? There shouldn't be any, but if there are, we've got sprays. Use them.'

'It's an animal,' said Firmon. 'We tried poison, and got a few, but now they won't touch the stuff. I had electronics rig up some traps. The animals seem to know what they are and we've never caught one that way.'

Halden glowered at the man. 'How long has this been going on?'

'About three months. It's not bad; he can keep up with them.'

It was probably nothing to become alarmed at, but an animal on the ship was a nuisance, doubly so because of this pilot.

'Tell me what you know about it,' said Halden.

'They're little things.' Firmon held out his hands to show how small. 'I don't know how they got on, but once they did, there were plenty of places to hide.' He looked up defensively. 'This is an old ship with new equipment and they hide under the machinery. There's nothing we can do except rebuild the ship from the hull inward.'

Firmon was right. The new equipment had been installed in any place just to get it in and now there were inaccessible corners and crevices everywhere that couldn't be closed off without rebuilding.

They couldn't set up a continuous watch and shoot the animals down because there weren't that many men to spare. Besides, the use of weapons in hydroponics would cause more damage to the thing they were trying to protect than to the pest. He'd have to devise other ways.

257

Sam Halden got up. 'I'll take a look and see what I can do.'

'I'll come along and help,' said Meredith, untwining her legs and leaning against him. 'Your mistress ought to have some sort of privileges.'

Halden started. So she *knew* that the crew was calling her that! Perhaps it was intended to discourage Firmon, but he wished she hadn't said it. It didn't help the situation at all.

Taphetta sat in a chair designed for humans. With a less flexible body, he wouldn't have fitted. Maybe it wasn't sitting, but his flat legs were folded neatly around the arms and his head rested comfortably on the seat. The head ribbons, which were his hands and voice, were never quite still.

He looked from Halden to Emmer and back again. 'The hydroponics tech tells me you're contemplating an experiment. I don't like it.'

Halden shrugged. 'We've got to have better air. It might work.'

'Pests on the ship? It's filthy! My people would never tolerate it!'

'Neither do we.'

The Ribboneer's distaste subsided. 'What kind of creatures are they?'

'I have a description, though I've never seen one. It's a small four-legged animal with two antennae at the lower base of its skull. A typical pest.'

Taphetta rustled. 'Have you found out how it got on?'

'It was probably brought in with the supplies,' said the biologist. 'Considering how far we have come, it may have been any one of a half a dozen planets. Anyway, it hid, and since most of the places it had access to were near the outer hull, it got an extra dose of hard radiation, or it may have nested near the atomic engines; both are possibilities. Either way, it mutated, became a different animal. It's developed a tolerance for the poisons we spray on plants. Other things it detects and avoids, even electronic traps.'

'Then you believe it changed mentally as well as physically, that it's smarter?'

'I'd say that, yes. It must be a fairly intelligent creature to

258

be so hard to get rid of. But it can be lured into traps, if the bait's strong enough.'

'That's what I don't like,' said Taphetta, curling. 'Let me think it over while I ask questions.' He turned to Emmer. 'I'm curious about humans. Is there anything else you can tell me about the hypothetical ancestor?'

Emmer didn't look like the genius he was – a Neanderthal genius, but nonetheless a real one. In his field, he rated very high. He raised a stubble-flecked cheek from a large thick-fingered paw and ran shaggy hands through shaggier hair.

'I can speak with some authority,' he rumbled. 'I was born on a world with the most extensive relics. As a child, I played in the ruins of their camp.'

'I don't question your authority,' crinkled Taphetta. 'To me, all humans – late or early and male or female – look remarkably alike. If you are an archeologist, that's enough for me.' He paused and flicked his speech ribbons. 'Camp, did you say?'

Emmer smiled, unsheathing great teeth. 'You've never seen any pictures? Impressive but just a camp, monolithic one-story structures, and we'd give something to know what they're made of. Presumably my world was one of the first they stopped at. They weren't used to roughing it, so they built more elaborately than they did later on. One-story structures and that's how we can guess at their size. The doorways were forty feet high.'

'Very large,' agreed Taphetta. It was difficult to tell whether he was impressed. 'What did you find in the ruins?'

'Nothing,' said Emmer. 'There were buildings there and that was all, not a scrap of writing or a tool or a single picture. They covered a route estimated at thirty thousand light-years in less than five thousand years – and not one of them died that we have a record of.'

'A faster-than-light drive and an extremely long life,' mused Taphetta. 'But they didn't leave any information for their descendants. Why?'

'Who knows?' Their mental processes were certainly far different from ours. They may have thought we'd be better

259

off without it. We do know they were looking for a special kind of planet, like Earth, because they visited so many of that type, yet different from it because they never stayed. They were pretty special people themselves, big and long-lived, and maybe they couldn't survive on any planet they found. Perhaps they had ways of determining there wasn't the kind of planet they needed in the entire Milky Way. Their science was tremendously advanced and when they learned that, they may have altered their germ plasm and left us, hoping that some of us would survive. Most of us did.'

'This special planet sounds strange,' murmured Taphetta.

'Not really,' said Emmer. 'Fifty human races reached space travel independently and those who did were scattered equally among early and late species. It's well known that individuals among my people are often as bright as any of Halden's or Meredith's, but as a whole we don't have the total capacity that later Man does, and yet we're as advanced in civilization. The difference? It must lie somewhere in the planets we live on and it's hard to say just what it is.'

'What happened to those who didn't develop space travel?' asked Taphetta.

'We helped them,' said Emmer.

And they had, no matter who or what they were, biologically late or early, in the depths of the bronze age or the threshold of atomic – because they were human. That was sometimes a frightening thing for non-humans, that the race stuck together. They weren't actually aggressive, but their total number was great and they held themselves aloof. The unknown ancestor again. Who else had such an origin and, it was tacitly assumed, such a destiny?

Taphetta changed his questioning. 'What do you expect to gain from this discovery of the unknown ancestor?'

It was Halden who answered him. 'There's the satisfaction of knowing where we came from?'

'Of course,' rustled the Ribboneer. 'But a lot of money and equipment was required for this expedition. I can't believe that the educational institutions that are backing you did so purely out of intellectual curiosity.'

260

'Cultural discoveries,' rumbled Emmer. 'How did our ancestors live? When a creature is greatly reduced in size, as we are, more than physiology is changed – the pattern of life itself is altered. Things that were easy for them are impossible for us. Look at their life span.'

'No doubt,' said Taphetta. 'An archeologist would be interested in cultural discoveries.'

'Two hundred thousand years ago, they had an extremely advanced civilization,' added Halden. 'A faster-than-light drive, and we've achieved that only within the last thousand years.'

'But I think we have a better one than they did,' said the Ribboneer. 'There may be things we can learn from them in mechanics or physics, but wouldn't you say they were better biologists than anything else?'

Halden nodded. 'Agreed. They couldn't find a suitable planet. So, working directly with their germ plasm, they modified themselves and produced us. They *were* master biologists.'

'I thought so,' said Taphetta. 'I never paid much attention to your fantastic theories before I signed to pilot this ship, but you've built up a convincing case.' He raised his head, speech ribbons curling fractionally and ceaselessly. 'I don't like to, but we'll have to risk using bait for your pest.'

He'd have done it anyway, but it was better to have the pilot's consent. And there was one question Halden wanted to ask; it had been bothering him vaguely. 'What's the difference between the Ribboneer contract and the one we offered you? Our terms are more liberal.'

'To the individual, they are, but it won't matter if you discover as much as you think you will. The difference is this: *My* terms don't permit you to withhold any discovery for the benefit of one race.'

Taphetta was wrong; there had been no intention of withholding anything. Halden examined his own attitudes. *He* hadn't intended, but could he say that was true of the institutions backing the expedition? He couldn't, and it was too late now – whatever knowledge they acquired would have to be shared.

261

That was what Taphetta had been afraid of – there was one kind of technical advancement that multiplied unceasingly. The race that could improve itself through scientific control of its germ plasm had a start that could never be headed. The Ribboneer needn't worry now.

'Why do we have to watch it on the screen?' asked Meredith, glancing up. 'I'd rather be in hydroponics.'

Halden shrugged. 'They may or may not be smarter than planetbound animals, but they're warier. They don't come out when anyone's near.'

Lights dimmed in the distant hydroponic section and the screen with it, until he adjusted the infra-red frequencies. He motioned to the two crew members, each with his own peculiar screen, below which was a miniature keyboard.

'Ready?'

When they nodded, Halden said: 'Do as you've rehearsed. Keep noise at a minimum, but when you do use it, be vague. Don't try to imitate them exactly.'

At first, nothing happened on the big screen, and then a grey shape crept out. It slid through leaves, listened intently before coming forward. It jumped off one hydroponic section and fled across the open floor to the next. It paused, eyes glittering and antennae twitching.

Looking around once, it leaped up, seizing the ledge and clawing up the side of the tank. Standing on top and rising to its haunches, it began nibbling what it could reach.

Suddenly it whirled. Behind it and hitherto unnoticed was another shape, like it but larger. The newcomer inched forward. The small one retreated, skittering nervously. Without warning, the big one leaped and the small one tried to flee. In a few jumps, the big one caught up and mauled the other unmercifully.

It continued to bite even after the little one lay still. At last it backed off and waited, watching for signs of motion. There was none. Then it turned to the plant. When it had chewed off everything within reach, it climbed into the branches.

The little one twitched, moved a leg, and cautiously began

262

dragging itself away. It rolled off the raised section and surprisingly made no noise as it fell. It seemed to revive, shaking itself and scurrying away, still within range of the screen.

Against the wall was a small platform. The little one climbed on top and there found something that seemed to interest it. It sniffed around and reached and felt the discovery. Wounds were forgotten as it snatched up the object and frisked back to the scene of its recent defeat.

This time it had no trouble with the raised section. It leaped and landed on top and made considerable noise in doing so. The big animal heard and twisted around. It saw and clambered down hastily, jumping the last few feet. Squealing, it hit the floor and charged.

The small one stood still till the last instant – and then a paw flickered out and an inch-long knife blade plunged into the throat of the charging creature. Red spurted out as the bigger beast screamed. The knife flashed in and out until the big animal collapsed and stopped moving.

The small creature removed the knife and wiped it on the pelt of its foe. Then it scampered back to the platform on which the knife had been found – *and laid it down*.

At Halden's signal, the lights flared up and the screen became too bright for anything to be visible.

'Go in and get them,' said Halden. 'We don't want the pests to find out that the bodies aren't flesh.'

'It was realistic enough,' said Meredith as the crewmen shut off their machines and went out. 'Do you think it will work?'

'It might. We had an audience.'

'Did we? I didn't notice.' Meredith leaned back. 'Were the puppets exactly like the pests? And if not, will the pests be fooled?'

'The electronic puppets were a good imitation, but the animals don't have to identify them as their species. If they're smart enough, they'll know the value of a knife, no matter who uses it.'

'What if they're smarter? Suppose they know a knife can't be used by a creature without real hands?'

'That's part of our precautions. They'll never know until they try – and they'll never get away from the trap to try.'

'Very good. I never thought of that,' said Meredith, coming closer. 'I like the way your primitive mind works. At times I actually think of marrying you.'

'Primitive,' he said, alternately frozen and thawed, though he knew that, in relation to her, he was *not* advanced.

'It's almost a curse, isn't it?' She laughed and took the curse away by leaning provocatively against him. 'But barbaric lovers are often nice.'

Here we go again, he thought drearily, sliding his arm around her. To her, I'm merely a passionate savage.

They went to his cabin.

She sat down, smiling. Was she pretty? Maybe. For her own race, she wasn't tall, only by Terran standards. Her legs were disproportionately long and well shaped and her face was somewhat bland and featureless, except for a thin, straight, short nose. It was her eyes that made the difference, he decided. A notch or two up the scale of visual development, her eyes were larger and she could see an extra colour of the violet end of the spectrum.

She settled back and looked at him. 'It might be fun living with you on primeval Earth.'

He said nothing; she knew as well as he that Earth was as advanced as her own world. She had something else in mind.

'I don't think I will, though. We might have children.'

'Would it be wrong?' he asked. 'I'm as intelligent as you. We wouldn't have subhuman monsters.'

'It would be a step up – for you.' Under her calm, there was tension. It had been there as long as he'd known her, but it was closer to the surface now. 'Do I have the right to condemn the unborn? Should I make them start lower than I am?'

The conflict was not new nor confined to them. In one form or another, it governed personal relations between races that were united against non-humans, but held sharp distinctions themselves.

'I haven't asked you to marry me,' he said bluntly.

264

'Because you're afraid I'd refuse.'

It was true; no one asked a member of a higher race to enter a permanent union.

'Why did you ever have anything to do with me?' demanded Halden.

'Love,' she said gloomily. 'Physical attraction. But I can't let it lead me astray.'

'Why not make a play for Kelburn? If you're going to be scientific about it, he'd give you children of the higher type.'

'Kelburn.' It didn't sound like a name, the way she said it. 'I don't like him and he wouldn't marry me.'

'He wouldn't, but he'd give you children if you were humble enough. There's a fifty per cent chance you might conceive.'

She provocatively arched her back. Not even the women of Kelburn's race had a body like hers and she knew it.

'Racially, there should be a chance,' she said. 'Actually, Kelburn and I would be infertile.'

'Can you be sure?' he asked, knowing it was a poor attempt to act unconcerned.

'How can anyone be sure on a theoretical basis?' she asked, an oblique smile narrowing her eyes. 'I know we can't.'

His face felt anesthetized. 'Did you have to tell me that?'

She got up and came to him. She nuzzled against him and his reaction was purely reflexive. His hand swung out and he could feel the flesh give when his knuckles struck it.

She fell back and dazedly covered her face with her hand. When she took it away, blood spurted. She groped toward the mirror and stood in front of it. She wiped the blood off, examining her features carefully.

'You've broken my nose,' she said factually. 'I'll have to stop the blood and pain.'

She pushed her nose back into place and waggled it to make sure. She closed her eyes and stood silent and motionless. Then she stepped back and looked at herself critically.

'It's set and partially knitted. I'll concentrate tonight and have it healed by morning.'

She felt in the cabinet and attached an invisible strip firmly across the bridge. Then she came over to him.

'I wondered what you'd do. You didn't disappoint me.'

He scowled miserably at her. Her face was almost plain and the bandage, invisible or not, didn't improve her appearance any. How could he still feel that attraction to her?

'Try Emmer,' he suggested tiredly. 'He'll find you irresistible, and he's even more savage than I am.'

'Is he?' She smiled enigmatically. 'Maybe, in a biological sense. Too much, though. You're just right.'

He sat down on the bed. Again there was only one way of knowing what Emmer would do – and she knew. She had no concept of love outside of the physical, to make use of her body so as to gain an advantage – what advantage? – for the children she intended to have. Outside of that, nothing mattered, and for the sake of alloying the lower with the higher, she was as cruel to herself as she was to him. And yet he wanted her.

'I do think I love you,' she said. 'And if love's enough, I may marry you in spite of everything. But you'll have to watch out whose children I have.' She wriggled into his arms.

The racial disparity was great and she had provoked him, but it was not completely her fault. Besides . . .

Besides what? She had a beautiful body that could bear superior children – and they might be his.

He twisted away. With those thoughts, he was as bad as she was. Were they all that way, every one of them, crawling –upward out of the slime toward the highest goal they could conceive of? Climbing over – no, *through* – everybody they could coerce, seduce or marry – onward and upward. He raised his hand, but it was against himself that his anger was turned.

'Careful of the nose,' she said, pressing against him. 'You've already broken it once.'

He kissed her with sudden passion that even he knew was primitive.

There were no immediate results from the puppet performance and so it was repeated at intervals. After the third time,

Firmon reported, coming in as Halden pored over the meager biological data he'd gathered on the unknown ancestor. Wild guesses mostly, not one real fact in all the statistics. After two hundred thousand years, there wasn't much left to work with.

Firmon slouched down. 'It worked,' he said. 'Got three a few hours ago.'

Halden looked at him; he had hoped it wouldn't work. There was satisfaction in being right, but he would rather face something less intelligent. Wariness was one thing, the shyness and slyness of an unseen animal, but intelligence was more difficult to predict.

'Where are they?' he asked.

'Did you want them?' Firmon seemed surprised at the idea.

Halden sighed; it was his own fault. Firmon had a potentially good mind, but he hadn't been trained to use it and that counted for more than people thought. 'Any animal smart enough to appreciate the value of a knife is worth study on that account. That goes double when it's a pest.'

'I'll change the cremation setting,' said Firmon. 'Next time, we'll just stun them.'

The trap setting was changed and several animals were taken. Physically, they were very much as Halden had described them to Taphetta, small four-legged creatures with fleshy antennae. Dissection revealed a fairly large brain capacity, while behaviour tests indicated an intelligence somewhat below what he had assumed. Still, it was more than he wanted a pest to have, especially since it also had hands.

The biological mechanism of the hands was simple. It walked on the back of the front paws, on the fingers of which were fleshy pads. When it sat upright, as it often did, the flexibility of the wrists permitted the forepaws to be used as hands. Clumsy, but because it had a thumb, it could handle such tools as a knife.

He had made an error there. He had guessed the intelligence, but he hadn't known it could use the weapon he had put within reach. A tiny thing with an inch-long knife was not much more dangerous than the animal alone, but he didn't like the idea of it loose on the ship.

The metal knife would have to be replaced with something else. Technicians could compound a plastic that would take a keen edge for a while and deteriorate to a soft mass in a matter of weeks. Meanwhile, he had actually given the animal a dangerous weapon – the concept of a tool. There was only one way to take that away from them, by extermination. But that would have to wait.

Fortunately, the creature had a short life and a shorter breeding period. The actual replacement rate was almost negligible. In attaining intelligence, it had been short-changed in fertility and, as a consequence, only in the specialized environment of this particular ship was it any menace at all.

They were lucky; a slightly higher fertility and the thing could threaten their existence. As it was, the ship would have to be deverminized before it could land on an inhabited planet.

Halden took the data to the Ribboneer pilot and, after some discussion, it was agreed that the plastic knife should supplant the metal one. It was also decided to allow a few to escape with the weapon; there had to be some incentive if the creature was to visit the trap more than a few times. Besides, with weapons there was always the chance of warfare between different groups. They might even exterminate each other.

Gradually, over a period of weeks, the damage to hydroponics subsided; the pests were under control. There was nothing to worry about unless they mutated again, which was unlikely.

Kelburn scowled at the pilot. 'Where are we now?' he challenged, his face creased with suspicion.

'You have access to all the instruments, so you should know,' said Taphetta. He was crouching and seemed about to spring, but he was merely breathing relaxedly through a million air tubes.

'I do know. My calculations show one star as the most probable. We should have reached it two days ago – and we're nowhere near it.'

'True,' admitted Taphetta. 'We're heading toward what you would consider the fifth or sixth most likely star.'

Kelburn caught the implication. They all did. 'Then you know where it is?' he asked, suspicion vanishing.

'Not in the sense you're asking – no, I'm not sure it's what you're looking for. But there was once a great civilization there.'

'You knew this and didn't tell us?'

'Why should I?' Taphetta looked at him in mild astonishment. 'Before you hired me, I wouldn't tell you for obvious reasons. And afterwards – well, you engaged all my skill and knowledge and I used them to bring you here by the shortest route. I didn't think it necessary to tell you until we actually arrived. Is that wrong?'

It wasn't wrong; it merely illustrated the difference in the way an alien mind worked. Sooner or later, they would have found the place, but he had saved them months.

'What's it like?' Emmer asked.

Taphetta jiggled his ribbons. 'I don't know. I was passing near here and saw the planet off to one side.'

'And you didn't stop?' Emmer was incredulous.

'Why should I? We're great navigators because we do so much of it. We would never get very far if we stopped to examine everything that looks interesting. Besides, it's not a good policy in a strange region, especially with an unarmed ship.'

They wouldn't have that problem. The ship was armed well enough to keep off uncivilized marauders who had very recently, reached the spaceship age, and only such people were apt to be inhospitable.

'When will we land?' asked Halden.

'In a few hours, but you can see the planet on our screens.' Taphetta extended a head ribbon toward a knob and a planet came into view.

There weren't two civilizations in the Milky Way that built on such a large scale, even from the distance that they could see it. Great, distinctive cities were everywhere. There was no question as to what they had found.

'Now you'll learn why they ran away,' said Taphetta.

'A new theory,' Kelburn said, though it wasn't, for they *had* left. 'What makes you think they were afraid?'

'No air. If your calculations are right, there must have been an extensive atmosphere a few hundred thousand years ago and now there isn't any. A planet this size doesn't lose air that fast. Therefore, it's an artificial condition. Who takes the trouble to leave a planet uninhabitable except someone who's afraid others will use it – and who else runs away?'

'They may have done it to preserve what they left,' suggested Halden.

'Perhaps,' said Taphetta, but it was obvious he didn't think so.

The lack of air had one thing to recommend it – they needn't worry about their pests escaping. The disadvantage was that they had to wear spacesuits. They landed on top of a great building that was intact after thousands of years and still strong enough to support the added weight. And then—

Then there was nothing.

Buildings, an enormous number and variety of them, huge, not one of them less than five stories high, all with ramps instead of stairs. This was to be expected, considering the great size of the people who had lived there, and it followed the familiar pattern.

But there was nothing in those buildings! On this airless world, there was no decay, no rust or corrosion – *and nothing to decay or corrode*. No pictures, tools, nothing that resembled sculpture, and while there were places where machines had stood, none were there now. Here and there in inaccessible locations were featureless blobs of metal. The implication was clear: Where they hadn't been able to remove a machine, they had melted it down on the spot.

The thoroughness was bewildering. It wasn't done by some enemy; he would have stood off and razed the cities. But there was no rubble and the buildings were empty. The inhabitants themselves had removed all that was worth taking along.

A whole people had packed and moved away, leaving behind only massive, echoing structures.

270

There was plenty to learn, but nothing to learn it from. Buildings can indicate only so much and then there must be something else – at least some of the complex artifacts of a civilization – and there was none. Outside the cities, on the plains, there were the remains of plants and animals that indicated by their condition that airlessness had come suddenly. Sam Halden, the biologist, had examined them, but he discovered no clues. The unknown ancestor was still a mystery.

And the others – Emmer, the archeologist, and Meredith, the linguist – had nothing to work on, though they searched. It was Kelburn who found the first hint. Having no specific task, now that the planet was located, he wandered around in a scout ship. On the other side of the planet, he signaled that there was a machine and that it was intact!

The crew was hurriedly recalled, the equipment brought back into the ship, and they took off for the plain where Kelburn waited.

And there was the machine, immense, like everything on the planet. It stood alone, tapering toward the sky. At the base was a door, which, when open, was big enough to permit a spaceship to enter easily – only it was closed.

Kelburn stood beside the towering entrance, a tiny figure in a spacesuit. He gazed up at it as the three came near. 'All we have to do is open it,' he said.

'How?' asked Meredith. She seemed to have forgotten that she disliked him. He had made a chance discovery because he had nothing to do while the others were busy, but she regarded it as further proof of his superiority.

It was hard to watch the happiness that her face directed toward Kelburn. Halden turned away.

'Just press the button,' he said.

Emmer noticed his expression. 'It's such a big button,' he objected. 'It's going to be hard to know when we find it.'

'There's an inscription of some sort,' said Kelburn loftily. 'This thing was left for a purpose. Somewhere there must be operating instructions.'

'From here, it looks like a complex wave-form,' a voice

271

crinkled in their radio – Taphetta from the spaceship. 'All we have to do is to find the right base in the electromagnetic spectrum and duplicate it on a beam broadcast and the door should open. You're too close to see it as clearly as I can.'

Perhaps they were too close to the big ancestor, decided Halden moodily as they went back. It had overshadowed much of their thinking, and who really knew what the ancestor was like and what had motivated him?

But the Ribboneer was right about the signal, though it took several days to locate it. And then the huge door swung open and air whistled out.

Inside was another disappointment, a bare hall with a ramp leading upward, closed off at the ceiling. They could have forced through, but they had no desire to risk using a torch to penetrate the barrier – in view of the number of precautions they'd already encountered, it was logical to assume that there were more waiting for them.

It was Emmer who found the solution. 'In appearance, it resembles a spaceship. Let's assume it is, minus engines. It was never intended to fly. Listen.

'There's no air, so you can't hear,' said Emmer impatiently. 'But you could if there were air. Put your hands against the wall.'

A distinct vibration ran through the whole structure. It hadn't been there before the door opened. Some mechanism had been triggered. The rumbling went on, came to a stop, and began again. Was it some kind of communication?

Hastily rigged machines were hauled inside the chamber to generate an air supply so that sounds would be produced for the recorders. Translating equipment was set up and focused and, after some experimentation with signals, the door was slowly closed. No one remained inside; there was no guarantee that it would be as easy to get out as it had been to get in.

They waited a day and a half while the sounds were being recorded. The delay seemed endless. The happiest of the crew was Kelburn. Biologically the highest human on the expedition, he was stimulated. He wandered aimlessly and smiled affably, patting Meredith, when he came to her, in the friendliest fashion. Startled, she smiled back and looked around wanly. Halden was behind her.

If I had not been there, thought Halden – and thereafter made it a point to be there.

Meredith was excited, but not precisely happy. The work was out of her hands until the translating equipment was retrieved. As the second highest biological type, she, too, was affected, until she pointedly went to her room and locked it from the inside.

Halden kept himself awake with anti-fatigue pills, in part because Meredith could change her mind about Kelburn, and because of that locked door.

Emmer tried to be phlegmatic and seemed to succeed. Taphetta alone was unconcerned; to him, it was an interesting and perhaps profitable discovery, but important only because of that. He would not be changed at all by whatever he learned.

Hours crawled by and at last the door opened; the air came rushing out again. The translating equipment was brought back to the ship and Meredith was left alone with it.

It was half a day before she admitted the others to the laboratory.

'The machine is still working,' she said. 'There seems to have been some attempt to make the message hard to decode. But the methods they used were exactly the clues that the machine needed to decipher it. My function as a linguist was to help out with the interpretation of key words and phrases. I haven't got even a little part of the message. You'll know what it is as soon as I do. After the first part, the translator didn't seem to have much trouble.'

They sat down facing it— Taphetta, Kelburn, Meredith, Halden and Emmer. Meredith was midway between Kelburn and himself. Was there any significance in that, wondered Halden, or was he reading more in her behaviour than was actually there?

'The translation is complete,' announced the machine.

'Go ahead,' Meredith ordered.

'The words will be speeded up to human tempo,' said the translator. 'Insofar as possible, speech mannerisms of the original will be imitated. Please remember that it is only an imitation, however.'

The translator coughed, stuttered and began. 'We have purposely made access to our records difficult. If you can translate this message, you'll find, at the end, instructions for reaching the rest of our culture relics. As an advanced race, you're welcome to them. We've provided a surprise for anyone else.

'For ourselves, there's nothing left but an orderly retreat to a place where we can expect to live in peace. That means leaving this Galaxy, but because of our life span, we're capable of it and we won't be followed.'

Taphetta crinkled his ribbons in amusement. Kelburn frowned at the interruption, but no one else paid any attention.

The translator went on. 'Our metabolic rate is the lowest of any creature we know of. We live several thousand revolutions of any recorded planet and our rate of increase is extremely low; under the most favourable circumstances, we can do no more than double our numbers in two hundred generations.'

'This doesn't sound as if they were masters of biological science,' rustled Taphetta.

Halden stirred uneasily. It wasn't turning out at all the way he had expected.

'At the time we left,' the message continued, 'we found no other intelligent race, though there were some capable of further evolution. Perhaps our scout ships long ago met your ancestors on some remote planet. We were never very numerous, and because we move and multiply so slowly, we are in danger of being swept out of existence in the forseeable future. We prefer to leave while we can. The reason we must go developed on our own planet, deep beneath the cities, in the underworks, which we had ceased to inspect because there was no need to. This part was built to last a million generations, which is long even for us.'

274

Emmer sat upright, annoyed at himself. 'Of course! There are always sewers and I didn't think of looking there!'

'In the last several generations, we sent out four expeditions, leisurely trips because we then thought we had time to explore thoroughly. With this planet as base of operations, the successive expeditions fanned out in four directions, to cover the most representative territory.'

Kelburn stiffened, mingled pride and chagrin on his face. His math had been correct, as far as he had figured it. But had there been any reason to assume that they would confine their exploration to one direction? No, they would want to cover the whole Milky Way.

Taphetta paled. Four times as many humans to contend with! He hadn't met the other three-fourths yet – and, for him, it wasn't at all a pleasant thought.

'After long preparation, we sent several ships to settle one of the nearer planets that we'd selected on the first expedition. To our dismay, we found that the plague was there – though it hadn't been on our first visit!'

Halden frowned. They were proving themselves less and less expert biologists. And this plague – there had to be a reason to leave, and sickness was as good as any – but unless he was mistaken, plague wasn't used in the strict semantic sense. It might be the fault of the translation.

'The colonists refused to settle; they came back at once and reported. We sent out our fastest ships, heavily armed. We didn't have the time to retrace our path completely, for we'd stopped at innumerable places. What we did was to check a few planets, the outward and return parts of all four voyages. In every place, the plague was there, too, and we knew that we were responsible.

'We did what we could. Exhausting our nuclear armament, we obliterated the nearest planets on each of the four spans of our journeys.'

'*I wondered* why the route came to an end,' crinkled Taphetta, but there was no comment, no answer.

'We reconstructed what had happened. For a long time, the plague had lived in our sewers, subsisting on wastes. At night, because they are tiny and move exceedingly fast, they were able to make their way into our ships and were aboard on every journey. We knew they were there, but because they were so small, it was difficult to dislodge them from their nesting places. And so we tolerated their existence.'

'They weren't so smart,' said Taphetta. 'We figured out that angle long ago. True, our ship is an exception, but we haven't landed anywhere, and won't until we determinize it.'

'We didn't guess that next to the hull in outer space and consequently exposed to hard radiation,' the message went on, 'those tiny creatures would mutate dangerously and escape to populate the planets we landed on. They had always been loathsome little beasts that walked instead of rolling or creeping, but now they became even more vicious, spawning explosively and fighting with the same incessant violence. They had always harboured diseases which spread to us, but now they've become hot-houses for still smaller parasites that also are able to infect us. Finally, we are now allergic to them, and when they are within miles of us, it is agony to roll or creep.'

Taphetta looked around. 'Who would have thought it? You were completely mistaken as to your origin.' Kelburn was staring vacantly ahead, but didn't see a thing. Meredith was leaning against Halden; her eyes were closed. 'The woman has finally chosen, now that she knows she was once vermin,' clicked the Ribboneer. 'But there are tears in her eyes.'

'The intelligence of the beast has advanced slightly, though there isn't much difference between the highest and the lowest – and we have checked both ends of all four journeys. But before, it was relatively calm and orderly. Now it is malignantly insane.'

Taphetta rattled his ribbons. 'Turn it off. You don't have to listen to this. We all are of some origin or other and it wasn't necessarily pretty. This being was a slug of some kind – and are you now what is describes? Perhaps mentally a little, out of pride, but the pride was false.'

* * *

'We can't demolish all the planets we unthinkingly let it loose on; there are too many and it lives too fast. The stars drift and we would lose some, and before we could eliminate the last one, it would develop space travel – it has little intelligence, but it could get that far – and it would escape ahead of us. We know an impossible task when we see it. And so we're leaving, first making sure that this animal will never make use of the products of our civilization. It may reach this planet, but it will not be able to untangle our code – it's too stupid. You who will have to face it, please forgive us. It's the only thing that we're ashamed of.'

'Don't listen,' said the Ribboneer and, bending his broad, thin body, he sprang to the translator, shook it and banged with his ribbons until the machine was silent. 'You don't have to tell anyone,' crackled Taphetta. 'Don't worry about me – I won't repeat it.' He looked around at the faces. 'But I can see that you will report to everyone exactly what you found. That pride you've developed – you'll need it.'

Taphetta sat on top of the machine, looking like nothing so much as a huge fancy bow on a gift-wrapped package.

They noted the resemblance vaguely. But each of them knew that, as a member of the most numerous race in the Milky Way, no longer feared for their mysterious qualities – despised, instead – wherever they went, there would never be any gifts for them – for any man.

There's a great difference between potential and developed power. The one is clearly visible and can be awe-inspiring. The other may take a demigod to recognize.

THE INTERLOPERS

By Roger Dee

For the brief time that the intercepting craft hung on the ship's foreign-body screen, Clowdis felt himself pulled taut as wire with the strain of uncertainty. When the expected finger of the communications beam reached across the distance and he saw the reddish reptilian face of the other commander, and the faces of others like him ranked in the alien control room behind, his sigh of relaxing tension was not an expression of relief but of resignation.

'Korivians,' Vesari said, unnecessarily, from the navigator's place beside him. 'T'sai bodyguards – and from the number of them, there's bound to be some T'sai aboard. We're going to meet the galactic masters at last, Ed.'

Without turning his head, Clowdis called: 'Shassil!'

Their Cetian interpreter came forward at once, his oddly angled body tensing and his narrow goatish face taking on the galactic's inevitable air of deference when he saw the faces on the screen.

'Find out what they want of us,' Clowdis said.

The Cetian touched his beard respectfully – not to himself, Clowdis noted, but to the Korivian captain on the screen – and spoke in a swift rush of sibilance. The Korivian answered in turn, beaked lizard-face expressionless as reddish stone.

Shassil touched his caprine beard again and turned from the screen. 'You are to shut down the ship's engines,' he said to Clowdis, 'and gather all hands below.'

Neither Clowdis nor Vesari, knowing themselves as far out of their depth as kittens in a computing room, considered demanding why. But Vesari paused at the down-spiraling ramp of a companionway and Clowdis, feeling a curiously unreal sense of experiment, paused with him.

278

'What do you think they want, Shassil?' Vesari asked.

The Cetian considered him gravely with long-pupilled eyes. 'When a T'sai is near,' he said, 'I do not think at all.'

A literal truth, Clowdis thought as he went with Vesari down the steep twist of helicline, and not one confined to Shassil nor to Cetians alone. A hundred thousand races from rim to rim of the galaxy – the least of them, so far as Clowdis had seen, older and wiser and infinitely stronger than his own upstart culture – suspended opinion when the T'sai spoke.

As if the T'sai were not flesh like other creatures, but gods. But *were* they flesh?

Clowdis smothered an incipient flare of resentment by reminding himself that he was after all a newt in strange waters, a minnow among sharks.

When in Rome one does as the Romans do, he told himself wryly. *When in space—*

'First things first,' he said aloud. 'We'd better break the news to Buehl in the engine room before we see Barbour and the colonists.'

Powermaster Buehl took the T'sai order with a bellicose impatience that was an index to his temper. A thick-bodied and heavy-minded man of middle age, given when off duty to solitary drinking and deadly serious absorption in his collection of Wagnerian tapes, he was devoted to his atomic charges with a singleness of soul which Clowdis, who had gone to space for the sheer restless love of seeing, had never been able to understand.

'Draw my men from their stations?' Buehl demanded angrily when Clowdis found him at his engine-room desk. 'Damp the piles, kill the ship?'

He had an incredulous mental picture of the ship not driven but drifting, helpless as a crippled fish in treacherous waters, an image sharply defined within the familiar bounds of his power section but growing vaguer when extended to minor reaches of cargo holds and crew quarters and many-tiered bunking cubicles filled with chattering, cow-eyed colonists. Control section and hydroponics, galley and hospital bay did not register at all in Buehl's regard because they lay in the seldom-visited and dispensable upper level; the power that drove the ship like a metal thunderbolt through space was everything to him, and he would no more have throttled it voluntarily in midflight than he would have taken a blade to his own throat.

'This is the moment we've dreaded since we first touched at Sirius ten years ago,' Clowdis reminded him. 'There are *T'sai* out there, Buehl. Get your men to crew quarters on the double, or I'll iron you and put Simmonds on the engines.'

The threat defeated Buehl as no other could have, as Clowdis had known it must. The powermaster gave the order from his desk communicator, but did not follow when his puzzled subordinates filed past him out of the power room. He remained in place, glowering through the uneasy silence that followed the sudden cessation of engine noise, long after the others had gone.

And slowly he began to realize something of the gravity of their position, piecing it together gradually from those accumulated bits of experience that had reality for him. The aesthetic had no existence for Buehl beyond his instinctive response to Wagnerian clamor; the social and economic intricacies of alien cultures left him as unmoved as did those of his own, and for the emotional drives that made men and not-men what they were he had only contempt.

But Buehl respected Power. He thought of it as an entity spelled out in upper-case symbols, a name synonymous with deity.

For Buehl was powermaster in his own sphere, and he had seen power beyond imagining.

His first stunning surmise as to what power could be like had come at the end of man's initial stellar jump – Buehl had been an engine-room member of that original expedition, but the glory of pioneering meant nothing compared to the feeling of mastery over the surging forces under his hands – to the far-swinging Sirian worlds. He recalled vaguely a swarming society of upright anthropoids, disturbingly manlike for all their chitinous jointure and wonderfully, if incuriously, courteous.

Their engines he remembered better.

The Sirians had outgrown atomic energy millennia before.

280

Somehow they tapped the force reservoirs of their giant sun, and a single monolithic station on each planet supplied power that could have pulverized a world but which instead drove their beautifully mechanized economy with the purring smoothness of a fine chronometer.

The Eridanians had used subatomic binding forces to make a perpetual paradise of their single slow-freezing world, and the Cetians, Shassil's people, drew limitless energy from the gravitic strain-currents that permeated space. A single building there housed a power more formidable than the total output of Earth's straining generators.

The hundred thousand other peoples of whom Earthmen had heard, but into whose spatial backyards they had not yet penetrated, had power as great and as varied. And over them all loomed the T'sai, the masters and mentors, the teachers and governors, who owned the secret of instantaneous transfer and who ruled with a word.

What, Buehl wondered, was power to the T'sai?

To the T'sai his own shining converter plant would be more primitive than Hero's steam engine. To them he was not a powermaster but a savage, squatting vacantly over the first-kindled spark of atomic force.

For the first time in his career Buehl, with his beloved engines silent under his feet, felt the frustration of utter insignificance.

Rumors of the emergency had already reached Barbour in his quarters, and he was – as Clowdis had expected, understanding as he did the agile thoroughness of his psychologist-propagandist's mind – busily organizing a program to reassure crew and colonists alike.

'We expected to meet the T'sai eventually,' Barbour said. He was a tall man, stooped and spectacled and balding, his mild light eyes normally veiled with habitual introspection. 'As well get it over with now as later, Ed.'

'They'll know about us from cultures we've visited already,' Clowdis pointed out. 'We're going to be weighed and judged and perhaps fitted into their scheme of things, Frank. The lot we draw is going to be largely up to you.'

281

Barbour sighed. 'I know, Ed, I wish they had caught us earlier, before we started to bring out colonists— we're trespassers to begin with, and to unload our surplus population out here without T'sai permission may prejudice them against us.'

Clowdis shrugged. He had anticipated such a development from the first and had opposed the colonization project; but political pressure at home, the necessity of justifying the enormous expense of interstellar exploration, had defeated his objections.

'We had to make the try, with that perfect oxy-nitrogen planet of Regulus lying unclaimed,' he said. 'And we'll have to do the best we can with the T'sai now.'

Clowdis moved on to the task he hated most, explaining to the colonists what might be expected of them.

Barbour, left alone, took off his spectacles and wiped them thoughtfully, his trained mind running carefully over the possibilities. Barbour, like Clowdis, had come to space under the lash of curiosity; not in his case to satisfy any restless yearning for adventure, but to push his investigations into the minds and manners of alien races as he had pursued them into his own society. The fact that intelligence was galaxy-wide instead of confined to his own insular sphere had fired his imagination from that first flight to Sirius – that that intelligence should follow such divergent paths, yet should always arrive at the same conclusion in the end, at once challenged and perplexed him.

Each culture they had touched, he considered, was older and wiser and immensely more powerful than Earth's, so far superior as to put his own handful in the position of a canoe-load of savages paddling wide-eyed through the harbors of a great city.

Yet these aliens were different after a fashion the nature of which had persistently eluded him.

The galactics traveled widely in pursuit of trade, making jumps of a magnitude inconceivable to an Earthman's mind. They lived in comfort and peace, without want or war, each society presenting a new variation of Utopia which only emphasized the homogeneity of the whole.

The nature of that unity came to Barbour now of itself, and he cursed himself with academic invective for not having seen it earlier.

There was no real progress out here – and had been none, obviously, for millennia. Each culture was balanced precisely to suit the demands of its own peculiar mores, but he had yet to skirt the fringes of an alien philosophy which was not founded on fatalism and *laissez-faire* resignation.

The galaxy was static. And what made it so?

The T'sai.

The realization brought Barbour a feeling of profound depression. So many promising beginnings intercepted and channeled to ultimate mediocrity by the super-race, so many vaulting young ambitions crushed to compliance with superior will!

And Earth?

Earth, Barbour thought, was the newest entrant to this cosmic kindergarten, the downiest yokel coming afoot in brash ignorance daring to blink at the bright lights of civilization. To be monitored and graded and assigned a niche, if found worthy of the trouble, in the T'sai economy.

To Barbour the truth behind the universal resignation he had seen was suddenly and chillingly clear. Why struggle, why toil and sweat for an ideal when the striving is doomed to failure from the start?

Earth, again.

Men, reckless of odds and intolerant of opposition, were never a docile people. Taken in hand by the T'sai, they might resent such regimentation forcibly. And then—

Barbour, like any good psychologist, knew when to drop a line of thought and close his mind to an unpleasant conclusion.

Clowdis was waiting with Shassil and the others at the conference-room table – Vesari fidgeting over an unwanted cigarette, Buehl a little drunk and more surlily taciturn than usual, Barbour humped moodily with his mild eyes fogged in thought – when Wilcox hurried in to take his place.

283

'Sorry to be late,' Wilcox said. His voice betrayed an habitual diffidence, an unconscious surprise that he should have been chosen to sit in consultation with the powers of the ship. 'I've been elected to represent the colonists, sir. I'll do the best I can.'

Clowdis accepted his presence without comment, avoiding his eyes because the man's meekness was somehow offensive to a spaceman's sense of fitness. Wilcox was a small, pale man with neutral hair and troubled eyes, a former hydroponics operator who had sold his job-registry rights in Greater Pittsburgh to raise fare for his wife and himself to Regulus. He had been chosen now, Clowdis knew, for the reason that Wilcox *was* the average colonist – anxious to please, inoffensive and without initiative or ambition beyond his own small interests.

'Good enough,' Clowdis said, and looked across the table at Shassil. 'What can you tell us now, Shassil?'

The Cetian sighed, revealing twin rims of cartilage that served him in lieu of teeth. 'Little, beyond the fact that the T'sai will board us soon for an interview. After that—'

'After that,' Buehl interrupted, 'the little gods of space will give us their word, and the word is Power.' There was a growl in his voice which he did not try to conceal.

'Easy,' Clowdis cautioned, 'we've passed on sufferance so far, Buehl, only because none of the peoples we've visited had orders from the T'sai to stop us. We'd be mad to make trouble now.'

Barbour looked up, his mild eyes sharp with interest. 'You said *the* T'sai, Shassil. Does that mean there's only one of them aboard the Korivian ship?'

The Cetian nodded. 'The T'sai travel seldom, and then singly. But the T'sai are not as we others – to them one is all and all are one.'

He rose from the table. 'My presence constrains conversation, I think. I shall wait for the T'sai in the control room.'

He left, for all his galactic politeness, without touching his beard in the Cetian gesture of respect. Clowdis, thinking of that goatish creature holding solitary sway over *his* control room, felt a quick surge of anger and quelled it as quickly.

284

'He's right, you know,' Barbour said. 'It's our problem, Ed, and we couldn't talk freely with Shassil sitting in.'

'What is there to talk about?' Vesari demanded fretfully. 'If we can't *do* anything, what's the use of talking at all?'

'We're not planning to do anything,' Clowdis pointed out. 'We're only here to assess the possibilities, and to wait.'

'The possibilities are soon numbered,' Barbour said dryly. 'They can kill us or imprison us, send us packing home again or ignore us.'

Clowdis said positively, 'They won't ignore us. I've made a hearsay study of the systems we haven't visited yet, and every one is an integral part of the T'sai realm. Personally, I can't see that we'd fit into such a scheme of things – I think we'll be lucky if they let us go home again.'

'Is it really as bad as that?' Wilcox asked in alarm. The face he turned on Clowdis had gone even paler than usual. 'I mean – we *can't* go back, we colonists. There's no place for us!'

Clowdis kept the annoyance from his face with an effort.

'The conditions of this Regulus expedition were carefully explained before the flight, Wilcox. Your people understood from the start that we were on shaky ground out here. You knew the chances you took when you signed away your job-rights.'

The colonist subsided, blinking. He was thinking at the moment not of galactic rights and powers but of his wife, of the child to be born to them in half a year and of the seventy-odd other couples waiting in the lower level for his report. To be turned back now meant more than a return to the desperately crowded warrens of Earth; with the surrender of their rights they held no status whatever, and the only course open was compulsory migration to a drab and driven existence, infinitely worse, in the domes of Mars or Venus or the moons of Jupiter.

The soft green planet of Regulus that lay short hours ahead was heaven by contrast. To give it up now, when they were so near—

They felt the presence of their inquisitor even before Shassil presented him, the slightest feather-touch of exploratory thought that was like a momentary, not unpleasant, itching at the roots of the mind.

The Cetian interpreter sidled into the conference room with a hand at his beard, his long-pupilled eyes down-cast.

'The T'sai,' Shassil said reverently.

They rose together, incredulous, stunned by the unsuspected possibilities opened by their first sight of a galactic master.

The T'sai was a man.

A small man, smaller by a head than even Wilcox, but looming like a Titan through the aura of power that hung about him.

'You think yourselves worthy of claiming our empty worlds,' the T'sai said. 'Prove it.'

And left them alone with their problem.

'. . . Not of the same species as ourselves,' Barbour said. Even an hour later he found the truth overwhelming, the wonder of it still blinding to reason. 'It's impossible! The straining of coincidence—'

'He's no oxygen breather,' Clowdis said. He felt like a man struggling up from drugged sleep, regaining the sharp use of his senses with slow labor. 'There was a sort of force envelope around him that held his air. The ears were different, and the hair, and he had more than five fingers to the hand . . . I think.'

He turned to Barbour in sudden suspicion. 'You don't think what we saw was an illusion, Frank? A projection of some kind?'

'I doubt that he'd go to the trouble,' Barbour said slowly. 'But it's so hard to realize—'

'Power,' Buehl burst out, astonishing them all until they saw that he had retreated to his own thoughts. 'With such power, they can do anything.'

It was Wilcox, who understood less of the wonder of it but whose problem was more personally immediate, who brought them back to reality.

'Man or not, he left us no better off,' Wilcox said. 'Do you remember what he said, commander?'

Clowdis' brain felt like an eye blinded by a light too powerful to bear, but he remembered.

'He suggested that we prove ourselves worthy of claiming the world we're reaching for.'

'It wasn't a suggestion,' Barbour corrected. 'It had the sound of an order, Ed. And he said *worlds*.'

'Power,' Buehl muttered. He stared hungrily at fingers that twitched for the feel of bottle and glass.

The others sat lost in blank surmise.

'He as much as said we'd have a free hand out here if we can prove ourselves,' Vesari said. 'What scares me is that he didn't say what happens if we can't.'

'Precisely,' Barbour said. He ran a palm over his balding scalp and was surprised to find it damp. 'If we can prove our worth. The problem is – *how?*'

They digested the issue in uneasy silence, facing it squarely for the first time and marshaling up, each after his own nature, the possibilities of satisfying it.

Clowdis moved first, linking his conference-room screen with the control-room. Shassil answered promptly, his goatish face blandly uncommunicative.

'Is every new race that develops space flight put to this test?' Clowdis asked. 'And what happens if they fail, Shassil?'

The Cetian shrugged oddly-jointed shoulders. 'The T'sai have always sought out the new cultures. You are the first to the T'sai.'

They looked at each other uncomprehendingly. To Barbour the information held a tantalizing hint of greatest significance, but he could not pin it down.

'Then the T'sai gave these other races their start,' he said. 'They must have—'

'Beside the point,' Clowdis cut in. 'What we want to know is this, Shassil: *What will the T'sai do if we fail?*'

The Cetian raised a hand to his own screen's control. 'I do not know. The T'sai do not confide in the minor cultures, nor do we expect it.'

The blanking out of the screen left them, Clowdis thought, precisely where they had begun. Barbour felt differently, but his nagging sense of significance concealed would not define itself for analysis.

'I'm out of my depth here,' Wilcox said, and stood up. 'With your permission, commander, I'll get back to my friends.'

Clowdis hesitated, foreseeing a risk more immediate than T'sai action. The ship's crew, including himself, numbered seventeen, while below decks a hundred and fifty colonists were already muttering uneasily among themselves. If they panicked, any chance of survival was gone at the outset.

He considered holding Wilcox until some plan of action should be agreed upon, and dismissed the thought because he knew from experience that no leaderless body of men could be kept for long in uncertainty without demanding reassurance.

'Go ahead,' Clowdis said. 'But remember this, Wilcox – our chances of surviving this thing depend as much on yourself as on us. If you can't help us, then keep your people out of our hair.'

When Wilcox had gone, Clowdis and Vesari and Barbour looked at each other doubtfully in a silence broken only by Buehl's heavy breathing.

'Maybe they won't panic,' Barbour said finally, without conviction. 'Not one of them can have any accurate idea of what we're really up against here.'

Clowdis shrugged helplessly. 'Have *we*, Frank?'

Wilcox went directly below and found the colonists' bay astir with rumour and apprehension. Men converged upon him the instant he set foot in the long metal room, voices clamoring for reassurance.

Surprisingly, he found it in himself to give it to them. The role of leader had been thrust upon him against his will, but their obvious dependence upon him now lent him a strength he had not known he possessed.

'We're being delayed for examination,' he told them. 'A kind of immigration clearance we must pass before we can claim the Regulian planet we're bound for. There's no danger. Commander Clowdis has the situation under control.'

But later, when the others had drifted away to talk in

animated knots, Wilcox sat with his wife in their cramped cubicle and discovered that his specious assurance had deceived her not at all.

'You're holding back something, Carl,' his wife said. She was younger than Wilcox, in her late twenties, dark-haired and moderately pretty even in her emigrant's cheap and sober clothing. 'They're going to turn us back, is that it?'

He shook his head helplessly. 'I don't know, Alice. None of us knows, not even the commander. This T'sai looks like a man, but he's more like a god. There's no way of guessing what he may do if we fail to prove ourselves.'

She tilted her head to look at him shrewdly, sensing with a perception clearer than his own something of the issues at stake behind their arrest in space.

'The T'sai never did this before. Carl, do you suppose they're going to judge the whole human race by this one shipload?'

He flinched from the thought. 'I hope not! The responsibility—'

Inevitably the possibilities rose to chill him: themselves rejected, wiped out or driven back to Earth; other scheduled expeditions banned from space; men restricted forever, perhaps, to their own barren overcrowded little ring of worlds.

But as inevitably, because he was from birth a simple cog in a complex economic machine and as such was experienced only in his immediate circle of concerns, his thought went back to himself and his wife and their unborn child and to the other colonists who had burned their bridges to make this venture into space.

They could not go back. There was no place for them on Earth, and the colonies were bitter hells for outcasts worse off than slaves.

We may as well die out here, he told himself. The thought took root and fanned to flame the smoldering spark of resentment that had burned in him, unaware, from the beginning.

'We're only trying to *live*,' he said aloud, and did not know that he spoke. 'The T'sai have no right to deny us that. They've no use for that planet, or they'd have colonized it long ago. There's no reason why we shouldn't have it.'

His wife put a hand on his arm and the touch brought him, as always, the warmth of more than physical support.

'I understand,' she said. 'I think the other colonists will understand too, Carl. If we can't settle out here, after sacrificing the little we had, there's no point in going on.'

They sat quietly after that while resolve built up in Wilcox.

'I think I'd better tell the others the truth,' he said finally. 'We'll give Commander Clowdis and his group every chance, but if they can't come up with a solution—'

Clowdis and Barbour, sitting alone in the conference-room when Wilcox came up again an hour later, had arrived at no sort of conclusion. Buehl had long ago given up a task for which he had no qualifications, and had gone to his quarters for whiskey and Wagner. Vesari had followed suit from sheer weariness, and was at the moment sleeping the sleep of the unimaginative in his bunk.

'We're no better off than when you left,' Barbour said irritably in answer to Wilcox's question. 'There's a gulf between the T'sai psychology and our own that makes it impossible to guess what he wants. He's not a man, for all his likeness, and there's no knowing how his mind runs. It may be a matter of ethics, and the proof he demands may hinge on a facet of personality unfamiliar to us.

'Suppose one of our ancient Earthly aborigines had asked admission to our own society – he'd have had to pass an immigration board, and his ethical code would have had to correspond nearly enough to ours before he could be considered compatible. Suppose he came from a culture that ate human flesh – would that sort of conditioning be acceptable? It would not, and you know it. It would make him unfit for citizenship, and the fact that he understood nothing of that unfitness would not sway us for a minute in denying him.'

'And if he tried forcible entry we'd deport or kill him,' Clowdis added. He lit his hundredth cigarette and scowled at the colonist with strain-reddened eyes. 'Frank is right, Wilcox. We've seen a dozen cultures at close range out here, and there's hardly a point of similarity between ourselves and any of them. Don't you agree, Wilcox?'

Wilcox was a little surprised at his own steadiness when he said, 'Surely we ought to know how long we're given to produce our proof. Have you asked Shassil?'

Clowdis and Barbour looked at each other in disgust.

'Out of the mouths of babes,' Barbour said. Clowdis reached for the activator button that lit his conference-room screen.

Shassil's answer had less meaning to them at the moment than the empty expanse of foreign-body plate behind him.

'You have until sunset of the present day on the Regulian planet for which you were bound,' the Cetian said. 'Some twelve hours from this moment, by your time.'

Clowdis ignored the information. 'Where's the T'sai ship?'

'The T'sai has gone to confer with his council. He will return at the appointed time.'

They looked at each other helplessly when the Cetian's screen went dark.

'Instantaneous transference,' Clowdis said faintly. 'Across the galaxy and back in twelve hours, with a conference thrown in. What's the use, Frank? Why don't we admit we're whipped?'

Barbour turned his hands palm up in silent defeat.

'But we've twelve hours to ourselves,' Wilcox said. 'We can reach Regulus in ten.'

He went on defiantly when Clowdis whirled on him. 'We're going to land on that planet, commander, if we die for it.'

They had no chance to argue. At Wilcox's call three colonists came into the room with heat guns broken from the below-decks small-arms store, and as quickly as that the ship changed hands.

Shassil, with his unshakable air of galactic resignation, took the new order without a murmur. With a heat gun at his back he sat before the commander's control board and took over the handling of the ship as readily as if the Korivian craft with its T'sai passenger had never appeared.

Wilcox and his contingent, now that the die was cast, seemed relieved of strain and as resigned as the Cetian interpreter.

'I suppose you're right, sir,' Wilcox said once when Clowdis cursed him for bringing annihilation upon them. 'But we're probably slated for execution anyway, and we colonists would rather die here than go back to Earth and be shipped out to the domes on Mars or Venus or the Jovian moons. You've seen those installations yourself, and know what it's like there.'

Clowdis did know. He knew, too, the bitter monotony of shuttling back and forth between those dreary hell-holes on the planetary runs he had followed before the advent of the interstellar drive freed him. Considering that the T'sai at best must have returned him to that drab routine awoke a certain sympathy in him for the colonists' stand, but failed utterly to compensate for the death he saw in the offing.

They brought Vesari up from his quarters, partly to check on Shassil's navigation and partly to keep Clowdis company, but Buehl they were forced to confine to his room. The powermaster had rushed to the engine room the moment the atomics came to life, and in his bull-like fury had to be bound hand and foot to prevent his interfering with the engine-room crew.

Twelve hours could be a wonderfully brief time when it measured the span of a man's life, Clowdis thought. Yet the flight dragged interminably; the ship seemed not to be flashing at twice light-speed through space, but stalled straining and motionless. Seated with Barbour and Vesari on a spare acceleration couch, Clowdis relaxed for the first time in hours and found himself nodding with exhaustion before he realized the strain he had been under.

He slept the flight through. When he roused, it was to see the soft green sweep of the Regulian planet rising under the ship, horizons rushing up with sudden dizzying speed to change from convex to concave.

'We're landing,' he said stupidly, blinking away sleep.

'As we set out from Earth to do,' Wilcox agreed. His wife stood at his elbow, her warm femininity startlingly out of place in the functionally male realm of control room, her eyes fixed on the clean sweep of hills and meadow below. 'Let the T'sai come and blast us now if they like. We've begun what we came here for.'

292

'Fools,' Clowdis growled. 'If you had to commit suicide, why didn't you bring the atomics up to critical mass and get it over with?'

But he thrilled a little nevertheless when the engines thundered in last-minute deceleration and the ship stood like a tall silver candle on the green plain.

'Now,' Wilcox said. His voice trembled.

Someone opened the locks below decks, and Clowdis could feel the stale air of the ship drifting out and smell the clean fragrance of growing things stealing in to take its place.

'We'll give you back your ship,' Wilcox said, 'as soon as we can get our supplies and gear unloaded.'

Clowdis looked at Barbour, who shook his head wonderingly.

'Men,' Barbour said. 'I've studied them for a lifetime, Ed, and I've never been further from understanding them.'

But both of them, while they watched the colonists hastily passing out their meager possessions, felt an unexpected tug of envy.

'I think we've been to space too long, Ed,' Barbour said when the last colonist left the ship. 'We've been too much interested in hunting out new worlds and investigating alien puzzles to appreciate our own species.'

Clowdis, lacking the psychologist's trained capacity for empathy, still felt a shattering change of perspective.

He *had* been out of touch. He had forgotten the pull of men toward the soil, the drive that made men fight and die for possession of a few square yards of it. He and Barbour and Vesari were in their own way pioneers, latter-day Boones and Houstons and Carsons, cramped when they saw the figurative smoke of other human occupation. To them in large measure was due the credit for man's early leaping across the spatial frontier, but now, as always, it was the settlers who carried with them the dogged unyielding spirit of humanity. Those poor idealistic fools going to their deaths out there were of the same breed that had slogged patiently in the steps of all pioneers, to hold the conquered land in perpetuity for their children and their children's children forever.

293

But not this time, Clowdis thought. *The T'sai*—

Wilcox appeared briefly upon the trampled grass below, turning a flushed face up to Clowdis and Barbour at the open port.

'You'd better take the ship away, commander,' he called. 'The deadline—'

Clowdis threw a glance toward the sunset washing the low hills to the west, and flinched when the T'sai ship sprang into view and blocked out the sun. His immediate reaction, curiously, was not the belated panic he had anticipated but a blast of red anger against the T'sai.

'Damned if I'll try to lift her now,' he said.

Then, before Barbour could move to prevent, he dropped down the personnel ladder to where Wilcox had stood.

'Here we are,' he shouted. He shook his fist at the lowering ship. 'Blast the lot of us and be—'

The T'sai appeared beside him like a solid projection that denied transit time, tiny face inscrutable behind his force field.

'Watch,' the T'sai said.

The alien ship grounded, feather-soft, on the grass. Korivian police marched out upon the meadow like orderly ranks of reddish reptilian automatons and bore down upon the huddled colonists. Clowdis caught the glint of late sunlight on enigmatic weapons, and stiffened with a sick chill of horror when he saw that the few colonists who had clung to their commandeered heat guns had aligned themselves before the rest.

He saw Wilcox in the forefront, keeping his wife behind him so that his body shielded her own. Her own and the other life not due for half a year, the unborn son or daughter they had confidently expected to inherit their share of the new Earth.

The T'sai raised a hand and the Korivians stopped like snouted statuary.

The colonists shifted uneasily and stilled. For a moment the tableau held fast in static suspense, a dragging eternity in which Clowdis forgot to breathe.

Then the Korivians turned as if on prearranged signal and marched back to their ship.

'The proof is sufficient,' the T'sai said. His voice, amplified without apparent mechanism, carried the length of the meadow. 'The world is yours.'

And left them alone with their victory.

The ship did not lift that night. Clowdis got roaring drunk with Barbour and Vesari and Buehl on the powermaster's whiskey, and put off questioning Shassil until late the next day.

The Cetian made explanation when they were sober, his lucid monologue falling with clear logic even upon their dulled minds.

'The T'sai ruled the galaxy,' Shassil said, 'before the first life crawled up from the sea of your world. They ruled because they, of us all, possessed both intelligence and initiative, the restless drive toward perfection that was somehow left out of the lesser races. The T'sai sought us out one by one and helped us up the long path to self-sufficiency, but they had despaired of finding another race with purpose like their own until you appeared.

'They watched over you from the beginning but without interfering; if your species was to prove itself worthy it would find its way to the T'sai when the time was right, and the T'sai would weigh it and pronounce judgment. You passed their test because your kind possesses the same initiative and idealism that made the T'sai what they are, the loyalty and belligerence necessary to make you their proper successors.'

They stared at him unbelievingly. '*Successors?*' Clowdis repeated. 'What—'

'The T'sai have grown old in fulfilling their obligations to the rest of the galaxy,' the Cetian said. 'And a renewal of lost racial virility depends upon their finding new fields to explore. Other galaxies are waiting for them, as this one waited for you. The T'sai will go when you are ready to step into their place.'

And in leaving their presence Shassil, for the first time, touched his goatish beard in respect.

295

EPILOGUE

Before and after man's troubled life we saw other humanesque races rise in scores and hundreds, of which a mere handful was destined to waken beyond man's highest spiritual range, to play a part in the galactic community of worlds. These we now saw from afar on their little Earth-like planets, scattered among the huge drift of the star-streams, struggling to master all those world-problems, social and spiritual, which man in our 'modern' era is for the first time confronting. Similarly, we saw again the many other kinds of races, nautiloid, avian, composite, and the rare symbiotics, and still rarer plant-like beings. And of every kind only a few, if any, won through to utopia, and took part in the great communal enterprise of worlds. The rest fell by the way.

Olaf Stapledon: Star Maker